PALO
THE WORLD IN HER LITTLE FIST

DR. AJIT PADHY

BLUEROSE PUBLISHERS
India | U.K.

Copyright © Dr Ajit Padhy 2024

All rights reserved by author. No part of this publication may be reproduced, stored in a retrieval system or transmitted in any form or by any means, electronic, mechanical, photocopying, recording or otherwise, without the prior permission of the author. Although every precaution has been taken to verify the accuracy of the information contained herein, the publisher assumes no responsibility for any errors or omissions. No liability is assumed for damages that may result from the use of information contained within.

BlueRose Publishers takes no responsibility for any damages, losses, or liabilities that may arise from the use or misuse of the information, products, or services provided in this publication.

For permissions requests or inquiries regarding this publication, please contact:

BLUEROSE PUBLISHERS
www.BlueRoseONE.com
info@bluerosepublishers.com
+91 8882 898 898
+4407342408967

ISBN: 978-93-6783-291-2

Cover design: Yash Singhal
Typesetting: Namrata Saini

First Edition: December 2024

Disclaimer: This is a fictional work. All names, characters, businesses, industries, institutions, places, events, and incidents in this book are products of the author's imagination and are used in a fictitious context. Any resemblance to actual individuals, living or dead, or real-life events is entirely coincidental.

Acknowledgment

To my dearest daughter, Aditi Padhi,

I cherish your frequent visits to my writing desk as this story 'Palo- The world in her little fist' began to take shape. You closely monitored my progress in the notebook and often shared hints with your mother, my wife, Dr. Swagatika.

Just as you both contemplated the conclusion of my writing, you were surprised to discover that the story was ready for another round of revision. I couldn't help it but always felt that this day was meant to happen before us.

With much love,

Papa.

AKP

About the Author

Dr. (Maj) Ajit Kumar Padhy is an esteemed Cardio-Thoracic and Vascular Surgeon practising at the renowned Vardhaman Mahavir Medical College and Safdarjung Hospital in Delhi. As a Professor in the medical field, he has an extensive collection of national and international research publications to his credit. Additionally, he had served as a short-service commissioned officer in the Indian Armed Forces in the past. Alongside his academic pursuits, he takes pleasure in singing and writing. His debut novel, "*Palo - The World in Her Little Fist*," is a captivating work of fiction that chronicles the inspiring journey of a young girl who embarks on the path to becoming a cardiac surgeon.

He is currently working on a new story titled "***Paro: The Daughter of Devbhoomi,***" which follows a soul's adventure through various lifetimes as it rekindles the flame of a forgotten spirit.

Your feedback will aid him in crafting his next novels more effectively. Now, you can connect with the author through these email addresses to share your thoughts or clarify any queries.

author.ajitpadhy@gmail.com

author.drajitpadhy@gmail.com

Contents

Chapter 1: # A Breaking News 1

Chapter 2: An Unthinkable Mess 14

Chapter 3: Beauty and the Beast 74

Chapter 4: A tragedy unexpected 111

Chapter 5: Believing in Self 126

Chapter 6: Dream Chasers 181

Chapter 7: A Dream comes true 237

Chapter 8: Justice to Disha 300

CHAPTER 1

A Breaking News

Juhu, Mumbai / December 2020

It is obvious that when a story clings to our nerves, it seldom fades away. And when a mystery treads through a multitude of possibilities, it for sure never gets away.

The scene in the farmhouse was noisy. The music there was explosive and deafening. Disha had drunk her favourite martini served by a waiter. It was not a hallucination to her real eyes. Their brutality lingered; the demons danced in her mind. She popped a few tablets with a sip of water and laid herself on a long sofa in her morning room. Two hours later, a loud rap on the door disturbed her. Still bound tightly with the morning grogginess, her eyes opened lazily to see the door in front shudder. She put a hand to her forehead, still throbbing with pain. Trying to orient herself, she just heard a familiar voice on the other side. She answered the door, rose listlessly and shambled towards it. She unlocked the door while holding the knob.

Her head spun. She swayed on her feet and crouched. "I want to lie down," she said to them. What she felt in her frigid state of mind was that they held her by the arms while she toed off across the hall. They walked her into the bedroom and then laid her on the bed. Fear built in her mind when they slammed the door shut. She did not like the touch. Without her realizing it, her physical safety was shattered as powerful hands, like a vise, pinned her down.

As she looked through the slit of her eyes, the man in the red shirt seemed unfamiliar, almost like a different person. If it wasn't him, then who was he who leaned over her in that dimly lit room?

He was in a red shirt and leaned over, taking her firmly by arms. She tried to wiggle free, but she couldn't. All she could do was splay her hands on the bed and tip her head up. As her eyes tracked through, she saw the other one, who hurriedly jumped to the leg end and slid the socks down before emptying a syringe full of a drug into her leg vein. In her senses, Disha, who they knew well, would have given them a hard shove with her legs. She would have fought fiercely. Her legs were gripped, and her body was frozen. Her little strength faded fast, and She felt outdone. Although she didn't tremble then, what it evinced in her also cannot be denied. She had a harrowing surge of icy cold emotions wash over her. The torture she endured was indubitably murderous. Her breaths turned shaky, and her vision blurred with tears. She panicked, "Was she frozen with any fear?"

There was no alternative left to overcome her susceptibilities except for pleading with them. She tilted her head and watched them with a sightless gaze before beseeched them, but that did not alter their minds. She had to believe then that her life was no longer relevant to them.

She could not shout. Her voice muffled when she asked the bringers of her death," I want to live my life. Why are you killing me?" Slowly, her voice trailed off into a strangled groan. She dreaded and even prayed to God for help when one decided to throw her out of the balcony. Suppressing a violent impulse in his accomplice, the other one abstained him from doing so as the daylight outside was still bright.

She became still. She heard one say, "She is dead." The other one even tapped her shoulder to check whether she was dead. They propped her up, and the tears trickled down. The ticking of the clock muffled...

She did not know what happened to her after that. Her heart **slowed down with a long pause.**

Two days later,

Yesterday, the news they heard turned out to be chilling like the cascading chilly weather. With the sun's first rays falling on a December Sunday morning, the city stirred from its slumber, enchanted by the tale of a middle-aged woman's mysterious demise. The unsettling report sparked doubts in many as to whether it was a murder or a suicide. It incited a wave of anger as the unusual circumstances left everyone perplexed, pondering whether their lives in the city were safe. Upon the television, a chorus of furious cries echoed in response to this unfamiliar and strange introduction of the day.

Today, it is an agreeably warm afternoon. The weather is bright and brisk. A noticeable congregation has sprung up outside Disha's house despite it being a working Monday in a busy city like Mumbai. The OB vans discreetly made their way into the narrow single-lane driveway. A passel of reporters still bounced around with their microphones to gather varied reactions. The public responded sensitively, with some arguing over the possibilities leading to the unusual death.

In contrast, others frowned upon the police action for not being hot-footed in any matter per se in the city. A few had settled their order with an uncompromising, truculent gatekeeper to enter the blocked building premises on a 'first come, first served' basis. To speak of his smartness, the next moment would reveal how long the order would prevail. Indeed, they all had recorded their timings with him to gain preference over others. It would not be incorrect to say that they all knew that they had been asked to snake out to the main road by a stern investigating officer of IPS rank, who had entered inside with his crack team in the early hours of the day.

A few journalists had already hooked a storyline beforehand to feed the entire country in total length with their exclusive hypothetical tidbit: A murder, not a suicide. Will their speculation be proved right? Only time will tell.

A Police -squad van blared its siren and hurriedly rushed past the crowd to enter through the guarded entrance and reach the main entry door of the building. Two policemen in khakis alighted swiftly and promptly placed the barrier tapes and poles at the entry door to prevent any unauthorized intrusion. The drill looked perfect to the crowd.

Their hour-long wait was over, and they heard the tap of their boots. As they could see Hanumat Shivdasani materialize outside the apartment, the journalists longed for a communique. They obeyed no rule to hound him before he could get inside a white police gypsy. They shouted, "Excuse me, excuse me, sir," from behind. Not to get deflected from his next action, he wanted to avoid their silly questions, but for a second, he thought, "Enough is now enough." He looked at his watch, and it was 2 PM. " No comments" could have been good riddance at that moment, but to ward off the reputation of the police, he stood there to engage with them as he was sure the need of the hour was to put a finger on it before anybody opened their mouth against the police.

He stopped and turned around to see in no time almost ten microphones pointed at his mouth just for a quick sound bite. The restless camerapersons fought for their best shots to cover him live. The channels had focused on him perfectly in the centre of their screen. It was not something unforeseen for him. He had expected it in advance.

After waiting for almost a day and a half since the incident came to the limelight, to them, the first-hand information from the horse's mouth carried more relevance in propelling their story forward than the all-cooked-up hypotheses by neighbours. They felt the constructed crime hypothesis, which arose from a neighbour's suspicion and guesses, was virtually inconceivable.

According to Hanumat, it was a cold-blooded murder. So, he emphasized in an authoritative tone, "The murder angle in Disha's case is being intensely scrutinized. We are hopeful we will reach a conclusion very soon. Our forensic team has found traces of narcotics and alcohol in her blood samples. So, based on the circumstantial pieces of evidence, we have concluded that this case merits further investigation. We are interrogating the key suspects in this case, and very soon, we will get back to you with the names."

As far as I know him from his police record of services, Hanumat Shivdasani is known in his circle as a calm, composed, zealous, and enthusiastic police officer. He is quite determined to end the crime in the city. In the past, he has solved many complex criminal cases and has won a slew of medals. A dedicated police officer like him is a rare breed in the department who always puts his heart and soul into a case when asked to solve it. He was roped into the crime branch for his unparalleled, matchless, fierce streak and bright professional record in solving murder mysteries.

All that, it emphasized, "At times, he becomes ruthless, unkind, cruel, and nasty to the monstrous criminals. His statements are always based on his experience and exposure; they are just unquestionable. There is not a shadow of doubt in his loyalty to the job. His works speak for himself." And the remarks just he made in front of the cameras were self-evident about the man's optimism. He did not escape the crowd with 'No comments on his lip.' Furthermore, it warned, "He is not a tight-lipped man to speak with, but when it comes to dealing with the criminals, he tightens the noose enough to keep their breath stifled inside."

The perception of the public was different. They felt that the police were always lax and unprofessional in handling the law-and-order matters in the city. The criminals always remained a step ahead of them.

An old journalist who knew Disha shouted from the crowd, "Is Salim Sultan's gang back in action in Bollywood? Have they killed her in revenge?" Another middle-aged fan, in a high, distinct voice, groaned coldly, "Police are protecting a murderer who killed her; how mortifying it is. Just a shame. Tell us, ACP, why has Dr. Pallavi not been arrested yet?" Another nosy reporter dissed, " If we understand correctly, you don't want to arrest her as you were once friends." Such jeers arose an unpleasant thought in him. It hit him hard to the nerves. "Now the journos will tell him what strategies the police should adopt." Something else, too, had in him to add to his fury when this name crossed his mind. Such a vehemence of an inner reaction erupted in him ever since he learned that Pallavi had a boyfriend, and she loved that kook. At that moment, it hadn't been easy for him to take their upsetting personal comments in stride, especially in a matter he was not a part of. Still being considerate of his uniform, he thought it would be nonsensical to lay a finger on them before he got some hard evidence to disprove them.

Hanumat entered his gypsy and rolled down the window. Such a tangent, critical remark about police action kindled anger in him. The awful reality for him was that he was live on air. Gesturing a stop sign with his voluminous right hand, he hushed them, and then he flashed a warning sign by pointing his index finger. His wrist jerked when he waggled his finger, and his face still bore the calmness while he remonstrated in a marginally roaring voice, "My dear ones, don't jump to any conclusions unless you know about the person. She is a renowned cardiac surgeon, and Disha was her patient. Being in a responsible job, it would not be sensible on your part to haul in someone's name like this without any concrete evidence. When I take on a job, I do a thorough investigation. The investigation process is underway. We will come to you again after completing the investigation." The calmness had withered away, and his face had turned red while suppressing a mild twinge of sympathy for his ex. Aside from silently suffering from indignation at the accusations, he had no other explanation beyond this to rescue himself from the taunts. And besides all of this, in his line of work, he had never proven himself insincere in his duty. He turned his face and looked away towards the road ahead. Withdrawing his hand back onto the steering wheel," he drove past them, saying in an indignant tone, " Let me go. Thank you."

As he strode off, his vehicle passed a few inches away from them. He tried hard to roll the window up. In yet another adventure, a few enthusiastic journalists accelerated alongside the gypsy for a few meters, seeking more answers to feed their puzzled minds. They panted, slowed down, and finally steadied themselves to settle down happily with a subtle triumph -the piece of information which they had gathered so far was adequate for the day to run their channels. They knew well that police had been groping in the darkness and were yet to discover the light at the end of the tunnel.

In a few minutes, he drove past the police headquarters and rushed to meet the forensic team studying the evidence shreds at their laboratory. He stopped in front of a square-bricked -three-story building at the dead-end of the street within the premises of Bombay City Hospital. It was well protected by guards. Like a diligent guardian of the law, he entered the premises while displaying his identity card. The halls inside were big and well-lit. The topmost floor had a concreted mansard roof laced with glass windows. The walls were also studded with ceiling-height French windows to allow natural sunlight inside while carrying out the post-mortem. A dead woman's corpse was laid on a table at the centre. It was swollen by two folds, the limbs were straight, the skin appeared white with blue marks over her protruded abdomen, and the eyeballs were puffed out with lids retracted halfway. The tongue was locked inside her half-open jaw box, and a large scar ran downward through the middle of her chest. There was an oblique ligature mark quite distinctly visible over her neck. There were track marks on both arms and a red pinprick on her leg. There was a putrefied stench in the air, and she was being intensely scrutinized by the forensic team inside when ACP Hanumat entered the hall on the top floor.

The lock was intact and not loose when the team broke open the door the previous morning. The latch of her bedroom was not loose; her body was hanging from a ceiling fan, her head looking downward, and her arms at her sides. "It was surely not a robbery," he overheard. They had discovered a few bottles of Johnnie Walker, some of them were empty on a shelf; a few disposable syringes with needles in a box, a few personal diaries, files in a cabinet, cash, and pieces of jewellery inside the locker of her almirah. A few medicine wrappers were scattered on the floor near the kitchen trash. TV and fridge were not missing. Two cut glasses half-filled with water, a few papers, and prescriptions were seen separately on the centre table of a big sofa set in the main hall. A few old diaries were rummaged around her book rack. The scene, the windows, the ledges, the balconies, the whole house, the neighbour's doors, surveillance cameras, and parking areas were photographed inch by inch. The photographs in a few hundred numbers were laid on a large table at the corner of the hall.

The bespectacled experts looked genius with black-rimmed glasses and very much experienced if someone reads by their half-grey hairs. Both were gloved but not masked. They discussed this while scrutinizing every square inch area of her body; they looked through a hand-held magnifier lens when in doubt. The junior-most expert was jotting down the observations on a post-mortem report.

According to the experts, there were multiple old, healed track marks on her body and cord-like superficial veins on her left forearm. "The findings are self-explanatory of a strong history of intravenous drug addiction," one said.

One young, enthusiastic expert from the first-floor lab, clad in a white lab coat, entered hurriedly into the hall, leaving behind his lab work in the middle to inform, "Boss, there are traces of anaesthetic drugs in her blood beside the narcotics," he said so while the other expert was corroborating to the former one's finding with the recovered medical reports in his hand. Interestingly, the case was taking a new turn for the experts.

It was 2'O clock by his watch, in a situation where the nation demanded urgent action; Ramdutt Shivdasani was bothered about the doctor's name and photo flashing on his TV screen. Sprawling on a big sofa in the main hall, he looked at the screen. His eyes fixed on her innocent face while his thoughtful mind traversed his past. The incident had a momentous implication on his son's life. He was increasingly desperate to know about the killer rather than being a little excited to watch his son featured on the screen of almost every news channel. In this case, the Pallavi he knew in the past was a prime suspect. He tried to console himself seriously many times but failed when he changed the channel to watch another. They had already started digging into her dreadful past. A question arose in his mind: "If she did, was this for any personal animosity?"

The channel repeatedly flashed his son's interview with a running breaking news at the bottom of the screen: "#someone was skulking". It had repeatedly flashed the blurred photo of the man who gazed over the boundary wall, resting his head upon it. It had been on the screen since last evening when the sentry made such a statement in front of the camera. The headline was hash-tagged: *"# who killed Disha?"* A few neighbours revealed their ignorance about the death. A few Hindi channels in their afternoon prime time hash-tagged "# *Disha -ke katil kaun?*" For many, she was the private secretary of a renowned film producer and actor, Late Sameer Malhotra, but to a few middle-aged who recollected her as a model turned starlet of their time 'Madhubala' from the picture which they just saw on TV.

*****

A supermodel, Diya Malhotra, a 32-year-old beauty queen of yesteryears, eagerly awaited her childhood friend on that wintry morning in December. She wore blue trousers and a clingy half-sleeved red top, unlike the eccentric ones she used to wear. She strode from one end to another in her terrace garden under the sun. All the phone calls she made to Pallavi were replied to by her secretary- "Madam is still busy in the OT. I am afraid that she would get disturbed."

Diya paused for a while in the middle of the garden and spread her arms out with palms up. She looked at the sun through her half-closed eyes and took a deep breath to embrace nature. She had not inhaled the freshness of the atmosphere better than this for almost a decade. It was purely non-alcoholic and suffused with the scent of Jasmine. The oxygen with every breath she inhaled made her feel full of vim and vigour. The natural, vibrant energy of the sun made her feel lusty. The warmth of the dull rays penetrated deep into her bones and warmed her growing flesh smoothly and uniformly.

As to speak of her, It had been almost two decades since they parted ways. Diya bared her heart in an e-mail. She finally conceded her defeat to win Pallavi's heart. As a friend, she had persuaded Pallavi to come to her flat in that condominium again. Knowing she had no one left to pat her back in good moments and hold her hand in bad times, she had been living as feral as an animal, quite uncared about others.

Like an extinguished lamp, the fame of her name simmered down from being a well-known identity in the city to a nonentity. The flame of Diya's life, which had once burned brightly to glory for a short span, was now completely burnt out. Her life had seeped surreptitiously into the darkness, surrounded by a cloud of smoke. Now, she felt ordinary and unshackled from the tag of a super-model in these years. Knowing fully well that she could no longer cling to the hashtag # highly paid or costliest - foxy model in the city, she had withdrawn herself from all sorts of a hot body and gym fit business.

Lately, people have called her -Ghost Aunty. There was a day a few months ago when her alcohol addiction was so intense that she carved and begged a peg from her neighbour in the middle of the night. She cried in a distressing pain in the abdomen. All that she complained about was the pain of being stabbed in her stomach. Her utter cry of pancreatic pain in the middle of the night had labelled her a "Ghost Aunty" by the mothers of small kids. The drawn memes of this short-fame celebrity popularized her as "Ghost Aunty" in that area. Brave kids who saw her in that condominium drew her caricatured image on the walls with details of her spooky goblin-like long, wiry, unkempt locks, sunken bleary eyeballs, skeleton-thin frame, thin wristed arms, lustreless skin, and talons like fingers, which had been perfectly superimposed on a distraught soul of a woman to give her a meme of a ghost.

Her fight with a half-decade-long battle of agonizing abdominal pain had withered away. She had recovered from intermittent attacks of pancreatitis and restarted a fresh life after undergoing pancreatic surgery three months ago. Her life-giver was a surgeon, her friend Dr Pallavi.

The morphological alterations in her body had been settling down and pushing her to a new state of physiological normalcy. She regained her lost weight and looked curvy again, no longer stick-like with a 'zero' figure. Her frailty had transformed to a few pounds of flesh, but her body was yet to acquire the delicacy of the super-alluring curves of her favourite formfitting jeans. Her anorexic aversion to food was abated, and she had regained entirely her lost appetite. She had tidied her daily routine in order.

She would ever be able to survive to this day; many surgeons were not hopeful. The disease progression was very extensive, and it had eroded the wall of a major blood vessel under the pancreatic tissue in her abdomen. After consulting almost a dozen top surgeons in the city, the only specialist whose name she was suggested by many was Dr Pallavi Rajhans, who had a high success rate in dealing with complex vascular cases.

She fussed over Pallavi getting late, but the impatience slowly melted down, and she waited in the hope that she would hear a knock on the door any time from then on. In her split attention to the selfie mode of the camera, she framed her face, smoothed down her not-so-coarse, little -dense -frizzy hairs with her fingers, pulled the bangs and adjusted them behind her ears, and jabbed the machine again on the number buttons.

The ailing days kept her cut off from all the city affairs. The cosmetic secrets of the glamour industry forced her to remain incommunicado with friends, and as a friendless person, she was wretched alone in the big city. The bitterness was unforgiving, which she spat out for Pallavi in the past. Would she recognize the difference in her manners? Her heart has turned pure and filled with love. She repented for her iniquitous mannerisms and all those jealous, hateful relationships with her in the past. Simply inane on her part.

If someone reads the chapter of her life, Pallavi was never the best dear to her on any of the pages, not even someone she counted as a friend in the happiest of memories. She resigned, "What a fool she had been as a classmate who always tried to ruffle her feathers for no reason! Can Pallavi recognize her as her best friend now? She had no idea to check on.

She sat on the swing, stared intently at the flowers, and slowly lost herself in her beautiful memories of the past. To proclaim herself she was the only daughter of the late Sameer Malhotra. Now, the awful reality is that she can spend the rest of her life with this identity. She has recovered sufficiently. She can start a new job with her own space and air to breathe. It would not be a suffocating job like before.

She looked into her phone's photo gallery and muttered to her image, "No, you have to pull yourself together, Diya; it is only a matter of days; you can't remain as a kaput forever; you may be worse off than yesterday, but your tomorrow will glow like Pallavi. Now is the time for you to manage your situation." She promised herself that she would again make herself presentable in all fashionable outfits. She would wear her favourite old hot togs and Spandex gear again. She would tint her hair, and her lips would look pink, glossy and full as before. She would be standing amidst the men as a strong lady like Pallavi. Once again, they will admire her carriage and stately walk on the ramp. After these long, dark, painful, sleepless nights, she will enter a new morning.

CHAPTER 2

An Unthinkable Mess

1989, MARCH, BOMBAY

Nature had blessed its most pleasant day in the film city, Bombay. The eastern sky of an early summer morning was painted with a subtle shade of liquid copper as it arched over Malad. Nature's best colour slowly faded away as the sun ascended westward a quarter in the sky and peered through the window of the parted feathery clouds. A wreath of dust swirled in the atmosphere, carried by a gentle breeze from the sea and settled down softly on the streets when the sweepers left the road for a brief rest. The clever squirrels took small hops, nibbled their nuts, shook their tails, trailed each other, and scurried up spirally to reach the top of an ancient mango tree while the vulnerable ants were picked up ruthlessly by the cruel mynahs who perched at the anthill under the tree.

Sagar Rajhans is an average-built man in his late thirties. He had been working tirelessly like an ant for a secured financial future for his family. He never believed in the pleasure of Carpe Diem like a grasshopper. He served his benevolent master with utmost pride. He parked his Sahib's long white Merc Benz under the mango tree, standing tall in front of his veranda. The canopy of the tree was large enough to accommodate the big car under it. He considered the place perfect for valeting the precious vehicle. As far as I know him, I can tell that the pride of his profession was inseparably embedded in his principles, one when it came to the maintenance of the car. The one principle in life he owned as a chauffeur was not to give his Sahib a chance to complain about cleanliness, be it in him or his car. The car must gleam brightly outside and remain scrupulously clean from the inside. Seemingly quite uncared about the tree falling over the costly car someday and he would get fired from his job, he parked the car with the greatest faith that it would cause no harm to it. He was not sure of his confidence but sure about his luck and destiny. His faith was that a branch would never fall free unless the tree wanted it to. He had seen the mango tree branches ever nodding to his terrace in cyclonic storms but had never seen them breaking and falling loose since he was five. Slowly, he stepped out and closed the door by gently pushing the chrome handle and muttered, " Another day is over."He was up since three in the morning. He shuttled his sahib's guests in that luxurious leather-seated car. Despite his performance of three consecutive night duties, one more duty in the day and one more in the night till the next day was expected of him. He appeared tired, and his eyes looked red and scummy. He yawned wide open, lifted his chin to the sun, and inhaled a breath to the maximum swell of his chest. He stiffly stretched his arms to his sides, squinted at the sun through his bleary, half-opened eyelids, and slowly exhaled. Huff....he arched his back to straighten his kinked spine. He was happy to have his work completed, but at home, his wife Laxmi would not be happy and polite to greet him like any other day. He repeatedly broke her sleep in the middle of the night in the last three consecutive days, and the reason was enough for her to sulk at him. She insists he should leave the job and says the same stock of narratives: "Take care of your health; enough is enough; your health is our wealth, etc."

 Over the past five years, he has mastered the art of handling such situations. He will listen with one ear and let those words out in the next moment with the other. Nothing would retain in his mind between the ears to argue with. He will never let himself be carried away by her insistence.

He stared above at the mango canopy. It had blossomed densely. He remembered exactly two years ago, by this time, he had thanked nature for finding a suitable name for her daughter "Pallavi." A newly blossomed flower of every season affectionately rekindled him of the cheerful day when Pallavi was born. Distracted again by a thought, "Laxmi will put forth her concerns and discuss the benefits of his serious subservience." He knew it well that the same discussion, one way or another, would loop like the song of an old gramophone vinyl record when the needle gets stuck to its spiral track and plays the same track again and again. The arguments will invariably end with no conclusion.

His friend Rajat narrates to him about his encounters with his wife. He coaches him on how to play witty and artful in ladies' matters. He boasts of his remarkable mastery in switching topics to a new track for a matter of new discussion when embarrassingly caught on the wrong foot. He was proud to call himself a faithful liar. He cannot be like Rajat no matter what it is; he cannot be a faithful liar like him.

He knew well that the root cause behind all these in his house was a feyly lived neighbour, Mrs Sinha, his wife's bestie, who stayed next door and taught them what they ought to do in any matters related to their life. He kissed the good luck rings to keep her away from their discussion.

The topaz rings he slipped on his fingers were all bought with his hard-earned money after consulting a clairvoyant pundit. He was the only expert in the whole city who prophesied right for the Sinhas; the rest were all frauds, as claimed by Mrs Sinha. Pundit Ji claimed that the stones could control the movements of all celestial bodies. They were as precious as his life. To get those stones, he stood like one of those crazy destiny seekers who gathered outside Pundit Ji's office and looked for their life solutions in the stones. He was such a kind-hearted pundit, that he generously offered him a discount much below the price he had thought of for the negotiation. He knew for sure that Pundit Ji didn't give any discount to the Sinhas, but he offered him a considerable discount because he was a chauffeur to Mr. Sameer Malhotra. Pundit Ji remembered him as the same person who once came to him with his Sahib and insisted on a big stone, which was, in fact, the biggest one he had in his coffers, the most precious one. He took the stone from his coffer and sold it to his Sahib at a hefty price. He prophesied the tallest stardom for him. It brought Pundit Ji a little confusion about where he would wear it, but soon, he dispelled all his confusion right there when he suggested a diamond-studded masterpiece wristlet for his Sahib's enormous wrist. The stone fitted to his wristlet so tightly that it never fell from its socket, even by an act of vigorous gyration around his index finger. The gyration was his style, but the sparkling diamond made all the difference. It brought him into the limelight only for this reason. As told by many, it brought him loads of luck in the film industry. He ought to believe in Pundit Ji's service when he once again proved himself right for his Sahib. His television serials clicked, and he became a superstar.

Pundit Ji was considerate to Sagar when he learned about the financial burden he bore on his weak shoulder after his mother's hospitalization. Never mind, when he visited his office, Sagar found himself as one of the luckiest ones in the queue, with a roof over his head. He was stunned to see the highest rungs of almost every field had been photographed with Pundit Ji on one or several occasions in their lives. He bent fates for their good health and fat wealth.

Sagar prayed Laxmi in a delightful mood, at least for the last time. He thought inside that it would not happen from tomorrow onwards. The only wish he wanted out of his stones was for Mrs. Sinha not to jump into their every discussion in one way or another. It was ten minutes past nine on the clock. On the other side of the hedge, Mr Sinha, a dear neighbour, had finished his morning rituals. He had circled his decade-old noisy mower, pruned the trees, and watered them with an old hose in his front garden. A lucky man on a ten-to-five job, he was proudly kick-starting his old Vespa Scooter. He tilted it once again after his third unsuccessful attempt. The engine revved in its usual clamorous mode on the fourth attempt and ejected a jet of smoke through its pipe when he was done. He sat on the seat, twisted his wrists down, and soon, in the next moment, he was off to the road. When he waved his hand at Sagar, he waved back weakly and gave him a perfunctory smile. Sagar knew that the next day, he would be granted a day off upon the arrival of his fellow chauffer Rajat, who happened to be on leave. Sagar had picked up the guests of his sahib from the airport and dropped them at Hotel *La* Plasma in Santa Cruz.

He would get a complete day off once Rajat rejoins. His kind-hearted sahib realized a much-needed break for him to celebrate Pallavi's second birthday, scheduled for the next day. After uninterrupted duties during the last three months, he was desperate to take this break. He knew his wife must be asleep by now with his two-year-old daughter.

He sauntered towards the door, then adjusted the topaz rings worn on the four fingers of his right hand before tapping on the door. He tapped twice gently. On the other side, Laxmi got up from the bed and glided slowly through the main hall.

"Coming. Wait a minute," Laxmi screamed after a few seconds and opened the door partly just to let him inside. He walked across the living room as quietly as possible, padding softly. Nothing of that sort happened as he had feared, so after a moment of silence, his dried voice asked huskily, "How is Palo? Did she sleep after I left?"

Laxmi said lazily, " Palo is sleeping. She was looking for you. She cried and asked me why I allowed you to go when she saw the pillow you left on her side to guard her from falling. She was awake to see you until an hour ago."

"Hmm," he sounded tired, then lethargically slumped to recline on his armed rattan chair, unable to add more words to his further conversations until she went to the kitchen and brought him a glass of water.

She stood beside him to collect the glass and asked softly, pronto, "Who were they?" He replied gently and cautiously, "They were Sahib's guests from Dubai. I picked them up from the airport and dropped them at Hotel *La* Plasma." She took the glass from him and stared at his face. She could see the weariness on his face and noticed the distinct dark circles around his eyes. She murmured, "How long will you continue like this? You look frazzled. You will fall ill. Palo is missing you immensely. She has become a demanding child; She demands more time from you. She always wants you to be on her side to clap for her playful activities. " After a pause for a few seconds, she asked concernedly, "Why don't you find a new job, a less tiring one with no outstation duty? "Sagar was ready to answer. He intoned convincingly, "Just to earn a little extra at this age." She looked closely at his face. It appeared pale, fretful, and worn out. "Hey, is everything okay?" she asked with great concern, staring intensely at his face. She then turned to the kitchen before he could initiate a reply. He rose, yanked open the curtains to illuminate the dim-lit room, then plopped down gently again on the rattan chair. His eyes sneaked a look at the littered floor with toys and squeezed pieces of paper, and then they moved to settle on a pen and ink drawn meaningful graffiti on a wall of the room. In the next minute, he sat with his eyes closed. It seemed like he slept, but he did not. He silently pondered on the event that happened in the wee hours of the day.

He dozed until she got him a steaming cup of tea. After a few sips, he said, " Laxmi, they were strange people I ferried today. Ill-mannered. They don't know how to speak with a chauffeur. Sahib will never approve of someone showing me such behaviour. My blood boiled, but I chose to remain silent and patiently heard their harsh words because, as an Indian, I understand what Atithi devo bhava means to us. We offer our best service to keep them happy, but the Emiratis were very. er."

"I don't believe you. You must have poked in shrapnel-like words in their ears. First, tell me what you did with them. Not everyone is like your wife, who will listen quietly to your cheaply drawn parallels. You must have gotten them into some arguments," She asked promptly, cutting him off to complete her remarks.

"Stop blaming me for everything, Laxmi. When I picked up their heavy baggage and bundled them inside the car, I smelled cocaine."

"How can someone secret away drugs in the airport? You must have smelled something else."

Sagar said, "No, the stink was so obnoxious that I couldn't enter the car. It was intolerable. After some time, my nose became stuffy, my stomach churned, and I felt queasy. I hastily rolled down the window to tamp the stink and get some fresh air. The guests sitting in the rear seat rudely objected. One of them used harsh words – "Are you the owner of this car?" When I resisted and explained that I needed some fresh air, the other yelled, "Bloody fool, you're just a chauffeur; stay within your limits, learn to obey orders, do whatever you're asked to do. Don't act smart." I rolled up the window but felt choked in my throat. His words were distinct; she noticed his brow contract as he disappointingly completed his explanation. She knew in her heart that the car he had been driving was more than a darling to him. They struck a chord in his heart by asking about its ownership.

"Will you report your Sahib about their ill behaviour?"

"My sahib is a busy man, and he never pays heed to such petty issues. He is least bothered about who is doing what. He enjoys his drink, chats with friends, and loves his stardom. Nothing concerns him beyond this."

"Still, I feel you should inform him about the incident."

"No, I am not going to report it anyway. He is overburdened with work and has no time for all these things."

"Arre, how can you remain silent? Will you not even speak to him about the cocaine?"

"Your concern is genuine, Laxmi, but Sahib knows about these things."

"He knows about all these!",

"Yes, he is aware of this. His hotelier friends use these drugs in their parties to keep the guests high. It sells well in the market. The consumption of drugs at late-night parties has become an elite-class fashion these days. So, the matter of fact is that telling him about his guests' mis- conduct will have no impact on his way of looking at this matter. He won't take this seriously. He may not like to intervene in such a matter when his stature is growing well in public."

"Very strange personality. You never told me about this side of him. Now I am sure your sahib must be taking these drugs, which is why he is supporting them".

"No, Laxmi, Sahib is 24-carat gold. He does not take such drugs. He is scared about the media. These reporters may dig the story further and find a cause to tarnish his image."

"I don't believe whatever you say about him."

"The film magazines are full of such stories, who hit whom when drunk? Who has the time to deal with such things? Disha madam has so much work to do. It will be better if I keep my mouth shut." He tried to convince her.

"I see no good in this job. Leave it," She said concernedly.

"I had ten long years of association with our Sahib before our marriage. How can I leave him without a justifiable reason?"

"Don't say our Sahib. He is your Sahib, and you keep worshipping him every day. Think about buying our taxi." She took the empty cup from his hand and walked towards the kitchen.

Sagar said, "The buy of a taxi will cost a lot of money, which we cannot afford." She stopped midway, turned to him and said, "How did the Sinhas buy their scooter?"

"The bank will take half a month's salary through instalments. .er...It is okay to be desirous, and it is okay to have our own business. Being desirous of earning money is not bad. But Laxmi starting a business on loan is like walking against a slippery slope where one rises less and falls more. Sometimes, mathematics settles at zero and even at minus. It is not prudent to set the score in minus. The taxi business would require a huge capital investment to reap profit."

Laxmi said with deep concern, "If it is so, why can't we sell our jewellery? As such, they are rotting inside the chest, unused after your mother's death. I am not very fond of wearing them".

"Our days have not turned so bad that we need to buy a car with the proceeds from jewellery. Laxmi, keep them in the chest. Those are three generations-old heirlooms. Tomorrow, Palo will grow up, and she will want to wear them. How happy she will be when she wears them. We must keep those pieces for her marriage. The send-off will look decent."

"You can't do anything in life. You have reasons to dismiss my proposal this way or that way."

"Don't be upset. I will receive an increment in a couple of months. I am very close to a five-lakh kilometre target. It's just a matter of a few outstation trips. Look at Sinhas; they are still paying for the instalments for their ten-year-old scooter."

"I can start a small business, like stitching, knitting, making pickles, and papads, for extra income. I don't like you being away on frequent outstation trips. Be it winter, be it summer, be it rain, be it a day, be it a night, someday you will be in Pune, someday in Shirdi, and someday in Ahmednagar, you never take a break. How long will you continue like this? Don't you ever feel jaded?"

"Laxmi, If I do not work hard at this age, when will? In my old age with all creaky joints? "

"My concern is your health. Your Sahib will not slap you on your back for your servility and subservience. An old mule is never a master's favourite. Besides, how the wheel of time moves in a job like this is highly unpredictable."

"I cannot compromise with Sahib's comfort. After all, I have eaten his salt. In this trying time, we shall stand deeply rooted to withstand the storm. Good hard work reaps good results always. Trust me, Laxmi, nothing is going to happen to my health. By the end of this year, I will have an increment in my salary. I feel you should spend time with Palo instead."

He turned the handle, pushed the door, and went inside the bathroom to get a bucketful of water to wash the car. He placed the bucket under the tap and opened it to fill it. Meanwhile, he turned to the mirror and peered into it. He set his comb back his Kamala-Hassan-type-hairs and his bushy- moustache covering his upper lip. He furrowed his brow lines, stared at his dark brown eyes, pursed his lips, and whistled in a little joy. He moved his fingers gently backwards over his scalp through his dense, wavy hairs in a mood of self-appreciation. The water spilled from the bucket's edge. Laxmi screamed from the kitchen, "Which fairyland have you landed in? No heroine will sneak behind you. Look at your bucket, water spilling over." He was interrupted, and immediately, his hand reached for the tap to close it. She walked across the hall to see him in the bathroom. She stood at the door with her arms crossed and left shoulder leaning on the jamb. Glancing at his act, she was amused. Her chubby cheeks dimpled with a flirtatious smile on her face, her lips curled. She bared her teeth and clucked," *Arre*, my handsome husband, what are you doing here?"

"Darling, how many heroines will fall for this face if I shave off these stubbles? Tell me, how am I looking? Like Kamala Hassan in Sagar? Isn't he looking like me? "He said with a coquettish grin on his face.

She stood straight and looked at him piercingly. Her eyes narrowed like a cat's before a fight. "My handsome- dear husband, a father of two years old, stay away from these white - white – pretty –pretty - heroines. Your job is to serve your sahib, not his heroines. Sippy Sahib surely will not cast you opposite your Dimple Madam."

" Laxmi, Sagar -2 is coming very soon."

"If he selects you in his sequel Sagar -2, he will take you as a zombie to wander around Mona. People will throw eggs and tomatoes at you when they see you as a horrifying zombie singing O Maria, O Maria. er…,"

" No, that can't be. Dimple Madam is always a hit, whether with Rishi Ji or me. I will play a good zombie."

"You play a good zombie, but Rishi Ji will surely break your head. Good luck."

" For what?"

"You know why. Ramsay Brothers will hunt you for their next horror movie - A Super Zombie in the Cellar, six feet under," she articulated with a half-smile and flashed claws with her thin fingers.

" Raja can take rebirth for his darling Mona in Sagar -3. Now don't stand there, my heroine, leave my way; Sahib has called me at 4 PM." He came out with a bucketful of water and closed the door behind him. He said, "What if Mona steals me from you."

"I will kill that witch who dares to do so." Crossing her arms in front, rolling her eyes, she promptly said, contorting a smile, and nodded, "By the way, your Mona will turn grey-haired till you take rebirth. How does it feel for you romancing with a *Buddhi*? What is the wrong in me that you discover as right in your Madam? tell me."

A glow of morning sun evoked on his face when she said these words in a gentle fury. He re-admired, "Don't kill me with your look, darling. My heart flips. You turn prettier when you become red hot." The clock's pendulum chimed ding–dong at 10 o'clock, which reminded him that he had to report for duty at 4 PM. He must drop his Sahib at the Hotel *La* Plasma - a five-star rated, pearly white hotel. He would host a gala dinner to celebrate his admirable acting prowess – a successful accomplishment of a hundred episodes of his TV serial.

He rolled up his sleeves, and with the bucket in hand, he tiptoed outside.

Sagar was a tidy freak. He followed every word of his sahib and Sahib's secretary, Ms. Disha, with utmost allegiance. As a rule of thumb, he should never score less than a hundred per cent on the scorecard—each word of his master he merited with firm compliance. As a matter of responsibility, the cleanliness and the maintenance of his Sahib's car were his foremost priorities. He used to clean the car every day without fail after every trip and log it in his twice-the-pocket size logbook.

He opened the side doors first, left the key in the ignition, and kept the engine running. He checked all the lights, then blared the music system with his favourite disco beat, engaging himself in cleaning the interiors while singing off -key every word of the song into the air. He seemed happy. After switching the engine off, he climbed out and walked rearwards to open the hatchback. Inside the boot, his hand reached for a bottle of Johnnie Walker that he had received as a gift of happiness from his Sahib. He was not an alcoholic, but how could he not hold the bottle that his Sahib had gifted him last year when he won the best actor award? The city witnessed and praised the gala occasion that the Malhotra House had organized. Every guest was made drunk until every stomach regurgitated to its neck. That was the last party at Malhotra House, where he and Rajat received a bottle. If his Memsahib had been keeping well, he would have earned another gift this time. He would have asked for a lovely dress for Palo instead of a bottle of Johnnie Walker. Her choices are undoubtedly glamorous. She buys good clothes for her daughter, Diya. How sad! The sophistication on her face has been withered away by cancer," he thought with a drawn silence on his face.

He recollected the day, on that very occasion when a tipsy waiter arrived with a drink on his tray, he could not say -No. On Rajat's insistence, he took the second peg; on Memsahib's insistence, he took the third one. He felt muzzy, and he couldn't recall the fourth one. In a befuddled state, the only thing he could remember was Laxmi, who screamed at him endlessly and demanded a vow from him never to touch alcohol in life. As a few words of defence, he replied to her with a lingering-slurred voice that he couldn't say no to his Sahib because of his profound love for him. In a wit, once Laxmi demanded a reply, "What if Sahib asks you to jump into a well? will you?" He said, "Yes, I can do anything for him. If Sahib says so, I will."

He covered the bottle with a cloth to protect it from the jerks. He checked all the pieces of stuff lying in the boot to endorse them in the logbook, as per the instruction he received from Ms. Disha. He thought about how lucky his Sahib was to have Ms Disha as his secretary, who happened to be a very strict lady, both as a secretary and supervisor. It would never surprise him if she randomly checked inside when any matter arose in her mind out of suspicion.

Sagar was happy to see her taking good care of his Sahib. He could not forget the day when she sensed a threat to his Sahib's life. She jumped out first from the car on the mid-highway before it stopped, taking a great risk of being trampled by the loaded trucks trundling behind. Then she hurried to the back and opened the dickey to see if any bomb was implanted there.

He wrote in his logbook, "Air pressure in the Stepney checked - found OK, Tool kit count was correct, Dusting grade of the car – good, Headlights, Music system, Indicators – functioning well, any servicing required- No, Total Kms run 43555". He only knew how much happiness he used to get with the rise of every kilometre on the distance meter. In contrast, others guessed to find no reason for it to be etched on his face. If his mathematics were set right, he would be completing his cumulative five lakh Kms at the 50,000 mark, which means he would get an increment of two thousand rupees. He thought about how much happier Rajat had become on that day to receive an increment of two thousand rupees when he crossed the five-lakh kilometre mark.

He cleaned the outside body of the car with water and smeared it with car polish. When his eyes fell on his white uniform, it appeared dirty and worn out, and the peaked cap was greasy. The uniform had become a year old. "What would Sahib's heroines think of him if they continue to see him in the same uniform?" He thought of getting a pair of new uniforms stitched from outside after he received a dress allowance. Laxmi had tightened the chest at the seams to see him slim. She does not know how much inconvenience it causes him while raising his arms. The stitch lines will give away at the armpit to constant exposure to a cup of sweat.

He locked the car, entered the house, kept the bucket inside the bathroom and washed his greasy hands with soap. The soap attacks the germs that the paediatrician instructed him about. He followed the instructions religiously before touching Palo. He noticed a volt-face change in Laxmi's temperament since she attained motherhood. She behaved like Lady Hitler, who otherwise was an even-tempered lady. He remembered the day when his Hitleri wife had become angry at him when he touched Palo with dirty hands. She may even bristle to chop his fingers someday if he doesn't follow what she says. On that very day, she warned him and gave him a mouthful of harsh words to swallow, repent, and ponder. His first and last unforgivable mistake taught him to take great care of Palo since then. He became more cautious about personal hygiene and germs.

'Oh, you finished cleaning the *Gaadi* car. You took quite a long time to clean today,' Laxmi shouted from the kitchen. He responded immediately, "*Jaanu* sweetheart, *Gaadi*, and *Ghodi*, a car and a mare are the ones known to give problems if not properly taken care of," hinting the latter thrown as a cue word for Laxmi to react, but his smile melted down as he did not receive a retaliatory response from the kitchen.

Exhausted, he took off his crisp, clingy uniform and draped a loincloth around his worn body. His face was smeared with a sheen of perspiration. The tiny drops of his sweat hung precariously as if adjusting their surface tensions before rolling down his brow in shimmering rivulets. He washed his face and stared at his one-day-old stubble before taking a clean shave with a new razor.

Images flickered in his mind of all occasions where the camera captured his swift movements as he quickly stepped out of the car, like a well-rehearsed actor, to open the door for his Sahib. Each moment replayed vividly, the flash of cameras illuminating the scene, showcasing his persona in the uniform. After cleansing his greasy uniform, he soaked under the shower and applied soap until a rich, foamy lather enveloped him. After the shower, he towelled off to dry and slipped into a top and pyjamas. A sense of tranquillity washed over him with this.

He inscribed a few lines in the to-do list of his diary. He learned the habit of writing a diary in the morning from Ms. Disha. Initially, it was to learn English; after that, it became a daily habit. With the arrival of every new year, she gifts Rajat and him an expensive diary to inculcate in them the habit of maintaining personal activities. According to Ms Disha, "The diary is a stockade of memorable events, so inscribe every page well." He spent a few minutes in puja before breakfast. Laxmi knew well that he was devout like his mother, so he was never to be disturbed until he came and asked for breakfast.

Palo had been asleep; it was quarter to eleven by the clock. Sagar recalled his mother telling Laxmi about Palo, "The longer she sleeps, the bigger her brain will be." He missed her presence, cooking tips, and skilful home remedies. She was the one who taught Laxmi how to make perfect gravy and taught her the herbal remedies for many diseases.

Laxmi adjusted the loose tresses behind her ears. Sagar's gaze caught her momentarily. Seeing her doing this, he wished, at least, Laxmi could have a quest for perfect hair. She should have learned some beauty tips as the sole inheritor from his mother, better than Mrs Sinha. What hadn't Mrs Sinha tried on her hair? A ton of *Multani Mitti*, Fuller's earth, to charm Mr Sinha by flaunting her long, silken, Dimple madam type, crowning glory hair. He knew well that Laxmi never felt comfortable unleashing her large bun. He missed his mother, who was no longer in the world to share such tips. Sagar had no siblings whom Palo could call uncle and aunt. Sagar's father had passed away when he was just eight, and his mother took responsibility for raising him to be a kind-hearted and God-loving soul. So, Sagar never ate his breakfast without performing puja in his mini temple. After the puja, he sat at the table for breakfast and praised Laxmi for her mastery of culinary skills. Laxmi knew well that Sagar would instantly spark with energy after breakfast but would lose it equally as fast if he couldn't make it for a timely lunch someday. Her biggest concern was Sameer Sahib's erratic work schedule. Lately, his lunchtimes have been irregular because of Sahib's tight shooting schedule and frequent hopping from one set to another.

"Sagar will fall sick if he doesn't care for his health," she thought concernedly.

"Laxmi, you finally learned how to make good food."

"Thank you, but you haven't yet savoured a bite, dear."

He shut his eyes and ran his tongue over his lips, "Yummy, mouth-watering, spicy scent." "My ears waited all these years to hear this from you, dear. I can't think how to react. You have a superb, acquired taste, you know. Why?"

"Why?"

"Because you liked the food when I hadn't put salt in it."

"No salt! But why?"

"Why No salt! I have been telling you to bring at least the essential rations for the last few days. But you didn't. You had no time. Now, there is no salt in the kitchen."

"Saltless diets today? Wow! You know, Laxmi, the doctors say it keeps your blood pressure under control."

"Don't increase my blood pressure now, Sagar. Can you ever become serious?"

It was eleven in the morning when Pallavi was woken up by their gossip. She climbed down from the bed and saw that her breakfast had been prepared and was ready on the table. Laxmi gripped her arm and dragged her away before she could put her fingers inside the porridge. Laxmi snapped her eyes at Palo. This is how the child is taught manners. She knew it as a mother of this cherubic two-year-old. She warned Palo not to put anything inside her mouth before brushing her teeth.

He burst into a fit of laughter when he saw Palo attempting a fistful of porridge by dipping her hand inside the bowl, unable to grab it with her little fist. Laxmi also enjoyed that moment. He made fun of her, saying, "How will you keep the world in your fist, Palo when you cannot grab the porridge?" Knowing that such an act beguiled her parents and set off giggles in them, she did it repeatedly. Palo demanded, "Give me the world; I will hold it." Laxmi said in fun, "You will have to make yourself big to hold the big world." A minute later, Laxmi spoon-fed her and said, "Finish the bowlful of porridge; then you will grow taller, stronger, and bigger." She asked, "Bigger than Papa?"

Sagar replied, "Yes, bigger than Papa." After a moment of silence, Palo drawled through a mouthful of porridge, "Papa, *whel wel* where were you? I missed you last night."

He amusingly replied, "I had gone to the market to get you a new frock and a few toys," while she swallowed. "Give me the toys, where are they?" Palo demanded after clearing her throat.

Sagar artfully replied, "The shop was closed, as the shopkeeper was sleeping with the shop closed during the night."

She asked him engagingly, "Why didn't you wake him up if he was sleeping?"

"To avoid getting disturbed from sleep, the shopkeeper had set a big dog free on those who knock at the door of his shop at night. The brute had long, sharp canines and gnawed on a bone. He stared at me through his big, wheel-sized angry eyes, grunted and came bounding down the stairs. He didn't allow me to meet the shopkeeper," he explained.

"Why didn't you give some biscuits to hush the dog?" Palo asked intelligently.

He said, "I took the biscuits but ate them up on the way when I felt hungry."

Laxmi intervened, "Finish your porridge; otherwise, your Papa will eat everything. He has a big tummy." She said while pointing her finger towards his tummy. She hurriedly ate the bowlful of porridge in her hand and spilled a quarter.

Laxmi said, "Allow your tired Papa to get some sleep so he can fight well with the barking dogs tonight, and you play with your toys."

As a child, Palo was playful, active, and intelligent. Her tiny hand picked up a crayon and effortlessly glided across a glossy drawing sheet. She drew some meaningful patterns on the paper like those she had drawn on the walls within her reach. Not settling with this act alone, she explored a few of her secret corners and showed up a few minutes later with a toy car and a bagful of plastic cubes. She wandered from one room to another, chasing her car. Then, she settled silently in the centre of the room with the cubes. At first, she tried stacking them one above the other. When it collapsed, she configured a different approach and succeeded. She switched to a victorious mode by clapping intensely and smiling sincerely over her achievement. Being engrossed with all the amusements, she proclaimed her victory to her mother by loudly and repeatedly saying, "Mama, I made it."

She toddled from room to room until she found her mother had left the kitchen open for her to play with the utensils. She helped her mother arrange her crockery and cutlery after she washed them in the sink. She had put her teddy bear on the bed, and to ensure her father had not disturbed it from its place, she ran to the bedside to see if it had been disturbed. Laxmi dragged her out of the bedroom and warned her not to disturb Papa as he was tired from waking up early. After a brief cry, she hunkered down on the kitchen floor with her other set of toys. It was a toy kit of household items: a gas stove, a pressure cooker, a few plastic plates, and bowls. She only took out the set when she watched her mother busy in the kitchen so that she could compete with her in making food. She pretended to prepare all types of imaginary dishes and served them to her mother, asking her opinion. She babbled on about the new cooking methods she used. Laxmi beamed at her such playful, childish activities, which she could never tell her to buzz off. Instead, for a moment, she carried on a conversation with her to show her interest and catered to Palo's demand for that moment. Palo needed patience while she elaborated on her newly learned culinary skills.

Laxmi woke up Sagar for lunch. He stretched on the bed to comfort his back and calf muscles. As soon as he woke up, Palo hit the bed with her new set of crayons. She asked for his assistance in selecting colours. It was 2 PM on the clock, so he left the bed and threw himself onto the rattan chair. Still, a part of laziness and drowsiness lingered in his body. Before serving him a timely lunch, Laxmi asked, "Have you paid the electricity bill for this month? We need to refill gas in the kitchen soon because the present one will finish soon."

He said, "No."

"Why don't you pay our bills when you go to deposit Sahib's bills?" she bristled.

"Laxmi, Sahib's bills come in thousands, and you know very well that I never mix personal work with my professional work," Sagar explained placatingly.

She asked, "Why don't you take some time for ours?"

Before he could reply, his eyes settled on the clock ticking 2:30 PM. He continued, "I will pay the bill once I withdraw money from the bank." Giving her a logical explanation, he said, "The day before yesterday was a nationwide shutdown called by the opposition party, and for the last two days, you have seen me, I have had no time to breathe comfortably. Every time I go to the bank, I stand in the queue for thirty minutes to withdraw the money. One person told me the government would introduce computers into the banks."

"Once it becomes computerized, I will no longer have to wait in the queue, and paying electricity bills will no longer be a big task." He tried to change the course of the discussion on computerization. Laxmi stood beside the table and said clearly, complaining, "Sinhas are getting a new telephone connection. Why can't we?"

"Who told you? All falsehood. It is not easy to get a telephone connection. You apply today, and then you get a connection after two years. The waiting period is too long. Mr. Sinha has never told me about this in the last two years."

"Why would Mrs. Sinha tell me a lie?" She said, "Mr. Sinha's company, Asian Express, is giving them a free telephone connection."

"Oh, that is the case. Who will pay the telephone bills, did you ask? She must have told you it is free, isn't it?" Sagar said laconically.

"Yes, she said so. She showed me a picture of the handset. It was very beautiful," she said, pronto. Sagar had nothing more to ask. He needed to stop the discussion before it got stretched inexorably long. Sagar was happy to change the course of the discussion, but the happiness didn't last long when Mrs. Sinha jumped into their conversation out of nowhere. Without wasting a second, he sat at the table and ate lunch. By this time, Pallavi was ready with her bowlful of rice mixed with dal and was trying to lift a fistful to feed her mouth.

After lunch, he wore his ironed uniform. He gave Laxmi a few hundred rupees and asked her to buy some balloons, a cake, and sweets for Palo's birthday party.

Laxmi served her food on the same unwashed plate Sagar ate to keep their love growing. Palo sampled a piece of pickle on the plate, which lit her mouth like fire. In a jiffy, she rushed to pick up her favourite tiny water bottle, which she had left in the kitchen while playing with the toys. Laxmi finished her food.

Sagar pressed a tender, loving kiss upon Laxmi's supple cheek before giving her a departing hug. He left the home waving goodbye. Through a lingering wave of hands, Laxmi's eyes sought a promise of swift return. Sagar's eyes twitched with an unspoken promise as their distance widened. Laxmi's eye followed him till he drove away.

At Sahib's residence in Juhu, he saw the parking lobby occupied by a large van from a news channel. His gaze caught from a distance that Sahib was busy with his interview, which was being recorded by a camera crew. With the keys in hand, he approached the security guard at the main gate for a security check on the vehicle. In the past, the guard had resisted him once for having a bottle of whisky in the car, but he later cleared him of this offence when he pleaded with a promise to keep it untouched.

He knew well that when such a press event happened at the Malhotra house in the past, Disha Madam got occupied with event management. She must be busy inside her cabin. Ms. Disha was a well-known face in the media houses. The former Bollywood actress is now Sahib's well-experienced private secretary and PRO. As far as he knows, Cheema, the hotelier friend of Sahib who owns *La* Plasma, introduced her to Sahib two years ago.

He entered the main lobby where the journalists were interviewing his Sahib, and in the room next to it, Ms Disha was busy preparing the speech for Sameer for the gala event at Hotel *La* Plasma. She signed the logbook and handed over a prescription to get the medicines for Memsahib, Madam Shreni, who was a television actress currently battling lung cancer.

If I were to mention a few things about Shreni, she used to smoke uninterruptedly. When asked to refrain in good times, she said the habit had been working wonders to control her weight. It was all she needed to suppress her appetite to start with, but when it turned into an addiction, she didn't recall. As a personality, she was pretty upbeat and ebullient, but the chemo made her wholly bedridden and dependent on a private nurse for care. A dedicated nanny was looking after her daughter Diya.

Sagar left for the shop to buy the medicines written on the prescription. "You seem to be in a hurry, sir. Wait for the shopkeeper who has gone to his stockroom to take stock of the consignment he received a while ago," a voice came from behind. He turned around to see a middle-aged man in a white kurta pyjama. Clean-shaven with a tall frame. He said, "Hello dear, I am Chunnilal; I am also here to take the medicines. It is very urgent, but we need to wait. There is no other shop nearby." The shopkeeper appeared there, making an apologetic tone, "Sorry, Chunni bhai, I couldn't deliver your medicines on time because of a complete nationwide shutdown. The medicines arrived today. They were supposed to be delivered two days ago. You know, who cares about the patients in the city? Besides politics, no one is bothered about those in distress and battling for life. Who cares?" The shopkeeper handed over the packet with the list of medicines to Chunnilal.

Chunnilal said happily, "Thank you, my wife was in urgent need of these medicines. I waited for two days but finally got them today." He left the place.

Sagar reached the Malhotra house after getting the medicines. The journalists were winding up. Ms. Disha kept the medicine strips and handed him one food coupon and one liquor coupon, which carried her signature at the bottom - Madhubala. Ms. Disha was also known in *La* Plasma by this name. She owned a new name, Disha, after starting her own Disha Beauty Parlour and Disha PR agency.

He dropped off his Sahib and Ms Disha at Hotel *La* Plasma in a few minutes. As per the schedule, his Sahib reached for a stage rehearsal at five in the evening. Three hours left for him to observe the guests rolling in for the party at eight. He waited outside the hotel's parking. A few BMWs and Jaguars filled the car lot. He listened to the clunk of the door being shut behind him and the cacophony of chauffeurs hitting the basement canteen as the TV was playing a live cricket match between India and Pakistan to entertain them.

He eagerly stood at the parking. His darting eyes long gazed at the glamour of the beautiful crowd entering. The paparazzi clicked them against a big banner carefully kept at the entrance. The minute hand crossed ten minutes past eight, his mind turned glum and restless, and his wandering eyes looked sullen. A moment later, his eyes suddenly gleamed bright when he saw his favourite madam appear in a flowery kaftan out of nowhere at the disembarking point. The crowd around her seemed to hold their breath in admiration.

The guests around her looked fresh with their well-lacquered hair. Such a moment was a visual treat to his eyes. His eyes lit up like a bolt of sunshine breaking through the faded clouds. He bore the freshness of a bloomed flower on his face. He smelled the fragrance in the air in a gush of breeze when he saw her sleek, dark, crowning glory hairs shimmering in the flash of camera light and swinging in the air. He looked at her until she made it to the lobby and shimmied down on the carpet at the entrance. The wind carried a mixed aroma of jasmine and rose towards him. He envied the man who escorted her into the lobby but went crestfallen for not having a sinewy chest like that bodybuilder.

The heroines looked tall with their high-heeled sandals and body-hugging slim outfits, and the heroes looked fabulous with their puffed-up bodies and tantalizingly swollen biceps. The squeal of excitement continued until the photographers clicked their last shot, who later headed towards dinner in the canteen in the basement. They all watched the remainder of the cricket match live inside.

The bartenders at the basement lobby bar doled out drinks. The dispensation signal passed from one person to another, pulling the crowd around the bar like ants hoarding around sugar. No more than one drink was allowed per coupon for hard drinks, and there were no such restrictions for soft drinks and food. Anyone could have as much as they wanted. Sagar made a whiskey and tingly Campa-cola cocktail diluted to the point where it filled a glass. In the past, he had left Laxmi rankled for a month for not apologizing for his drunken act. "Not more than one peg," clucked in his mind. He felt happy not to have Rajat around for the first time. Had he been there, he would not have left without making him drink less than a quarter of the bottle from the bottle of Johnny Walker he kept in the dickey. He was the one insisting on having the bottle inside the car.

Sagar knew a few of them personally as they regularly showed up at every party. They discussed secret affairs, marital discords, breakups, wages, and perks in B-town. A few narrated the story of their struggling days in Bollywood before becoming a chauffeur. Sagar's attention was drawn to a circular table in the extreme corner of the hall. He met ASAP, and his full name was Adarsh Satyabadi Alpabhashi Pattanayak.

I know that ASAP was a witty and resourceful secret agent in Bollywood. He carried all the secret information about the inner circles of B-town. Usually, he kept people engaged until he vomited every piece of information churning in his stomach. He spoke only the truth, whether it was brunt or bitter. Adarsh was in his early forties, with premature baldness evident on his head. The scalp was covered by carefully combed few strands of fine, thin, black, and wispy hairs. His brow always bore a red tilak in the centre, and friends often greeted him as Guruji. He was a chauffeur to Ms. Vanya, who was the female lead in Sameer's tele-serials. According to him, the B-town gossip was not easy to understand due to too many cross-connections: a mess of secret conspiracies and agreements for all illegal purposes.

Ms. Vanya had tried to enter Sameer's life before Shreni, but her castle of love was smashed to smithereens when Sameer proposed to Shreni in a dance show. The Shreni-Sameer pair ruled the screen for years before getting bonded in wedlock. Due to a long battle with cancer, Shreni left the show, and Vanya replaced her on the persuasion of Cheema. According to ASAP, Cheema was a married man, the father of a two-year-old son, and Vanya was his paramour.

Vanya and Shreni knew each other from their struggling days in B-town. In Bombay, they stayed in the same working women's hostel. Vanya was the one who orchestrated a zero figure for Shreni. The mantra she gave her was to smoke to lose weight. Their quest to stay in shape was aided by Cheema, who owned the hostel and became a supplier of illegal cigarettes to the residents. He had a gambling instinct as big as his luck. Over a few years, he transitioned into a hotelier and owned *La* Plasma. As a skilful businessman, Cheema knew how to expand his empire. To increase sales in Bollywood, he entered the glamorous world through his film connections. He had a long list of contacts in Bollywood, and Disha was one of them. Sameer learned about Cheema from Vanya and later became close associates in the film production industry.

Cheema has become a financier for Sameer's projects. Now, he has invited two drug dealers from Dubai to invest in Sameer's project. Sameer was not oblivious to Cheema's illicit and unlawful activities, which he carried out under the guise of a hotel business.

Joining him at the table, Adarsh asked, "How is your boss?"

He replied, "How would a person feel whose wife is not well?"

Adarsh sniggered after taking a sip of whisky and said, "Are you aware your boss is dating Madam Vanya?"

Sagar's cheeks flushed angrily, and he said, "Stop it, Adarsh. These are all rumours."

Adarsh gazed at his angry face and said, "Telling you the truth, the sole truth, cent per cent absolute truth."

"Absolute truth!"

"Whether you believe me or not, your sahib is courting Madam Vanya. The intense coochie cooing scenes say a lot. These scenes were not in the script when it was written."

"Did you write the script?"

"I am happy that I am a driver. I drive cars, sell stories, and earn ten times what a scriptwriter does. Have you seen that song? Like that Abdul fellow in that song, I keep tabs on everything happening around me. Your Sahib is in the television business. It is a family entertainment show. All family members sit together and watch him and what he does. Lately, those scenes portray significant revelations about your Sahib."

"About Sahib's what? Extra-marital affair with your Madam Vanya! All nonsense. No, I don't believe you."

"Believe me or not, these filmy people have a very complicated, tangled-up past. They are addicted to having many affairs. After number one, they will die for numbers two and three; God only knows how many. Numerous, potentially even more than can be counted. They sing soft, romantic songs under the moonlight. The terrace door remains open. The heroine stands at the doorway. The candlelight flickers in the gentle breeze and gets extinguished, and finally, their desires unleashed."

"My Sahib is 24-carat gold. He believes in one life, one woman. Despite life giving him roller coaster rides on the personal front, he keeps himself going with work on the professional front."

"Nope. I am eager for you to ask around if I am wrong."

"I am his chauffeur. I know more about him than you."

"Don't pretend, Sagar. I don't like it."

"What do you know about my Sahib? Say it clearly. Don't circle the words like a Jalebi. Be straight."

"Relax, Sagar, I know because I want to know. You don't know because you don't want to know."

"Okay, tell me what you know about Sahib."

"There is a conspiracy going around your Sahib. Cheema is eyeing your Sahib's property. He has made a secret deal with Madam Vanya."

"What secret deal?" Sagar asked.

"Do you know who the men you picked up from the airport were? Did your madam Disha say who the persons were? I am sure she hasn't."

"They were Sahib's friends. Ms Disha asked me to pick them up from the airport."

Adarsh grinned and said, "That is why I am saying they made a fool of yourself. Your Sahib is too straight to understand the conspiracy around him."

"Open up how?" Sagar blurted.

"Conspiracy, a deep conspiracy. Cheema called the firangis. Both are Cheema's overseas partners in the drug business. They are drug suppliers. Cheema and Madam Vanya are persuading your Sahib to invest in big projects. Are you aware that Cheema has loaned a few crores to your Sahib to see your Sahib's estate and house pawned someday? He is lucky because his serials clicked; otherwise-."

"Otherwise, what would have Cheema done?"

"This is not new. Cheema's entire motives are mercenary, whether right or wrong. Tactically, in the past, he has foreclosed on many producers' property by delaying their projects. He is such a low-level man who would trade his wife and son for money. Forget about your Sahib. He is a greedy money lender like a Lala from a Hindi movie whose appetite for money is so whetted that he can go to any level to own his property. Honesty is an oddity in him. He is dipped in black business from head to tip of his toes."

"Is he that dangerous as a man? My Sahib needs to be careful."

"I want you first to be a little careful. Your unwavering trust in them will put you in great trouble. Someday, you will get caught with the drugs, and these firangis will fly away. Your Sahib will also be in great trouble. Cheema is very shrewd; he will take all his properties."

Sagar started believing that Adarsh's every word was the "only truth." He had never thought about it. He pondered, "What would have happened if the police had stopped his car in the morning?" He had finished his peg but wanted to delve deeper into the conversation to know more from ASAP. He got to his feet and went to the bartender to order a second round of paid drinks, one for him and another for Adarsh. He thought to himself, "Yes, he is right. The firangis had brought drugs in their bags."

"Say more about these conspirators, Patnayak. I want to know," Sagar asked after gulping a large sip.

Adarsh said, "Madam Vanya called your Sahib and asked him to send you to the airport, saying I was sick. Do you see any problem with my health now? I am quite hale and hearty, perfectly fine. I always keep myself fit."

"No," Sagar replied.

"It was a solid plan to-," Patnayak stopped.

"What plan, Patnayak?"

"Vanya Madam is a bit of a wild schemer type of lady. She knows when to act and when not to. *La* Plasma is not far from her house. She used your car to pick up the cocaine from the airport, not hers. Interestingly, four hours later, at seven in the morning, she sent me to Hotel *La* Plasma to pick up a packet and a bouquet. The packet was gift-wrapped. Do you know why?"

"Why?"

Adarsh said, "She kept the packet and brought the bouquet to give the guests at the party." After gulping, he added, "Listen, these masters think we are some fools. But we are not. What was the urgency of getting the bouquet when the party was in the evening? It was a well-orchestrated plan. Are you getting what I am saying? What was the hurry to get the bouquet from the hotel when she came here in the evening? We came at five in the evening for a program at eight. My name is ASAP, and they cannot fool me. I smelled the packet; it dispersed the scent of cocaine."

"What is she going to do with that?" Sagar asked.

"Of course, not to throw them in the drain. Vanya Madam will consume it secretly," Adarsh said.

"Is it?"

"Yes, once I had a peek into her vanity van. I was surprised to see her taking a packet from a sanitary pad. One cigarette means a bundle of confidence, which she desperately needed for the party. What do you think? Where does the confidence exude from?"

"From these contrabands! "

Sagar was very involved in the conversation. He bought them a third round of drinks to continue further with ASAP. Sagar asked, " Does Ms. Disha know about this drug business?"

Adarsh replied, "She is one of those knowingly unknown beauties in B-town, A victim of debauchery. She knew Cheema when he was a nobody. This Cheema, who owns this Hotel, was once a coolie in the railway station. Now, he has jointly taken a farmhouse in her name, and she doesn't know how the farmhouse is being used, er, misused."

" Misused! " Sagar asked.

" Yes, misused. Criminals and drug barons come and stay there. Everything is happening under her nose. The plot was registered in her name so that she would be caught if ever raided. Cheema can wash his hands off easily. So, Sagar, you be careful. " ASAP cautioned.

Sagar's eyes narrowed. He asked, "How do you know so much inside B-town Patnayak? Adarsh suddenly shrieks with a smug nod, " I know because I want to know. Bottoms up."

- II -

Ramdutt Shivdasani, aka Romy, lived in an imposing house in Dharavi, Bombay. The spherical lamps on the gate posts cast light upon the roads in the front. The light above the shingle illuminated "Ram Dutt Shivdasani and Briksha Roy" distinctly. The letters were golden, glittering against a background of black stone.

The clock hands had moved into the small hours, and it was 2 AM by the clock; Romy was in his study. He was working on a presentation that he had been preparing since evening for a board meeting scheduled in the morning. He had almost consumed three mugs of coffee after dinner. His eyes settled on the grandfather clock, which struck three. He rose from the couch and walked towards the window. He stood there with his hands on his hips and leaned backwards to unkink his sore back. In the next moment, he put his hands inside the pocket of his kurta and glanced at the road outside from his balcony. He was looking anxious. He desired to have a fourth mug.

Meanwhile, his wife Briksha entered the room, breaking her sleep in the middle, as evidenced by her hanging tresses and unkempt hair. Staring at him through her sleepy eyes, she asked, "Aren't you getting any sleep tonight? What are you doing here?"

Romy said, "Just watching the bustling city and staring at its roads. From here, I have seen the traffic weaving through the roads at night and joggers charging in the morning, but why do they only ask me where I am? Their adoration for me is still immense. They are the same old roads that sheltered me in my struggling days until you came into my life. **A new road lies ahead, adding a new turn and a new chapter in my life tomorrow.** It will surely change the course of my destiny, surely to prosperity. But can I leave them behind for a new highway? They inspire me every moment, telling me who I was and who I am."

The words emotionally challenged Briksha, who couldn't find any words to atone.

He asked her, "Why am I feeling so restless, Briksha? I want to know. I was a nobody in the city. You came into my life, and everything changed after that. You gave me the courage to advance in life and showed me a direction."

Briksha replied, "We have enough time to discuss it later, now you go and sleep. Papa had called from Singapore, and he was asking about your promotion."

Romy said, "I don't know why I am feeling so anxious today, so please sit by my side for a while. I want you to always be by my side, Briksha."

They both sat on a swing. The brightness of the full moon spread all over. They sat hand in hand, with her head resting on his shoulder. Romy said, "I forget all my worries when you sit like this. Do you remember the day when we met for the first time?"

She said, "Exactly five years ago, you forgot to wish me a happy meeting anniversary today."

"So sorry, darling," he said apologetically.

Romy asked, "You never told me why you chose me in the interview. I want to hear from you today."

She said, "The good quality in you was that you were true to yourself. You had a sense of being yourself despite being anxious. You were blunt, too. I was delighted to choose you for the company when you pronounced super confident towards the end of the interview instead of becoming arrogant. Do you remember when the question was thrown to mock your dressing sense? How brilliantly you defended without giving yourself a chance to evade the question. Others might have chosen over the rest because of your prowess in convincing people, but my way of choosing was different."

"Different?" Romy questioned.

"I chose you for myself because of your shirt for the interview. Still, you haven't told me where you got the shirt from and where you get your confidence from. You are not just an ordinary man; within you reside an extraordinarily talented man."

Romy still didn't reveal about the shirt he had bought from a jumble sale raised for a charity of street urchins. Romy replied, "You made me super confident that day. I was nervous initially, but you were so beautiful and radiant that I could not hold my confidence back. I unleashed the horse within. I didn't know I would ever get you as my wife. You never told me who they were asking for your hand before me?"

Briksha said, "Let me tell you today. No one could capture my emotions that day. That was the prime piece of the interview. It was the moment when you saw me through my eyes; I, too, saw those beaming eyes of yours. You ought to be selected, my heart said. I followed what my heart said. I was smitten."

After a pause, Briksha asked, "Have you finished your presentation? If not, can I help you?"

"Yes, all done, thank you. People curse me, saying I stole their good boss and kept her caged at home. You didn't tell me when you will join the Singapore company."

"Let them find a new boss. I am not going to leave you and Honey. I have left everything up to the management to decide. If management decides to absorb me here, then it is fine. Otherwise, I would resign. I am not going to leave India at any cost."

Romy said, "Call your parents from Singapore if they can stay with us."

"Have you gone mad? After all these--" Briksha said.

"All those bitterness has been patched up now. They have accepted me as their son-in-law. I don't see any problem now."

"You call them if you want, but I will not call. When did they accept you? They accepted you when Honey came into my womb," Briksha replied.

Romy replied, "Let bygones be bygones. Look at them in a new light. You would like to see them again." The pride was at stake. She said, "I disagree. Some aches are not so easy to forget."

She yawned hugely. It was 3 AM on the clock. Briksha rose from the swing and said, "Have we gone mad? Is this the time to discuss such things?" She pulled him inside the room, and her arms went around as she gathered him. Looking at his face, she said, "You are crazy." She smacked a kiss and then nudged him to the bedroom.

The morning light appeared dim through her glass window, the alarm clock on her side table beeped, and she groped to stop it by pressing the button at the top. She glanced through her sleepy eyes; its hands, in a straight line, struck six. She fell back asleep. Half an hour later, the phone rang in the drawing room, and the sound disturbed her. She woke up. The light had become brighter outside. Honey had shifted his position from the middle to the leg side of the bed. She removed the wet diaper wrapped around his waist and replaced it with a new one. The toddler had not learned nocturnal bladder control, so she had to do it regularly every morning.

Standing before the portrait of Lord Shiv in her bedroom, she clasped her hands in prayer, seeking happiness for her family. She murmured a few words with closed eyes before moving to the kitchen to prepare tea. That was her strength – the ability to do what was right, not just a reason to ward off all evil eyes. The sound of the doorbell interrupted her routine, prompting her to accept a milk delivery.

As she settled with the morning newspaper, a headline caught her eye: "Asian Express Private Limited Reports $1.5 Billion Profit." Reading about Ram Dutt Shivdasani's accolades, her tears of pride welled up. The MD had high praise for the efforts put in by Romy, who had brought the company to a worthwhile level. She couldn't hold the good news for long. The boy who once strolled on the street searching for a decent job had made a big way in the business. Such brilliant work! She felt proud of him and felt good about herself for choosing him for the company over the rest when she headed the HR division. She still couldn't understand why such a brilliant person decided to wear a jazzy outfit for the interview. The tone of his voice was remarkable when he confidently bluffed to the selectors that the brand was famous for making high-quality stuff at a lower price for the commoner. Although she was not convinced as a selector, the confidence he exuded had given her goosebumps.

She noticed the same confidence on his face while he was interviewed a few days ago. The other side of this man was that he never took this art of convincing people too seriously. Still, the brand of the shirt he wore that day remained a big paradox. He picked up the marketing strategy so well to lure the ordinary men. He made it to the highest-selling company in Asia in software products. He was happier with his black Toyota Corolla than a Merc Benz or BMW offered by the company. He didn't even ask for a chauffeur from the company to include the savings as a profit.

The tea was ready on the bedside table at 7:30 AM. The aroma of the freshly brewed tea filled the air and the room. She gently woke Romy, who was not in a deep slumber. There was a bit of reluctance, but she couldn't help it. A helpmeet's mind weighed heavily on her. Her foremost concern was The thought of him not being late for the office. He should be ready for the presentation well before the time. 'The board of directors would surely notice if he arrived late for the presentation,' she pondered anxiously.

Romy turned to his side; his eyes rested on Honey for some time. He caressed Honey's tiny hand and shook him slightly for fun to gauge his reaction, but Honey remained in the blissful embrace of deep slumber, oblivious to the world around him. Romy rose from the bed and sipped the steaming cup of tea, feeling invigorated further by a cheerful morning wish from his wife, who was standing a little distance away, observing all this.

Briksha served the breakfast to her eager companion at the table. While he savoured each bite, she took out the floppy disk from his computer after checking the contents, carefully packed it inside its cover, and kept it inside his attache case. She was going to keep the newspaper folded for him to read in the office, but then she decided to show him the news highlighting his company's accomplishments. She waited until he finished his breakfast. He was in such a hurry that he had forgotten to zip up his pants. She teased him for this and, with full laughter, asked him to keep his zipper shut before the board could question him about the brand and cost of his underwear. Her words were enough for him to become self-conscious. He had been consumed by the thought of his presentation in front of the board for a brief time while having breakfast. She brought him back to the real world by showing him the newspaper. It was 8:30 AM by the watch, and he was not too late for the office. It was the usual time for him to leave the house. Briksha enveloped him in a warm embrace and bestowed a tender, loving, departing kiss on his brow before handing him his attache case. She watched him go and waved goodbye.

As she sat down to eat her breakfast, the thoughts of Romy continued to play with her emotional centres uninterruptedly. Despite her efforts to avoid anything related to Asian Express, the waves of memories and contemplations refused to subside. She was so engrossed in her inner turmoil that she didn't even notice when the maid came and started sweeping the floors.

Suddenly, the presence of Honey beside her snapped her out of her reverie. The child had woken up and was demanding his special food. An hour later, the shrill ringing of the telephone interrupted the tranquillity of the morning. She picked up the receiver and said, "Hello," her voice tinged with a hint of curiosity. Her father was on the other side, calling her from Singapore to share the news he had read in the Singapore Daily about an hour ago. He sounded happy for Romy.

He asked, "What have you decided about joining the Singapore firm? Honey will stay with us if you join here, and you can attend the office."

Briksha replied, "Papa, you never change. You always think about me. Have you ever thought about how Romy will live without me? He is such a wonderful person who always speaks highly of you. He was thinking of calling you, and you are trying to keep me away from him. I am inseparable. I live for him and die for him."

He said, "Don't take me wrong, Beta. I am also thinking of inviting him to Singapore. If he had not been considered for this promotion, I would have offered him a job in my company as a business manager. But I am not forcing both of you to quit and join me; you don't think I have any personal interest in this. I had a false perception of his abilities. I considered him an ordinary man, but he proved me wrong. He is a self-made man, and I am happy to have him as my son-in-law. The decision lies with him or both of you."

Briksha reminded herself that she should remain silent if she didn't have to hurt her practical father. For him, the news wasn't warm when he learned about her affairs with Romy, so he cut the links. All those years together, for him, her sister Brinda was a darling daughter as she chose an Army officer as a groom. She would prefer to resign from the company rather than consider a shift to Singapore. Finally, she silenced her father by saying, "The company appreciates his work, Papa, and the directors feel that he should continue here in India for a few more years."

Honey strode in and picked up a toy gun lying on the centre table in the room. He reached nearer to the telephone with the toy gun and triggered it to produce a musical burst sound aimed at the ceiling. It caught his Nana's ear. "Nana ji wants to speak with you, Honey." Briksha pressed the receiver to his ear and made him talk with her father.

"Nana ji pranam."

He asked affectionately, "What is my Honey Beta doing?"

Honey replied promptly, "Nana ji, I am chasing the thieves, bye." He ran away. She put the receiver back on the cradle.

Romy reached the office sharp at 9 AM. He saw MD's car parked in the lobby. He wasted no time asking the guard about his arrival. MD had arrived at the office half an hour ago. It seemed quite unusual. MD was never seen to enter in before 9:30 in his last five years of service. Curiosity piqued. He chose the lift to go to his office on the 3rd floor. MD's office came first in the corridor. He took longer strides, and all his steps were brisk. He stopped pacing once he crossed MD's cabin. Soon, he turned around to respond to the morning wish of Nutan, who was the most faithful among all his secretaries. The boss could rely on her for all occasions-always punctual and cheerful.

" Good morning, RD sir," Nutan said, her voice brimming with enthusiasm. "I noticed MD in a very delightful mood when he came in the morning. He came a little early to meet with the two directors from our Singapore company. To my surprise, the first thing he asked me was about your file before asking me for a glass of water," She added, her eyes sparking with curiosity, no doubt sensing Romy's own interest in the matter.

"My file!"

"I took your file and placed it on his table. He was happy to read the newspaper today, speaking all good about our company. Boss has asked me to type the appreciation letter for all employees and mentioned, in the end, a special appreciation for you for your humongous effort."

RD asked, "Which file of mine was he desperately looking for?"

She said, "Your record of service, sir. Congratulations on completing five years in the company today. I am sure you will get a big bonus."

RD took a deep breath. It crossed his mind, "Thank God he didn't ask about the Singapore project file, which he had been laying hold of as his nurtured pet project for quite some time. He takes it home. It shouldn't be in someone else's hands before he presents his plan at the gathering. Yesterday, he couldn't even discuss the project with MD as he had to leave early to beat the traffic."

The peon appeared there with a plateful of biscuits, three mugs of coffee, and three glasses of water on a serving tray. Before he set foot in MD's room, RD seized him, raised a glassful of water to his mouth, and chugged down. The peon beamed at his throat in surprise, then returned to the kitchen cabinet for a refill.

Seeing him anxious, Nutan asked, "Is everything fine at home, sir? How is Madam Briksha? How is your baby doing?"

"I am not worried about me, but I don't know what to answer if he asks me about Briksha."

"Is she not going to come today for the meeting?"

"No, Boss is banking on me to get Briksha back into the company. Briksha is still firm on her decision. I have no answers. I cannot be rude to him by saying find a replacement."

"Why replacement, sir? No one can be like Madam Briksha. She is very sharp and intelligent and is one of the company's founding members. MD will never allow her to quit."

"Briksha is very firm on her decision. She will not go to Singapore. I am just caught between my wife and the management. Neither can I convince the management, nor can I convince my wife."

"Don't worry, sir. I have read her file. Boss is happy with her working from home. The pen picture in her record is very good. It's okay to work from home when you have a small baby."

"It has been almost three years since Briksha worked from home. The boss may not like the terms and conditions she will put before the committee. Anyway, I must handle it. If they decide to vet a new employee as her replacement, he would have to accept it unconditionally."

Nutan said, "No, sir, they plan to send you to Singapore. In such a case, you can move to our Singapore branch together."

"Ah! That's good news. Thanks for this piece of information, Nutan."

The telephone on her desk began to ring, and she picked it up. Before she could say hello, Romy could hear his boss's voice distinctly on the other end of the line. The tone revealed that the boss was eagerly waiting to know about his arrival. Nutan placed a hand on the mouthpiece and whispered, "Boss is on the line."

"Yes, sir, I will ask him to join you in a minute," she spoke into the receiver. Nutan placed the receiver back on the cradle and said, "The board room meeting has been rescheduled for ten. The MD wants you to meet the directors from Singapore. Go inside." RD looked at the watch. It was twenty-five minutes past nine. He went inside after opening the door.

"Good morning, gentlemen," he greeted as everyone's eyes landed on him. The MD gestured, and RD sat across from him.

"Let me have the pleasure of introducing Mr. Ormond, the Director of Marketing, and Mr. Frost, the Director and Head of the Technical Wing. They are from our Singapore office. They have come here especially to meet you."

He shook hands with them. He had a sense of what his boss was going to say next. A part of him was sure that one of these two would replace Briksha in Bombay.

Mr. Ormond said, "Hello, Mr. RD, we have come here to meet you."

"Me?"

Taking a moment to think about the financial expenditures the company had to bear for their travel and stay, RD asked, "What made you fly down from Singapore? You could have spoken with me over the phone if the matter was important to know from me. I am always just a phone call away from Singapore. I hope that in the future, we will all be meeting over a video conference, considering the pace at which thousands of kilometres of fibre-optic cables are being laid in the submarine trenches. The day is not too far when we will all be sitting at home and chatting with each other using our handheld computers." They watched him displaying his naturalness and knowledge in future technical adventures.

Ormond said admiringly, "You turned right, as your boss told us. I heard so much about you from your boss. Now I believe it. We are impressed by your knowledge of your technical field and its suitable implications in the market—a talent of rare combination. Everyone should learn from you. We left a voice mail, but you had left the office by then. We had eagerly been waiting to meet you personally. We feel lucky today for this coincidence of coming here and attending your presentation. May we have the pleasure of inviting you as a trainer for a month? The employees out there are eagerly waiting for a pep talk from you as their mentor. We will be grateful if you oblige us with your affirmation."

RD's heart had stopped racing by now. He had no time to realize that the expansion opportunity was growing for his company, both for him and for the employees. "I am so sorry for not having checked the voice mail after my interview with the print media."

After a pause, RD asked, "What exactly would you like to know from me during my talk? "

Frost said, "We want to know the secret of your shirt theory and how you made this company achieve a magical $ 1.5-billion-dollar mark in a single quarter."

Romy's lips curved into a subtle smile, but he remained silent. The MD added to their conversation, "Go there with Briksha; it would be a nice business-cum-holiday trip for you." Romy's composure, however, remained steadfast. Though the smile on his face lingered inside, he was carefully considering how to react and what to say. The air around him held too many expectations. Nevertheless, he refrained from voicing his thoughts aloud.

It was five minutes to ten. Nutan, ever-diligent, gracefully entered the MD's office. Her footsteps were light, and her demeanour poised. "Sir, the board meeting is about to begin. Everyone has arrived," she announced. They reached the boardroom. The projector was ready.

Romy reached into his attache case, which was placed on a chair designated for him behind a desktop. His fingers brushed against a card—a flash of colours through which he could read, "Best of luck." It touched him deeply. Romy felt a surge of warmth, silently appreciating Briksha's unspoken support during the meeting. He took out the floppy and shoved it into a box.

MD had taken the chair at the head end of the table, while the other ten directors sat on both sides when RD took a chair behind the desktop.

"Good morning, gentlemen. There is going to be a paradigm shift in the global communication system. The world is shifting towards wireless communication. After a year or so, the present landline telephones will be of no use. The breakage of wires, replacement costs, labour charges, and maintenance is too much of an expenditure. Our professionals have developed a new software system where communication can be established through a wireless network. Emaar Singapore has come up with their new hardware, the cell phones which can fit inside the pocket. The cordless handsets that we devised a month ago need immediate improvisation. From a heavy handset laced with limited features, we have moved to a new generation handset to launch in the market."

Everyone looked at the new product on the screen. "We are also coming up with a short message system, recordings, and a digital display screen. Now, you may ask me, how? For all of us to know, the dense wavelength signal transmission cables transmit a few terabytes per second, which is much better than any satellite transmission these days. The globe is sweating to use this opportunity for all commercial utilities. The banks, the airports, and the offices will soon be computerized. So, with the short messaging and digital display screen, we would be the first global company to launch the product in the global market."

"The technical wing is being inducted with all research facilities under Mr. Frost. He is going to work on a colour display system in our new house in Singapore. Ms. Briksha has been working on this new project, and her suggestion to hire a hundred software engineers was approved in the last board of directors meeting. Gentlemen, one Chinese company wanted to collaborate with us, but we found Emaar Singapore is much ahead in making quality hardware. Mr. Ormond and Mr. Frost have personally visited our company to discuss our new project investments."

At the end of his last slide, the room thundered with a massive round of applause.

Ormond stood from his chair and said, "Greetings from Singapore. As our new MD is not present here, I will briefly review the project on her behalf. We are going to provide better RAM and a colour display system. Besides these, we have been working on its design. The basic digital computing system will remain the same. Still, we are working to improvise the gadget with advanced features: a digital camera with a resolution of 3.0 megapixels and multiple ring tunes in our next launch. For different tunes, we are working in unison with a renowned American Jazz band and Indian classical musical maestros.

Most importantly, the demands at the consumer end were to reduce the weight. We expect the gadget's weight, including the battery, to be approximately 100 grams, almost 150 grams less than our competitors. Our batteries will last for six hours on one recharge, which is better than the products our competitor plans to introduce. The production cost may increase marginally by seven to eight per cent."

"I am looking forward to RD's visit to Singapore to work on this product. I want to introduce him to our Research and Development team for his technical input. Lastly, I am thankful to all of you for this merger. Our combined efforts will be highly productive. I believe the telecom sector will enter a new revolutionary era with this merger. I extend an invitation to RD to join us in Singapore with his family."

MD, at the end of the presentation, nodded his head. "I must say, I am pleased to be associated with you. We will work together on this new revolutionary technology. Thank you, Mr. Ormond, for your presentation. Gentlemen, the company has experienced significant growth, with a 1.5-billion-dollar turnover in the last quarter, and I give credit to all your efforts. We should be grateful to all the people who have supported us. From our scientists to the administrators, even our staff who work day and night in the kitchen to provide you with good food for lunch and dinner, they have saved your precious time to spend in the company. Each of you has worked hard and put your life into this achievement. I appreciate every employee of our company for their contribution. Now, I propose a name who has worked tirelessly for our company on this project from the beginning and has been able to steer our ship through the toughest tides and turmoil. Only one name comes to my mind today, and he is none other than Mr. Ram Dutt Shivdasani. I propose him for the position of Director."

The other directors seconded the proposal, and the room filled with the sound of applause. RD stood from his seat. There was no smattering of reason for him to deny the new responsibility. Indeed, he had worked tirelessly for these five years, day and night, working on market strategy, sales, research, production, and more.

He beamed with confidence and said, "I thank our MD, Mr. Sridharan, Mr. Ormond, Mr. Frost, and the board of directors for placing their trust in me for the position of Director. I pledge to work towards the company's vision with unwavering commitment and utmost sincerity."

After the meeting, while he was tidying up the files and the project floppy, Ms. Nutan entered and congratulated him. She informed him that Ms. Briksha had a phone call regarding the presentation. She told her the presentation had started half an hour late and was ongoing. RD, with a blossoming smile on his face, thanked her and went to his office like a bird taking a flight to meet his dear one, so he called up Briksha to share the news of his promotion.

He asked her to arrange a dinner party before the Singapore guests departed. Briksha placed the receiver down, her hands clasped together in prayer, stood in front of Lord Shiva, and expressed her gratitude for the blessing that had been bestowed upon her family.

She picked up the nearby telephone directory and dialled a few numbers to share the joyous news. She dialled one hotel after another. She called Hotel Tazz, Hotel Maurya, and Hotel Lalita to book a perfect venue to host a celebratory dinner party, but each one politely declined her request. The ordeal ended when she called Hotel *La* Plasma. The receptionist received the call and transferred it to the booking manager. The booking manager broke the news cautiously: 'Madam, a big TV star has booked our banquet hall for a party tonight. We are expecting a large crowd. Your guests might face parking issues.' Despite the initial hesitation, Briksha persisted, and after much persuasion, the manager agreed to accommodate her party of a hundred guests.

She drove down to the hotel, eagerly handing over the booking amount. On her way home, she stopped at a beauty parlour. She chose a red-coloured saree with golden embroidery, a riot of colours that matched the blouse for the occasion. The party was scheduled to start at 8 PM. She invited Mr. Sridharan, all the directors and their wives, and a few known neighbours. Romy invited Mr. Ormond and Mr. Frost separately.

The clock struck six, and Honey was playing with the maid. The maid was called to keep Honey engaged until midnight. Briksha convinced her mother to stay at her house that night. The maid was happy to stay during the night with Honey for a reward of a few rupees and a new dress. She had stayed once before when Briksha was pregnant, and Romy had gone out of town for a day. She enjoyed watching a movie on the VCR with Memsahib. She was a movie buff, and Briksha had a big home theatre to cater to her interests.

Romy reached home. He honked to signal Honey for an evening joy ride. His car horn echoed in the distance, but Honey did not respond and remained engrossed in playing Pithoo, trying hard to break the stalk of plastic cubes with his rubber ball. The maid was leading 1-0. Heeding his mother's warning, he played indoors like a most obedient and dutiful mama's child.

Briksha heard a tap on the door. It was in her mind that Romy had left the office an hour ago, and she had been expecting him by then. Unmindful of the snacks still half cooked on the stove, her exulted self rushed towards the door and opened it before the fourth tap. The pleasure of the promotion was at its peak. The excitement had sped up her work in the kitchen. She had prepared snacks for Romy and cooked Honey's favourite dish: rice-dal-potato paste rolled in a ghee paratha.

She saw him at the door, his face flushed with joy. A smile appeared on her face. She offered a hand just before he stepped into the hall. Their hands met. "You are simply amazing," she swiftly said, dragging him inside the drawing room and hugging him tightly for a minute. Unmindful of the attache case in his hand, she put her arms around his neck. The instant arousal of a passionate hug was so magical that it washed away all his tiredness. He steadied his feet beneath him, then with the attache case in hand, he pulled her closer against him fervently. The rousing stint of possession they felt for each other was so evident that they heard the symphony of their hearts thumping hard in synchrony. He whispered, "I missed you in the office."

"No hard feelings, Romy. I am always with you. I can't leave you till my last breath."

"Then reconsider your resignation."

"My decision is final. I had an incredible experience working with Asians."

"Your resignation is not accepted yet."

"I know, but I am not going to withdraw. My decision is final. Let them underline this once and for all. It is final, means final. I can't leave you and Honey for a moment."

He would never be able to change her mind, but happy moments are to be enjoyed. The thought made him ecstatic. He kept the attaché beg on the sofa, then lifted her in his arms in one fell swoop. "Let's celebrate this moment."

"I have already made arrangements in a hotel as Singaporeans will be leaving tomorrow."

"Such a great darling you are," he kissed her before making her land on her toes.

He opened the attache case and took out the red leather box. She saw the exotic diamond necklace, a replica of the one she had seen in a magazine while onboard for a London trip. He put the necklace around her neck and gave her the matching earrings. She looked stunning in her red saree with the diamond necklace.

Romy said, "Darling, you always keep smiling. I live for this smile. I live for you, and I would die for you." She hushed him and placed her hand over his mouth.

"May God add my life to yours, but never say this again." The seriousness on her face slowly faded into a smile, which brought a vibrant expression to his face.

It was 6:30 PM, and she went inside the kitchen to make him tea. After the tea, he rushed to take a bath. She had kept a blue tuxedo with a bow tie for him, which she had bought from London Square. It was just for a change to match the party mood. "I was thinking of wearing it for a long time," Romy said.

Honey bolted into the room with a whoop of victory. "I won; I won, Mama! Papa, I won! Meera Auntie lost the game." Romy rewarded him with the toy set from his attache. Honey rushed to the kitchen with the toy set to show his Mama, but she grabbed him by the arm to tell him how dirty his hands and legs were. "You are now a big baby, and you should learn to wash your hands after finishing your play." She dragged him to the bathroom, ignoring all his protests. "Go, wash your hands and legs properly. I am watching you." She blocked the entrance to the bathroom until he washed his hands by rubbing them thoroughly. The mother-self within her knew how to teach a playful child good habits.

She served the snacks on the dining table. For them, it was fun to watch Honey munch and suck the softer end of the roll. No matter how hard he tried to keep his hands dry, they always ended up wet after he shoved the roll into his mouth. He pulled his hands away in surprise and stared at them. Looking at his thoroughly wet hands made his conscious mind sullen. "What will Mama say? She will want them clean again," he thought. Soon, he jumped from the chair and went to wash his hands.

"Where are you going, Mama?"

She replied, "I am going to get you some chocolates, dear. Do you want cakes as well?"

"Mama, did you like the gift Papa brought me?"

"Yes," she replied.

"Papa, will you play with me until Mama comes back?"

Romy replied, "I will help Mama find nice gifts for you and make sure she buys the best chocolate for you. How about an ice cream, beta?"

"Take me along, Papa. I will choose for myself."

"After we leave, robbers may barge in. Will you guard Meera Aunty with your pistol?" Romy asked.

"Yes, Papa. If the robbers dare to enter, I will zap them all in one burst." He picked up the toy in a style that showcased the pride of the police. He swished the toy with a series of splutters. Romy tapped his back and said, "Bravo, my brave boy."

Briksha instructed Meera to entertain Honey with a game until midnight and told her to serve dinner around 9:30 PM. Before leaving for the hotel, she confirmed that the telephone had a dial tone buzzing and that the receiver was properly placed on the cradle. She told Meera to answer when she called. Honey waved goodbye. He would never feel cooped up with Meera if his play continued. They left the house in their black Corolla. The back seat was filled with the bouquets he received from his colleagues after the promotion.

At a quarter to eight, they were inside the Hotel La Plasma. They entered the banquet hall on the first floor. She felt ecstatic and slid an adoring gaze around. She released a euphoric sigh and said, "Wow," when she saw that everything was arranged properly.

The tables were circular and placed with sufficient gaps in between in that large hall. They were covered in well-decorated cloth. The chairs around the tables were not sufficient in number to accommodate all the guests at a time. However, she knew the delicious snacks and refreshing beverages would keep most of them on their feet at the dispensing counters. The food was getting warmed by the spirit lamps underneath. Romy took a soft drink, and she took a glass of water.

A few moments later, the guests arrived, and they greeted them by shaking hands. The instrumental music in the background was soft and soothing. Briksha's joy intensified when she met her office mates, Mr. Ormond and Mr. Frost. The managing director joined after a few minutes with the news that *Trion* is coming up with touchscreen features for which they are looking for a processor like ours. He hinted they should move away from button presses to a touch screen. Ormond nodded his head and shouted, "Possible."

Mr Ormond started conversing with Briksha, "Glad to see you, Madam, after a long time. We will wait for you in Singapore." The smile on her face was a guise for uncertainty, as her mind was thinking, "Sorry, Ormond, you have to find a new boss for yourself."

"I am not sure if I can go overboard," Briksha said.

"Really?" A surprising note was in Ormond's voice.

"I am sorry I was not there at the meeting. After this merger and corporate takeover, I am glad you have taken over the Singapore branch nicely. The Managing Director is on cloud nine."

RD breezed in and said, "Briksha, MD, is pleased to send us on a trip to Singapore. It's a little jaunt of training and business trip type, you know? I forgot to tell you before. I also came to know this morning."

The managing director refused to accept the hints dropped by Briksha on several occasions that she would no longer be continuing in the company. He came with a glass of whisky and said, "Briksha, the date of the walk-in interview needs to be finalized as soon as possible. You need to work on this."

Briksha replied, "I have planned it best in accordance with the ground rules. The ground rules say that fifty per cent of professionals are taken through campus selection, and the rest are taken through a periodic walk-in. You know, new ideas and new minds."

MD said, "New minds! But their inexperience will not be an excuse. You will have to train the fresh lot. How would you plan for that?"

Briksha replied, "If you want to run a marathon in this business, then repeated training is required to keep pace with evolving technology. We will sit together and outline a few modules for their training."

Her gaze shifted towards the Training Director, who nodded in agreement.

MD asked Briksha, "I heard you make good coffee at home. You and RD should invite this Techie to your home on the weekend and prepare a training manual. I am planning Singapore as our new training centre."

Frost said, "What a fantastic idea!" Slowly, everybody grabbed their drinks, and the party continued.

*****

The hotel lobby was crowded with the presence of the public. Everyone seemed consumed by the cricket match between India and Pakistan, which had taken an exciting turn. Everyone's gaze shifted towards the large, ceiling-height glass entrance door when the guests started rolling in.

A well-pitched voice greeted him, "Sameer sahib, come in." The man wore a black uniform. He led him to a hallway, a mystical stretch through which he emerged through the doors one after another. He noticed the guards at each door greeted him warmly. He needed to be respected. Inside his mind, Sameer felt like a king's guest. He flashed them a smile before he stopped in front of a lift. Sameer yanked the gate of the lift and pressed the button for the 20th floor.

Cheema was waiting for him in the office. He entered Cheema's cabin when the red light turned green at the door.

He could understand the drill well. He was mindful of some third eye keeping a tab on him from the entrance. He had heard from many that Cheema had specially ordered spy cameras from the USA, like the ones that blinked a few meters away while he walked. There was one every twenty meters. He heard him discussing the film project with the two Dubai men when he entered Cheema's office. Cheema chanted, "Come in Sameer."

After a brief exchange of greetings, the Dubai men congratulated him on completing the 100th episode. They had agreed to invest their money in films in an overseas distributorship agreement. The deal was made; Sameer signed the papers, and Cheema needed to announce the film at the party.

Cheema's euphoric mind finalized Vanya to act opposite Sameer, as people had started accepting them as a lead pair. Vanya entered a moment later. Cheema's voice was hoarse when he greeted her. He told her that the deal was done. 'I will write the script for both of you,' Cheema said.

'You will write the script?' Sameer asked.

'Yes, I will write all controversial stories about both of you. You need to shed some fake tears from your eyes, Vanya.'

Vanya gave a startled screech, 'Sounds interesting. Cheema, I will do anything that you want.' Covering her slender body, she embraced him passionately. That hug was brief but tight.

Cheema said, 'I am here to exaggerate the controversy until people realize a final breakup between you two in the next six months.' Sameer looked at Vanya, her face flushed. He didn't understand what excited her so much.

Vanya said, 'Sameer, this is the trade secret. There is nothing wrong with it. Many have done this for instant success on the big screen.' She looked at him passionately. Vanya added, 'Moreover, you should be happy to launch your 200th episode at the end of next quarter before our film. We will blame each other, understandingly. You are welcome to share your viewpoint if you don't like this. Tell us otherwise; how should we go about this show business?'

'I am ready. Go ahead,' Sameer said.

Disha later entered the cabin after inspecting the hall. Disha was asked to plan their itinerary accordingly so that they would show up for all parties within India and abroad.

The festivity started at seven when the guests arrived. The photographers were ready at the entrance to click their best shots for their newspaper and magazine. The hall where the event was planned was big and could accommodate five hundred people at any time. A red carpet in the hall's centre ran from the backdoor to the stage. The hall was packed by 8 pm. Two anchors, one lady and another gentleman, appeared on the stage.

They said, "Good evening, ladies and gentlemen. Welcome to the eve of success. As you know, Bombay has always been kind to shower its love on Bollywood. The production company, The Dreamz, has completed the hundredth episode of the serial "Sunaina." Without wasting your time, I would like to invite the very famous Sultan and Sunaina to the stage. Everyone, please put your hands together. Here come the dashing Sultan and the lovely Sunaina." They were greeted with applause.

Sameer played the characters of Sultan and Vanya as Sunaina. It was a series based on the story of a prince and princess - where the prince loses his eyes while hunting in the jungle. When the charming prince was refused by his beloved princess for marriage out of his blindness, he fought with the princess's father to know why he was deserted. The princess explained to him through a letter about the cruelty he had shown towards the innocent animals of the jungle.

Sameer and Vanya entered the stage from opposite sides. The flashlights followed them. They strode, looking at each other's steps to enter onto the stage at the same time. They saw a sea of admirers through the applause before they stared at each other passionately. They had done a good rehearsal an hour ago. They replaced both the anchors, and after introducing themselves, they delivered a few dialogues from their written scripts. The hall was filled with waves of applause. After this act, they called Cheema to the stage to announce their next project. It was a live show. The big names from the film industry were present. Cheema was one of them. From serious artists to aristocratic socialites, everyone found a reason there to listen to Cheema. He bustled through the cacophony, "Aryabraaaaat is the name," and he announced it as a mythological fiction created to give a message of nonviolence to the masses. Our Eastern brothers and our overseas partners are present at this gathering. I want you to welcome them with a round of applause. Cheema said through a round of applause, "They have invested in our production house. They will be our partners for overseas distribution, and not only that, but they have also sponsored this gala event, and they have agreed to conduct such events in Dubai in the future. We are eagerly waiting to accommodate more partners to support us. The film will be ready by the end of next quarter. Soon, we will announce the release date." Another round of applause spread all over. He announced that the bar was still open for beverages and the buffet was ready in the neighbouring hall, a very big one, communicating through a door.

Bhairav, over six feet tall, looked extremely powerful. He appeared raw and menacing with his jet-black long hair, hooked nose, and cold eyes. To someone's horror, he looked like a bandit from the Chambal Valley. Clad in black attire, he walked over to Cheema and said that the Dubai guests wanted to see the weapons, and the arms dealer had already reached his cabin. "The meeting is only for fifteen minutes." He whispered in Cheema's ear to whisk him away from a crowd of imposing men around him. After a pause, Bhairav bellowed like a bull, "Your Ferrari is ready at the gate, Hazoor, for your night out."

The ride was an instant plan he made after receiving a new Ferrari. He hoped it would be exciting to go with Vanya, who suggested it as a last-minute idea to generate excitement in his restless soul.

Cheema hefted two AK 47s in his hands. He asked Bhairav to gift-pack one for Sameer and keep the other for himself to dragoon Chunnilal. "If he refuses to comply, then pin him down."

"Hazoor, he has gone underground. He didn't show up at the inaugural meeting of the railway station. The organizers kept waiting for him. Someone told me that he was shunning away from party politics. He is now almost like a dead man, broken by his wife's ailments. His daughter is studying in Delhi, and he is also planning to shift out."

"The snake will remain dangerous if not held by the hood, remember Bhairav."

Bhairav's allegiance to his master evoked an immediate reaction, "If you wish, I will bump him off in public. Forget about shouldering him on a bier, Hazoor. No one can find a trace of him to ignite him on a pyre. As such, he has many enemies within his own party. No one will suspect us."

"I can't wait, Bhairav," there was annoyance in his voice. "I need that piece of land at any cost. I am ready to pay. That is not a place for a children's park. I want a shopping mall there. Coerce him. If he doesn't yield, you buy a chaplet with that money to lay on him."

Bhairav understood the master's mind. "What is not possible through words, Cheema makes it possible by coercion."

After dinner, the chauffeurs made their way towards the entrance. Cheema invited them to spend the rest of the night in his farmhouse at Panvel. It was 11 PM. The guests had started leaving. Sameer and Vanya agreed to his offer. They called Disha to accompany them. She nodded after thinking for a while.

The main lobby looked almost empty. They headed towards the main entrance. Vanya signalled Pattnayak by raising her hand to return from a distance. Cheema slipped into his new Ferrari for a ride. He controlled the wheel, and soon, Vanya joined him in the co-driver's seat. Sameer and Disha made their way towards the Mercedes, slowly accelerating towards them. Sagar stepped out after halting the car to open the rear door for his Sahib. Disha sat next to Sameer in the rear seat. Sagar slowly moved out to hit the main road.

About half a mile up, Cheema stopped at the intersection to call Sameer for a race up to his farmhouse.

"We can't think of excluding you, Sameer. If you want a truly thrilling experience behind the wheel, now is the time. It won't come too often."

Behind the wheel, Sagar heard Cheema's voice from the Ferrari window. The sound was the real voice of Cheema. He could see the excitement on his Sahib's face through the mirror. Those words had suited his nerves. He accepted the invitation to participate in the race. He forgot all his to-dos before replacing Sagar behind the wheel, asking Sagar to stop the car.

Excitement welled up in Sameer's champagne-oozing mind, making him restless and crazy. He let the moment consume him, enjoying it thoroughly. Sagar was stunned. He was aware that his Sahib was unstoppable when called by someone for a race. He had a horrifying experience in the past when his Sahib took over the steering wheel. His tongue started to dry up. He felt choked at the back of his throat. Like a submissive child, he got out of the car to allow his Sahib to take the front seat. Disha came out to sit next to him in front.

Suddenly, the car swung off the road when he pressed the accelerator hard and down. Within seconds, his Mercedes was ready to chase Cheema's Ferrari. They reached the highway, and Sagar watched the speedometer indicator sway past 120 Kmph in a few seconds. He clung to the front seat, sighing as his heart raced faster with the speed and slammed against his ribcage in fear. He closed his eyes and tightened his grip. His chest heaved intermittently after a few shallow breaths. He muttered, "No… no…" before calling upon all the Gods in his prayer.

Sameer was racing parallel to Cheema on the highway. He further accelerated to overtake Cheema, and in a second, he lapped the Ferrari. Sagar perched at the edge of the rear seat, and his grip tightened. The Mercedes had raced past much ahead of Ferrari. Before Sameer could realize it, the Mercedes paced to make violent contact with the side of another car running left to it. Sagar was dazed for a moment to see what happened. Before he opened his eyes, the Mercedes had gone far ahead for him to notice the car behind. The race did not stop till they reached the farmhouse. Sagar was asked to go back. There was a coldness in Vanya's words that Sagar didn't like. Vanya didn't want him there that night. While returning home on the highway, he heard the emergency siren and saw a speeding ambulance behind his car in the rearview mirror. In a second, the ambulance crossed his car. Many awful thoughts arose in his mind before he could calm them by muttering all the names of God. After a few miles, he felt a coldness in his palms and feet when he saw the police van behind his car. He sped up and reached his house after midnight.

He parked the car and knocked on the door. Laxmi opened the door and closed it behind him after he entered. He was panting when he asked for a glass of water before saying anything. He chugged it and asked for another one. He heard a knock on his door. He slowly opened it and saw a pair of boots. His face turned blank when he lazily gazed up, seeing two policemen standing in his doorway, waiting for him to give them some information. The police had identified the vehicle from the black scratch marks. They had done a thorough inspection of the body of the car. They asked for the key to inspect the inside. They recovered a bottle of whisky from the trunk. One of them took out a machine to analyse his breath. It beeped for high alcohol levels.

Palo woke up from sleep and rushed towards the main hall. She shouted, "Where are you taking my Papa? He is not a thief! Inspector, please do not take him to jail." Palo cried and tried to stop him by pulling his clothes. They had put handcuffs on his hands. The neighbours were aroused by the sound and looked at him with surprise.

Cheema said, "Sameer, I know what you are thinking. You are not going to tell the police who was driving the car. Forget that you have ever caused this accident. It was just an accident, and the car you hit was also speeding. Why do you think this was your mistake when the other car's driver couldn't control it and crashed into the pavement? Remember, you have a wife who is sick and battling terminal-stage cancer. You have a two-year-old daughter. What would happen to her future? Who will look after them when you go to jail? You must complete the current project. What would happen to the remaining episodes? You have invested all your money in the next project. I have also put in a lot of effort to finance your film. What will happen to our money if we cancel it midway? We would all go bankrupt. What will happen to the people earning their bread and butter from this project? What will happen to their families? Think about them for a moment."

Vanya said, "Sameer, we have worked together, and people have accepted our chemistry. They want to see more from us. We are entertainers, and we are in show business. People wouldn't like to see their hero rotting in jail. You are a present-day superstar, and the time is yours. You cannot afford to waste your productive life in jail."

Disha asked, "Then what should we do, Vanya?"

Vanya replied, "Sameer caused that accident that night; no one knows except you, me, and Cheema."

Sameer asked, "What about Sagar? He was there with us, sitting in the back seat."

Vanya replied, "Yes, he was in the back seat but drunk – my sources confirmed. The spy camera recording in the hotel showed he was drinking alcohol, and he was at the wheel before you hit the highway. They found a bottle of alcohol in the car, and the alcohol level in his breath was above the acceptable limit. This piece of evidence is enough to prove him guilty of a crime. The blood report is awaited, and if he tests positive, he will be sentenced to five years in prison. We will take care of his family. Learn to live for yourself, Sameer and for the public- your big extended family outside." The inspector came to write their statements. Sameer stated that he had witnessed the crash when Sagar was driving.

A fortnight later, a bereft Romy woke up from disturbed sleep. He popped up pills, but nothing could erase the memory that had frozen in his mind. The pain of losing his wife in a second had broken him mentally. He cried, sobbing, standing in front of her portrait as if the time had not moved forward by a single minute. The car was pushed to the kerbside, and it swerved after mounting the kerb. Before realising anything to change the course, he could see them spin within the car before hitting the ground. The light from the streetlamps that fell through the broken window was enough to show him his wife's face. It was smashed and contorted. Her brow was depressed and laid open. Something curd-like poured down from the gaps onto his chest. He saw her neck whipped and her head stooped down to his side. The eyes were swollen and had come out from their cavities. The blood was pouring down. He felt the wetness of her drenched hair. The glass pieces had pierced her face like shrapnel. The steering wheel stoved into his chest discomforted him, making breathing difficult. He was unable to cry for help. He felt paralyzed with the heavy compression on his arms. He tried to come out and pushed the leg down but could not. Her tilted body was still resting on his broken shoulder. A moment later, he felt dizzy. It was almost impossible for him to drag air into his lungs. A curtain of darkness dropped before him, with the eyes rolling up beneath his drooping lids. The darkness deepened further until he lost consciousness. However, he did not forget the numbers on the back of the Mercedes.

*****

CHAPTER 3

Beauty and the Beast

At 4 AM, Disha arose clumsily and disturbed after a few hours of fitful sleep. It was not a usual time to get up like this. Nothing of the sort could help her lie comfortably without turning sides. The thought of uttering falsehood after palpating the holy Bhagwat Gita bothered her. Guilt indelibly seared into her mind. She intended to save two lives in Sameer's life: His wife Sreni and daughter Diya. She did not consider it wrong at that spur of time. She could not tolerate the whimpers of pain, the pitiful sights in Malhotra House. She had seen them all.

Her eyes witnessed the moment when Sagar stood silent, and the judge pronounced the verdict. The reason was obvious – his loyalty to the salt he had consumed at Sameer's place.

What disturbed her most was Sagar's wet -innocent eyes. They had stopped at Laxmi in the courtroom. The verdict was - Six long years of imprisonment in a hit-and-run case. Laxmi cried utterly after hearing this. The presence of guilt lingered in her mind. The scene remained in her mind. She strained to hear nothing. The shrilling cry, not even it muffled for a moment. The voice echoed in her mind was as real as hers.

She circled around a pillow drawn close to her chest, but her thoughts refused to dwindle away. The sound of her soul emanated from the heart, echoed between her ears, and remained uneliminated. Outside the courtroom, the little girl clinging to Sagar sobbed, " Papa, you don't go. I will not be able to stay without you."

There was no respite from her thoughtful mind. Disha heard voices around her. The story was her own. The forlorn figures from the neighbourhood wailed. Her mother broke her bangles with an utter chest-thumping cry. Her vermillion on the head had been smudged. That day, her father died of cerebral malaria. She cried from her mother's lap. At age three, she learned that her father would never return to her life. She was drawn to her awful past when she lived in a small town in Bihar. The voice in the courtroom dropped. She felt lost in her memories. A curtain rolled up in her mind slowly, and memories ran through her mind.

It was the year 1965, "Madhubala' – A name she bore from Urvashi's womb. Her mother was a background dancer in Mughal-e-Azam. The pundits prophesied of a girl child. Her mother, Urvashi, ascended the temple a thousand steps barefoot to keep Lord Shiva and Goddess Parvati pleased. She was born a milky-white-skinned girl, and when she grew up, people praised the artwork of her beauty chiselled flawlessly by nature. Her gently arched brows, almond-shaped eyes, and glinted brown hair made her a simulacrum of Madhubala.

Her upbringing was solely maternal. She wishfully yielded to the imposed patriarchal restrictions by society, just like her mother. She would surely have made it into an IIT if she had not been born to her actor parents. A dance teacher was hired to teach her the steps of art instead of an academic tutor to teach her the principles of science. Though she grew physically, she did not grow academically enough to know that H_2O is water and that the process by which plants prepare food is called photosynthesis. She mostly spent her time shaping her body in the gym. Her mother forced her to binge on salads and cucumber and kept her deprived of her favourite sweets and delicious cuisines. With the surge of gonadotropins, she looked full. A cheer rose from the streets when she appeared on the balcony. At times, from the rim of her cup, while sipping tea, she noticed that the boys in the street seemed excited to catch a lazy glance of her. Otherwise, they would have shown their fallen faces to each other in crestfallen, blaming surely on their forlorn hopes. During play hours in the evening, while she skipped alone on her rose-strewn rooftop, she noticed the boys sneaking into her deck in search of their cricket ball. She was aware of their plausible excuses. She catered to their desires by aiding them in their search. It was a physical attraction that kept them milling around her house all the time. She gazed out at the courtyards behind her house; they looked abandoned. Her friends no longer visited them. As a child, she had played hopscotch with them. She strolled alone and strummed chords on the guitar in private while her friends enjoyed the joyful rides on their new bicycles. Her friends attended college while she learned to walk the ramps. She climbed the ladder of success and stood tall in the glamour industry. Many called her 'modern Anarkali'.

She celebrated her eighteenth birthday. The doorbell of her house rang once. Urvashi opened the door. A middle-aged man in a black coat and pants appeared before her. Quite a charming personality and claimed to be a talent hunt manager linked to a big advertising agency. He entered and sat on the sofa when her mother gestured. The deal he proposed to her mother was not to sign for any commercial ad but to feature Madhu in a photo shoot for a calendar. A private airline had been arranged for them to fly to Goa. Madhu was one of the twelve lucky girls the company had approached for the shoot. When Urvashi accepted the deal, the man rose from the sofa, bowed gently to shake her hand, and left her house with a thankful note of happiness, which exuded through his smile.

They boarded the flight from Patna airport on the next day. As briefed, they reached Hotel Parijat in Goa. It was a comfortable journey, but their flight slowed down in the air. They reached the destination ten minutes late owing to unfavourable aerial conditions. The receptionist fretted about seeing them because the man to whom she allotted the room had not only arrived before the scheduled time but was also a close friend of the hotel owner. Just a minute ago, she received a call from her boss in Dubai, instructing her to accommodate the gentleman in one of the rooms for a week.

Regretfully, the girl at the check-in desk announced, pointing towards him, "Madam, the gentleman in the black coat is Mr. Salim." Madhu glanced at him from a distance; undoubtedly, he carried an aristocratic look. He was pulling out notes from his wallet to give tips to a bellman, gesturing for the bellman to take his big suitcase. Her eyes settled on the diamond on his pinky, and the golden wristlet had an impeccable taste for jewellery.

"He is here for the same photo shoot you have been called for. He is an important guest to us, and it would be kind of you if you could wait for an hour. Can I ask our bellman to help you place your luggage carefully inside the cloakroom?"

"Why can't he wait? The room was booked in our name. It would be best if you let us in," Madhu frowned like a harried customer.

"I wish I had a vacant room to accommodate you. Just a minute ago, I received two phone calls, one from the coordinator of this event and the other from my boss. They want him to be well taken care of. Since he is a very important guest and he needs to be attended to with utmost priority, I allotted him the room where you were supposed to stay. I understand your discomfort seriously, but I am helpless, madam. I have been told that Mr. Salim is here in Goa as a selector to pick up the real modelling talents for his company, which manufactures and exports ladies' garments and ornaments worldwide."

No matter how intensely she tried to convince Madhu, she could not provide her with a justifiable reason for her deeds. "Probably, this girl is also being richly rewarded for it. She would deal with this girl at some other time," Madhu thought.

After a minute of silence, the girl added apologetically, " He owns a private jet to fly and has many fancy four-wheelers to zip around. He does not stay here in Goa for long but comes every November to shoot calendar girls. He is a very precious guest of November for this hotel, and I am sorry I couldn't deny him. "

"Why have you made him so precious? This guest of November does not even have the courtesy to exchange a hello; forget about a thankful smile," Madhu frowned and shot him a resentful look.

"He brings us a lot of overseas business, which helps us maintain a good reputation in the city. The supermodels, the film stars, the crew members, the fashion photographers and big banner producers all prefer to stay in our hotel. And to tell you, we organise the beach carnival every year, and Mr. Sameer is one of the carnies who makes heavy donations for it." She praised him endlessly.

When she heard a beep, the receptionist darted her eyes to the board, displaying the vacancy status above the pegboard. The red light turned yellow before she cleared her throat twice. She swiftly adjusted her voice and intoned moderately to impress her with an expression: a blend of her humbleness and genuineness. It was undoubtedly aimed to please her, "Madam, it is very kind of you to excuse me for this inconvenience. The good news is that one VIP suit will get ready for you in less than an hour." She tweaked it immediately. A verbatim message to impress Madhu was, "Madam, we are known for our remarkable hospitality, and we treat every guest as our God."

"Oh...I don't mind waiting an hour if that's the case. But before that, I intend to tell this God of November through you that it is not right to use clout in every matter. The ordinaries, too, have a voice to speak for their comforts," said Madhu.

She said, "Madam, he is a nice gentleman. I will mediate to patch up this matter by extracting his due apology."

"Oh...no! It is not just a matter of his apology. See his superciliousness. He is such an insensitive man who will never understand the predicament of others," said Madhu.

"No, madam, he has all the concerns for you. That is why he arranged your travel and a comfortable stay in this hotel," The receptionist said.

" My dear, he must be thinking about his profits from all these. Who knows? After all, he is a businessman." said Madhu.

"Madam, my apologies. The talents he has discovered so far are now ruling the silver screen, and if you have that within you, then you will feel lucky that Bollywood will be your next destination. Not many obstacles will come your way, and no one will dare to strike your name out of the list in the industry once this man approves your name himself. I have heard from others that he is kind-hearted and takes care of all their needs in Bombay. All someone needs is to pack the baggage and move with him."

In the evening, from her room, she stared at the pool. The scene was something beautiful. She rocked back on her heels when she saw him diving into the pool. He began his lap like a dolphin slicing its fins through the water. He curled, then pushed off against the wall at the end, not staring at others, full of oneself. After a while, he reached the coping, took the steps and climbed out. She grabbed her binoculars and eyed him through them for a closer look. She looked at his drenched body. A sigh burst out from her, " Wow." Water dripped from his damp, sinewy arms and flat belly. Seeing his humongous calves contracted to give a good grip on the ground was a treat to her eyes, leaving behind his wet footprints on the floor.

Should she go to meet him to say hello? She was not clear in her mind. She had heard stories about such people. They do not give a damn to any stranger. She retook her position and saw him wrapping a Turkish towel around him. She muttered, "Don't close my views, stay away" as someone came in between.

She ought to believe that at least he has some manners left behind, unlike the beauties who had been on display of their scantily clad body like an art show on the couch next to him. They had no errands left except to lure such rich men into big hotels.

He eased back on the couch and read a fashion magazine. He struggled, trying his best not to pay attention to the bathing beauties around him. It must be his natural way. After a while, he looked at the western sky. He waited to see the sun setting before him, leaving behind a short time to glow. Her gaze crossed the gardens as she looked at the waves slapping the shore. The returning sailing sloops glided towards her with every return wave. The sea was almost calm. How strange both their eyes were fixed on one point, the dimming orange hue of the setting sun. Her heart jumped with all romantic thoughts. She looked back to the poolside, but he was not there.

They met the next day during a morning photo shoot with the rising shade of the sun in the sky. It glowed with an ochre hue in the background. While sailing on a cruise, she posed for a few snaps wearing a branded fashionable body-skimming water costume that emphasized her thin waist. The session was called off around ten when the sun glowed intensely in the morning sky. Those who did not come for the outdoor shoot were the ones who wished to be picture framed in silk negligee-style costumes with tangled hairs on charpoys.

The snorkelling expert was called in for a few underwater shots. One by one, they jumped into the water in the mid-sea with their oxygen heads. With them, who also jumped into the depths, was - Salim. After a fun-filled underwater view, they all surfaced to get on the cruise. They all assembled in the large dining hall after an hour for merrymaking, which went on till the evening. They all dined, wined inside, and enjoyed the spectacular view of the town from the cruise. She looked straight into his eyes and could read his secrets. Such an event brought Madhu closer to Salim. By the end of their seven-day trip, they grew much closer to each other. Salim gave them the departure hug before leaving for Bombay. And he left a departing note for Madhu in a closed letter: *"Roses are red, and violets are blue. See you in Bombay; only I & U ."* The address he had given her to meet him in Bombay was Hotel Blue Diamond. On its reverse side was a phone number written distinctly with a sign of love at the end.

*****

December 1983, Hotel Blue Dimond, Bombay.

Inside the bar, A paunchy, middle-aged, jowly-faced, proverbial director of Bollywood lecherously gazed at her from a distance. As swift as he could have been, he reached her side and stood a breath away. His camera-like eyes first set on her face, then screened her from top to toe. He murmured, "My... my... Madhubala, what a knockout beauty." Sotto Voce. His wife cut him off before he could say hello to them through his gaping teeth.

" *Jaanu,* sweetheart, we got a table. Please come," The lady who screamed from behind looked all overgrown and round. Although unusual for the place, she had trussed herself up in an expensive *Berhampuri silk Patta* saree to look slim. She was adorned with gold from the top to her toes. That was her style. A sliver of flesh at her waist bulged outside the chair above her broad hips when she sat. A hump of fat at the nape of her neck looked prominent above her round shoulders.

As he knew Salim before, the director hurriedly extended a hand towards them for a handshake. Madhu spoke slowly - *Namaste.* His hand hung in the air until it was met by Salim's. In a brief conversation with her, he was boastful about launching raw newcomers and mentioned the names of a few stars he mentored to make them big and successful on the silver screen. He implied that he would mentor her for the films. She remained silent momentarily and said, "That's nice of you, sir." A wry smile appeared on her face. The director laid a hand on her shoulder. " God, when I walked in, I saw you. You are very beautiful. I was attracted to you. You look like Madhubala." She was heated, but the desire and passion to be on a big screen softened her. "Well, I hope we can work together someday." He took a business card from his pocket and placed it on their table. A convincing smile erupted on his face, and his eye twitched at the angle when Madhu picked up his card. Madhu noticed that glint of mischief, which evaporated before he turned to his wife.

Though she did not bring out a visible sign on her face to reciprocate, she felt delighted to meet a person like him whose eyes detected her as Madhubala at first sight. Madhu felt excited about the chance to take her to the silver screen. The screen her mother had ever dreamt of being on.

Breaking the discord in the hall, the DJ played the romantic tracks segued one into another. It brooded romance in her mind; her eyes settled on his angled features, and his eye settled on hers. She looked ravishing and attractive. Her oversized updo on the back and the long tresses at the sides coaxed as ringlets displayed her charmingly feminine look. She looked luminous and radiant when a flawlessly cut diamond in the necklace sparkled between the gentle bulge on her chest. It attracted many greedy eyes to stare at her. She looked straight into his eyes and sank into the ocean of love. He had been thinking the same thing for her, and affectionately, he let his hand be placed on her hand and then gripped to say, " You look amazingly beautiful." Their eyes settled silently on each other.

On the dance floor, the tempo of the music grew louder. The twist of the whirling bodies went coarser, and a few swayed madly on their feet when the track "You Shook Me All Night Long by AC/DC" was played. On a Punjabi beat, the atmosphere warmed up. As the sticks on the drum thumped rhythmically, the ladies raised their arms and shook their bangles, creating a lively jangle. Their male partners, too, enjoyed flagging their handkerchiefs to match the cadence.

She beamed at his strong, chiselled chin and prominent aquiline nose. The features strongly depicted an Afghani look. He took out a pack of cigars and stuck one in his mouth. He torched the tip of it with a lighter. She inhaled the musky, sweet scent of the smoke while he jetted out through his nostrils. He gestured towards the dance floor after dinner. They got up and left their table. He ran a hand down her back before placing his hand on the small of her back while he glided her across the hall. They danced to the smutty item numbers which the DJ played on the dance floor. Her curvy hips made a few sultry moves while the ample-hipped Director's wife amused herself by twisting gently to her sides and clapping out the tune with her hands.

They waltzed around the floor, holding each other's arms. She could feel his breath on her, his eyes glistened while on hers, and hers, too, seemed lit up.

"Hi Salim," Jeba, a short-haired gamine, sneaked up on him, dodging the crowd while they twisted. She raised her hand. He detangled his fingers from Madhu and reciprocated from a meter's distance by waving his hand while twisting his body. She came closer. The stench of alcohol wafted in the air with every word she mouthed, "Hi dude, who is this babe? New *murg*i Chick in the industry? Nice choice. Looking pretty like Madhubala."

A gentle smile lingered on his face when she let out those words. He replied swiftly, " Let me introduce her. She is Madhu, a new face in the industry and an aspiring actress. She is Jeba, a supermodel."

"Are you from Pakistan? The fashion magazines were always full of your photographs during our school days." Madhu said.

" That's her talent. But she doesn't look that old." Salim said.

Jeba darted a surprised glance, "No way for sure. She shouldn't be the same girl." She is trying to recollect the story of this girl.

"Duplicate Madhubala, Umm, yes! Are you that calendar girl - **Anarkali Patnawali**? " Jeba asked.

Jeba gestured to them towards the bar. " Join me for a snifter." She hoped Madhu would reciprocate, but Madhu did not show any interest in the drinks.

"Sorry, can't have it after dinner," Madhu said pronto.

Such an act never happened to Jeba. Madhu's rejection took her by surprise. Jeba felt insulted and frowned, " *Kudi*, girl, the industry replaces them who leaps out of a request. Come on, get drunk."

When Salim himself asked her to have the drinks, at that moment in life, she could not decide what was good and bad for her. Madhu took the hint and followed them to the bar. Jeba lifted her gin and toasted, "Cheers!" Madhu drank gin and tonic with ice and lemon, which she had never tasted.

"Is she an artist?" Jeba asked Salim.

"I am just waiting for the right time to launch her in the industry," Salim said.

" Oh, now I realize she is your girlfriend. She is very pretty. I would give her a ten out of ten as her look is ditto to Madhubala's."

With the first gulp of drink, Madhu raised her hand to her chest and patted her burning chest.

" Sultan, you kept this a secret. It amazed me," Jeba said.

Jeba's eyes caught sight of a tobacconist who was selling cigars and pipes. Madhu even picked up the cigar lit by Jeba and got carried away at that moment, overtly appreciating her beauty.

For the first time, she smoked marijuana. It shattered her mental equilibrium. She slipped into another world and felt like scaling the sky. "*Kudi,* you can look in on me sometimes," Jeba left.

She lurched as she leapt from the chair behind the bar. Salim escorted her to the room on the fifth floor. Inappropriately, he grabbed her waist inside the enclosed cubicle while riding the lift. She could not squirm free. She felt uncomfortable with his groping hands. If she hadn't been drunk, she would have resisted. She would have fretted and screamed. She experienced a queer numbness in her mind as he led her into the room. She bundled herself onto the bed and pulled a blanket over her. She could feel the mattress dipped next to her. After a few seconds, a fuzzy sensation arose in her mind before she drifted into a peaceful night's sleep.

At dawn, she woke up to a phone call made by the hotel receptionist. She realized she was probably not fully dressed when she came to bed. The bitter irony was that she had no one to blame but herself for that state. She had collapsed onto the bed, but it was unlikely an intentional act to unfurl those encapsulated body-hugging detachable linings. "Did the drink she had tripped her up to do so while in bed?" she thought. She found her necklace on the bed and her hair unkempt. She took one glance around and noticed that the door was not latched. "She certainly would have come here after the drink and forgotten to latch it. Salim probably left with Jeba after the drinks. What could have happened last night? It was completely my fault. I shouldn't have had the gins. Mom, I am sorry. It was not practically possible to stay away from the drinks. That's something I listened to my mind. Sometimes, it happens; I am sure you would have approved my actions had you been with me. What I did last night after dinner was not wrong. My feelings for you are honest, but Mom, everything happened so quickly I couldn't call you to ask. I will explain to you in detail when I come to you." Such thoughts shuddered her before she tried to fall asleep again.

Within her closed eyes, her nerves surreptitiously recollected the glimpses of the moments she shared with Salim and her mother: he stared at her, "I do feel something for you, Madhu." " Sorry, my mistake for coming late and making you wait, Salim." "Don't apologize, Madhu," "Can I call you by your name, Salim." " you can." "Salim, the Goa trip was the best part of my life." "I am glad you got me right, Madhu. My apologies if I have caused you any trouble in Goa." "Being fair and honest, I like you, Madhu." " During the shoot, his hands touched my skin, mama." "Perhaps the fault is in you, Beta, for not properly dressed." "Go and live your life, Madhu. Now, Patna is not your place." "You are the best, Mama, and I love you." "Take care, Beta. You are going to Bombay for the first time." "Mama, you and Aunty keep this number of the hotel. Let me know if there is anything I can buy for you from Bombay."

She woke up again to hear the telephone ringing. Was she actually in her senses to believe that the telephone had rung? She pinched herself. She raised her hand and picked up the phone. It was a trunk call made to her by a neighbour in Bihar. Disha heard voices in the background. One said, "Your mother has suffered a serious head injury and has been admitted to the hospital. Come soon. She was found lying unconscious in a pool of blood. No one heard her screaming in the neighbourhood."

She flew back to Bihar upon hearing this news about her mother, who had become unresponsive after a fall in the bathroom early in the morning. She hurried to the hospital and arrived there in the evening. Her heart sank to see her mother on a ventilator. Panic swept over her as she noticed her mother in a fragile state. Her mother had a brainstem haemorrhage from a head injury. Madhu's stomach twisted with dread. She felt a lump in her throat before asking the doctor about her mother's condition.

" Doctor, I would feel much better if you could tell me she will be alright. It doesn't matter over one month or two months."

Madhu said in a subdued voice, with hollow eyes and tears trickling down.

"If you want to feel better, pray to God, Beti. We are trying our level best to save her."

Her Aunt said, "I had dinner with your Mama last night. She said she was going to sleep. We had planned to go for a walk in the morning. When I went in, I saw her in a pool of blood." She blew out a long sigh. " Who knew she -"

She was utterly unprepared for what the doctor had to inform her of. There was weeping, and she froze as the news broke to her.

"Your mother now had a cardiac arrest, and the doctors gave her cardiopulmonary resuscitation ."

She sobbed. It seemed to her someone was there to hold her when she was falling. No, it was her imagination. All the memories of her mother's warm embrace, her soothing voice and her unwavering love flooded her consciousness. She felt helpless. There was no certainty of her mother's condition. Her mind was consumed with hopes and prayers. There was no Salim to support her at that moment. She slumped onto the chair.

For a moment, she was not certain that she ever existed in the room. She only heard, " You are a sensible woman. Please tell her we are sorry. We couldn't save her mother."

The doctors declared her dead. She wept at her bedside. She cursed herself for not being with her and leaving her alone at home. Her mother left the world with an unfulfilled dream. She always wanted to see her on the silver screen. She felt orphaned. No one in her close relations had been left behind whom she could look up to in distress. She decided to shift to Mumbai permanently after her mother's last rite.

She did not have enough means to support herself in Bombay. She had no academic qualification for a decent job in any office. She was desperately drawn towards Salim. His craggy features had attracted her, and she felt smitten. It was not an easy decision to leave Patna. She was aware of the future challenges for her. She reiterated to herself, "From now on, it will just be your hard work, Madhu. Go ahead and take life as it comes."

The air inside the station was thick with the damp, musty smell of wet clothing and the heavy exhalations of impatient passengers standing nearby. Madhu had never experienced such a day in her life. She covered her nose with a handkerchief; her luggage settled on the floor. The concrete floors were squeaky underfoot as the throngs of people shuffled in the platforms, leaving muddy footprints all over. The announcement system crackled to life. The lady's voice was barely audible above the cacophony of voices, clanging luggage carts, and the patter of rain on the sheds. Weary travellers huddled against the train carriages, their faces drawn and shoulders hunched under the weight of their luggage. Children wailed while harried parents attempted to maintain a firm grip on their hands as they tried to enter the already-loaded trains. Besides all this, the crowd's patience grew thinner with each minute delayed by the raging storm outside.

A brawny six-footer coolie with rugged features approached her, his voice a raspy croak. "*Namaste, madam.* Which train are you searching for? May I help you get in? It has been raining cats and dogs outside. The runway at the airport is flooded, and all the flights from Patna airport have been cancelled. You can see the station unusually overcrowded today." He eyed her with recognition. "It would be my pleasure to serve you, madam. You are quite popular in Bihar. A few days ago, I had seen your photo in all these magazine stalls on magazine covers. Who does not know you? Everyone knows you now as *Madhubala*, our own '**Anarkali Patnawali**.'

His gesture conveyed a sense of dependability. Madhu liked his steadfast offer of assistance. She didn't realise she had become famous by a new name until then.

Promptly, she replied, "I am looking for the Bombay Express."

"Do you have the berth number ?" asked the coolie.

"No, I don't have a reservation," she said. She looked at the ticket barrier, still packed with people. He looked at her and understood the plight of a single unaccompanied lady intending to travel with too much luggage. She gazed at the crowd alighting from the carriage outside and rushing into the station. She was very aware of the standards of train services in an unreserved coach. She had by then rightly understood that she would never get into any of these trains in her life with all her luggage.

He said, " Madam, if you say yes, I will contact my people to arrange you a berth. You will have to pay a little more. Everyone out here calls me Coolie Number One, and my name is Cheema."

When she nodded, he helped her to get a place to sit in the restroom before leaving to arrange a ticket. An hour later, he succeeded in getting one. She pulled out a wad of notes from her purse. All notes were in the fifties and hundreds. He pocketed those notes. The next moment, he lifted her luggage and placed it under the allotted berth.

While she travelled, the director's words echoed, "You can be a great star of tomorrow." When many girls like her wandered Bombay's streets without a job, she felt fortunate to get a job offer. All because of Salim's company in that unknown city.

The streets were illuminated to greet her that night. It was seven on her watch when she stepped off the halted train. She responded to a taxi driver waiting for a prospective customer. He aided in dumping her luggage into his Taxi and dropped her at the hotel in a few minutes. She got into her hotel room, had dinner, and slipped into a deep sleep.

It was nine in the morning when she woke up to a phone call from the receptionist. After a good morning wish, she ordered a cup of tea in a lazy tone, paying a little attention to the follow-up words the receptionist wanted to convey. Fifteen minutes later, the bell at the door rang. The room bearer served the tea with a note-' Meet Mr. Salim at 4 PM in his office.' Was it for a love affair she did not know? After reading that piece of paper, she was sure her feet were not on this planet. It was such good news that she hoped for a great deal to act in a film at the next moment. She would become famous. Riffling her suitcase for a smart outfit, she picked a skin-tight white top with a pleated red skirt. Not finding it suitable for the occasion, she wore a red suit over it. She spent a few hours inside the hotel room till 3 PM. Wearing her newly bought matching square-toe cowboy boots, she left for Salim's office after lunch. Her demeanour was unbelievably pretty.

The edifice by the beach stood tall amidst all. The crashing waves on the pavements were adorable for the couples who dotted its edges. Their bodies leaned in close, heads nearly touching, caressing each other with delicate tenderness. For them, love mattered, nothing else. The salty air in the atmosphere whispered in her ears something good, "This city is the perfect place for you, Madhu, to live in," as she entered the tower.

"Madam, Salim sir wants to introduce you to the people sitting inside. They have been here to show you your new house. It has everything that you want. It was recently constructed with stylish interior designs. It will suit your lifestyle and taste. To meet your needs, the house is stuffed with luxurious installations. I just scanned the complete set of papers that they brought along," the desk clerk, Toofani, briefed smilingly.

" Why is she doing this for me?" she asked in a surprising tone.

Toofani replied, "He keeps the frame ready before he paints the picture of his heroines. He is a wealthy guy. His shoes spread across the globe, all over Dubai, Pakistan, Afghanistan, and here in India. He has innumerable mansions sprawled over a quarter of this city. He has a fleet of long cars; He owns many hotels. He gifts those big cars to those he likes and keeps the girls as queens in his palatial bungalows. The girls feel safe with the security arrangements he has made for them. All his guards carry big guns. Madam, you are lucky because Salim Sir has called you directly. Before you, many girls came here, but nobody earned a gifted house like you. Madam, it is a two-storeyed mansion with pillared verandas, a well-manicured big lawn in front of it, and a swimming pool in the centre. It is a big, all-sided -walled house facing the sea. You will enjoy watching the sea from your balcony. Many girls in this fashion industry are struggling to make their career in Bollywood, and for you, the opportunity is just waiting at your door. He has many connections in Bollywood. He can make or break someone's career at the snap of his fingers."

"Is he that influential as a person?" She asked.

"Yes, madam. His likings and dislikes depend on his mood. He likes a girl who never says no to anything," Toofani replied.

Before she entered inside, Toofani asked her to sign the papers. "Madam, please place your signature here," she gestured to a space. This bungalow is going to be yours for ninety-nine years. These papers will be given to the person handing over the bungalow. Madhu took the pen from her and asked, "Gold?"

"Yes, madam."After signing the document, Madhu hefted the pen before returning, "Heavy! very nice."

"A birthday gift, madam."

"From Salim?"

"Yes, Madam."

As she entered his office, in a momentous transformation, his depraved mind leered at her, though his demeanour seemed friendly. The Love for him was so blind that her vile mood had turned into an intense feeling of excitement after meeting him. She was grappling with the feel of his breath and his hand's touch. She marvelled at his pointed nose and his angled features. She did not know what his intention behind this was. It came to her as a big surprise. Was she being considered by him for marriage? Although he had often revealed his heart to her for a serious relationship, they never discussed marriage.

The sound of crashing waves and the salty sea breeze filled the air. As she stepped out onto the patio of her new beachside bungalow, she could see the gentle tides lapping at the shore rhythmically. That morning, she gazed at the blue stretching horizon meeting with the sky. The warm sun caressed her soft skin. She thought all good things for herself, relaxing in a cosy chair. Her little paradise is here. She and Salim, nestled right on the beach, are everything one girl can dream of. The worries of everyday life get washed away with the rejuvenating scent of flowers from her garden. At that moment, she was entirely at peace in her new house.

"Sorry, madam, here, no one is allowed to go out without Sultan's permission. This point is the last limit of someone's freedom."

It annoyed her. "I have to purchase necessary items. Sultan is my friend."

" The servants are here to look after your every need. They will provide you with all sorts of assistance while you stay." The guard grinned. The words were unpleasant to her ears as he said gruffly.

"This is torture and deprivation of my freedom. You can't do this to me." She continued to frown," Let Sultan come. I will ask him to teach you some manners."

She walked back to the bungalow. Somehow, she did not feel like going inside. It has been a week since she has been shifted to this place. "Everything went according to Salim, but when will he come? Nobody knows. Toofani was right. He has hundreds of houses in Bombay, but it doesn't mean that She should be left in the care of his slaves. Next time she meets him, she will tell him the list of complaints," she thought.

Madhu felt like a dumped mistress in a fort who had little clue about the people who lived next door. She was being poorly treated within the four walls. Everything inside was quiet and dull. Nobody even had a charming smile to show to her. Even the maids were like that, not wanting to ease away with her. The team of mercenaries that he had left for her in the name of security all carried serious looks. All tight-lipped.

In her dreams, she had never thought of his weird see-sawing behaviour. The time they spent happily together playing Frisbee and ball in the tiny waves on the beach, moving together on a bike in their baggy shorts in the streets at midnight, tanning their chests brown together under the sun, running on the Goa beach was it all just meant for the sake of fun? Was he not emotional when he intended to ask her company for his whole life? Undoubtedly, from his side, it seemed a serious confession. She had liked his straightforward style without considering that an accomplished flirt could seriously make the tones. Can he deny that the photo shoot of her being laid on a canopy with a male model was not called off by him on that day? Was he not possessive about her on that day? She dreamt of becoming a big starlet in Bollywood but could never contemplate that someday it would end like this. A selfish itch to travel the world with him proved to be a fatal trap for herself, of which she had been entirely unaware.

As a homeless itinerant in the city, she needed a strong shoulder to lean on for support, which she desperately wanted at that spur of the moment. The silence inside her heart was somehow interpreted as her agreement. She wandered at a sedate pace, from wall to wall and corner to corner, often restlessly walking in circles across the large central hall around the sofa. At times, the room suffused with the fresh air by the lift of curtains from a gentle breeze through the window, but the suffocation in her life lingered uninterruptedly within. She felt bemused and gloomy like a caged bird. Her wings were clipped, and her birdie's desire to fly in the sky had been trampled to crush under his feet. She will never allow someone to destroy her life like this. Her cheeks flushed red in anger. Her life remained no longer colourful and cheerful as she languished in that bungalow.

Two weeks ago, she had carried a large suitcase. She had dresses and jewellery in it. She could not recollect where the maid kept it. She even did not know where her cosmetics were. She had been wearing the dresses kept for her in the wardrobe.

She thought of remissing herself for not taking good care of herself. Something had happened wrong with her groins. The skin had become very sensitive and bruised. She could have been hurt inside her lower part. Her chest had never been so painful and tender before. She had never felt restless like this before. She felt powerless. She had difficulty articulating words as if the tongue cleaved to her palate, and she could not utter her words smoothly. She had an indescribable hardship, both mentally and physically. Every nerve in her body screamed with pain.

At that moment, the only recourse left for her was to offer a prayer, hoping that God would grant her emancipation. "Oh God, what has this man done to me? Isn't it a sin? Does this nefarious man realize what he does is cruelty? Is this man sane enough to understand that denying someone freedom is not a small offence? Can she ever shout protestation against this powerful man and secure her freedom? When will she be able to get rid of this barbarism?"

By then, She understood that a hideous monster was masked behind a nice-mannered gentleman.

The door opened slowly. The old man entered, saying," Lunch."

Karim Cha Cha entered and walked across the main hall with a tray with a plateful of rice, a bowlful of Daal, vegetable curry, and a bowl of kheer. He dropped it on a centre table laid in front of the sofa. The tray rattled. He was an old, white-haired and thin-built man.

"Cha Cha, don't send me too much food. I cannot eat them like before. My lips are burning and sore." she said softly in a slurred deadpan, leaning back on the sofa. She sat with sprawled legs.

"That is why I came here, to ask why you are returning the food untouched. What happened to you, Beti? I don't want to be a whipping boy for not feeding you properly."

"Cha Cha, I want to return to my home, or I will explore another place to stay. This palace is not for me. Send someone to take out his portraits from my view. I don't like them." She piqued.

"Many girls came to stay here, but–"

" But, what? Are you hiding something serious?"

"They were numb skulls, but you are different. If you do not like to stay here, then start liking something else. Anyone who comes here to stay is never allowed to go out clean."

"What else is there to like?"

"Cha Cha, I feel unwell. The sight of food makes me feel nauseated. Every day, once or twice, I get fever spikes. I do not know what ails me with this fever."

"Eat this healthy food, and you will be all right in a day or two."

"My lower body pains intensely once the effects of injections wither off. I do not know what is happening to me. I feel knotted up here. I want to go to a refreshing place where I can breathe properly."

"Sit there on the balcony. Look at the sea for some time. You will get some fresh air."

"I am not dependent on anyone for my living expenses. I came to him for my dream, A dream of a lifetime to act in cinema. Now, my life has become no less than any tragic cinema."

"I know one day you will become a successful actor, but for that, you need to survive. Eat this food, and your fever will subside."

"I want to break free from this monster's grip. Please help me, Cha Cha. Besides food, I also need a doctor to see me. I am like your daughter. Please help me get out of this place. I do not know what these men are up to and their intentions," she said distressfully. Her face looked pale and contorted, with noticeable facial tics and tears rolling down her eyes.

Cushioning her sorrow, his voice choked, and there was a visible sadness on his face. Karim Cha Cha said, "I have been staying in this place for many years. He brought many girls here, drugged them, and treated them like some exporting goods. He exported them to different countries."

"You mean to say the house was not bought recently for me? I was lured to stay. Whatever Toofani said was a constructed lie. I was made to sign all fabricated documents !"

"Those lines were broken to many girls before you. The exterior, the facade, the sea-facing view, the big lawn, the palatial bungalow. That is a trap." After a moment of silence, he said,

"Other than my work, I am asked not to interfere in any other matters, so only I can say-"

"Tell me, Cha Cha, complete your sentence. Why did you stop? Tell me, what is the matter? I want to know. Here, no one speaks. Everyone's mouth has been stitched."

"The walls have ears, Beta. When you do not remain in your proper senses after the injection, you are served to the guests as a cake on their platter. Each one of them bites a piece of you. May Allah give you strength and courage to fight with these monsters." he said.

Cha Cha's panicky mind was attuned to see the torture calmly for years without a trace of resistance to keep his family out of these monstrous atrocities he was to inflict upon. He said, "When the time comes, I can help you sneak out covertly in my tempo, which I take out every day to buy groceries and vegetables, but promise me you will never take my name in any unfavourable circumstances if faced with. The sentries have their orders, and they will never let you go out in any situation if they see you escaping."

"I will not take your name, trust me, Cha Cha."

"He is a monster. He has killed my son. My son was a wrestler. First, he lured him with quick money through drugs, then sent him for extortion and turned him into a dreaded criminal. Who later was killed in an encounter."

Madhu was initially drugged through her drinks and then injected shot after shot to make her body a listless and meaty one to serve on the foreign platter like a ravishable item. She knew at least about herself and what she was subjected to after those shots of injections.

Her freedom was snatched. She yielded to the force of the monster. Her life became colourless and dull. She mourned the decision to mingle with this man. Through her growing wisdom, she could see that the man had never meant love as a beautiful emotion. For him, Love was a game of attraction, a series of chemical reactions and a surge of hormonal secretion. He lured many girls with fame, Bollywood, easy money, and a life of luxury. She sobbed in silence. She looked pale, weak, and frail. She lost a few pounds of flesh due to her fever. She waited until she could gain strength well enough to walk. She wanted to get rid of the caged life. She mustered the courage to venture out from the monstrous cage. On a Sunday morning when the security was thin, she bundled herself inside a jute sack to be driven out by Karim Cha Cha to the city's real world. She reached the police station and lodged an FIR. An arrest warrant was issued immediately against Salim for the crime he committed. She accompanied the police to his office. The medical reports confirmed sexual assault, narcotics in her blood, and leakage in her heart valve.

"None of your prisons can keep me longer, Inspector. Even if thousands of your men guard me in the strongest of your jails, in the deepest of the ground, they can do nothing to me. My men will take me away right under your nose, and you will see me as a mute spectator with your hands tied. Mind you, inspector, they will not spare you nor any member of your family to live on this earth." He gritted his teeth and cowed.

Madhu shouted, "Inspector, take this man to the prison. This man cheated hundreds of girls, exploited them, drugged them, and trafficked them to Dubai." Her voice thundered, and the veins of her neck stood prominent. She was not as timid as she used to be. She displayed the courage to stand against his threats.

"You stupid girl, you should know who I am. I will crush you like a pesky fly. I loved you so much, and you handed me over to the police."

Walking closer to him, not letting someone intervene, She gestured to the police officers not to react. "Love, what love truly is for you, everyone saw within those four walls. The names in your diaries, the phone numbers, and the price at which you sold those girls to the brothels abroad have also been seized from your office. Enough for your lifetime to rot in jail, you heartless scoundrel."

"Rot in the jail? I will send you to the hell. You stay with your mother. The men are still free who conked your mother."

It maddened her. "I will kill you, you scoundrel," she shouted, and her eyes opened with a jerk. It was her dreadful past, something unforgettable, something bonded with her nerves by strong emotions. She lost her mother.

With a jolt, she woke up from the bed, her head aching to leave the comfort of the bed. However, reaching over, her hand grasped the worn leather handle of the suitcase hidden in the storage drawer beneath. Pulling it out, she flipped open the lid. Her hand reached for a file of medical reports. She had an appointment with Dr. Pradeep. She needed to hire a taxi. She was very disturbed by Sagar's imprisonment.

The incident weighed heavily on her mind, a constant source of distress. Her fingers, sifting through the stack of medical files within, picked up a crumpled paper and a tattered diary from the suitcase's contents. Still, she could not believe that she had been sold out. How she had been betrayed, her signature adorning a lifetime contract to work as a domestic helper in Dubai. The document carried her real signatures on all pages. Was that the job of Toofani? She was nowhere to be found by the police in all of Mumbai. She did not remember when she had kept this diary in her suitcase. Many questions in her mind remained unanswered in the last seven years since the incident occurred. 'Where is Kareem Cha Cha?' Is it Kareem Cha Cha who kept the file and diary in her suitcase? Where is this Omar transport? She could not find it in Bombay. Was it really a transport company? Was there any plan to transport me with the suitcase? She went through the medical reports.

That day, She had palpitations and shortness of breath when she was taken to Dr Pradeep's cabin for the first time. That day After Salim's arrest, his words reverberated intensely off the wall umpteen times, so also hers: "I will kill you, you scoundrel. You Killed my mother!" The colour of her cheek turned crimson, and her blood boiled and gushed inside her arteries. The flow thundered in her heart. She felt the pain. There was palpitation, her heart raced and hammered to the chest, and the chest heaved, her head pounded, there was a shallowness in her breath, and she was engrossed with a feeling of running out of oxygen. She felt her energy draining out, her body turned a red hot iron, her eyes burnt, the fury soared up, and she collapsed in the police station. When she came to her senses, she found herself in a hospital bed.

Two days later, when she felt better after hospitalization, she asked, "Doctor, is there anything serious?"

"Ms Madhu, a valve in your heart is leaking and requires fixing," Dr Pradeep responded.

" How did it happen, Doctor?"

" It is a serious infection of your heart valve, which has made a hole in it. You got it through the infected needles that were pricked into your blood vessels."

" How will you fix it?"

" By replacing your diseased valve with a new one."

" How do you do that?"

" It is an open-heart surgery."

" Surgery! You will cut my body, no Doctor. I do not want any surgery. Prescribe me some medicine. I will be alright."

"Don't worry, my dear. The surgery will be painless. We use general anaesthesia. After the surgery, you may get little pain or discomfort, but that can be managed effectively with the tablets. You need to spend at least a week in the hospital. You have to come for the follow-up visit after that."

"Doctor, I am scared of this surgery. Can you manage it with only antibiotics?" Madhu asked.

" No, You must take these antibiotics for four weeks before the surgery, and Surgery is necessary. Here, the problem is that the valve in your heart is leaking significantly, and you will never have any relief from your symptoms until we fix it. It has already caused significant damage to your heart. You better be prepared for the surgery. Trust me, There will be no pain,"

"I am not worried about the pain, but I am worried about the cut on my body. I am in show business, and any scar over my body will ruin my career," she said in a wet-throated voice.

"Every moment in life is lively if lived with perfect health. Ailing life is conditioned to drain out its colours, and the livelihood stumbles at each step, which will impact your career even more seriously. A minimal scar will be visible in the midline of your chest, which you can later conceal with a beautiful tattoo or any makeup. The approach to your heart is through your chest bone, and we will keep in mind the final cosmesis at the end of the surgery. If you consent, we will proceed with the necessary investigations before the surgery. The decision is yours, whether to continue with antibiotics or get yourself operated on," said Dr. Pradeep.

"Okay, Doctor, I will let you know after the course of antibiotics," she said.

As he said, she felt her life took a new turn. She looked frailer with the ailment. She lost all her future assignments following the lapse of time-bound contracts she had signed with big business houses in a better state of health while in Goa. Madhu felt desolated in the city. She was emotionally exhausted after her mother's demise. She telephoned her neighbours in Patna with a lingering desperation, but no one answered. She was physically drained as well. The biggest fiasco in the public glare was her name, which every newspaper published as 'Salim's Anarkali'. It brought her public infamy. Her name was linked with the gangster. She ran from pillar to post to get a second chance at survival. But nothing worked. She had been replaced by new entrants in the industry. Her bank balance went thinner and thinner with every passing day.

A couple of weeks passed, and her health condition deteriorated further. She consented to surgery, and the recovery was uneventful. After a week, she was discharged from the hospital.

As a temporary engagement, she started a new job as a beautician in her salon. She began her life journey in a new direction within the ambit of her experience in giving beauty tips and bridal makeup solutions to her clients, with a new name and a new identity: " Disha."

Almost half a decade later, a big car stopped in front of her salon. A lady alighted from the car. She looked beautiful, with her long, wavy hair mantled over her shoulder. She looked tall, wearing high-heeled sandals. She entered her salon accompanied by her tall, rouge-looking husband. He was a hotelier, and his eyes darted to every corner of her salon, and then he approached her with his heavy gait. She could distinctly hear the chink of metallic keys in his trouser pocket as he walked heavily. When she turned around behind her desk, his eyes widened, and he surveyed her from top to toe. Cheema could not believe his eyes - she was the same supermodel Madhubala he had once met at the railway station.

Time changes, and so does fate. People change, and so does their destiny: some climb high, and some fall. The time brings luck for some and hope for others. Like in a tragic movie, goodness prevails in the end. Her life was turning into a new path of happiness. Happiness, when it comes, it comes like an uninvited guest -when and where no one knows. It brings along a myriad of changes with certainty and stability in life. In these five years, Cheema had turned from a porter in the railway station to a hotelier. He offered her a managerial post in his hotel.

These flashbacks made her feel better. She stared at those medical reports and kept the rest inside the suitcase in the storage drawer of the bed.

3 (II)

1990, Bombay:

Those who had links with Salim scurried away like rats to shelter in other countries for their safe confinement. Those who complied to remain fugitives stayed away from the city's affair, and a few non-compliant handfuls of narcotic traffickers were dealt with an iron fist. Incidences of gang wars in the city sloped down tremendously. At times, the curve trended downward and intersected at the lowest point. The underworld was in a panic mode following Salim's arrest. The enemy country changed tactics to peddle narco-terrorism for geographical expansion, slowly gripping the rest of the country with its deeply penetrated tentacles in the society. The conspirators had joined hands with the smugglers for a regional arms race. The national agencies stood alert following the arrest and turned every page of Salim's chapter. With their stern actions, Salim's chapter was closed forever within a few years.

The cordless phone in his pergola rang. Cheema picked up the phone and said, "For reasons of my own, I could not deliver the stuff, Peter bhai. The situation is a little tight here."

As Sameer noticed, Cheema's laugh melted, his face contorted. The expression on his face went from happiness of his company to a stunned silence of the dead.

Cheema said, "I do not think Sultan can ever be released in this life, Peter Bhai. Almost six years have passed since he has been in jail. What have they not tried to set him free? Nothing worked. They can't release him. "

"They have sealed the border, Cheema. The Army at the border killed my men and destroyed my refineries."

"What are you saying, Peter bhai? Border sealed! Crackdown on opium refineries! Hello, hello, too much crackle on the line. Just a minute, Peter Bhai." Cheema's face was dead and pale. He rushed inside his house with the cordless phone, giving a hard shove to the servant. "Give me way. Do not stand here. Don't you know we are discussing something serious?" He was desperately annoyed.

"What happened to you, Cheema?" Sameer said.

"Hold on, Sameer. Shut up for a minute. Let me think about what I can do." Cheema bolted up with the phone. He lifted a hand to her chest. He patted his racing heart.

Sameer thought of being ridiculed by a conceited soul. "Is this manner out of some distress? Which gets worse in odd moments. He should have gotten the contract signed then and there last year just after the announcement."

Sameer heard Cheema saying on the phone, "Listen, if the news is correct, then we have to find a new partner, Peter bhai, who can supply us in time. Let the stuff rot there at the border."

"Wait till Azgar finds some solution. He is waiting for the right time." Peter said.

"I can't wait for any right time, Peter bhai. That right time will never come. Ten of your men have already been knocked down at the border. The Don is in jail. Withdraw your men; otherwise, the rest will also get knocked down. I do not want to get you into any trouble. I will presume I lost a big wager amount."

"You will lose all your stuff, Cheema."

"Peter Bhai, I know it stings hard, but we have now no option left. They sealed all our borders. That Pakistani, Azgar, will devour all our money. That Omar Afghani is an idiot, Peter Bhai. He should not have sent our stuff without a nod from you. That Omar chap is good for nothing. Mark my word, you can't expect anything good from him."

In the face of adversity, through a cloud of confusion and fear, Cheema could not decide how to act or react to the news. Sameer had to say something as Cheema cut the phone. Sameer scanned his face; Cheema's petulant expression was still evident.

He slowly started to understand this side of Cheema. An instant of despair shrouded his thought process as he did not reply to anything after hearing what Sameer had discussed with him about the investment.

"Sorry, Sameer, my import-export business is spread all over. There are so many problems you do not know who calls from where. I do direct business. I have kept no middleman." He leaned over to make tea for Sameer and said, "After a month or so, we will work on the set. Give me some time to get my money back. At present, there is a lot of activity going on at the border. All my trucks are stuck. Don't close it off. I will see how early we can start."

Cheema was a shrewd businessman. He knew how to manoeuvre a deal for his profit. Things have changed in Bombay, but he has not. Does he need to revise the contract if Sultan gets free?

3(III)

There was not even a hidden place left where the poppies were not being grown on these mountain lands of Afghanistan. The secret cultivation in this place on the earth is no longer a secret. The green farmlands on both sides of highways all have poppies in them. Such a place is where a blue and clear sky would be a perfect day, and a rainy one would be the worst day for its farmers. For ages, they have not heard any screams of police van sirens stopping them from growing poppies because the police have understood the rationale of incentives and disincentives in that job. The strong hands of the youth still have the confusion between grabbing a rifle or a spade as there is a big cash flow in either way. Every season of poppies is a harbinger of their wealth, especially for people like Omar Afghani, whose trucks and containers relentlessly trundle down the highways of Pakistan, India and Afghanistan.

This man in his late fifties wore a grey Peran o Tunban and a brown turban. There was dismay on his face when twenty-eight of his trucks returned from the Pakistan border without delivering the goods. No delivery slip had the required permit stamps beyond the border. He wandered along the returned trucks, examining every truck, all hoarded up with many buckets, each full of opium pastes collected from his farmlands. When a Pakistani diplomat visited him with a satellite phone, everything was ready to be transported back.

The Diplomat intoned twice from behind," Omar, Omar, Azgar Saab is on the line."

Omar turned around to see him. The Diplomat promptly handed over the satellite phone to Omar. The diplomat had sharp features and amber eyes, revealing his sophistication, while Omar looked dirty and suntanned.

Omar was an illiterate, stubborn man who threw his half-smoked cigar into the air and said "Hello" through the mouthpiece while ejecting the mouthful of smoke. There was a satellite lag in communication.

"Azgar Zardari this side, *Janab*."

Omar said, " Salaam, Azgar saab, I pray to the Almighty that you flourish, and your enemies should flounder."

"Why did you call me *Janab*?" Azgar said.

Omar said, "Azgar Saab, we have grown bumper crops worth three hundred million dollars this season. Take care of them before they get rotten in the fields."

" *Janab*, a few of your trucks are about to cross the border, and this time, you will find your diesel tanks, which will reach their destination, all loaded with your stuff."

"Azgar saab, when should I send these trucks that are sent back from the border? There is enough in stock now to make India doped along its whole length and breadth for a year."

"Don't worry, Janab. My men are on your job, taking all sorts of risks. Very soon, your stuff will reach India. Our sole mission is to destroy our enemy with drugs."

Omar asked, "Peter *bhai* has withdrawn his men. Is that true?"

Azgar said," No problems, *Janab*, I have a young brigade. They will not stop whatever may come their way. We will snatch Kashmir at any cost and ensure our enemy bleeds from every pound of its flesh. It is my duty to see your trucks reach India."

Omar said," Azgar saab, I am happy you are ready to lift the rest of my stuff."

Azgar said, " *Janab*, your wish is my command. It is also our happiest desire to see every youth of India doped with your opium. Grow more crops next time."

"Azgar saab, I heard that the situations at your end are becoming more unfavourable."

" No problem, *Janab*. Peter has no idea how to handle the situation in India. Our tiger will come out of the cage very soon. I have sent a bunch of commandos from the eastern side. They have already crossed the border."

3(IV)

Kathmandu

Azgar Zardari called the airport, "Are you Mr. Gomes, the security officer?"

"Yes, speaking," Gomes replied.

"I am Azgar from the Pakistan Embassy. I want to meet you, *Janab*."

"What is the matter?" Gomes asked.

"Mr. Gomes, with me here is Mr. Bhola. He is a priest and a state guest. After his stay at the king's place, he will go to Delhi tomorrow afternoon. The king desires a quick security clearance."

"You request diplomatic immunity for him. Already, two names have come to us from your office. We will add his name to the list," Gomes said, putting the receiver down.

Gomes opened his diary and noted Bhola's name. Three names he wrote on a piece of paper: Mr. Bhola, Mr. Burger, and Mr. Shankar. He handed it over to the police inspector, Thapa, to facilitate their quick security clearance.

Azgar put the receiver on the cradle. Moments later, the heavy oak door swung open. Rauf entered his cabin without knocking on the door. Azgar sprung from his chair behind the polished Mahogany desk and extended his hand, his grip firm. He welcomed Rauf with a hearty handshake. Rauf took his seat across from him.

Azgar pressed the call bell beside his chair. Two more people waiting for Rauf in the lobby entered his cabin and took their chairs.

Azgar lifted a heavy suitcase behind the desk and placed it on the table. He opened the lid and rotated the suitcase towards them for a display. What they saw inside was: one Kalashnikov, attached with a loaded magazine case and a folded butt, was shining in the middle. There were also two more magazine cases loaded with live rounds, along with two pistols, one hand grenade, and three holy books wrapped inside saffron velvety clothes.

Azgar took their Passports and ID cards from his drawer and said, "Here are your ID cards. Rauf, you will get inside the airport as Bhola. Abdul, you enter as Shankar, and Zia, you as Burger. You will clad the attire of priests. You would gift Three holy books: one to Inspector Zameel and another to Mr. Gomes, the airport officer. The Third one you will gift me in front of Mr. Gomes,"

"Why all this saffron cloth drama, Azgar? Take us straight away to the departure lounge," Bhola asked.

"It is not for Zameel and not for Mr. Gomes. It is to show the passengers that you all are priests and not to give them the slightest clue that you are there to hijack the flight before you reach mid-air."

"Where will we land?"

"For you, the safest will be Kandahar Airport."

"Why not Islamabad," Rauf asked.

"No. Do not make that mistake. Listen to me carefully. Our commandos will take you to Quetta from Kandahar Airport by truck."

"Truck!" Rauf asked.

"You all will be provided radio sets to communicate with each other at the airport. But Your location can be traced by the international spy agencies. It will not surprise me if the agencies fit half a button-size transmitter chip on their clothes or boots while handing over our tigers. There are Faraday cages placed in a few of these trucks. You will move in them. They will protect you from getting detected. It is Omar Afghani who will take your responsibility in Afghanistan. I want Salim and Masoor in Quetta at any cost.

After a while, clad in the dignified robes of the priesthood, they headed to the airport. One by one, the pristine white ambassador cars arrived, and the travellers alighted after their journey of an hour. The boarding announcement was echoing through the entire corridor. Passengers were steadily making their way towards the Indian flight, IC-47, with some already settled into their seats.

Three priests were introduced to Inspector Thapa as the royal guests of Nepal by Azgar. As per their plan, they were swiftly escorted through a non-frisking passage. Azgar handed over the suitcase to Bhola. In no time, they were comfortably aboard the business class.

The aircraft gracefully lifted off the runway. Fifteen minutes later, the crew members assumed their designated stations following the initial announcements. The flight soared and juddered in mid-air after a while. Eventually, the pilot's voice echoed through the cabin, informing the passengers that they had entered the air space of the Indian subcontinent. So far, the transition into Indian airspace has been smooth for all passengers. While everyone enjoyed the landscape below, the cities and winding rivers, Rauf sprung from his seat, opened the suitcase, picked up the weapons, and declared a hijack.

Rauf entered the cockpit with the Kalashnikov rifle, took the pilot at gunpoint, and shouted at him, "This plane has been hijacked. Now, you follow our command. If you do not follow what we say, we will blow up this flight in a second. Zia proceeded towards the tail end; Abdul took a position at the head end of the flight."

Amritsar's Air Traffic Control tower contacted the Prime Minister's office in Delhi to break the news about the hijack of flight IC -47. Before the officer could inform the secretary, the PM had planned his scheduled visit to the USA on the same evening. The secretary-level talks had been initiated. The Foreign minister and the home minister were in the same meeting for a discussion on foreign diplomacy with Southeast countries and the growing narco-terrorism in the continent. The Secretary took a minute to think before speaking with the PM. He was in constant touch with the diplomats in Afghanistan. When he broke the news at the meeting, the PM cancelled his visit. He was concerned about the lives of 176 passengers. Their safe return was his utmost priority. The unanimous decision was to release Salim and Masoor and send them across the border safely, unharmed, and taken by the house floor in the all-party meeting.

CHAPTER 4

A tragedy unexpected

1994, Mumbai.

"Hello, hello," Chunnilal shouted after picking up the phone receiver.

Natasha said, "Papa, my flight is departing late from Delhi. It has been rescheduled to 10:30 AM, and I will land in Mumbai around 12:30 PM. Don't be late to pick me up like last time."

"Beta, don't worry. I have not kept any meetings scheduled at the party office this time. I will reach there on time." He put the receiver on the cradle and swiftly pranced towards his car parked outside. Suddenly, a white van came from nowhere and stopped in front of his gate. Two masked men slid open the door and hopped down. They trespassed through the main entrance and approached him with hockey sticks. They looked strong and muscular. One held his collar from the front, and the other helped push him into the van. Before he could take a glimpse of the driver, his head was covered with a black cloth, and the van took him far from his place. The thought of his daughter waiting for him at the airport worried him throughout.

Minute after minute, hour after hour passed. Slight darkness covered the city as she waited outside Juhu airport, madly looking at the departing crowd leaving one by one in their reserved taxis. Incessantly, her mind raced with worries, contemplating any possible mishap her father could have faced en route in such bad weather. On and off, her eyes sneaked a look at the main road, which appeared hazy through the streaks of rain. Her face gleamed with anxiety, and her legs became tired. She shifted her weight from one weary foot to the other. As she strained to adjust the curls behind her ears, she ran her hand through her voluminous permed hair frequently while scanning her golden wristwatch fastened to her other hand. The clock struck six in the evening. Just as she was about to turn towards the waiting lobby, an autorickshaw driver called out loudly from a few meters away. "Madam, madam." She gazed at him in a strange look.

"Madam, are you Miss Natasha, daughter of Mr. Chunnilal," he intoned low after clearing his throat.

She replied, "Yes, I am Natasha, and I am the daughter of Mr. Chunnilal."

"Madam, I am Sagar Rajhans. Your father, Mr Chunnilal, has sent me to receive you."

"Tell me, why didn't my father come here? How do you know him?" She asked with great concern, and she looked anxious. Her brows met with each other.

"Madam, your father has been admitted to the ICU of Bombay City Hospital. His body is crippled with fractures. I discovered him on the roadside, quite distressed. I could recognize him as I knew him before. I took him to the City Hospital in my auto-rickshaw. He collapsed at the hospital gate. Throughout the ride, he uttered your name and asked me to pick you up from here. There was a traffic jam en route, and I reached here half an hour ago. I waved a placard, but you probably didn't notice."

"Oh, I am sorry, I never expected it this way," her brows puckered, her eyes turned moist, and her throat went dry. Her voice turned low. She looked down, dragged her suitcase, and bundled into the rear seat. Her face turned pale and blank. She asked, "When did it happen?"

"I saw him around two in the afternoon, about when the rain had gone a little milder."

"Hurry up, Sagar," she urged.

"Madam, I know this place inside and out. I know every road around the airport. I used to drive a taxi in this area. There is bumper-to-bumper traffic on the main road. I will take you through an alternative, less trafficked road," he boasted in an authoritative voice as the proud owner of the autorickshaw.

He took a sharp left turn from the intersection, and soon, they reached a wide lane between two rows of houses. They strode slowly across the middle of the road, flanked on both sides by covered drains. The water was ankle-deep there.

"Don't worry, madam. The water is not very deep. We can get through easily," he said in a convincing tone.

"Are you sure this road is okay to pass through?" she feared.

The clouds boomed with thunder, and the lightning flickered incessantly. Within minutes, the rain grew stronger. The noisy wind blew it sideways.

"Sagar, I can see that the water current is high, running from one side to the other, and the water is whirlpooling ahead," she alerted.

"On this side of the city, people throw garbage on the road. That is why the storm drains are clogged and the road is inundated. Do not worry, madam. This auto rickshaw is a new one and is adequately powered to pave us through even knee-deep water. I just bought it recently, and nothing will happen to us," he boasted.

"Sagar, please stop here. I sense something is wrong ahead." Before she could speak another word, the auto-rickshaw toppled over, and the current of mid-thigh-deep water carried it away. She gripped the sidebar, and the autorickshaw bobbed with the ripples of water, which rippled back intensely towards her when it hit the pavement on the other side. It got anchored. Through the dim darkness on the road, she could see him caught in the intense forward flow towards the whirlpool. He cried for help, but with the blink of her eyelid, he was dragged into the pit of the whirlpool. He vanished from her sight within seconds. She cried for help, but the crowd had stopped very far from her sight. The inhabitants of the nearby houses had no idea what had happened on the other side of their tall boundary walls in that fitful rain.

No one reached there for any help. Her body was drenched with the muddy water, and her feet went numb. She panicked and prayed for the rain to stop. Finally, the rain stopped, and the flow of water slowed down. She lifted herself from the ground, but the auto-rickshaw remained on its side.

Every word she let out seemed stammered, her throat went dry, and she felt choked while explaining the incident to the crowd that came to help her. Someone from the crowd uttered the presence of an open maintenance hole in the middle of the road. The workers had left it uncovered after cleaning and placed a small stone next to it as a warning sign to slow down when the road was dry.

*****

The darkness enveloped the city slowly. A genuine question from Palo, "When will Papa come?" made Laxmi anxious. The gas lamp in her house flickered. The wind outside turned violent and pierced to whistle through the glass windows before the rain lashed and swept the streets again. It tapped the windows heavily for a few minutes before it turned mild. The glass windows had been smeared with mist. The sky thundered. The sea roared with big tides. Sagar was expected at home by eight. Slowly, the hands of the clock approached ten, and the clock chimed ding-dong. The backstreet houses had closed their doors. Mr. Sinha's house was dark as usual, around ten at night.

The light emanating from a few windows in the street through the gauzy curtains was not sufficient to illuminate the road. There were no streetlights in that stretch; not even a single dog was out to bark at the strangers. She heard the splash of water close to her window when she watched a torchbearer hop to negotiate a small ditch before approaching her main door. His face was dark. She opened the door before a tap on it. His voice was not familiar like his shadow. His khaki was half wet on his back and folded up a few centimetres at the legs. The narrative he placed before her was devastating. It stunned her. She felt a sudden high-voltage lightning stroke hit her heart, and she stood paralyzed. She was unable to understand what happened to her. The sadness in the message ripped her apart in the middle of herself. Several more minutes passed by, and the silence continued without an utterance, not even a sound of a word. The news she heard after the evening weather forecast on the radio cracked heavily on her head. Her own self refused to believe that Sagar was no more.

Palo stared at the police without blinking her lids. She broke the silence of the room by screaming. She abandoned her cake on the platter and seized the half-swallowed bite in her throat to unleash a long scream. She cried, "Papa, you cannot leave us like this. You must come to us wherever you are." Palo paused to hear a deep sigh from her mother between her screaming, who cried in front of the portrait of Lord Shiva with apposed palms, tears streaming down her cheeks as she did so. "If you exist, If I have ever prayed to you with utmost honesty, then bring him back into our lives," she cried. Her unquestioning faith in Lord Shiva generated a wave around her to believe he was safe. She stopped weeping. The duty-bound policeman stood by the door in silence, behaving as a mute spectator since then. The family's reaction to the news shook him with the land itself. His legs trembled, and eyes grew moistened; he could do nothing to counsel her in this matter except pray for strength for the family to bear the loss.

*****

Palo pulled a sketchbook from a bag in her cupboard, which Sagar had bought recently. On the pages of it, she had laid down her artful patterns, everything she imagined about the school where she would join, the classroom where she would study, the children with whom she would befriend, the parks inside the premises, and her nicely stitched colourful school uniform.

The admissions in the school were over for other children, and the chance for her was tragically stolen by the incident in the family. She was disheartened. Laxmi left no stone unturned to find Sagar's body. From the municipality to the ministry, they had no clue where he was. Any amount of ex gratia would not bring Sagar back into her life. The municipality's negligence came to the fore when the reporters churned out the story. The authorities had no statement to deliver to ward off their skin in public. They preferred to remain mute in this case. The ones who approached her as responsible authorities finally left her alone with a few kind words of consolation. They had no other words left except saying a "big sorry" at the end. A week had passed following the incident. When his body was declared not traceable, Laxmi was hopeful that Sagar was alive in some corner of the world. He would come back someday.

Palo insisted on going with Laxmi to the market on a Saturday afternoon. Her tiny hands clutched her saree before she moved to catch an auto. She would not stay at home under the supervision of Mrs Sinha anymore in her absence, which she revealed as being a little stubborn. She pleaded to be with her during her weekend shopping. She tried to impress her generous thought of helping her mother softly in a sugary voice, listening to which Laxmi could not deny. So, finally, she declared her victory over her motherly heart with a big smile. The words she spoke to help her mother by carrying her little luggage with her tiny hands attracted a silent affirmation from her mother, and she received an instant nod.

On a Saturday afternoon, the phone of the casualty medical officer of Bombay City Hospital rang for a very brief period, less than the expected time for him to attend the call. He was a busy man. He was seeing the patients. His experience over the years about the callers is that either the caller was in a hurry or did not have the patience to talk. If there is enough reason to believe and not to hold the telephone exchange responsible for every call drop, it was one of them. It was undoubtedly not a technical snag, as the essential conversation had not yet started to be interrupted by a beep.

The survivors could not believe their eyes that they were alive after the bomb went off in the middle of the market. Many lives were lost on the road. Babies who withstood the impact were left to cry on their mothers' silent laps, bodies flung like crumpled torn paper sheets and Walls of shops painted with red blood. A few drops were still trickling down to settle before falling onto the ground. Animals -cows and dogs grounded motionless, and birds fled. The balmy breeze turned to a cloud of smoke in a few seconds and suffocatingly cascaded the lives on that street. The thickness of the air was further compounded by the burning of tyres, creating intense darkness in the atmosphere. A few cars and houses had received cobwebs of fracture lines on their glass windows. Laxmi was pinned down by a splinter with minor scratches on her body. Palo was standing next to her and shouting, "Mama", but her words were not clearly reaching her mother's ears. Her eardrums had failed to receive any decibel of sound after the impact, and her chest slowly became too heavy to breathe.

Ambulances, fire tenders, and police jeeps arrived at the ravaged site in no time, blaring sirens. As appropriately said by a wise man, "Life is a bubble; uncertainty lies in the time –few bursts early and few burst late, but it bursts." A few had died on the spot, a few were dying, and a few were alive but would be dead later if not hospitalized on time. The medical and paramedical team had already started triage. Both Palo and Laxmi were considered to be stable at first sight. Still, Laxmi was later evacuated to the hospital with a written note, "Urgent attention - ICU care for lung injury", on a band that circled her head. Palo accompanied her to the hospital.

*****

The unspoken patient emotions and palpable tensions among ward nurses always coexist. The nurse in the Trauma care ICU looked at Chunni angrily for a while and said, 'Huh, what happened to you now? Your daughter must be coming; we have informed her. Nothing is going to happen. Don't be so restless." His searching eyes paused on her. The nurse felt his heart rate quicken on the monitor, and his breathing became long and deep. She turned to him quickly. He drew deeper breaths in seconds. With every breath, he was muttering, 'Natasha.' It got even worse. She placed an oxygen mask on his nose. The life-giving air rushed to fill his lungs, providing a momentary respite.

"Natasha Beti, Chunni needs urgent heart surgery," Dr Pradeep intoned with great concern. His concern was how Natasha would react to this piece of information. She has no one in the family except her father to consult. Destiny had snatched her mother from her three years ago.

"Uncle, why does he need heart surgery?" she asked, panicking.

"Yes, Beti, open-heart surgery. He developed breathing difficulties; we suspected some embolism in his lungs. Performing an echocardiography on him, we saw a large blood clot sitting inside his heart and ready to migrate to his lungs at any time. There is an imminent threat to his life if it is not addressed in time. That is why he was shifted under my observation from the trauma care ICU."

"Uncle, what about the risks involved in this surgery?" she asked.

"I can only assure you that he is in safe hands. The threat to his life is definite as the clot is massive. If he is not operated on now, We may lose him at any time. I do not know why he is sulking and not willing to talk to me anymore. Why is he behaving with me as a stranger? After all, I am his childhood friend," he showed significant concern.

Natasha said, "Uncle, I know the reason. He has not yet erased that incident of the past. He still feels Momma could have lived a few more years with us, even in the last stage. Both momma and you hid the truth that she had cancer."

"It is not the truth. I am misunderstood. By the time your Momma revealed it to me, it was a terminal-stage metastatic breast cancer. We offered her whatever palliative treatment was possible for Divyani at that stage, but despite all this, we failed to save her. We are not God. Chunni huffed and thrashed me on that night when Divyani died and unleashed all kinds of rants that aroused in his mind in frustration, but I have forgiven him, and there is nothing within me now to say -I hate you," He said.

"No, uncle. It is not the matter, but for you to know there is something else I know. Before you meet Papa, I want five minutes of your time. Look into this letter." She picked up a letter, handed it to Dr. Pradeep, and said, "I discovered this letter in his room in the morning while I was cleaning."

"But, Beti..."

She cut his words off and said, "Uncle, if you permit me, I want to meet Papa in the ICU. I will try to convince him."

"But, Beti, don't engage with him for a long time. Don't keep him off the oxygen mask for too long. He is on high-flow oxygen."

Dr. Pradeep went to his cabin and opened the letter addressed to him. Divyani wrote it before her death.

The imprint of her writing pattern and pearl-like circular letters were unforgettable. While he was studying in medical college, she used to write to him regularly, at least one letter a week. He used to sneak out during the interval period between classes and mooch around the post office on the weekends when he did not receive a single reply for months. He was sure their friendship was so deep that she would not turn down his proposal, a commitment to a lifelong relationship. However, she withdrew her steps back and went on her knees to propose to Chunnilal, their common bosom friend of childhood. His every question remained unanswered. He blamed her for his single status and vowed not to marry another girl since then.

Dear Pradeep,

  By the time you receive this letter, I will have left this world. I am penning my last few words because I do not want to leave this world by keeping you in the dark any longer. I want no one to pine for me. Probably, it will help you bear a deceit. While stating this, I accept with great honesty that I deeply liked you because of your sincerity and dedication to serving humanity. I had a mild youth and fanciful ambitions about life, imagining love in everything. I was fond of your becoming fashionable, your dressing sense, and your kind-hearted words, quite uncareful about the little notice from the friends in school carrying deeper sympathetic words for me. As I could sense you as a very simple soul, I treasured all your growing sense of love for me in my heart.

  The words you wrote in your last letter shook me to the core. You accused Chunni of snatching me away from you. After learning the truth, I hope that you will agree that my choice and decision to marry Chunni were never wrong. It pained me when you fought with each other during my last stage of life. Chunni is a very composed man who has never been a harried husband, nor does he have any less of an outgoing persona.

  You blamed Chunni for my ailment, of which I was quite unaware of the severity. Little knowing about it as a big form of cancer, I underestimated the ulcer. I hid my ailment from him. It angered him when I revealed it to you first instead of him. He left no stone unturned in trying to save me, but it was too late when he finally found out. He is just as caring a husband as he was a friend.

You always asked me why I proposed to him for marriage and not you.

It all happened on the same day while you were on a summer vacation. Your kite soared out to the bank of the river. You tugged on your kite string in excitement. When you cut the string of my golden frilled Japani kite, you smiled in victory, celebrated, and danced joyfully. My heart sank slowly and slowly with the fall of my kite. My loss mattered to me. That kite was special. It was my birthday gift. No kite would have replaced it. Chunni had a knack of reading my soul before my eyes. I appeared to him as someone lost and helpless. He saw my heart breaking beneath me from a distance. Without hesitation, he jumped into the muddy backwater and drenched himself completely to rescue my kite from falling into the water. I could see a thorough gentleman on the other side to his flip side. I lost my heart to him. He remained no longer an ill-mannered idiot for me after that. The love words for him clogged my throat, but they came out incessantly. There was nothing around me looked more beautiful than him that day. I proposed to him smugly for the marriage.

My family had never disapproved of you; they all had been very close to yours. I had to take this step against my family. That was not an easy decision. I was labelled defiant. Until then, for everything, I looked upon my parents. There was never a mother like my mother and a father like any father in this world, but it proved me wrong. I didn't bend to anyone. They called my marriage improper. I lived with a new identity, Divyani. Many a time, I thought I would go to them when the right circumstance arose, but that day never came.

You always blamed him that he snatched me away from you. I hope you change your mind. You will always remain a good friend to me. Your words give me the strength to live longer, but I know I won't survive for too long. My last wish is to die in his arms, and I hope you will understand why I did not reply to you. Lastly, if you meet Ammi and Abbu, tell them I missed them every moment.

Best wishes

Love you always.

Zara.

*****

"Uncle, why didn't you talk to doctor uncle when he came for rounds?" Palo said in a dulcet voice. She was observant, and she deciphered something wrong in Chunnilal's expression.

Chunni replied, "Beta, I do not dislike him. I wish I could speak, but I am afraid. Doctors jab big injections."

Palo knew what the matter was. "Doctor Uncle was so affectionate despite you quarrelling with him. You seem to be a good human being. Such behaviour doesn't look good on you."

"Quarrel! Who said so? I am a good human and don't quarrel with anyone," replied Chunni.

Palo smiled and said, "You are a good human being. I am pleased with how you rescued Aunty's kite. Tell me more about it."

Chunni asked, "How did you know about it?"

She bit her lower lip to keep the truth from him.

"Are you going to tell me? How do you know?"

"A tweeting bird said." She smiled away and said, "Big people never quarrel."

Chunni said, "Okay, I will say sorry to him. Now, will you tell me how you knew I rescued my wife's kite?"

"It just evaporated from my mind. How, I don't know. I am a kid; don't give too much value to my word."

Chunni never expected a tiny tot to be so observant to upbraid him this way. To him, she seemed pretty mature beyond her age.

"I don't know anything about it, uncle."

"First, you look directly into my eyes and then say." He exclaimed, "Did Pradeep say about it?"

"Uncle, I swallowed my words. They won't come out so easily until you promise me not to fight with Doctor Uncle."

Before he could utter a word to ask Palo, he was interrupted by the nurse who came to his bedside with a spirometer. She asked him not to speak and to do breathing exercises with it.

An hour later, he felt a slight discomfort in breathing. Palo realized that Chunni uncle had removed the oxygen supply line during the spirometer exercises and had not reapplied it after finishing it. Immediately, she went to his bedside, pulled out the oxygen line, and helped him to set it onto his nose. When the nurse arrived, she assisted in propping him up on the bed. When Dr. Pradeep came for an evening round, Palo asked, "Uncle, how happy were you when you cut Aunty's kite string?"

"Did Chunni say anything?" Pradeep asked her softly.

"Uncle, Nothing. I am just asking out of curiosity. I promise. He didn't tell me anything about you?"

"I don't believe you."

"OK, you can ask him."

Dr Pradeep asked Chunni, "What have you told her about me?"

"That's what I was going to ask you, Pradeep."

"How did she come to know that I cut kite strings?" Asked Pradeep.

"You tell me, how did she know I rescued Divyani's kite."

"I didn't tell her. She will only be able to tell," Dr Pradeep said.

They turned towards Palo. She was getting the pleasure of their conversation. Natasha entered inside to meet Chunni. "Hello Uncle, how are you papa? What discussion is going on?"

Palo jumped into their argument. "Pradeep uncle, In the afternoon. You were busy in the operation theatre. I saw this machine on your table. I listened to my heart sounds. And I read the letter you had left on your table."

"Palo, these are bad manners. You should not read someone's letter like this." Pradeep said softly.

Chunni asked him, "Which letter is this? And What is she talking about?"

"Yes, papa, it is the same letter which Mamma had written to Pradeep uncle during the last few days of her life, which you had kept hidden in your library. I discovered it while cleaning your study," Natasha replied.

Emotion welled up in Chunni's heart. "I had kept that letter as the last voice of my wife as she could not speak and express anything through her mouth. This letter was her last expression, and how would I waste it like this? Forgive me, Pradeep, for this. I was upset because Divyani chose you to reveal her ailments first, not me. That letter demolished my aversion spell. I wanted to apologize to you, but that moment never came. Anyway, destiny made it happen this way. This little girl made me realise what I owed to you."

"By the way, uncle, half the credit goes to Natasha Didi. She planned to see you together again as good friends, and I just acted."

Chunni asked, "Beta, which class are you studying in?"

"Uncle, I didn't get admission to the school, but my mumma teaches me at home."

"What do you want to become when you grow up?"

"I decided to become a doctor, nothing else. A heart surgeon like Pradeep Uncle."

"Don't worry. I will try to get you the best school here in the city. You will become a doctor one day."

Dr Pradeep was amazed to listen to her replies and her extraordinary confidence. Who hadn't even stepped into the school, claiming at the top of her voice to become a heart surgeon!

He reached Laxmi's bed. After auscultating her chest and viewing the X-ray of her chest, he advised her to start walking and do spirometry exercises. Her oxygen saturation level had improved, and she required a very low oxygen flow to support her lungs.

*****

CHAPTER 5

Believing in Self

Once, It was a fragmented piece of land dropped directly from nature's canvas with more shrubs and trees. The breeziness was awesome. The freshness of blooming flowers was a treat to every amused eye. The earth herself had embodied the moistness of a lush green blanket without any human interference. To someone who had seen the meadow before, it was a constituent of something set in dreams.

Towers rose quickly, and a maze of roads crossed across her heart. Slick vendors had their shops perched alongside. A few unapologetically dumped their garbage. The streets were drowned out in the rains. The hawkers who once sold their foods at traffic signals slowly provided space for dining on a large table below the fantasy lights where they learned every trick of their trade and could sell their rubbishy items under the garb of ambience and polite conversation. The cultured crowd was not nervous about spending money bigger than the size of the hole in their pocket in the casinos. A few real estate transactions were found on paper, while most went unnoticed off paper. There was not even a trace of guilt among those who decided not to put the deal on official records. All the sympathetic glances shifted to the poor and the orphans on the streets. The social guards who assured the public a good service when they collared pickpockets released them after dragging them to some drafty places in the want of a quick bonus. There was always a brief tug-of-war between politicians and police to decide their superiority in public mightiness. Those who were sugar-coated were the lawyers, who prospered with an armful of files on their tables. While a crowd enjoyed the gardens, a few struggled to get tickets for the movies of their favourite movie stars in the cinema halls. Their madness was so real that with every new release, it didn't stop until pushing someone to bleed. The moonlight fainted under a smoke cloud every evening. The atmosphere had turned so sour.

The City High School was constructed half a century ago to provide education to all sections of society, from the rich to the socially downtrodden. Most students it produced were bright and prosperous. The roll of time over the decades produced several students who successfully ruled the globe in all fields. The alumni further contributed to reshaping its infrastructure, making it an institute of excellence in the city. An echelon of regulators decided the admission process.

With time, the lush green meadows around the school shrunk. The only greenery left behind sprawled inside the boundary of the school. This corner of the city turned into a special economic zone, flanked by warehouses, lumberyards, and sawmills. The vehicles transporting goods in its immediate vicinity had made big patches on the road, almost making the traffic standstill for hours by the afternoon.

Chunni had spent forty-five years in this city. Those were the best days when he saw the surroundings clean and green. He was well acquainted with the school and the function of its regulatory body. The construction of inhabitation around it further influenced the admission process. The rich found it convenient for the admission of their kids by tweaking the admission rules. The school set criteria for admission for a privileged group who lived within a closeness of three kilometres.

Chunni was one of those people who always went forward to help others. Such a quality of ministration was ingrained in his nature. He perceived Palo's misfortune seriously and didn't want to waste his political clout elsewhere without helping her. The promise he made once to himself that he would take care of her studies was to be kept by any means. No matter how difficult it would be, he would leave no stone unturned. So he acted promptly as soon as he recovered. Chunni entered the school premises to meet the principal for a mid-term admission. The deadline had passed three months ago. He was accompanied by Laxmi and Palo when he entered.

Getting an appointment with the principal of such a reputed school was not easy for him. 'Miss Joseph, a lady with grey hair in her mid-fifties, the school's principal, loved the school so much that she settled down within the premises to safeguard its flora and fauna spread over hundreds of acres, far from public nuisance. She had denied unfettered access to strangers inside the school premises. However, she had ample time for the social workers who arranged charity for the school or the politicians who could release the funds on time. How could Chunni be denied access in such a case when he was a prominent party worker from the state's ruling party?

He walked through the turnstile and, after taking a short flight of steps, entered the corridors. Everyone he met there seemed to be in a hurry. He stopped at a pebbled glass door at the end of the corridor and merged into a silent corner before taking a turn when he spotted a shingle of the Principal's office on the wall just above the door. He then confirmed from the peon standing at the door about Miss Joseph inside her office. Palo and Laxmi also followed him up to her office. Palo saw the students coming out of the rooms, the walls outside of which were daubed with graffiti. The students were in red monogrammed jackets. She checked out each room as she came across it while walking down the corridor with one side open to a playground. The stretch was very noisy during the tiffin break. After a few yards, she stopped at the corner room, where they were asked to sit in a furnished waiting room. Palo did not doubt that the door on the other side would soon open with the door to her fortune. She was going to be interviewed, as Chunni had told her. 'The time has come now,' Palo thought. There was no sign of any anxiety on her face. Her eyes followed the fish as they playfully swam inside a small aquarium in front of them.

Laxmi said, 'I am worried. Such schools are sophisticated, and I have heard they are starving for money. Miss Joseph may not accept her.'

'Fret not, I am hopeful. Palo will be accepted. The school will get a real gem,' Chunni said.

He pushed open the door and said, 'Good morning, Miss Joseph, may I come in.'

Miss Joseph stopped writing with her pen and stared at the stranger intently. He had a charming expression on his face. 'Come in.'

'Miss Joseph, I wrote a letter to you a few days ago, but probably you have not received it. I am Chunnilal.'

'I received it but didn't find it meaningful to us.'

'Thank you for keeping my request to meet you personally.'

'Netaji spoke about you. I have no time to engage in a lengthy conversation with you. Be brief. Please tell me what your problem is, Mr. Chunni. Why are you standing there? Be seated.' She didn't like him towering over her. Miss Joseph gestured for him to sit on the chair across her table.

'Thank you, ma'am. I have come to you with great hope, and..' he said before he could finish the sentence. She cut him off to end the conversation.

She said, 'If your request is about admission, then I am sorry, Mr. Chunni, we have no mid-term admission policy. None of our students leave the school.' She rejected his request. Her eyes shifted from his face to the papers placed on her table. 'You may come next year,' she murmured. 'I am sorry.'

'Madam, the girl is poor. She cannot afford expensive schools. Who would have thought of this bad luck? She lost her father three months ago. Her mother is also recovering from trauma. Show some kindness.'

Miss Joseph glanced at her wristwatch. Such problems often occur with the pupils. These are not new to me. You are simply wasting my time. Admission is not in any way possible. She gave him an annoyed look. She picked up a file and opened it to skim through it quickly. She thought this would make him leave.

After a pause, he spoke, 'It is my sincere request, madam, that you meet with the girl once. You will be fortunate to have her enrolled.'

'Sorry, please come next year,' she lifted her head and looked at his face. 'There is a board that decides. I don't decide. I can't help you,' she said.

'Please, interview her once, madam. She is quite intelligent. You will regret not accepting her in the middle of the term. You can accommodate her through the management quota. The board will listen to you if the recommendation goes from your position.'

'Sorry, Mr. Chunni. I am under a lot of pressure. I can't touch the management seats. There are only two seats left,' she said.

'You will regret it later if you don't interview her. She lost her father recently, and her mother also had to undergo a lengthy hospitalization. It would be a sin if the child is denied a chance to prove herself. If you allow me to, I'll call her inside. She is waiting outside your office with her mother.'

She looked at him and said, 'No need to plead for her, Mr. Chunni. I reiterate that we do not make exceptions in such cases. A committee decides the admission process, and I am sorry, but we cannot accommodate her in the middle of the session. The admissions for this academic year have already closed, and now nothing can be done,' she showed a bit of rudeness in the latter part of her statement.

'Madam, this girl lost her father in an accident. Have you heard about the maintenance hole incident? On a rainy day, one man was trapped inside a maintenance hole. The news was regularly featured in the newspapers for quite a few days.' She said. "Yes, I heard about it. The incident came in the newspaper, "The Sagar Rajhans case," But in the end, the municipality accepted its callousness, and the government agreed to compensate for the loss, didn't it?"

Emotions exuberated. He said, "Certainly not! Like every time, they attributed the weather for its unpredictable entry into the town before the preparedness. This syllogism is the biggest lie of this monsoon. But who will compensate for the time his child has lost? What about the education of his child? She could not take admission owing to her father's death, which happened exactly a day before her admission. The family is experiencing a tattered time without its breadwinner. Try to understand her genuine problems," he said in a deep and heavy voice, showing genuine concern.

She had not realized the matter could be so serious. The entire system has ignored the family. If she does not listen to her inner voice, then God will punish her for this sin," she feared.

Despite a first declination, he successfully persuaded her. It overturned her decision of disallowance to a positive action with conscious guilt. She turned her head to the air to listen to her inner voice. "I will interview her as an exceptional case. Please call them inside."

The peon let them in after getting a nod from the principal. Palo entered the office with Laxmi, hand in hand. They walked straight to her table. The plimsoll she wore squelched against the floor. She was wearing a red frock. Miss Joseph stared at her momentarily from top to toe as she stood by her side.

"Good morning, Madam." Something pleasant to her ears, which put her in a delightful mood.

Miss Joseph responded in a moderate voice, "Good morning."

"Come, sit, both of you," she gestured for them to sit.

Palo saw many portraits of children wearing red monogrammed school uniforms hung on the wall, and another wall bore a large portrait of Miss Joseph clad in a long black academic gown and hood receiving an award from an older man.

"So, my dear," before she could utter her name, Pallavi introduced herself, 'Madam, I am Pallavi Rajhans. She is my mother, Laxmi Rajhans.'

"So, my dear, you want to study in this school, right?"

"Yes, madam, I want to study in your school," Pallavi said, nodding. Her tiny plait of hair with a ribbon at the end shook on her back when she nodded.

"Tell me, why should we take you? Give one best reason."

Palo said, "Because I am interested in studying. What could be a better reason than this? If you ask me for two reasons, I have just completed the books for class three, and I know the tables up to 25. If three reasons..."

"Stop here, stop here! I had only asked for the one best reason."

A smug smile appeared on Palo's face. Laxmi's tempestuous look faded with a gentle smile when she heard the answers.

"Can you tell me who they are?" Miss Joseph pointed at the portraits of national heroes hanging on the wall.

"Madam, the old man with a stick in hand is Bapu, our father of the nation. His name is Mohan Das Karam Chand Gandhi. He got us freedom from the clutches of Englishmen. People call him

'Sabarmati ke santh.' Mama was saying he never used violence against the Britishers."

"Madam, next to him is Pandit Jawahar Lal Nehru, our Cha Cha Nehru. He is the first prime minister of our country. He also fought for our Independence."

"Tell me the time on the clock."

"It is fifteen minutes to ten o'clock."

"Okay, one last question," said Miss Joseph.

"Yes, ma'am. I am ready. You can ask me," Palo said.

"Tell me the time on the clock where the minute hand joins with the hour hand, and the number of minutes required to complete the hour is the same as the hour it is going to strike," asked Miss Joseph.

Palo paused, her gaze steady on Miss Joseph, The silence in the room for her had the very rhythm of time itself. She thought for a few seconds and replied, "Madam, it is ten minutes to ten where the minute hand meets the hour hand."

Ms. Joseph's face lit up with delight, a smile spread across her face. She exclaimed, " Ah, Right answer." Her tone had a warmth of welcoming embrace, " I am overjoyed to meet this girl, Palo's mummy." She said so, turning to Laxmi.

Laxmi asked, "Madam, so, Are you accepting her-- "

Before she completes the sentence, Ms Joseph said, " Your child is a true gem. We shall place her directly in class Two. We have a vacancy for pupils of straitened circumstances. We will especially consider that seat for her. I am sure she would qualify for academic scholarships in Class Three."

Laxmi's hands came together in a gesture of profound gratitude, her face aglow with joy. Tears of happiness welled up in her eyes. She breathed, her voice trembling with emotion. "Madam, I have no words to express my happiness. Her admission to this school is the greatest virtue of your kindness. May God give you all the happiness and prosperity."

Chunni said, "Thank you, Miss Joseph."

Miss Joseph quickly added, "Mr. Chunni, thank you for introducing me to this extraordinary student. I will get all her paperwork done today. I want her to join us tomorrow if you are all prepared."

Palo said, "Thank you, madam. I will always be grateful to you for this. I will prove myself sincere and disciplined." The words came out spontaneously from her mouth as if spoken by a twenty-year-old adult with the conviction of a seasoned scholar.

Squelch...squelch...squelch... produced under her feet as she walked across the floor. Laxmi said outside the Principal's office, "Thank you, Chunni Bhai. I had not expected the school to accept my daughter." He said, "I have done nothing. Palo deserved such a school. She can study up to her matric, and the results are good here. The teachers are quite concerned about their students. In today's world, a dumb priest never got a parish."

*****

"Mama, I miss Papa today. Had he been with us at this moment, how happy he would have been. Last night, he came to my dream. He congratulated me, cuddled me, lifted me by my arms, and kissed me on my brow. I found myself standing amidst the sea of glittering stars, shining brightly around me, at a stone's throw away. Papa wished me good luck, and soon after, he began to dissolve, dispersing like tiny particles into the galaxy. I tried to call him, but the words caught in my throat as if a bumble bee had lodged itself there. I tried to wave at him but could not. I felt paralyzed. I tried to catch him but could not. I felt trussed up by a strange force."

Her emotion-filled words for Papa brought moisture to Laxmi's eyes. Palo realized the pain in Laxmi's heart. She prayed that no one should ever suffer from the harsh, cruel blow of destiny like this. She promptly lied, "But, Mama, do you know he looked so thrilled and told me he would return to us soon, just as he was melting ." She articulated to keep her cheerful disposition intact. Deep down, she knew her father no longer inhabits the earth. He is a heavenly abode. Laxmi seemed happy to appreciate the nimbleness in her daughter's mind, who lied instantly to soothe her mother's sobbing nerves.

Laxmi braided Palo's hair tightly and added a ribbon flower at the end. Palo stood beside her, wearing her new white top and red skirt school uniform. She piggy-backed her new school bag after putting on the monogrammed red jacket. She carried her books, a water bottle, a lunch box, and an umbrella to school. She hugged Laxmi tightly at her waist. Laxmi dropped her off at the school by taking public transportation.

They arrived at the entrance of the school early. She was overly excited. She read the school's name and was exhilarated to enter the girls' school. She would make new friends, play with them, dance with them, sing with them, etcetera, etcetera. She pranced her way to the classroom on the first floor.

The hall was big, and she was standing there alone. "Wow," her breath escaped and echoed. Tables and benches were dusted and lined up across the length and breadth of the classroom. The aisle was wide. She stepped forward, touching all the tables as she crossed them. She reached the last row and turned back slowly to eye them again from the front row. She knew those were not just a few pieces of logs motionlessly mended to be kept there. They might have seen many stories, the glory of the past, the nobility of teachers, and the goodness of students. They might have touched many scholars. She felt with her hand a kind of mute benevolence. Despite being struck hard many times with the palms to any rousing cheerfulness in the classroom, these non-livings never ceased to fawn on. The holiness of the place seemed to her as a temple to a learner. Something unbelievable on her part when she thought about the justness of this temple of learning - providing moral values rather than existing to enlighten for possession of any substance or any satisfying benefits in the future. The niceness in her decency was obvious; with a smile on her face, her eyes carried the innocence of a child mixed with a soft feeling about the atmosphere. She cared for them. Introducing herself to the non-livings was undoubtedly not less than any goodies she could offer them. "I am Pallavi Rajhans. I want to become a doctor. I salute you for producing great scholars and wish you will continue to endow your support to me as well."

She slid her bag and kept it on the table. She treaded to the window. The light rays from the morning sun warmed her bare hands when she looked at her palms. She clenched her fist and then closed her eyes. All those things sensible to her danced in her mind. She discovered them in her heart. If she needed anything inside those fists, it had to be her promise to herself, which she was bound to keep. A promise to tell her mother someday, "Look, what have I found? The world, mama." Her thought paused when she heard the bell ring. She looked away through the windows, and the children arrived at the school gate. The bell at the main gate rang to tell them to hurry up. She shrugged; the clock on the tower seemed a little slow. Someone might not have noticed it, or she might have turned up a little earlier than others. The feeling of warm sunlight was something different on her first day. She unclenched her fist.

A few minutes later, the girls entered one after another. She stood in the front row, occupying a desk with her bag. She kept standing. She had a beautiful smile with her tiny teeth and an amazing seraphic look. All eyes in the classroom were set on her. They studied her face. She looked different. The ribbon at the end of her plait attracted many to giggle. A few watched her boots, not the costlier ones like they wore. A few who couldn't hold back their grin whispered, covering their mouth and chin with their hands, "She should go to a parlour." Unimpressed with the style, even one struck at the plait from behind and said, "Latest fashion, you village girl?"

When Diya swaggered into the classroom, there was a long silence. Everyone in the classroom seemed very scared of her. Diya was the class monitor and often muscled in on the teachers' interaction. A few things about Diya: They all knew Diya would freeze one out of her gang, the D-gang, if she disliked someone, even if they were aware that any disliking about her would bring them the punishment of those harsh categories. Nobody would dare take her on directly. A few were also amused by the things that would happen with the new girl. The class teacher was supposed to arrive in the classroom fifteen minutes later. A few laughed, sounding "Hi. Hi.. and a few Hee. Hee. Amidst the silence, they were staring at each other. It was up to Diya to decide where Palo will sit.

Palo extended her hand, "Hi, I am Pallavi Rajhans, and today is my first day in school." Palo retracted when not met by one of Diya. A few girls did not like this gesture of Diya, while a few stuck their tongues out as a mark of their innate unhappiness.

Pallavi then offered her a friendly hug, and Diya became angrier. Her face turned red. " You need to dress warmly. How dare you to touch me with those dirty clothes." Diya pushed Pallavi's bag down from the desk. Pallavi grabbed it with a jerk. The water bottle beside it lurched and rolled down. It broke at the lid, and a few drops spilled onto the floor.

Embracing the fury, Diya kept both hands at the hips; she sniggered, "Maybe this is just a little loss. Don't dare next time. I am Diya Malhotra, and I am the class monitor. I will decide where you will sit."

Palo lifted the bottle and settled on the desk. "Hey, you. Don't act smart," Diya shouted and looked into her eyes.

Pallavi came face to face and said," I don't want to know who you are and why you are behaving this way with me. I want you to behave good with me ."

Diya slid her hands into her pockets. Turning to face the other girls, she spoke with a hint of sarcasm," Saying us to behave suitably, girls. This poor girl doesn't know that she has on her no class ." The classroom was instantly abuzz with laughter. The girls exchanged amused glances. A few beat the desk. Diya's words created a sense of acceptance in the background.

Palo protested, " We are all friends. We all are here to study. Come on, Diya and don't stir things up unnecessarily. You have a nice name."

" Don't utter my name in your ruddy lips, poor girl. You don't know who you are messing up with. I am Diya Malhotra. I am the daughter of famous star Mr. Sameer Malhotra. Now I am as your class monitor ordering you to go and find a place in the last bench."

" I know you are trying to study me. You all are trying to figure out who I am and where I come from. Which school was I studying at before? Isn't it?"

" What the hell is wrong with you dirt- poor girl? Why don't you go to the last bench?" Diya was becoming ridiculously impatient for her inability to create fear within the newcomer.

" Diya, be an expansive girl. I have come first to the classroom, so let me sit here ." Pallavi sat down on the bench.

" In the front row. With me? No way."

" Stand up, Move from here. I can't take your chatter like this for much longer. I will drag you to the Principal's office and punish you for this disobedience."

" Why can't I sit here, Diya ?"

" Don't you have a brain to understand that you are not like another us? You smell poor."

Ignoring the prickly words as the inane remarks of a rich star kid, Palo said, " I am very much aware that you will first make me feel that I have made a mistake coming here, you will make me angry, and when I will become then you will go and report to the class teacher about me. Customarily, I suppose, you all are curious to know about me. How did I join in the middle of the academic year? ..etcetera. I have a grey matter, and I can see a few faces are still studying me. How did I get into this class? I'm being ordinary." She spoke like a twenty-year-old girl.

Diya's head spun at the narration. She yelled at Pallavi, " For you to understand that this front row is only reserved for the girls who have scored more than eighty per cent in the class. I have scored eighty-five per cent, which is why I have been made monitor of the class. It is me who will decide where you will sit. Get your bag out, and you go to the backbench. My deskmate Taruna is absent today, but I will keep this desk vacant for her. I will not allow you to sit here beside me."

The class teacher entered in the meantime. Every student rose from their seat for a Good morning wish. Her eyes fell on Pallavi, who stood quietly after everyone had taken their seat. Diya had sat almost crossing the midline, leaving no place for Pallavi to sit.

The school teacher asked, " What happened to you, my dear? Why are you standing here like this? Why don't you sit down there? Diya, move up a little and let her sit in Taruna's place." Palo said with a smile," Thank you, ma'am."

Diya leapt up from her seat and screamed, "Madam, I don't concur with what you just said. Allowing her to sit beside me would be a wrong practice. She does not deserve the first row as she has come in the mid-term, and we do not know whether she will be able to get good marks. Who knows, she may fail. Let her sit in another row, but not in the front row on Taruna's seat. Let her take the challenge to compete with me to prove ."

The class teacher cut her off. "Diya, don't say anything to her, which you have to atone for later."

Pallavi stood and said, 'Madam, I have no problem with where I will sit. As I entered the classroom earlier than others, I preferred to sit in the front row. I was not aware of this rule in the classroom. My humble request to the monitor is that reshuffling every day is the best way to keep the front row occupied and the back rows vacant, giving the backbencher a chance to benefit from the front row. There should be no reservation policy in a classroom. Madam, this reminded me of how Gandhiji was thrown out of the first-class compartment and forced to board the third-class compartment. But in the end, he threw the British rulers out of this country." Her voice was composed and smooth. She sounded like a twenty-year-old girl teaching the classroom about -Inequality. The teacher stood appalled at the logic she just heard from Pallavi. She had never expected this from a girl of class two. Diya, however, was seen happy throughout the day, keeping the desk vacant. She rejoiced over her victory.

As time passed, with every difficult question asked in the classroom, Diya grew red-faced as the teachers' eyes paused at Pallavi. They always focused on the last row with great expectation that at least Pallavi could tell the answers. Sometimes, Palo was quick, and it was unbearable for Diya to see Palo holding her head high after answering the question she already knew. During leisure, girls heard the thunder of the door slamming at Palo. One can imagine how unhappy Diya was to see her in class. She threw scrap paper balls at her desk to invite her to take offence, but Palo didn't engage with her in verbal dualism; instead, she spent time learning literature and participating in all cultural activities.

In the classroom, from the backbench, she could stare past the blackboard over the shoulder of the teacher so well that she needed no front-row sitting. She scored almost a hundred per cent in all subjects. The class remembered how she explained every answer by standing and gripping the edge of her desk. The answers she explained were not only straight but also carried her voice, which displayed her qualities of modesty and humility.

*****

 Many things have changed since Pallavi joined. However, What had not changed was her smile, which stayed on her face; her hairstyle, with the ribbon hanging at the end of the plait; Her voice, as she sounded reasonable in every new happening in the class and her seat; the same last bench where she sat. And her glorious academic record. She had imagined that her survival depended only on hard work, so she dealt with her life differently. At her age, she was perceptive of the fact that she didn't have the same luck as others to spend emeralds on pleasures to say - "what a lovely meal it was, friends", in the canteen. Also, she didn't have the annoyance of losing it all over in embitterment over any careless generosity of unpaid bills. She looked happy. She looked at life this way. She had to help her mother with household chores. It was a meandering path she was treading in life, like the path she and her mother used to take to reach the school.

 By then, Pallavi had won prizes in many literary competitions. She was like one of the pupils, always hanging around the library and the school cultural club during her spare time. Even at times, when everyone else in her class had gone home or to the diner at the rear end after the last bell, she would head straight to the study for a while to turn another page of another book before Laxmi came to pick her up after two in the afternoons. She could wrestle with a balance between her poverty and her studies. She could not think of wasting a single penny and a single minute. If the traffic went smoothly, by her calculation, her mother reach the school by 2 PM to pick her up.

 Pallavi was pushing boundaries. Diya couldn't stop worrying about Pallavi's growing popularity among the school girls and teachers. At the same time, Pallavi became the apple of every teacher's eye. Diya missed no chance to criticize her for sometimes falling asleep at the desk during a break. Sometimes, she even swayed towards her to shove her down from the stairs. Pallavi never defended herself and tried to set these matters aside. She never took Diya seriously. Whenever their eyes met, Diya would toss her head and turn her gaze to the other side. Diya had lost the battle in academics. To her misfortune, Pallavi was much ahead of her. She destroyed Diya's ego by leaving her behind by a considerable margin. It had pushed Diya into a highly uncomfortable position in the classroom. The harsh words Diya had ever kept for a squabble lay there in a deadly silence inside her throat. Diya couldn't find a reason to engage with Pallavi in a big fight. The biggest setback for her was that none of her ideas mattered important to her friends anymore.

Pallavi knew well that when exam days were near, she had to get up early to avoid the unnecessary exam pressure of last-minute preparation. Pallavi loved doing her best whenever she was assigned a task. It gave her the opportunity to interact with students from other classes. Teachers, by then, knew enough about her academic and social progress. Pallavi had made considerable progress in academics and became a known face as an intelligent girl in the senior school circle. The senior girls guided her whenever she sought their guidance. Her name for the role of Lord Ram was also recommended by a senior girl to the drama teacher.

The students of Class Four gathered in the grand auditorium. The air buzzed with hopes and despair about the students' performance during the audition. The Class Teacher awaited for the Drama Teacher to submit her feedback.

"Teacher, I heard both Pallavi and Diya perform the role of Lord Ram. Pallavi delivered the dialogues with poise and clarity like a mature artist. She is the perfect choice for the role of Lord Ram. Diya can play another role this year," the drama teacher said.

And so, Pallavi was selected to don the role of Lord Ram in the play 'Ramleela,' a dramatic fixture played every year by the junior class girls during the festivities of Dushera. Diya, however, had her heart set on playing the role of Lord Ram. She had even gone so far as to purchase a brand-new crown and order special ornate clothing for the part. The disappointment on her face was palpable as she learned that Pallavi had been chosen instead.

Diya's fury bubbled to the surface. Seething with rage and voice in extreme resentment, she asked, "Why, ma'am? I have been playing Lord Ram for the last two years. I want to play his part again,". Yet the teacher stood firm. "Pallavi's audition was simply superior, my dear . You shall play the role of Ravana this year."

Diya's loyal D-gang girls stormed to the teacher's office, determined to protest the decision, but one stern glare from the teacher sent them scurrying back, their faces flushed with embarrassment.

As the day of the final rehearsal arrived after a week-long practice, The activity hall was abuzz with students' actions and emotional reactions. Pallavi, clutching her bag, entered the space alongside her friend. The other students who had attended the dance class made their way towards the exit, creating a thin crowd at the doorway.

Suddenly, Diya emerged from the group. Her face was etched with fury. She stormed up to Pallavi. Without hesitation, Diya shoved Pallavi forcefully against the wooden panelling of the wall, punching her repeatedly in a fit of rage. "This is the prize for you in advance. You will remember the punches while aiming the arrow at me in tomorrow's final play." Before the teacher arrived, Diya left Pallavi with a stern warning, cautioning her against participating in the play in the future to avoid any unpleasant consequences.

"Hey, Diya, save this fury for tomorrow. I'm glad you are getting into your character nicely," Pallavi mocked, placing her hands on her stomach.

Pallavi's friend helplessly watched this. She could do nothing to rescue her from the swirling D-gang engulfing Pallavi from all sides. She lifted the bag and slung it on Pallavi's shoulder. She warned Pallavi not to provoke Diya until the play was over.

As they entered the classroom, Pallavi stood at the front, her gaze sweeping across the girls in the D-gang row. With a steely note in her voice, she declared, "Girls, there are witnesses who want me to name those who attacked me in the activity hall. I am not considering this matter lightly. I feel I must inform your parents when they come tomorrow to watch the play." A silence fell over the classroom, thick with tension. "Today, you have disappointed your parents. How will they react when they learn that you girls have been indulging in violence? They will curse themselves for this kind of upbringing," she continued, her voice unwavering. One girl stood up, her shoulders slumped, and apologetically said, "Sorry." However, a few girls remained seated, defiant.

Pallavi continued, her eyes narrowing, "Don't make your parents ashamed of your cowardly act. I always considered you all as my friends. I know some of you have been following me and reporting to your master where I was going and who I was meeting. But were all these exercises to keep me out of this play? Do you girls have no brains? Today, you have committed a crime." The girls in Diya's faction realized the gravity of their mistake.

The tense atmosphere in the classroom thickened as a few more girls hesitantly rose to their feet, fidgeting nervously to apologize after realizing that Palo's balanced mind called them friends and that she could have complained about them to the drama teacher, but she didn't.

Diya's face contorted with disdain as she sneered, "Oh, Gandhi's little child, next time we punch you, show your other cheek. Please don't lecture us. Go and take your seat. Neither are you a Mahatma here to champion your thoughts upon my friends nor am I any Martin Luther to love my enemies."

Pallavi knew Diya's unapproachable nature all too well. She calmly replied, "Your fury can no longer hide your wistful mind, Diya. This is not a theatre. This is a classroom. Enough of this nonsense. I could have taken your name, but I didn't when the teacher asked about my bruises." Pallavi's words struck a chord, and Diya's expression transformed from rage to fear.

Pallavi's words carried a weight. Turning to Diya, She continued, "Try to change yourself, Diya. You are the centre of all this." She implored, her gaze steady and unwavering. " I know you are jealous of me." Pallavi's tone was not one of condemnation but of understanding, as if she could see the depth of Diya's inner turmoil. " Bapu is my inspiration. You can't mock him like this." Turning to the D-gang girls, Pallavi's voice took on a softer, almost pleading tone. " Friends from the D-gang, your leader is deceiving you, but don't think that she will ever protect you if you get expelled from this school." Pallavi could see the D-gang girls, once trembling in fear, now seemed to feel the weight of her words.

"I am not any lecturer to lecture you here. Bapu's life is an example for us to know about our real potential. We must trust our potential within. Everyone in this hall is somehow talented. Someone is blessed to be a good dancer, and the other is a good singer. Find your talents and make the best use of them. If I am selected for a play, then why has heaven fallen? I request you again, don't waste your talents and time after a bad leader."

As Pallavi stood her ground with her words, the D-gang girls turned to Pallavi, burying all the animosity. They all, in unison, uttered, "Sorry, Pallavi." Their voice carried a tinge of contrition.

Diya, however, remained defiant. Her face was etched with a mix of fear and resentment. Her face turned crimson; she trembled and looked affronted. Pallavi knew the big-headed girl surely would try to slap her down at any moment when she noticed Diya glaring at her grimly. Sure enough, In no time, Diya cut loose on her. In a swift motion, she pulled out the hairpin from her own hair and charged towards Pallavi, intent on causing harm. But Pallavi, anticipating Diya's attack, quickly grabbed her arm and, with a steady grip, pushed Diya's hand away, preventing the hairpin from reaching her neck. Pallavi's other hand ran through Diya's thick, loose hair and swivelled her to coil them around her neck. It foiled all her attempts to escape from her tight clutch. Diya was not ready for this. It was something she had never expected from Pallavi. Eventually, Diya's strength waned, and she reluctantly yielded. Her expression morphed from one of rage to a mask of defeat. She dropped the hairpin. The D-gang girls once united in their opposition, now stood silently, their faces reflecting a growing sense of unease and discomfort at witnessing their leader's humiliation.

The class teacher made an announcement for an out-of-school trip as part of an academic activity. The official circular, bearing the principal's seal of approval, was prominently displayed on the notice board, sparking anticipation among students. These trips were more than mere excursions – they were opportunities for the young mind to share their thoughts and it clearly stated that the students would choose their places. These are occasional documents where students are asked to speak their minds before teachers push their suggestions. Students are heard, whether it be a community cleanliness drive or any other adventure trip. This time, the suggestions were for an academic trip. This is one way the teachers find it interesting, and they go out of their way to go with them on the trip. Everyone in the classroom seemed happy when the teacher announced the date. She asked students to suggest places they would like to visit.

Diya sat quietly, her gaze fixed on the announcement. She was brimming with happiness as, through the bustling chatter around her, nothing had been spouted off from the back bench. She stood and looked around. Her gaze caught the sight of Pallavi. Then she turned her face back to the teacher and suggested, "What about exploring the local food courts and the vegetable market nearby? We can have a wide choice of foods like piping dosas and mouth-watering pizzas. I don't think the last benchers will support my idea." Diya was not prepared to accept something that could crash her castle of tasty foods down in mid-air before it formed. Pallavi certainly would protest.

Pallavi rose and said, "The backbenchers suggest visiting the nearest planetarium, ma'am." She whisked away the moment to discuss the matter further before getting the acceptance of her classmates. The mood of the class seemed to ebb and flow with Pallavi's every word. Be it for any occasion as if her influence held a magnetic pull over her peers. Diya had no control over that. A few girls also came up with their suggestions of visiting a handloom and public library.

The majority of hands raised in Pallavi's favour. Diya's heart dropped with the opposition. Undeterred, Diya pensively tried to put forth her point to the class. She poured her heart into advocating for a food market tour, painting a vivid picture of tantalizing aromas and the opportunity to learn healthy eating habits, nutritional values of food and whatnot. Pallavi, in turn, explained how the planetarium could provide a breathtaking view of the movement of planets, the origin of the earth, the formation of landscapes and the wonders of the universe beyond. Pallavi could sense the swelling tide of Diya's discontent behind her dropping face as she was finishing to talk. She quickly added her last sentence by saying, "Ma'am, besides all these benefits, It would be intriguing to know about the astronauts, the spacecraft, and the universe beyond this world if we visit the Planetarium." Pallavi's supporters slapped the desk in victory. With this shifting dynamics in the classroom, Diya's eyes raged.

In a way, it was all possible for Pallavi to convince the class because of her excellent conduct and broader view of any subject.

It also impressed the teachers. Diya doubted herself as if some other person lived within her to whom her friends no longer paid respect and attention. Taruna, her desk mate, standing in support of Pallavi, was the biggest blow to her belief. Taruna said, "Madam, we can learn about food by sitting inside our kitchen or visiting a restaurant on the weekend. Even local vendors who carry vegetables and visit our doorsteps can tell us more than we want. If we were to visit only one place, then there is nothing like the planetarium. We all support Pallavi's point of view in this case." Diya sizzled with anger. She thought of giving a massive nudge to her stomach in detest. Her lips began to shiver. If anything that ignited her mind to get infuriated, it was Taruna, who could never be at loggerheads with her. They shared the same desk. Diya muttered to Taruna, "You have broken my rules. I will break your legs. No other girls ever dared to disrespect me by taking Pallavi's name. It was your first mistake and is going to be your last. This ruse is not pardonable. I will see how long that Pallavi takes care of your interests. What made you think differently? I know Taruna. I am not a fool to understand you."

It startled her when Pallavi's eyes met hers when she turned to see her on the last bench. Diya returned her gaze angrily. She muttered, "If today I am to promise myself only one thing, Pallavi, I will put you where you deserve. If I can't do it, I will tweak my ears and slap myself a hundred times on my cheeks." To add a little salt to her wound, when asked to, one by one, other students from the D-gang students uttered, "The planetarium is the best option, ma'am."

"What the hell is going on? Everyone is singing Pallavi's tune." She slid her boot on the floor, then stamped heavily on Taruna's foot. "This all happened because of you, Taruna. I won't forgive you. I will teach you a lesson that you will remember for a lifetime. You will now see my true colours of enmity. I will not spare you."

"Now, in this classroom, it's just me and myself. No one is with me," Diya thought and looked at Taruna discontentedly. "I will see how you mingle with others."

The next day, The schoolyard was abuzz with activity as the students assembled, eager to embark on the planetarium trip. A long table, laden with an array of tempting snacks, stood at the centre of the open space, beckoning the hungry young, tiny minds before boarding the bus. Diya joined the orderly line of her classmates, making their way from the classroom to the schoolyard. However, the path leading to the schoolyard was not smooth. The patch was devoid of grass, replaced instead by a scattering of broken stones. , hastily laid to patch the uneven terrain. Undeterred, the students made their way across the gravel-strewn landscape, their footsteps crunching against the sharp stones.

Diya squirmed past everyone to reach Taruna through the throng of students slowly heading onto that gravel-filled land. She swiftly wrapped her arm around Taruna, pretending it to be a warm gesture. A facade of warmth masking the simmering anguish beneath. Taruna's eyes met Diya's, a pleasant smile crossing her features as if to maintain harmony like before. But the facade soon crumbled as Diya's harsh and rude voice cut through the air, her words laced with venom. Diya grumbled right at Taruna's ears, "I will kill you" The madness in her eyes, burning with ferocity, caught Taruna off guard. Taruna's expression changed; her friendly smile evaporated, her features hardening into a fearful, unfriendly grin as she walked past Diya, only to be met with a sudden, unprovoked attack. Diya's leg swept swiftly through Taruna's, causing her to stumble and tumble to the ground, her nose and knees bearing the brunt of the impact. And she bled.

Taruna sat on the ground, her knees drawn to her chest, blood trickling from her nose and staining the cotton of her shirt. The madness in Diya's eyes was something she couldn't decipher in time, her fault. This kind of madness wouldn't have surprised her if it had been directed at someone else, but at her loyal friend like her - It was accepted by her with great reluctance, especially when she saw the blood drops falling to the ground. Her nose bled profusely, and her knees skinned. Palo looked back as Taruna screamed, but Diya had already left before Pallavi could reach. Pallavi, ever the caring friend by nature, rushed to her aid, gathering the first-aid kit and tending to Taruna's wounds with the practised skill of one who has witnessed such injuries before.

It was an opportunity for her to learn when her mother was hospitalized. She had learned the art of dressing wounds by looking at many screaming patients with their wounds bleeding courageously. Since then, on and off, she happened to visit that room at the end of the narrow hallway with her mother, and what fascinated her was the stitching of wounds that her eyes almost rested upon with full attention while talking with Uncle Pradeep. She gloved her hands and gathered gauze pads from the kit, pouring saline onto one. She then touched Taruna's wounds, causing her to wince with a hiss of pain. Pallavi cleaned her brown-black bruises over her knees and the blood caked around them, saying, "It will take the edge off in minutes, Taruna." Then, she applied a little antiseptic ointment and bandaged it perfectly. Taruna cleared her throat and said, "Now, I feel better."

Diya came to see her, like one of the many who circled around and shrugged as if it wasn't a big deal. "Taruna is a brave girl. She doesn't need your sympathy, Pallavi. These are minor scratches," she uttered. Pallavi was almost red- hot, and angry inside. Diya added, "She has not bled much. Why are you making a big fuss? We fall every day and walk off. Why are you so sympathetic to this girl, Pallavi? Hurry up, run, run, the bus is waiting for you gals."

Pallavi's voice rose sharply, her words cutting through the tension like a knife."When she was bleeding, you disappeared from the site. You didn't bother to help her. You gave the girl a bloody nose, and she bled because of you. Now, you're asking her to run to catch the bus."

Diya's retort was laced with defiance ."Don't act like a doctor here when you're not one," She snapped.

Pallavi's scream echoed through the air, "Don't show me this arrogance, Diya. Instead, feel sorry for yourself for what you have caused with your desk mate."

Diya's eyes narrowed as she turned her attention to Pallavi."Pallavi, you, too, don't show your arrogance as a protector of this silly girl. You are unnecessarily delaying the whole class. Are you getting any sort of pleasure out of it?" Diya spat.

Pallavi's expression hardened as she levelled a stern gaze at Diya. "Do not investigate my conduct, Diya. Rather, correct yours. Everyone knows how arrogant you are. Your arrogance disturbs everyone in the classroom," Pallavi said, her words dripping with a mixture of frustration and authority.

Diya's chin lifted defiantly as she retorted, "I have the badge of honour of a monitor. The teachers support me, the girls fear me, and I discipline them. That is not arrogance," Diya claimed, her voice brimming with a sense of self-importance.

The clash of wills and the underlying tensions between these two classmates were palpable, creating an atmosphere of discord that threatened to disrupt the entire class.

"Mind you, Diya. The badge of honour you are holding on your chest has been passed on to you because I didn't want it," Pallavi said, ruthlessly slashing Diya's arrogance. "I didn't want it, considering that someday the responsibility will bring a change in your behaviour, but you... you will never change. I can snatch it back any day if I wish to. As it has given you some responsibility, you are expected not to show your relaxed side in such a situation. You cannot even deviate yourself today by saying you were busy elsewhere. You are standing right here, in front of me."

Inside the planetarium, Palo watched as the stars twinkled and then glowed bigger and brighter in the sky. She saw them moving closely around her and felt radiant when a bundle of rays emanated from those stars and beamed at her. Her real self was engrossed in an intense surge of a strange feeling of déjà vu - a visitation from her father who lives in the stars, as she once dreamt of. She tried to search for her father among the starry crowd when she sensed his presence at a hand's distance, speaking directly to her affectionately, riding and circling around her on a big moving star. "My child, my flesh, my blood, I waited for you to come. I want to embrace you in my arms. Come near, my child," he said. Every word he spoke sounded natural and engaged with the drum of her ear directly, not as a whisper but as a big bang right there. Her little eyes glittered and welled up when she discovered him in those celestial reflections. Moisture shined at the angles of her tiny almond eyes. She brushed her hand at her eyes but could not stop the tears from rolling down. All she dreamt of earlier was dancing again in front of her as a repetition of reality. She could now hear her father asking, "How will you hold the world in your little fist, Palo when you cannot hold the porridge?" She remembered saying, "I will hold the world in my fist one day." She inhaled sharply and stretched both arms to embrace the universe, her soul emanating from her real self. She wanted to chase and snuggle up to her father before he could disperse as tiny molecules in the universe again. But she turned back in despair, not touching him again. She stood among the stars motionless and paralyzed, screaming, "Papa, don't go," her voice buzzing like a bumble bee choked inside her throat. The reverie was interrupted by the illumination and the room's noise after the show, taking the moment away from her.

*****

The classroom fell silent as Mrs Lawrence, a middle-aged woman dressed smartly in a vibrant saree, swept in alongside the teacher. Her intellectual bearing and well-spoken manner suggested a woman of great wisdom and experience. Everyone noticed as she conversed with the teacher while entering. There were a lot of reasons to get closer to the students – One of which was that she couldn't remain in the school as an unrecognizable face. She was a social worker and a former student of the school. It had been almost twenty years since she graduated. So, she spends a few moments there, speaking to students once a year.

She had suddenly hopped into the school for an informal meeting with the students to learn about them and their future. She was often seen as a vital link between the school's most talented students and their mentors. Silence fell as she entered, and the students scrutinized her, supposing she was a close friend of their teacher. They waited for the teacher's introductory words about the silver-haired lady. Pallavi needed to know what could have brought this lady here.

Mrs. Lawrence announced, "The state's Chief Minister has expressed her best wishes to all of you. She will be coming to your annual meeting scheduled for next week. I am here today to meet and get to know you all. Madam chief minister will reward the best talents of the school at the annual meet."

Palo asked, "Madam, will she be meeting with us?"

Mrs Lawrence replied, "There will be an hour of direct interaction with the students. You can ask any questions related to your school, study, social issues, or scientific inventions, but the questions will be subjected to scrutiny to avoid duplication. Each class will be allowed to ask three questions. The class teacher will send the questions to me five days before the meeting."

Mrs. Lawrence adjusted her bifocal spectacles, looked at Pallavi and asked, 'Are you, Pallavi?' Even though Mrs. Lawrence had heard about her, she had never seen her in person. 'I hope you have many good times in this expensive school, Pallavi.' These words aimed solely at her seemed to have a degree of derision for her poverty, which Pallavi could sense before anyone else could catch wind of it. What did she mean? All she could do was nod with a smile and say, 'Yes, Madam, I am Pallavi,' in a gentle voice.

Mrs Lawrence then uttered, 'Do you know the chief minister will be happy to meet underprivileged girls like you who have been given free admission to this costly school?'

The messenger of the minister, wanting to be loved, would speak such words far from her expectations. She looked severely disappointed. Her pride was wounded and trampled upon by such a silly and derogatory remark. Indirectly, Mrs Lawrence was discussing money, fixing an invisible price tag on her free education, and trying to insinuate a profit in an indirect way. Pallavi understood by then that Mrs Lawrence was treating the students as milch cows for profit, especially the children whose parents sleep with crushed money under their mattresses to buy seats. It seemed to Pallavi that Mrs Lawrence was cracked up by the privilege of getting closer to a chief minister. She didn't know when to speak, where to speak, and what to speak. Pallavi felt insulted. The guest intended to say, 'Look how kind-hearted the chief minister is?' It filled her heart with anger and resentment. The messenger of the minister, in her misguided attempt to appear generous, had revealed a callous disregard for the struggles of the less fortunate. Pallavi tried her best to cover her anger behind a silent-looking face.

The teacher could recognize the sign that Pallavi would blurt out a befitting reply. Diya looked back to snigger at Pallavi. There was indeed an overt sign of pleasure which she displayed on her half-smiling face. With this image in the classroom, Pallavi's anger finally boiled over, and she rose to her feet. Her words were a scathing rebuke that shook Mrs Lawrence to the core.

"Madam, you helped me join this school. Today, it seems to me like you are rejoicing over this action, but when will you mourn over my father's death? It is you who dragged me into poverty. You didn't utter a single word against the chief minister who hid behind me for the failure of the state machinery. Who made me poor? I lost my father because of the negligence of your municipality. I got admission to this school as part of a compensatory package that the minister announced after my father's death. Will she be able to return my father alive if I leave this school? Your words today brought great displeasure to me, but I still respect you as a former student of this school. As you stated that we would be allowed to ask questions, I would ask the chief minister only one question: Where is my father? My mother has been waiting for him for so many years. Was the manhole a man-eating dinosaur which devoured his body without a trace? No, it was not. Your madam did not use a single diver to search his body inside and not even in the sea at its exit. My mother still believes he is alive."

The young girl's raw, unapologetic demand for answers about her father's fate left the older woman puzzled and speechless. Mrs Lawrence stood in mute shock. The words sent a shiver down her spine. Her body trembled; she shouldn't be there even for a second. She took to her heels the next moment and quickly jumped in her car to move out.

The teacher watched the exchange of words with a heavy heart. Probably, her prayers for the healing of Pallavi's deep-seated pain echoed in the silence which led to abrupt departure of Mrs Lawerence . **She recognized the extraordinary maturity and insight that had forged Pallavi's remarkable character-** *That was a testament to the resilience of the human spirit in the face of unimaginable loss.* She prayed, 'May the angel heal your deep pain within you, Pallavi. The almighty will do justice.'

"As all of you know, the annual meeting is the most enjoyable day. The senior girls will conduct the event, and I expect all of you to help them. The outstanding performers will be rewarded, and, to tell you, the parents are invited to this gala event. There was visible excitement on everyone's face after the teacher made the announcement.

The rush of parents was as usual near the gate when school time was over. Laxmi was already at the gate and peeping through the school gate. She could see Palo from a distance, who seemed more excited than the rest as if to announce the biggest achievement of the day in the next few seconds.

"Mama, the teacher announced the date of the annual day celebration, which is scheduled for next week. All parents must attend and cheer up the students on that day. I want you to be present in the hall when I perform on the stage."

"I have so many garments to stitch before these boutiques bite my head off," Laxmi said.

Laxmi knew well that her income relied on the prompt delivery of orders. It would slash off the customers if she fails to deliver the products on time. A single parent managing a business and a household was like taking on tasks more than she could chew. She ought to have a firm hold on her business in the competitive market when a section of the capitalist class was slowly venturing into large stores in the city. They could stock ready-made garments for a larger crowd. A few had turned into big players in the market ecosystem through their scrambled merchandising. The ravishing film stars posed on daily flyers with designer outfits, luring many youngsters to be like them. People had no kindness. In the past, many customers had bitten her head off for the delay in delivery, and even a few had turned absolutely ungrateful in asking for their money back when something went wrong in the measurements and fittings, nothing which they blamed themselves for having gained weight after their quarter-a-century-old recorded measurements.

"Mama, if you say no this time, I will not perform in any of these events." They talked while walking hand in hand, and a moment later, they reached the bus stop to catch the bus.

They entered the bus. Palo insisted on a middle seat over a seat at the rear end. She knew well over these years that travelling in a city bus is no less than a bumpy ride on a camel.

Both sway with equal jerks. And the jerk is more pronounced at the tail end.

The potholes had grown bigger and deeper over these years. There is no solid repair at all. Those temporary solutions with macadam never withstood a single lash of heavy rain on these city roads. She saw it closely over these years: many weak spines had crashed down to a state of paralysis. The files which hopped from one table to another someday either died of their own death after a time or were trampled to smother under the weight of a big-fat file. Ultimately, the champions came up with their best temporary solutions as an interim arrangement to such a sordid city affair. The clever Mandarins took advantage of the fact that public memories are short and repair works are to be done just before the elections, giving no chance to the public to raise hands in public meetings to question the exploitative state rulers.

A medium-sized, deep, maroon-coloured car stopped in front of Laxmi's house. It was twilight, and they probably needed to stop at the first big mango tree on the lane in front of someone's house. The figures alighted from the car and headed towards the veranda. One knocked at the door, and a few seconds later, Laxmi opened the door. She appeared surprised to have Chunni and Natasha at the doorstep. She greeted them inside, and they sat on the sofa. After a brief interaction, she went inside the kitchen to get some drinks for them. Laxmi sat on the couch across to participate in the chat that Chunni would start. He seemed to clear his throat first to start the conversation.

Chunni started by saying in a soft and persuasive tone, "I am touched that you remember us. The reason I wanted to see you is Palo." He paused, letting the words sink in. "She's gone out to play with her friends."

He continued, "The government has announced a new scheme for the girl students over ten years old ." At this, Laxmi's face flushed with interest.

Natasha chimed in, "As part of the scheme, the government is distributing cycles to the girl students, and in my opinion, Palo is entitled to one. If you agree, I can proceed with the application." Laxmi could not bring herself to disagree.

Chunni cleared his throat, " And there is one more request before we leave; I apologize for asking you this, but both of us feel that you should accept the ex-gratia money still lying with the government." Natasha added, "The compensation may get quashed if the next government takes over and the election is around the corner. Please, don't say no this time."

Laxmi sighed, "If it is a scheme, I have no objection to applying for it." Laxmi signed the papers for Palo's free cycle. Chunni was uncertain if Laxmi would ever sign the documents.

Chunni hesitated and then continued, "Your anguish at the state machinery is irrefutable. I agree, but how long will you continue sewing for these boutiques? Your clients profit more from your dresses than you do. Why don't you start your own boutique with the money you will receive?"

Laxmi rose from the sofa and went towards the shelf to pick up a trophy. Holding one in her hand, she said, "Look at this: Sagar was a national-level swimmer; he won this trophy. He was christened Sagar because he could swim in the sea when he was ten. He was strong and brave." Laxmi's eyes glistened with unshed tears.

Natasha tried to interrupt, "But, someday, you must accept it. I saw Sagar getting funnelled into the..."

"Stop, Natasha," Laxmi cut her off. "I cling to my deep faith. The light of eternity will dispel the darkness in my life someday. Sagar will return to our family. Like me, my Sagar must be finding difficulties without me and Palo."

Natasha sighed, "But Laxmi, we searched for him in the city. He was nowhere to be found."

Laxmi complained, "The water treatment plants and the exit area at the sea could have been searched properly. My anguish should not be perceived as meaningless. All my emotional appeals to the so-called proverbial chief ministers and her mandarins that day were not listened to."

Pointing her finger towards the trophy, Laxmi said, "How can a national-level swimmer go missing with the flow of water like this? My heart says he is still alive in some corner of this world."

After a pause, she said, "With all certainty in my mind, in hope, keeping faith in Lord Shiva, I have not wiped my vermillion over my brow. Taking the money from the government will be like accepting his death. I cannot live to hear that my husband is dead. I knew there was a cyclonic storm, and the city was drowned under the water, but still... if the government wanted to search for him seriously, then the chief minister could have exercised all the state force."

Chunni said, "I pray for his safe comeback if he is alive in some parts of the world."

*****

The winter was midway to wither, and the days were short. The sun had moved westwards. The squirrels were leaping from one branch to another in search of new offshoots on the mango tree. The worker ants were hibernating. The climate was a little nippy with less intense sunlight. The breeze was skin-deep and cold enough. To ward off the cold, Laxmi wrapped a thin, warming shawl around her shoulders. The ding-dong clock on the wall chimed once and struck one o'clock.

The program was to start promptly at two in the school. Laxmi had to reach at least half an hour before the arrival of the chief guest. She had finished dressing and had worn her favourite golden-bordered whitish saree. She looked at herself in the mirror and turned slightly to each side to scan her middle-aged appearance. She hallucinated a shadow of her husband by her side, mocking her, "*Buddhi ghodi lal lagam.*" Like a grunt of a harpy, she would have let out in retaliation, "*Buddhe hoge tum.*" But the shadow at once disappeared into the surrounding silence behind her. It crossed her mind, "Was this shadow a mental form of an effectuate?" She repented for mocking him as a zombie in happier days.

"Stop moaning, Laxmi. Have your faith in Lord Shiva," her inner self said. Her soulful belief was not ready to accept the harrowing truth. "I miss your those monosyllabic banters for me , Sagar. I will discover you someday, wherever you are. You have to come for Pallavi." She grabbed her handbag and hurriedly headed out to catch the bus.

She settled in the middle row of the hall. All eyes turned towards the chief guest as the spotlight fell onto the chief minister. The chief guest delivered her speech in the opening sequence after lighting the inauguration lamp. Palo received an award for outstanding performance in class six. The proud parents clapped and cheered the students for their performance in different fields. The children played jazz with the band led by their music teacher. Palo appeared as a butterfly among the bunch of others who swayed as little flowers.

The laughter in the hall grew louder and more regular as the students mimicked their least favourite teachers. In an act of bravery of a nervous child, one portrayed an anxious kid who stuttered with a constructed narration consisting of all mixed-up words of pain and pleasure in answering as the other questioned deftly, mimicking the monopoly of a terrorizing teacher. Their act constantly changed the delights in the viewers' minds as the word -by- word stuttering sentences amused their senses instantly. In the end, not to put off their amusement, even the students got so nervous that one ran for the loo by raising her pinkie, and the other, as a teacher, ran for water, complaining of a dry throat due to fear.

They looked sweet and carefree, like little angels in their fancy dresses. The claps in the hall didn't pause when the viewers' eyes caught one charming character who satisfied their amusement. Laxmi could not stifle a loud laugh when she saw a tiny girl in a police officer's attire walk into the gangway, circling the crowd with a whistle in her mouth. She whistled to gesture and teach the parents some discipline.

The speakers roared behind her, "Dear parents and students, we regret that we will not conduct the program, the close talk with the chief minister, due to a shortage of time. We need to wrap up the function here. The girls need to eat their dinner before leaving for their houses. I request all parents move to the waiting area of their children's respective classes. The students took the backstage to go to the canteen. The thought of Sagar was still swirling over her head. How happy would he have been today? Her mouth twitched at an angle, and her eyes grew moist in that moment of joy. The parents started moving from the main hall towards the waiting hall in the next moment.

Their wait was not too long. The atmosphere in the waiting hall was changing with the arrival of the participants. From every corner of the hall came delightful cheers from parents, and they echoed upon the arrival of their kids with prizes in hand. A few were still curious to know what their children would get. Pallavi exited her class with the award cup and headed towards the waiting area. "Whoopie, this is my prize, mama." She had a lot of things in her mind to tell, holding her award cup in her little hand, but couldn't. Laxmi's gaze had shifted elsewhere.

Laxmi saw a familiar face approaching her. He wore the same look he had nine years ago in the courtroom. Not much had changed on his face except for a golden spectacles on his nose. Within the hero's virile persona, she had found a villainous werewolf who devoured everything in her life that night. She understood by now that the bait of law begets only the innocent toddlers hooked; otherwise, the privileged giant fishes had all the royal prerogatives on when to hunt. Something in his manner prevented her from being emotionally pushed out of that place. That dreaded face had a smile of recognition. His palms came together in a prayer-like gesture. He uttered, "Namaste." It was a matter of conjecture why this man said Namaste. Does he have no shame left? She had shattered his ego by returning his financial help, which he had given after Sagar's conviction. She refused to accept it, saying she smelled blood in those paper notes, and she was right in saying so. She reciprocated with apposed palms, too.

Sameer said, "I came here to meet Pallavi's parents. My daughter Diya is her classmate. I didn't know she was your daughter. I can't believe my eyes; she is the same girl crying that day outside the courtroom and grew up to receive the Best Student of the Year award. Laxmi, I cannot bring back your happy days. If you can believe me, I apologize today for everything with a heavy heart. Then, I had an ailing wife and a two-year-old daughter, Diya. All my money and my house was mortgaged. Although the world knew me as a rising star, behind the screen, I was a broken man. I came to your door when I learned that Sagar had been released prematurely. I was sure he would forgive me because his heart was as big as the ocean. Though, in his words, he forgave me, he politely refused to accept my offer to rejoin duty. He said he had his own auto-rickshaw. Later, I learned about the tragic incident that happened to him."

Laxmi cut him off, "Palo speaks about Diya often at home."

Sameer looked down, stared at Pallavi, and said, "Pallavi beta, Diya is a very disturbed child, and her mind resists every order like a stubborn. The teachers are worried about her high-headed behaviour, so I request that whenever a situation arises and she hurts you for anything, do not take her words seriously."

Pallavi said, "Don't worry, uncle. She will always remain a friend to me."

Sameer thanked Pallavi and Laxmi for this conversation and headed towards the classroom.

*****

The road was narrow and open. It was smeared with a layer of mud after a brief rain. The potholes scattered over it gave her a troubled cycle ride. Adding to her problem, her backpack intermittently popped up from the basket and clung to the handlebar. After every jerk, adjusting her balance with one hand, she pushed the backpack into the basket with the other. She made many serpentine movements to avoid the potholes but could not escape one near the intersection ahead. The sidewalks were almost encroached on both sides by hastily parked big vehicles. She slowed down for a bunch of careless wanderers walking freely to cross the road. She signalled her tin-tin-sounding bell to prevent a direct hit with one such wanderer and applied the brakes.

Her cycle skidded off. She fell along with her backpack at the camber. The crowd around her screamed and came to help. One exclaimed, 'Arre Arre,' and another said, 'Thank God, not a single scratch on her body.' She took a moment to get up, lifted the cycle to make it stand on wheels again, pushed the backpack into the basket, and brushed her clothes to remove the mud clots with her little hands.

A white Merc Benz stopped a few meters away in the middle of the road. Diya opened the rear door and climbed down to see Pallavi in that state, and Rajat chose to sit behind the steering wheel. She tossed her head up once and then pranced towards Palo. She stood a meter away with crossed arms in front of her chest, sniggered and said through her teeth, "I could have given you a ride in my expensive car up to your home, but sorry, I can't. You poor girl don't deserve this." Indirectly, she hinted that to befriend rich pupils, preppies like her should yield to their whims and fancies. While turning back, Diya said, "You deserve only a cycle."

Pallavi's heart wrenched to hear the awful, offensive words. She winced inwardly, then thought of Diya as a selfish mouth and an insecure girl of a wealthy father. This is not her fault but an offshoot of her rich culture. From her words, Palo understood by now that a rich kid boasts about two things: one was the status of her father, and the other one was a luxury car. It was her fate that she didn't have either.

With every passing day, she turned sharper and sharper both in the field of academics and in her social life. She pulled an all-nighter for every exam. She excelled in her studies. It panicked those shopkeepers who took her just as a kid of thirteen. They were unhappy with her rapid and correct calculations. The shopkeepers knew by then that Pallavi could not be shortchanged and not be bullied in any haggling. Their tampered weighing machine readings were caught by her sharp eyes, questioned and objected to. She ticked them off for cheating customers with the expired grocery items.

*****

The scheming socialites showered Mrs Sinha with all high praises, marvelling at her ability to entertain her guests with her captivating tales of her shrewd financial machinations- *The art of making all profit, no loss business.*

Daring not to prove himself as an unsupportive husband, Mr Sinha had always been in a state to dispose of his old car at a reasonable price ever since his wife went ahead with her thought about buying a new car. Mr Sinha had adopted a different daily ritual recently – he would park his gleaming white Ambassador at the front of his house and lavish it with meticulous attention, polishing its every surface with utmost dedication. He would pleasantly greet the eager neighbours who would visit, showcasing his car, regaling them with the vivid heroic encounters of his daring exploits behind the wheel, not just about the ones on easy roads but through every manner of negotiating the challenging pot hole rich terrain. To someone, his arms swaying in action with every word reflected his inner enthusiasm. One way or another, the stories ended up with a significant round figure with multiple trailing zeroes, making it common knowledge that the car was up for sale in the neighbourhood.

Pallavi knew well that her mother could never finance her studies if she bought the car.

She had once heard Mrs Sinha telling her mother, "Laxmi, you wouldn't believe it. Sinha Ji didn't accept the cheque from a prospective buyer because he liked the car very much. It's his life. It's like a good luck charm. We take care of the car like our baby."

Pallavi had borne witness to these events over the years. Even at a young age, she often heard Mrs. Sinha declare to her guests during any festive occasion, "A widow lives next door, and her daughter is preparing for her matriculation exams. I haven't invited them because of that ." Mrs. Sinha would then proceed to blame Pallavi for every misfortune in the neighbourhood, accusing her of embodying some doomed destiny.

Hearing such venomous words from a neighbour's door would bring tears to Pallavi's eyes. The list would be long and unforgiving if she tallied the curses directed at her.

She often heard wild bursts of cacophony from the Sinha's house. She would listen to the lady playing music much louder during her afternoon rest when her mother went to the supermarket to sell her products.

Pallavi stared at the clock, then settled on the chair with her eyes closed. It reminded her every time that she should manage her time wisely. "Let me rest for ten minutes, then I'll settle on the chair until Mama comes."

She saw an unusual outpouring of affection in the past few days, with Mrs. Sinha approaching her main entrance door with a plate covered by another plate. She had heard the people who visited the Sinhas last night laughing hysterically at the party. What disconcerted her was when she heard Mrs Sinha narrating her guests about her father's death. It made Pallavi realize how her mother had been raising her since then. Everyone she knew as a close friend had learned about Mrs Sinha's charade of becoming sympathetic towards Pallavi in recent days, but in reality, she had suffered from high blood pressure ever since she heard Pallavi would be appearing for her matric board exam in a week's time.

Sitting on the chair with her gaze fixed on Mrs Sinha, she pondered how she would go to the examination centre. The exam would be conducted at a faraway centre, approximately twenty-five kilometres one way if she took the shortest road she had discovered on the Bombay city map.

She opened the door. Mrs. Sinha was not a woman who spoke less. She looked at Pallavi and commented, "It's not good for your health to stay awake until late at night. During exams, you must sleep adequately, beta." Pallavi had never heard such a caring and soothing response from her. She was taken aback by the uncharacteristic warmth and concern in Mrs Sinha's tone.

"These sweets are for you. Sinha Ji is going to Singapore on an official trip. His friends came to attend his success party last night. These are some sweets for you. I thought Laxmi would have come by now. How is your preparation going, beta?"

"Going well, Aunty."

"Sinha ji is going to buy a new car. I was hoping you could tell your mama to buy our old car. You don't have to pay much. The car is still his life. His lucky charm."

"Aunty, don't sell it. After this Singapore tour, I have heard that the company is considering a pay hike for Sinha uncle."

"How do you know, beta?" Mrs Sinha gave her a surprising glance.

"I heard it last night. One uncle said they would promote him to General Manager after the training in Singapore. You will get a big house to stay in." This surprised Mrs Sinha.

After taking the plate from her hand, Pallavi said, "Aunty, the way I see it, you're lucky charm may turn unlucky if you sell it to us. Think it over."

"Hmm... I need to rethink before selling it to you. It is in decent shape. What else were they saying?"

"One of them was considering buying your car."

"Beta, you are very nice." She put a gooey piece of sweet inside her mouth. "I will tell Sinha Ji. He will be incredibly happy. Beta, I only insisted he sell the car; otherwise, Sinha Ji has no interest in selling it off."

"Aunty, what is the price you have kept for your car?"

"Oh, Beta, we are not going to sell it. I told you, na, it's Sinha Ji's lucky charm." Palo's words had found their way deep into Mrs. Sinha's heart and started vibrating her mood with joy. She had nearly dropped the idea of selling the car anymore.

"I will tell Sinha Ji... he will drop you for your exams. Your Mama said, 'They kept your exam centre very far from Malad.'"

"Don't worry, Aunty, don't take the pain for us. We will go by our auto."

"Don't say no. I will tell Laxmi not to take you by auto. Why lose the rent of a day?"

"But, Aunty."

"No, Beta, you are just fifteen. Listen to me. Don't argue. I will not listen to you. Sinha Ji will drop you at the exam hall by car on the first day, that is final. He knows the roads in the city. Your father is not alive today to drop you at the examination centre... so what? After all, as your neighbour, we too have some responsibilities." Mrs Sinha hurriedly went to her house to give the happy news.

Palo studied hard as the day of the exam came closer. She began a strict regimen. She slept at midnight and rose at four in the morning. The pre-exam vacation in the school made her friends in the neighbourhood relaxed. A few were still playing on the ground, which she noticed while studying at the corner table close to the window. She experienced a form of hidden energy beyond the point of exhaustion.

Palo suggested, "Mama, staying in a lodge next to the examination centre will save us a lot of time." Taking a moment to think, Laxmi said, "Not a bad idea, Beta. I was also thinking so. You will not feel rushed, at least before your exams."

"Yes, Mama, I don't want to go with Uncle Sinha. I have seen him struggling almost every day to start the car. I can't take the last-moment exam pressure like this." Laxmi noticed the sneer on Palo's face about the Sinhas.

A Day before the exam, on a Sunday morning, staring out the window, she saw Uncle Sinha trying hard to start the car. He looked pitiful. He called a few chaps from the neighbourhood to help push the car. Not wanting to admit his failure and determined to conduct his mission to start the engine, he opened the hood and checked everything inside thoroughly to the best of his understanding about the car.

The sight of it worried her. She waited for Laxmi to tell Sinha Ji, "We are going to stay in the nearby lodge, not to put so much effort into the car for us."

Sinha Ji didn't stop there. She saw a few young men chatting and laughing at his actions as they made their way towards the car while passing by.

" Thank God, Mama, God listened to us. I pray that Sinha Uncle will never find the solution to his problem today."

Palo heard the clock chime " ding doing ten times." She had washed and dressed and opened her copy to revise maths. As the minutes ticked by, the engine of his car revved up. She saw Laxmi's face displaying a low level of nervousness. Mrs. Sinha was coming to their house. As if her mother tried to convince herself that she would not let herself be influenced by any of her wrong advice. It is a matter of Palo's career. She was certain she would resist Mrs. Sinha if she asked them to stay put. The engine stopped again. Laxmi could see Mrs. Sinha's feet slowing down. She turned back and headed towards the car, which had stopped again on the main road. A smile appeared on Laxmi's face, and she said, " Let's go beta before the engine splutters again."

Pallavi flipped through the last few pages, which she had gone over in detail earlier. She went out with her small suitcase and went towards the main road.

" Sinha Ji, don't take so much pain for us. We are going to stay in a nearby lodge." Laxmi said.

He tried to convince them that there was nothing wrong with the car. He checked it several times.

Pallavi looked at the sky to take notice of the clouds forming up as if someone from there wished to tell her, " Don't worry, Beta. I am there to deal with Sinhas. You will reach your destination on time."

They reached the lodge by four in the afternoon. Laxmi carried the bag full of books. The pudgy manager helped them to bundle their luggage up to their room on the first floor. The room was clean. They had planned to stay there for a week until the exam was over. Both looked very tired. Palo went to the kitchen to ask for a glass of water. It was five in the evening. The evening daily newspaper was just delivered. The manager handed over the newspaper to her to read. She took the paper and sat on the sofa quietly. Her tired eyes started closing. She didn't open the paper to read the news. When the butler came, she took the glass from him and drank. She felt refreshed. Leaving the newspaper on the Centre table, she left the place.

They came for supper. She saw a long wooden table laden with food. Palo had a light dinner in the dining room. Her eyes fell on the newspaper, which was still on the centre table. She glanced through it and read the weather forecast ."Heavy shower is likely to lash the city tomorrow ". It would not have been better if they had stayed home and waited for Uncle Sinha to drop her off at the centre on exam day." Thank God we are just a stone's throw away from the centre," Palo thought. She remembered how she once was thoroughly drenched in the rain on an exam day for not taking her umbrella, considering the clouds were not that thick and dark to pour down. Carrying an umbrella, Diya shot her a cold look by chewing bubble gum while she dashed across the school garden, almost drenched. " You have no umbrella, you poor girl? Get drenched", she had cried at her loftily. Such a curtly unforgettable remark from Diya kindled her to remain extra careful during the exam days.

The Model school is not far from here, as the autorickshaw driver told them.

"Mama, should we go to the school side now and check how far it is from here? If I heard the name correctly, the driver mentioned "Model school, " Palo asked.

It was nine o'clock. "No need to be on tenterhooks before the exam. Concentrate on your studies," Laxmi said. "I have already checked with Mrs. Sinha, and it is somewhere close by."

"Come on, Mama, who did you ask, Sinha aunty? Please, mama, let's go and check where the centre is."

"Okay, baby...You read, and I am going downstairs to check with the manager." Laxmi went to the reception and asked about the location of the Modern school.

" Don't worry, madam. You don't have to go too far; it is next door to our hotel," the manager said.

Palo got everything off her mind. Her mind concentrated with vim to conquer the exam pressure. Someone knocked briskly on the door. A woman in a grey suit appeared. " Hi, Dear I am from the press. May I use your balcony to fix our cameras, if you don't mind? We will just fix the cameras, please. Our crew members will be staying downstairs. No one will disturb you. The basketball match is in the morning at seven. Players are staying in this hotel. So ...," the woman said.

Laxmi returned from the reception.

"Can we fix our cameras on your balcony, madam? We must telecast the final basketball match, which is being held on the court of Modern School."

"Of course not? My daughter has exams. She must prepare for her exam. You can't disturb us."

"It's a final match, ma'am. There is no place left for us on the pavilion side. Your room is the perfect place where I can secure my cameras if it rains. Please..."

"The final session is in the afternoon. A brief practice session is in the morning. We will not disturb you. Please allow us..."

"Okay, you fix them."

"Thank you so much, ma'am."

"By the way, have you come for the matric board exam? I have seen your daughter somewhere. I can't remember exactly."

Palo said, "I know you very well. You are Minakshi Joshi from Timeline News. Last year, you covered the entire science exhibition in our school."

"Yes, you are right. Are you the same girl? What's your name... let me recall... Pallavi... Pallavi Rajhans, right?"

"Yes."

"I still have the recordings of the interview. You want them?"

"No, thank you, ma'am. Let me now focus on my exam. It's tomorrow."

"Sorry for causing you this inconvenience. I am extremely excited about the final match between City College and Rajdhani College. The practice session is at seven. That's why?"

"Good luck, Pallavi. I am sure you will do well in the exam. Looking forward to another interview after the exam."

"Beta, I am going to the dining hall. The room is crowded today. Players are there for their breakfast. I am going downstairs to order our breakfast. You come soon."

"Ok, mama. I will be through my revisions in ten minutes. I am just practising the last two possible exam questions from the previous year's test papers. Then I will come. Mama, buy one water bottle for me."

In the next few minutes, Pallavi exited her room. In her hand, she carried a book. Its pages were still open, and her eyes rested on one page. The soft click of the latch echoed as she closed the door behind her. She took the key from her purse and twisted it in the keyhole.

"Excuse me, I think you have dropped this paper," the boy said.

"Thanks."

"Oh! It's my admit card," she said to herself. "How can you be so stupid, Palo? Could it have happened while she rooted for the room key in the purse?" she worried.

She swung round towards him. The boy was not there. She saw him walking towards the stairs in a tracksuit with his back facing her. His hair combed back, and both hands were tucked inside the side pockets. She read the monogram, "City College. No.5."

"Thank you so much, dear stranger. I don't know who you are, but I am grateful to you." Pallavi thought. The love for the stranger crammed in her heart and then surged through her mind. She swooned at him from his side view while he descended the stairs. The expression of a smile had appeared unwittingly on her face. Her hand was in mid-air to wave to say something as if he were to begin a talk. She gazed at him until he took the last step to vanish from her sight. A moment later, she was amazed to catch up with herself in that state. She quickly snapped out of her daze. Her mind had gone off balance to a point, nearly convincing her to follow him where he was going. However, she was stopped. A part of her nerve said, "Don't be stupid, Palo; these are raw emotions. How will you show your face to your Mama if you fail the exam?"

She reached the dining hall. The food was piping hot on the long table. The butler came with a bowl of porridge and placed it in front of her. There was a brief hesitation to start eating at once. Soon, she heard someone say in her eardrums, " How will you hold the world in your fist, Palo? Don't forget, Beta, you have a bigger challenge in life today. My best wishes are with you. Do well in the exam. "

Students trickled down to the exam centre. The crowd grew thicker with the tick of time. Pallavi watched Diya throw a critical look at her while she walked past her.

Diya seemed engaged in some serious conversation with a boy from another school. His aristocratic charm seemed to be wholly taken over by her hotness as it appeared to many by the wicked grin at the angle of his mouth. There, too, she noticed a kind of nervousness on many faces.

The gatekeeper announced, "Fifteen minutes to open the gate. Check your room numbers from the display board. Keep your valuable items, books, and bags outside. You can take your water bottle, Geometry box, pencils, pens, and admit card." Laxmi waited outside the school gate for a while and returned to the hotel room.

"You will find your roll numbers on the table. Sit accordingly." She heard the announcement upon entering the examination hall.

As the minutes ticked by, Palo glanced at her watch. Ten minutes before the answer sheets were handed out. She began filling the first page with neat handwriting. The question papers were distributed next when the bell rang, precisely at dot ten on the clock.

Palo carefully read the question paper, and then she began to write. By the end of ten minutes, she had completed the answer to the first question. By the end of two hours, she had solved all the questions. She double-checked her answers and made minor corrections. And she waited until the last bell rang. Palo noticed Diya was struggling to finish her paper a few seats away. The examiner dragged Diya's answer sheet before he gathered the papers. Pallavi smiled at Taruna, and they walked out of the room. Diya stared back at the boy who she was speaking with.

Laxmi looked at the paper. It was quite tricky. But she was happy to see the tick marks on the numbers against each question.

"Mama, I wrote the paper well." She arrived at the hotel. She ate lunch. There was a little shower on the ground. The court was covered with tarpaulin cloth. The gallery was empty. It was two in the afternoon. Her first thought was when she would read science. From the balcony, she saw player no 5 on the ground, surveying the court and aiding the staff in covering the court. He appeared in a white knicker and a red vest. Hair combed back and a little curly. He had the muscular figure of an athlete.

"Palo, read, you are not here to waste time." Laxmi's voice came from inside. " Should I go and thank him now? "a part of her also bothered her. Her gaze followed the boy to the ground. What a serious-looking boy, not even lifting his head off the ground. At least I can wave my hand now. I don't even know his name." What will the people around him think?... Shameless, " Palo thought.

After an hour, she noticed from her balcony that there was a slight drizzle; he flung himself up and threw the ball. It fell directly into the ring. She clapped. But the boy still didn't notice her.

She heard the sound from inside her room. Her mother was budging the bed away from the wall.

"Why are you doing this, mama?"

"I hear a lot of noise on the other side of the wall. The boys are ill-mannered. I can't withstand the noise they produce on the other side. Meenakshi said they would pack their bags tonight after the match and that a few would leave tomorrow morning."

"My child, please come inside. Draw the curtains and rest for a while. The boys are still in their room."

She needed only a few minutes of solitude from her mother. She contemplated knocking on the neighbouring door and inquiring about his name. Palo thought to herself.

She peeped onto the ground, but the boy was not there. After the match, she looked around the marquee on the ground, but he was nowhere to be found in the dribs and drabs. As she last saw him, his impatient supporters scrummed inside the court in want of the ball when they saw the overhead hoof receive the last basket of the match and heard the gong sound twice. The boy dropped to his knees and kissed the court.

The market square is nearby, and she can get him there, but the thought of excelling in the exam crossed her mind. The canteen jukebox played some good numbers, and the music filtered in. "No distraction can break my resolve. I must outdo it to become a doctor. Now, nothing can deter my determination."

She heard the skirmish noise from the neighbouring door, and it seemed they had lost the match. Quieting them was quite formidable, and she had not gotten a moment to waste time mediating them.

Like a contentious mother, Laxmi had kept the Science book on the table and called, " My child, sleep for a while. Do not stare outside. The exam is over your head. You have no liberty to see the match."

She laid down on the bed with slight reluctance. Suddenly, there was a knock on the neighbouring door. Her determination to stay focused started swirling around her thoughts, and they refused to settle down in her mind. Pallavi opened the door and saw a butler with a big tray in hand, a big flask, and many paper glasses standing in front of the neighbouring door. The person who came out was a different guy wearing a yellow vest. He must be from Rajdhani College. She thought, "I wish I could see player number 5 coming out. I will ask Minakshi about his name; she must be familiar with the players playing for City College."

"Beta, I told you that these boys will vacate the room by tomorrow morning. Don't pay attention to what they're doing."

Pallavi closed the door and opened it briskly when she saw a glimpse of one side of his face as he descended the stairs.

"Mama, I want to have a cup of tea. May I go downstairs?"

"Open the flask and pour yourself a cup. It is on your table."

"Alright, Mama."

"Mama, I have heard about a botanical garden nearby. Shall I ask the manager for directions?"

" Beta, I have been telling you not to get distracted by all these. Focus. I have been seeing that you are not taking science seriously. You must achieve high grades if you seriously want to become a doctor." There was quietness in the room next to her. "Probably the boys have left." She expected a knock at any time as Minakshi had not yet turned up.

"I had seen you earlier meticulously reading the chapters word by word uninterruptedly and not even letting me in between those words. What has happened to you? How is it that suddenly you want to visit the Botanical Garden?"

She sat there with her books, reading them attentively. Minakshi Joshi came for a brief time to wind up her camera and cables. There was not much interaction between them except for a short exchange of hellos. Palo didn't feel inclined to indulge with her to inquire about the boy.

After a light supper in the dining room, she continued reading until midnight. She heard footsteps crossing her closed door. Someone stopped for a minute, but she didn't hear a knock on the door. "Please knock on my door, stranger." She silently prayed.

"Whose handkerchief is this? " his friend Ajay asked.

"Her name is Pallavi something I don't remember the full name. It was written on her admit card; I don't know anything beyond that. "

"How are you so certain that it is her handkerchief?"

"I found it outside the room where she stayed. Look, "P" is written on it."

" So, Are you serious?"

"Serious about what?"

"For a friendship! Let's go back to the hotel room." Ajay said.

"Absolutely not. Let's go. Papa must be waiting for us." The boy said.

*****

She burned midnight lamp oils to become the highest scorer in the matric board examination in the state. All the efforts she made and the courage she displayed to face the difficulties and challenges in life paid off well for her. She attracted the headlines in the newspaper.

That day, all eyes stared at her. Her heart thumped hard with excitement. She was speechless. Laxmi answered cosily when interviewed by Minakshi. Pallavi was interviewed by Minakshi and photographed. She posed alone in her study a few times and, in some moments, with her mother standing next to her. She revealed her dream of becoming a doctor in front of the camera. She remembered her father and how happy he would have been that day. To one question, she replied, " My father has been a great force throughout my studies, whose words always inspired me to work hard."

It seemed Sameer Malhotra was not with himself that day. Disha read to him the utility bills, the expenditure on a big car and sophisticated designer glad rags. He strode up and down on the terrace, leaving behind a scheduled vigorous exercise session in the gym that morning after reading the newspaper.

He had no control over himself to give a break to his thoughts. The glamour bug had already bitten Diya before he could plan something else. However imperious and eccentric she may be out of her quick temper, she carried a regal persona of all elitism in a happy mood. Her dreamy eyes, confident look and well-pitched voice, seemed perfect for someone's acknowledgement in the film industry. She would not mender like thousands in the glamour world for acting. To someone like her, the gene comes unmutated as a birthright. He plopped onto the chair and bobbed his head when Disha read the party's guest list.

The Malhotra family was planning a big celebration in the wake of Diya Malhotra's success in the tenth board examination. The result was declared first in the daily newspaper, and upon seeing her academic promotion, her father's chest swelled with a surge of pride. It was a long-awaited dream come true moment for him. He had planned a future for her in acting. Being a successful actor in the television industry, he wanted to nurture the naturally talented acting abilities within his daughter. To mark this occasion, he held a lavish gala dinner on the weekend.

Diya was asked to invite all her friends. She invited all her friends except Pallavi to preserve her happy mood at the party. As such, she never endeared Pallavi and another reason to believe that her growing popularity forced Diya to feel jealous of Pallavi. She found this was the only way to keep herself away from the uncomfortable questions related to her academic performance at the party. "Pallavi would steal the show if she attended the party", she thought in her mind.

The Malhotra house was adorned with a variety of coloured electric bulbs. The string of blinking bulbs spread all over her house that night, keeping the outdoor attraction lively and captivating. Guests began to enter. Diya was dolled up in a Western outfit —an exotic, elegant, pearly white sleeveless peasant top baring her midriff above the fitting coffee brown velvety skirt specially tailor-made by a renowned designer for the occasion, bearing a high-end price. She chose from the rest in her closet. She was bored with her indigenous handmade traditional garments. She was entering into an arena of visual culture founded entirely on fashion where education takes a backstage and matters least. The bold details of the attire wrapped on an aesthetically built body get precedence in the news over someone's natural talents. The more skin it reveals, the more appreciation it earns as the outfit in the game of show business. The outfit had accentuated her waistline. The diamond-studded necklace and earrings she wore sparkled to attract the gathering. Many eyes were arrested on her smokey eyes. Her large, inky, shiny hair curls hanging up to her mid back with swirled right-sided frontal tresses complemented her beauty. She had a perfect face to earn the tag of a beauty pageant winner. She glitzed up the party. That party just gave her an entry pass to join the rich kid club. She was introduced to many celebrities in different fields. Some of them were prominent news reporters of trendy fashion magazines, and her actor father specially invited them to the party.

They captured her photos, focusing on her potential as a new face in the fashion world, much like Palo grabbed the media attention for her academic achievements.

She longed for her deceased mother to be alive to see that momentous occasion. It, indeed, would have brought her boundless joy. The party setting exuded an energetic atmosphere, with the continuous playback of the top ten music tracks playing in the background while people were busy conversing with each other. In minutes, a dozen impeccably dressed liveried servants hired for the evening served the guests the drinks. Their glasses were filled with effervescent colas and alcohol, and they chewed the morsel served by these servants. The guests included the prominent socialites and their family members. As the party progressed, the gathering gradually moved from her living room to her spacious lawns, where affluent adolescents comforted themselves for a smoking race in a corner behind a tree. A few of them who were new to this habit highlighted their talent by puffing smoke rings and throwing smoke jets from their nostrils. Diya also tried a few puffs with them behind the corpse secretly so as not to be frowned upon by her father. Butlers roamed from one group to another, randomly offering starters. She particularly liked the cheesecakes on the stick and cutlets. She summoned a butler, who was serving alcohol, to the treeside and got everyone's glass refilled. A member of the rich adolescents' gang hit the dance floor and requested the DJ increase the music volume. The ' pop beat' got louder with every request until it became noisy enough to distract people from their conversations. The loudness of the cacophony was too much for a late night. The intensity was almost at the brink of crushing the eardrums. A few joined the dance floor, while others remained busy chatting to settle their business deals. The crowd enjoyed the fancy buffet in the meantime, and the party continued until midnight.

CHAPTER 6

Dream Chasers

From the corner of his eye, he saw her wave a hand at him. When their eyes met, an electric current seemed to pass between them, sending shivers down his arms and making his hair stand on end. Some magical, invisible energy was transferred into him when she extended her hand to take that piece of paper. Awkwardly, when his eyes met hers, his mind wanted to know more about her. Was she a girl who indeed looked upon his face? Who was she standing in front of his door? Truly, in that moment, he felt their minds speaking to each other through their eyes. They were trying to study each other as strangers. For him, there was something else in the way she said -Thank you. There was a gleam in her eyes and a smile on her face when she stood frozen. A voice rose within him, speaking something nice to him. He felt as if he was drawn close to her. He recognized her as someone he had known from the past.

Upon recovering from his lost thoughts, though he was not certain whether the thought was aligned well in her mind in an equivalent way, he knew his heart was seeking consent from him to enter inside her heart. But the fear was whether the permission would be granted on a mutual agreement of their minds.

They both stood like that for a while before he shifted his eyes and walked past towards the stairs.

Once again, she eagerly struggled to meet his gaze while he sat down to kiss the ground. Far from the ground, he couldn't decipher what emotions it sprang in her. He, too, stared at her, avoiding everyone's gaze. He could not speak to his best friend, Ajay, about what he felt within, even though there was no secret unshared between them. His mind had cautioned not to reveal anyone, but the handkerchief in his hand unveiled everything. He was too uncertain that he would ever find her in life. It sprang mild jerks in him when he saw her on TV. He was impatient, wondering if she would not recognize him. God only could help him. He kept wrapping himself tightly in the blanket and repeatedly sought comfort and solace.

Romy knew that anything that couldn't be easily broken was Honey's sleep. He had shifted his position from one side to another at least ten times in the last half an hour. Romy's patience finally broke. Honey's last moment of nightly comfort has now ended. He was struck by one question, which made him wonder once how his son could sleep through the buzzing of a phone beside his bed.

Romy walked into Honey's room and ruffled his hair. "Beta, it is seven now. You must go to your practice sessions. The breakfast is ready. Get up."

After a few seconds, Honey turned to his left, snuggled up with a soft pillow, and said in a sleepy voice, "five more minutes, papa. Today is Sunday ."

The telephone on the bedside table began to ring.

" No five minutes. You are getting late for your practice, Beta. Get up."

"Papa, Please answer the phone." Honey slurred in a husky voice.

"Ajay on the line."

"Ajay!" Honey stretched his hand, drew the receiver and said, "Hello."

"Honey, pick me up today. My bike broke down last night," Ajay said.

"Okay, I will see you at quarter to eight," Honey replied.

Honey woke up and hurriedly rushed to the toilet. By the time Romy returned to the kitchen and got the breakfast for them, Honey was ready at the table to have breakfast. While Honey was munching, Romy pulled a chair and sat across the table. He looked at him and said, "Brigadier had called in the morning."

"To say what?" Honey asked.

"Abhimanyu cracked the NDA exam."

"That's good News. Brigadier would have made his life a hell otherwise."

"Speak with Abhimanyu when you find time."

"Okay Papa"

"How is your practice going, Honey? December is not far; there are only six months left."

"I know Papa, still seven months in hand before the zonal."

"Beta, this is the time you should practice daily. After the intercollegiate, you are concentrating neither on your studies nor the game. I see you have turned into a slob."

"No, Papa, I am just the same as before."

"No, you were never like this before. There is no regularity in your life. Who is this P in the handkerchief? I discovered it in your grimy clothes before washing them."

"P for Player, probably someone who knew me by this name had dropped in front of my room following our victory. I liked the motif, so I kept it." Honey explained.

"Player! It reminds me of my time. I used to be a talented player, but I never had the opportunity to pick up a dropped handkerchief like you. Our coach never taught us about all these things, but defence is equally important in a game like this.

Sometimes, you need to learn to be a good defender to win. All that you need to learn is to touch the ball a little to alter its course. When the ball changes its course, the opposition loses the target at once. "Romy reminisced.

"Papa, I must leave now. I must pick up Ajay. Honey finished his breakfast and said, "Bye, papa."

Honey had worn aviator goggles, a dark blue sports jacket and trousers. He reared up the sports bike, did a small wheelie, zapped past his lane, and reached Kaul's house on 44 -Kashmiri Lane in a few minutes. He blared the horn, and Ajay came out of the front gate. They left immediately.

"What happened to your bike?' Honey asked.

"I will tell you; it is a long story. Let's reach the ground first. The coach must be exasperated for not seeing us in the field," Ajay said.

Parking the bike outside the field's lobby, they ran into the sports arena. Some had already started their warm-up rounds. They joined them, too.

"You guys are late again. I am worried about how you will make it to nationals. If you are not interested, then do not come," The coach said.

Ajay said, "Sorry, sir, it is because of me. My bike broke down last night, and we clubbed together on one from my house, where Honey came to pick me up."

"I have seen your university rounds, Honey; you must improve your footwork and defence. Ajay, you must work more with the rings."

The coach demonstrated the footwork, body swifts and jumps, then moved to the next player, uttering, "Practice, Practice."

It was eleven in the morning. The sun was glowing bright and intense. The warm breeze forced them to move towards the shed near the pavilion end. They sprawled on the grass. Honey pulled out his sports bag, took out the water bottle, and offered Ajay a drink. Ajay gulped a few sips, then handed over the bottle to Honey to gulp a few sips.

Ajay said, "Ballu tailed me to the market. Not alone, with a gang of five. He asked me to withdraw my name from the list."

"Why didn't you break his snout? If I have to break in him, the one thing is his snout."

Ajay asked, "If two things?"

"I will see. What I can." Honey said.

"Don't break him now. The coach would not think twice to fix you." Ajay suggested.

Ajay continued, "He came with a gang of five, each with a hockey stick. They broke my bike."

Honey's blood boiled, and he said, " I knew this scoundrel would do like this with us someday. This time, I will not leave him; I will smash his snout flat. Bloody scoundrel, son of a pig. He won't change."

" His father is a politician", Ajay said.

"So, what! Where is it written that the son is also licensed to act as a state minister? Who is he to decide our fate? Thanks to the new coach who took our side. Otherwise, he had made all arrangements to keep us out of the team." Honey said.

"Yaar, just listen to me. He has politics in his genes. Be wise. He is trying to instigate us for a fit of vengeful anger. To pick a fight with him now will surely get us either disqualified on the field or imprisoned inside the jail ."

"So, what! Shall we even not resist?" Honey said.

Ajay said, "He may go to any extent to use his political clout, and his father may go to any depth to take him out of any unfavourable situation if ever get caught with. Revengefully, he may put us behind bars if we take the law into our hands. The school days were different. Now he moves with a gang of four beefy hooligans."

Honey said, "You, too, think like a son of a lawyer. Look, we need to be good defenders. When the ball changes the course automatically, the opposition loses its game. All we need to do here is to touch the ball before it reaches its target. We need to break his teeth once to keep him away from us. Then he will change his course and will never cross our way. Let them be twenty in number; we two will be enough to fight them out."

Ajay said, "I knew you would react like this. You aspire to become a police officer. Once a police case is registered against you, you will be ineligible to sit for the exam."

Honey said, "Damn with my aspirations. We must retaliate once; otherwise, the snake will raise its hood and spew venom. We have to teach such people a lesson soon."

Ajay said, " A lesson? You can teach these snakes after becoming a police officer. Until then, you hold your horses."

Honey asked, "What have you decided about joining the police force?"

Ajay said, "I don't know yaar. Now, I cannot dream of something against my father's approval. You know it well."

"Discuss with him. He may agree." Honey said.

Ajay said," Discuss! Almost five years have passed now, and he still has not recovered from the trauma. Do you think he would ever allow me to sit for the civil service exam after the incident with Didi and Jiju? Never. He wants me to become a lawyer like Didi, but never in his life will he want to see me in a police uniform. I don't want to give him another jolt. Any form of revolt will push him further to a hopeless state."

After a pause, Ajay said, "He sailed through a tremendously distressful life. He would never–" Before he completed, Honey asked, "Any news about your niece, Parvati?"

Ajay replied, "No. When the police came in the morning, a mourning neighbour said that the one who killed my sister and brother-in-law inside their house in Bandipora had picked her up and ran away towards the jungle in the darkness. The other terrorist who Jiju killed was a Pakistani. Only God knows where our Paro is. Paro was one year old. Now, she must be around five. My mother prays every day in the hope that someday God would be kind enough to bring her back into our lives."

Honey swiftly switched the topic with a joyful tone and uttered, "One good news: Abhimanyu Bhaiya has cracked the NDA exam. He will be joining the Army very soon."

Ajay said, "Wow, that's great. Congratulations. How are the twins doing? Tapasee and Shreyashi."

"They are good," Honey said. After a moment of silence, both stood up and walked towards the bike. While they walked, Honey said, "The freshers will be joining tomorrow, so let's plan something."

"Oh, we should," Ajay said.

In the next minute, they left the playground for home.

*****

He was neither a lady-pleaser nor a spoiled-rich-brat-skirt chaser. His friends unanimously agreed that he was a 'Macho guy'. He looked tall, heavy, muscular, and outrageously handsome. Like an elite hipster, Honey flaunted his beefy biceps under his rolled-up sleeves and the prominent pectoralis of an athlete with the opened upper shirt buttons. He jammed his 2.5 kg equivalent hands in the trouser pockets, often revealing the top of his underwear. Whoever could see him from a distance could distinctly read 'Macho' over the strap. People who knew him said, 'He is a tad conservative on his ethics. His manners had no incivility; however, his mighty hands would find no time to ground opponents with his heavy punches when whetted for the wrong reasons.'

Diya decided to pursue the arts stream for higher secondary education. On her inaugural day at college, she donned an elegant and expensive frock, portraying herself as a princess. She was the head turner for many who saw her in a new Merc Benz, which stopped at the college's main entrance. As she stepped out of the car, her chauffeur opened the door for her. Upon entering the crowded corridor, the boys whistled and made inappropriate remarks after recognizing her as a newcomer. It amused her when one boy exclaimed, "Hi, pretty face, you take my breath away." Other girls listening to this secretly pulled their faces in displeasure and walked away.

Bhavna, A senior girl, was happy to vent out all her frustrations and anger, which she had experienced last year in that unforgettable razzing, which everyone called ragging. She was thorough in her mind that none of these juniors should get inside the classroom without her permission. How can she not be happy upon the subjection of juniors to a full day of ragging?

Bhavna put the girls awkwardly into a situation where they were to shout " Honey sir " twice after every question the seniors uttered.

"Who is he? Every girl likes to marry him. "One of the senior girls screamed. The reply in chorus came as "Honey sir, Honey sir."

"Who is the man we all call Superman," The reply came as "Honey sir, Honey sir."

Honey felt quite awkward about being referred to in this manner for everything. Bhavna won't change. What a stupid idea she had. Had Ajay been there today, he would have suggested some suitable means.

Soon, he was introduced to the crowd as - Hanumat Shivdasani.

Honey ordered everyone to sit on the floor of the corridor. Bhavna's idea was to drag them all to perform a monkey dance. The super hit idea of mocking them flopped when Honey posed as a teacher to teach them the first lesson in college - How to behave with seniors?

There was a noticeable resistance on their face while they sat on the floor. Whoever pronounced little resistance was asked to stand facing the wall in a corner and warned not to glance at them all for the day at all lengths.

"Listen carefully. Any doubt, boys, you call him Honey sir, and for you girls, call him Honey boy," Bhavna said.

Bhavna called Diya to her side. Diya rose to her feet, walked up to her and stood facing the students who sat on the floor. She declared, "Diya, from this moment onwards, for a year, we declare you as the beauty queen of the college." One meddled, " But mind you, your willingness to carry the title will also burden you with another tag for a year, " *Honey ki rani."* Another girl stepped back and took a long look at her, then tipped a finger under her chin and uttered, " *Hai, hai ye Chehera nyurani, Banegi kya Honey ki Raani."*

Honey's face flushed. "Stop it, please. It is silly. I am not going to get along with any girl for a year."

The boys were asked to become respectful to Diya for the title and were warned not to put an evil eye on her. "If the warning is ignored, then prepare to face its disastrous consequences. Is that clear to you all in the first years ?"Bhavna blurted.

Honey's eyes fell on the girl, who entered the main lobby with a stately bearing not less than that of a beauty pageant winner walking on a ramp, pleasing enough to melt a block of solid ice. The curtain of all that boastful cold-man's oddity in his mind dropped in the next moment. It was her he had been waiting for a month and a half. A part of him was desperate to keep his image up. He was reluctant to initiate a talk to avoid dropping any silly words. He tidied up his dress buttons and combed a hand through his hair before she came closer.

Pallavi looked absolutely stunning in her natural beauty, even prettier than the rest of the girls. He felt his heart aflutter before it stopped for a while.

Is it his fortune that he is seeing her again? Her expression shifted to a puzzled look when she saw him. He paused his eyes from a snap and fixed his gaze on her for a while. A part of his mind let out a drawl to warn himself, "Girls are not your priorities, Honey. Just stay away. You can't fall in love. "

Meanwhile, the other part of his mind said, "That doesn't mean you stop gaping at her eyes, Honey. Don't be unfocused. She is the girl made for you. Extend your hand for a shake and introduce yourself."

"No, Honey, you are in great trouble. Don't try to mess with her. Believe me or not, she is the same girl you met the other day at the hotel. You are not in a state to match her spontaneity, which you saw on TV. Don't say anything silly which she would twist to stifle you with one of hers, if at all needed; converse with great caution." It followed a brief silence till further order came from within, " Honey, go and at least ask her name. She will tell you her name, Pallavi Rajhans."

"No, that would be unnatural. Just return her handkerchief, and if she identifies it as her own, then you say you have mistakenly lifted off from outside of her door."

"No Honey , She is not a bimbo like Diya. She is a real combination of beauty and brains. The most deserving girl to bear the title of beauty queen, er Honey ki Rani."

He welcomed her, and their hands met for a warm handshake. Pallavi responded to his friendly gesture. As he did, others, too, followed him. His crazy mates, too, shook their hands with Pallavi. Sitting in the crowd of freshers on the floor, Diya was surprised to notice that the seniors who had put her in a beauty pageant winner frame and oohed and aahed over her tinted brown hairs of high-heeled society a while ago suddenly turned onto Pallavi. They all behaved differently with her. "Pallavi was greeted warmly, while for her, it was cheeky! That was something indigestible. Having yielded to the thought of being made light of, she asked herself what she really lacked. "Stupid jerks giving importance to an ordinary girl who has no traits to match with her, leaving behind a girl of extraordinary smartness and beauty around them! Disgusting", she grunted.

It made her feel jealous of Pallavi. Her dark eyes turned red in anger, and she looked disturbed. All her past stories of school came rushing back. What she had thought and what did happen was the opposite.

Diya had thought of getting a spark of her dream man, who would collide with her, and the books she clutched close to her chest would fall. Their eyes would meet, and their hands would brush while helping her gather those. He would pause, then he would throw a smile. A thousand bells would jingle in the background when he would ask for a coffee, and she would say " no" like any romantic movie. Then he would swoon at her feet for a proposal, but nothing of this sort happened on the first day. She exclaimed, "The boys didn't hover around her, unlike bees do around a scented flower. They didn't flock to her and ask for her address. Which Lane does she live in? What is her father doing? Instead, the moment turned differently for her. Pallavi was introduced to them as someone 'intelligent, pretty, witty, and whatnot! They said everything in her praise before they stopped. She had prayed a million times that Pallavi should not appear before they dispersed, but it happened. How humiliating it is going to be when she discovers her sitting on the floor. What about her coming in a luxury car, getting the doors opened by the chauffeur, and wearing an expensive dress - do they really have any impact on these silly boys? ' She doubted. What she cherished as a delightful moment of happiness a few minutes ago was soon obscured by sourness and gloom. The happiness of winning the 'Beauty Queen' title slowly faded on her face.

It seemed to some senior girls that a sort of jubilation surrounded Pallavi after her arrival. One of them examined her face. "It is real, no powder. Pretty chick, ye chehera nyurani, kya banogi –." Honey dived into this wryness before she could take his name. Amidst the rising flurry in the background, Palo heard one saying, "Now she has become Honey's interest."

Pallavi was looking anxious about being late for the class. She did not want to miss the first class on the first day of college. After all, she had to sprint meters chasing down the town bus to reach the college when it was about to leave the bus stop next to her house. Standing in a crowded bus in a busy city like Mumbai was not a comfortable ride. All the pain she took was to chase her dream. One girl, taller and stronger, appeared in jeans, shirt tucked in the waist, grabbed her by the arm and tried to swing her around in pleasure. Pallavi whirled, and the books dropped. She crouched down to re-stack them. A helping hand came forward and helped to sort them in order. Their breath mingled. A dim view she carried for the boy so far changed. Grabbing the books, she rose and said, " Thanks."

"My pleasure," Honey said.

Palo joined the science stream. The only thing on her mind that day was the classroom and the lecture. Her heart was impatiently racing faster. The seniors were neither letting them go from their clutches nor teaching them anything useful they would have learned in the classroom. Amidst all this, a few passing remarks were made, calling them a bunch of jokers, and a few named them a group of young monkeys. Such words from their mouth had further aggrandized a panic reaction in her mates. It kept their minds in terror when they looked into the eyes of the seniors. She did not want to spend much time standing there like an idiot saying 'yes sir and no sir.' She dared and meekly begged permission to leave that site without paying much attention to the students sitting in the crowd. She was permitted without any objection from the group of seniors. No one dared stop her as Honey had allowed her to go.

Her heart was constantly on a race ever since Honey came into her view after that brief encounter at the hotel. His eyes were so close to hers that she thought of getting lost in their depths for a moment. However, her modesty managed to mask her feelings, and she looked away. Far away in the corridor, she heard a mix of laughter every step she advanced. By the time she reached the classroom, the handkerchief she squeezed in her hand was dabbed with perspiration as she found no one inside except her.

She was a strong-willed girl who always believed that her conviction and hard work would sail her through her career's difficult and most challenging parts. She wanted to crack the pre-medical test in a single attempt. She befriended the senior girls preparing for their pre-medicals in the library. Her determination was unshakable; she was predetermined to spend all her time studying, so she did not have much space for her friends who wanted to waste time. Such a mindset of her's brought her only a countable number of studious friends closer. While she was busy studying, Diya was busy attending the canteen calls to make friends. The rich kids club could reach out to Diya for a membership, which she accepted with pride. She smoked with them, partied with them and skived off the classes. Academics was her last priority in the list of her life.

*****

A sports bike made a skidding effect as the rear tyre stopped suddenly beside her. The bystanders agreed that the boy was a sport, not from the helmet at the top but his sports shoes and the muscles protruding through his spiffy sports outfit. They all cared to admit that it wouldn't have been impropriety in his action if he had rebuked the bus driver by taking him by the collar to question him why the bus had stopped suddenly. The reproved words of a flurry for the state transport's casualness came out of their minds as if they were nagging for years inside to come out someday.

Pallavi would have gotten inside the bus if something had not dragged her attention. Soon, their attentions switched to see a puppy on the road wriggling in pain. A little while ago, the pup had been gambolling beside her, racing in circles around its mother.

To her, it seemed the driver didn't intend to hit the pup, certainly not, as he remained there to apologize to the bystanders who reproved his action. Somehow, he left the place so as not to take any more scowls from the passengers for the delay.

The puppy couldn't stand to run. It screamed. The mother dog turned to him without caring for the other vehicles passing by, endangering her life by pulling the puppy with her mouth. The puppy screamed more. She dropped and started licking its legs.

The biker cradled the puppy in one hand and carefully supported its limb with the other. The puppy felt a little comfortable and stopped screaming. He asked Pallavi to help him take the puppy to the nearest veterinary clinic at the marketplace. The mother dog probably comprehended that the baby was in safe hands, and she did not resist. She licked for a few minutes and licked the biker's hand to get familiar with him. Pallavi took the puppy from his hand. When she cradled it, the puppy snuggled its head into the crook of her elbow and settled down comfortably without any pain.

"Hop on," patting the pillion, the biker called.

She perched on the pillion with the pup in her hand. "Are you comfortable?" he asked. He didn't start the bike until he got a nod from her. For Pallavi, saving life was more important than knowing about the biker under the helmet.

An observant Diya to the whole fiasco followed them to the market in her car. They bought some medicines from the chemist. Diya could see his sports bike parked in front of the chemist shop.

A curtain of darkness just fell in front of her and dissipated in a second. She couldn't believe her eyes; she saw Pallavi standing beside him. The biker had taken off his helmet. Honey stared into Pallavi's eyes, and she stared back at his. The waves of that discomfited sight swept over Diya, and she turned furious. In that moment of quandary, she didn't know how to react. "That jerk of a girl is still holding his hand."

Her inner beautiful girl begged permission to meet Honey, but the wicked one had something rotten to do. Her heart slammed against her ribs loudly; it evoked a reaction in her mind. Her pulse quickened, her nose wrinkled in anger, her lips quivered before she picked something sharp from the ground and went close to his bike, then she sliced the seat of his bike with that sharp object. Muttering, "He will never give you a pillion ride again, Pallavi," she started back down the way to a lane where they couldn't see her.

*****

On the next day, About five in the evening, Pallavi came out of the chemistry laboratory. Her bright eyes had turned red-rimmed and runny. Someone had mischievously spilled a bottle of formalin near her desk. Hurriedly, she took off her laboratory coat and stuffed it inside her bag. Without looking anywhere, she headed towards the bus stop. The traffic was unusually scanty, but she waited at the bus stop.

No one in the college would have ever thought that the atmosphere on the road would turn hurly-burly. She was baffled by the sudden crowd bursting onto the road. A few familiar faces looked panic-stricken, while others dispersed hither and thither as if they just saw a man-eating tiger. However, this was not the case. She saw a police van and an ambulance at the spot from a distance.

Pallavi eavesdropped on a conversation between two men sitting at the bus stop. One explained the incident, while the other interpreted it with his remarks. She heard about a clash between two guys from her college and five from another college. "The guys from the other college waylaid these two guys in the middle of the road while they were on a bike and attacked them with rods and hockey sticks. The pillion rider, who hadn't worn a helmet, got a direct hit on his head and fell from the bike. But the other guy, my God, what a fighter he is! He showered punches and smashed their faces. He heaved the bike into the air in a retaliatory rage to throw it at them. He would have let it on them if the police hadn't arrived in time. What a rage! The pillion rider is being taken to the hospital by ambulance to the City Hospital."

She could see Honey from a hundred meters away when the crowd completely dispersed. He was pushing the stretcher into the ambulance with the help of the stretcher bearer.

She walked past the police personnel and a few students. She saw Honey a few meters away. His clothes were torn, and he had bruises all over his arms. The student lying still on the stretcher had a blood-stained face, and a white bandage was wrapped around his head.

For a moment, she was struck with the thought that the exam was next week. If not superb, standard preparation would take a few days to cram. She was supposed to be studying for the exam. The next moment, she was split by the thought of whether to go with them. She knew the hospital inside and out, as well as many medical staff and doctors. Finally, before another moment compelled her to rethink, she decided to accompany the critical life battling between life and death.

The nurse who accompanied the injured person recognized her and screamed, "Pallavi Didi, Pallavi Didi... Here!" She looked at her sitting inside the ambulance. Pallavi recognized the nurse as Payal, who worked in the emergency division of City Hospital. She used to go out regularly for ambulance cover when called by the hospital. She was popularly known in the hospital as "Resuscitation Didi" because she once saved a life while aboard a flight.

Pallavi asked, clutching the ambulance door, "Shall I accompany you? I know many doctors in the hospital."

Honey nodded and gestured towards the ambulance, saying, "Go inside." Pallavi sat beside the nurse on the side seat, and Honey sat close to the door. The ambulance then left the scene. Honey sat with his left arm on his lap and the palm of his other arm cupping his cheek. He looked at Ajay's face, which lay silently with closed eyes. His eyes had turned black and swollen up.

After a moment of silence, Pallavi asked, "How did all of this happen?"

"They attacked us." After a brief pause, "Who were they?" asked Pallavi. "The MLA's son and his gang."

"Why?"

Honey replied, "They don't want us in the national team."

"Basketball?"

"Yes."

Her assumption about the game was spontaneous. However, a sudden shiver ran down her spine in anticipation that he would ask her something else. This wasn't really an assumption they both knew. Nonetheless, she made it so he could recount the past days at the hotel. Now it was his turn to ask her, "How did she know?" But it seemed to her that his side of the wall was too big to see this tiny hint inside her curious mind.

Twisting her body a little, she took in the sight of his battered face. "Hey Bhagwan! What am I seeing?" she asked herself.

"What a fighter he is!" A mental image of Honey appeared while she was thinking about the men who verbalized so at the bus stop. What continued to trouble Pallavi was the sight of Honey. How it was then and how it is now. The sight of his side flashed in front of her repeatedly. Now, it was much closer to the nerves in her thought process. This boy is now sitting so close to her that her mind couldn't think of running away anywhere, leaving him alone in his period of stress. Also, asking him like a reporter conducting an interview wouldn't be wise. She didn't know why, but for her, the time had just halted with the exclusive sight of him. He is the same cheerful boy with whom she spent a beautiful day of her life yesterday.

She shuffled, tucking one leg under the other. There was not a shred of grimace on his face. The blood had clotted around his lacerated brow on the right side. Her gaze shifted to his white linen shirt, which was now drenched with sweat and smeared with blood. Through the torn windows, she could see the bruised skin on his back. She looked at his faded blue jeans, smeared at places with patches of mud. Despite his outward composure, she could feel he was seething with rage inside. His eyes, at the angles, had rimmed as red as his blood. She hesitantly placed her hand on his, hoping that her touch would give him some solace.

"Calm down, please." After a few moments, Honey turned his head and caught her eyes. Slowly and gradually, his breathing slowed down, and his fury subsided.

As the ambulance pulled into the hospital premises, the blaring siren stopped.

Pallavi said, "Payal, I am going to the Neurosurgery ward to call Dr Gagandeep. You take both to the trauma care emergency."

"I am Okay," Honey said. He hobbled through the hallway while pushing the trolley.

With her expert ministration, Palo emerged in the emergency room with Dr Gagandeep. The resident doctors who accompanied him immediately in a fierce spirit sprang into action. Not holding himself accountable for the delay, one resident doctor took out his examination kit and grabbed his flashlight to check the patient's eyes. As he continued with him, he checked all his injury sites: the spine, abdomen and chest. It was clear the situation was critical. She wandered off to a corner when Ajay vomited a mouthful of blood with food particles splattering all over the floor. She noticed this with a pang. The sight put her into consternation.

Before one could scrounge the trolley to shift another patient, Dr Gagandeep asked his resident doctors to get a head CT scan urgently. There was a wafting smell of chemicals as the floor was cleaned. Honey felt queasy, though the reaction on his face was silent. He was recovering from the jolt of the revelation that his friend might have to undergo a brain surgery where every need had to be fulfilled quickly in a situation like this.

Dr Gagandeep stared at Palo and said that the patient needed to be cared for urgently with urgency in his voice. "To me, it appears he has internal injuries in his brain," said Dr Gagandeep.

Ajay's life was in the hands of neurosurgeons. There was little time left, and any delay could be fatal for him. The team sprang into action, doing their best to stabilize him on a trolley before embarking on the immediate surgery.

They arrived at the glass passageway, where the glass door slid open automatically upon their arrival. The guard allowed Palo after a familiar nod, and he asked Honey to stay back before he crossed the red line. He cautioned Honey not to enter the radiation zone. Two men wearing lead aprons pulled the trolley and hurriedly took Ajay into another room. The room was big, and at its centre was a sophisticated giant, loop-like scanning machine, a wonder of science that could scrutinize every millimetre of the body in minutes to tell you what is wrong inside. The men in lead aprons carefully shifted him onto another trolley attached to the machine and fastened his body and head with the belts after adjusting his head on a headrest. Upon completing the positioning, one of them flashed his thumb.

Pallavi stood near the console inside the console room, where the radiologists viewed Ajay through a distant glass window. With a press of a button, the upper half of his body was pulled inside the machine, activating it to run while slowly retracting him back to his original position. The men in lead aprons helped him onto the trolley after the radiologist gave instructions through a loudspeaker in the CT scan room.

The radiologists continued to discuss the issue among themselves, analyzing the black-and-white images of his brain and spine and pointing out the location and extent of the lesion. They collaboratively drafted the report, eventually reaching a unanimous agreement. They concluded that Ajay had an extradural hematoma compressing his brain and he would require surgery, and only then did they inform Pallavi about the findings. The lady doctor, with a ponytail, who had drafted the report, handed it to Pallavi with a recognizing smile and said, "Take this report, Pallavi. I will inform Dr Gagandeep over the phone about the findings. And send the films directly to his chamber ."

The guard quickly turned around and stood at the passageway, holding the sliding door open for a swift transfer to the operating theatre.

Palo asked Honey to inform Ajay's parents to sign the consent paper. Honey knew it well and thought, "What would be the state of his father, who is yet to come out of the trauma of his daughter's death? It would be better if he could call his father Romy to inform Ajay's mother."

It was 6:30 PM, and Ajay was wheeled in for brain surgery. Avinash and Aradhana (Ajay's parents) decided to stay in the small enclosure, a cubbyhole, where the relatives are counselled and asked to remain there until the surgery ends. It was a different area, adjacent to the waiting area of the ICU cum operation theatre, as the guard requested them to stay there to sign the consent papers for surgery. They saw their son's head being shaven in the pre-op area before he was taken into the operation theatre. They would have sprung through the door to meet their son if the guard had not stopped them. The distance was not much; their son was lying on a trolley just a few yards away.

While Ajay underwent brain surgery, Honey and Palo walked to the dressing room. As the corridor was congested with trolleys and patient relatives, Pallavi guided him to walk in an alternative corridor. Honey sauntered across the hallway.

Payal walked to them and said, "Pallavi didi, the dressing station is clean and ready now. You can bring him in."

Pallavi gloved her hands while Payal removed the sterile instruments from the tray and a few sterile gauze pieces from a sterile drum. She poured a little antiseptic solution into a bowl inside the dressing kit.

Honey found the atmosphere quite nauseating, causing him to even forget about wanting a glass of water. He disliked the smell of the chemicals being smeared on his body. When Pallavi swabbed the brow wound with an antiseptic solution, one could have reacted strongly, hissing and squirming, but Honey stifled a scream by turning his head away for a while.

The guard treats and greets the relatives in the waiting lobby of the ICU like guests in his private office. The guard had been doing that job for ages. By making a bold choice, bolder than others, he was there for his duties, which may not be good for many persons who must always deal with only stressful people in that deadly silent hall, what they call a waiting room.

Even people who lived in luxury were found sitting on the bench and spending nights. The lucky ones were those who had been allocated the areas where the recliners were placed.

He had known Pallavi since she was a child. Like a record keeper, he knew many people by their names. There was a sincere regret on his face as the lobby was packed. The row of recliners to accommodate the relatives of patients was also occupied. He printed their names on a big register on a centre table and handed over a key to a locker to keep their belongings. He provided them with a corner place where they could lay the thin cotton mattress on a bench and take some rest if they intended to. He looked at Honey intently, at his blood-stained torn clothes, and empathized with him. Honey settled on one of the benches placed along the corridors. Palo arranged for him to wear a working dress from the resident doctors in the ICU. "Go clean up in the bathroom," She said.

Pallavi left him there to get him some food. She brought a few pieces of sandwiches and a water bottle with the money she had in her bag. When she returned with the provisions, she noticed Honey's absence in that place and in the lobby. Honey had gone to change his shirt and trousers. Pallavi glared at him sternly when he emerged in that new attire. Honey looked like a perfect gentleman. Pallavi thought if a grievous injury had not struck his friend, she could have seen Honey in a joyful state.

Honey was surprised by Pallavi's remarkable energy. Even seasoned players like him felt exhausted at the end of the day. She was supposed to be sleeping in her bed that night, but instead, she was prepared to spend the whole night sitting on a bench, just as he was doing.

Pallavi pulled out her handkerchief and dabbed his face to clean the sweat beads of anger. "You know, Honey, your anger has drained all your energy." The anger still lingered, and Pallavi tried to put off his worry by asking questions about his parents and friends, but all his answers were yes or no. There was no monologue, not even once.

All the others in the lobby were getting ready to sleep. Pallavi thought they should eat something. After giving him the packet of sandwiches, she kept waiting for Honey to open it, but he didn't. "Now, come on, throw your anger into the basket, Honey. You need some food." She knew he was unable to endure his friend's battle for life.

"I am neither angry nor hungry. You pray for my friend. There is too much noise in my mind. I have known Ajay for years, since my childhood. We were classmates, playmates. We trekked mountains together. He is battling for life. How can I -" He stopped. An emotion filled his heart.

The tannoy had announced twice, with soft instrumental music in between, but no announcement had been made for them.

As Honey sat in the dimly lit hospital waiting hall, his gaze drifted to the silent doorways and corridors. He was still unsettled with the surroundings. He couldn't help but wonder about Pallavi's presence and her well-being. The clinical setting was far from the world he was accustomed to. He thought, "As a player, he had stayed outdoors many times, but what about Pallavi? Her parents must be worried about her."

Meanwhile, Pallavi hesitated to interrupt the recovery room, her analytical mind grasping the gravity of the situation unfolding within. An invisible force directed her to get inside the recovery room for an update, but she resisted. Like telepathy, the announcement came right at that moment. Dr Gagandeep wanted to meet Pallavi and Ajay's parents.

In the first instance, Honey turned to Pallavi, his eyes pleading with her to speak to the doctor. Pallavi perceptively understood Honey's unspoken request. He was not in a state to handle any bad news that might arise from the briefing. Her observational skills allowed her to read him like an open book. How terrified he was.

Pallavi witnessed that moment and observed how Dr. Gagandeep handled it, something she had never seen before. A passionate professional has the skill, knowledge, and ability to handle such situations.

Pallavi said, "Dr Gagandeep said the operation was successful, and Ajay has been shifted to the Intensive Care Unit after the surgery." Her words were like a soothing balm on Honey's anxious soul.

He loved Pallavi for comforting him with her words. The anxiety knot in his chest of losing a friend had loosened. Half the lights in that hall had been turned off. They sat in silence for some time. It was an hour past midnight. If that moment could have been captured appropriately, the nascent love between them was blossoming. Honey realized that Pallavi had also skipped her supper, so he opened the packet of sandwiches, and they ate together.

While eating, Honey asked," Your parents must be worried about you. "

Pallavi said, "Don't worry about me. This hospital is like a second home to me. I have taken permission from my mama, and she said yes."

"Second home? This hospital? It is a horrible place. I feel uncomfortable coming here." Honey expressed his discomfort.

"Stay with me for a while, and you will start liking this place. I come here on Sundays and spend almost half a day."

"To this hospital on Sundays? You should rest your body and mind on the weekends instead of coming to this hopeless place, Pallavi."

"I do not agree. My soul drives all my actions. When the demand comes from my soul, my mind and body ought to act.

You appear to be a perfect doctor in this attire, Honey," she said with a smile.

"Not everyone's calling is to become a doctor. Mere observation and patient interaction will not make me a doctor, either. One should have enough knowledge about the diseases to treat them. I have heard you must clear many exams to get a degree. I am afraid I am not that type who possesses such qualities." Honey said.

Pallavi replied affirmatively, "My uncle, Dr Pradeep, once told me that doctors learn medicine by observing patients. That is exactly what I do here at the weekends. Sometimes, I visit alone and other times with the members of a social welfare team."

"Stupid, you are being naive. Merely observing is not enough, as I said earlier. One must also learn how to treat them," Honey retorted.

"Honey, what is more important here is how one perceives it as a human being." After a pause, she continued, "I try to uplift those who have lost their hopes of living. Some of them are battling cancer, and a few have lost their limbs to accidents. There are victims of acid attacks and many more who are in distress."

Honey was left speechless. There was a complete silence in the hall. The music playing in the background had ceased. Carrying their respective thoughts in their mind, they sat on the bench with their eyes closed. Honey's head had slumped onto her shoulder, and she sat there motionless, not disturbing him till the next morning. That is how Pallavi spent her weekend, and now Sunday had arrived.

*****

A distraught mother, her voice trembling with emotion, shared her story, expressing her faith in Lord Shiva, "Beti, my father was a priest in a Shiva temple in Kashmir. All his life, he devoted himself to the worship of Lord Shiva. He foresaw a life of abundance and success for my Ajay. His predictions have never been wrong. He named him Ajay, symbolizing his invincibility in the battle of life."

"I know, Aunty. Your son is a true warrior, a fighter to the core. The times may be tough, but he will emerge victorious." Pallavi reassured her.

"My faith in Lord Shiva says that he will protect my son from all the evil powers. He cannot be so cruel to me again. I lost my daughter five years ago, and he cannot snatch away my other child."

"Nothing will happen to your Son, Aunty. Maybe the almighty is testing our faith in him," Pallavi said, trying to comfort Aradhana.

"If this is a test, I will walk to the door of Kailash, barefooted, to beg him for my son's life. I will pass any test to save my child. He cannot ignore my distress like this. I will compel him to open his third eye to destroy the evil forces around my son." Thick tears welled in her eyes, rolling down her cheeks and dropping to the ground, a testament to her anguish. Aradhana sobbed.

Pallavi saw that the mother's cry for her child was so intense and penetrating to her core. She felt equally heavy-hearted and stood by her to counsel. Pallavi stood by wordless as the mother's words echoed repeatedly in her mind, settling on her nerves like a heavy load of emotions. It took a few minutes for her to start a counselling talk. She thought that Lord Shiva could not be so cruel again to her.

Pallavi softly said, "Aunty, I spoke to Dr Gagandeep this morning. Ajay is breathing on his own, a good sign. Soon, he will regain consciousness. He is hopeful that within a week, the swelling in his brain will subside, and he may no longer need ventilator support. You will see him walking before us again."

Aradhana wiped her tears, and a small smile graced her face. Her eyes were still glistening and damp.

After a moment of contemplative silence, Pallavi suggested, "Aunty, I know about an old Shiv temple nearby, just a short walk away. I feel we should visit there. I believe our prayer to the deity will never go unheard." Ten minutes later, they stood before the temple, their bare feet absorbing the sanctity of the ground.

The air around the temple streamed the scent of incense sticks and flowers. Aradhana reverently prepared an offering, a basket filled with coconut, bel leaves, bananas and diyas. She bought them from the nearest stalls and placed them in a wicker basket before entering the temple. Pallavi accompanied her.

As they walked towards the main entrance, they were seized by a hungry cow. Pallavi panicked at the size of the cow and her long-pointed horns. Pallavi stepped back and dragged Aradhana by her arm a little behind to keep her away from the cow. Aradhana, unfazed, went close to the cow, soothed it with a palm, and then muttered to herself, "I am certain you must be feeling starving." She offered the cow the bananas, which it happily munched on. It was a pleasure for Pallavi to watch as the cow was being fed. Pallavi also had an urge to soothe the back. She hesitated for a moment before doing it. Her hand moved over the hump and then the forehead. The cow felt extremely comfortable and gave Pallavi a lingering look while munching. Its hunger was sated, and there was contentment in the hiss of the breath when the cow departed.

Aradhana's eyes were drawn to the serene sight of a saint under the tree, his palms raised in the gesture of blessing. His words, spoken in a divine tone, echoed around her, "Kalyan ho beti Tera, may your son be blessed with a new life. May Lord Shiva bless you. You fed a hungry pregnant cow." With the blink of an eye, the saint disappeared into the trees. She hallucinated about a flowing river in the background until the saint was there.

Aradhana turned to Pallavi, her voice tinged with wonder, "Did you see the saint? Did you hear him?"

Pallavi replied, "No, which saint Aunty? Where is he?"

"One near the tree," Aradhana said.

"No, Aunty, there is no one here except you and me. You must be hallucinating. Let's go inside the temple. It happens when we are distressed and think about something repeatedly." Pallavi's response was one of concern.

Aradhana's gaze drifted towards the tree as she recalled the saint's words. "I saw Ma Ganga flowing in his background; he resembled my father."

Pallavi said, "It must be a nearby river ashore which you have visited recently or any other river you saw on TV. You must be thinking about your father too much, which is why you see him everywhere."

Aradhana's eye shone with a conviction that defied Pallavi's scepticism."Whether you believe me or not, he also said that my granddaughter, Parvati, would one day return to me. My father always used to say that my granddaughter has a shade of Goddess Parvati. *Our Paro is the daughter of the sacred land,* *"Dev Bhoomi"*. Aradhana's voice grew wistful as she recalled the moment of connection with Lord Shiva. "I was in Rishikesh when Paro was born. As I dipped myself in the water, I felt my closeness with Lord Shiva. The connection was eternal. I sat by the bank of the river Ganga for a while, filled with confusion. I couldn't think of what Lord Shiva whispered in my ears. He said my granddaughter Paro is a human form of Parvati, and her genesis from Adishakti is for a big cause. She is a blessing to humanity. When I told my husband, he didn't acknowledge it."

A moment of silence fell upon them as Aradhana's voice trailed off, her emotions reminiscing about her past.

Pallavi listened intently, and she pondered the vast difference between their worlds. But she tried to find some similarities. Yet, she found a glimmer of understanding, "Many a time, I experience hallucinations where I hear my father speaking to me from the stars, but in real life, he is not. He died a long time ago. Still, my mother thinks he is alive, and he will come back."

Aradhana acknowledged Pallavi's perspective with a nod, "Beti, you are right. I am sorry. I overthink these days. Maybe it is my hallucination." They reached the temple and worshipped the deity of Lord Shiva, the air filled with the fragrance of incense and soft chanting of prayers.

As they descended the temple steps, Aradhana turned to Pallavi, her eyes glistening with unshed tears. "I prayed to Lord Shiva that everyone in this world should be blessed with a daughter like you. Your mother must have done some holy work to have a daughter like you. How happy she must be to have you as a daughter?" Her voice trembled with emotions. She continued, "It is very rare to find someone like you these days praying for others, Pallavi."

Pallavi's heart swelled with affection, "Auntie, you are like my mother, and Ajay is like my brother. I prayed for a speedy recovery, and I am sure Ajay Bhaiya will soon be standing on his feet and running to play basketball."

Ajay's father suddenly arose from his restless slumber, disturbed. It was as if he saw something unpleasant in his dream. How can a father sleep when his only son is admitted to the hospital, fighting for his life? Abhinash's gaze drifted across the hall, observing the other anxious families waiting for the news about their loved ones.

Beside him, Aradhana stirred on the recliner. Her own sleep was fragile and fitful. As her eyes fluttered open, she noticed Avinash sitting upright. His expression was tense and troubled. She understood the pain of the father, who hides his tears behind his eyes so as not to express the inner turbulence and grief to others. But as a wife, she knew his feelings through his eyes. She asked him to sleep for a while to feel refreshed in the morning. It was the fifth night after five days had passed without any obvious sign of progress in Ajay's health.

Avinash's voice was heavy, and he felt a sense of dread as he confided in Aradhana, "Probably the moment we are going through is a part of some divine retribution of my past sin. That is why such things happen in our lives. I still remember Briksha's murder case, where a mother cradling her baby had cursed him after the judge had handed down the jail sentence to her husband. She blamed me for the proceedings that I made against her innocent husband, "Avinash murmured, the woman's words still haunting him.

"Yes, you had told me," Aradhana acknowledged, her heart aching for her husband's burden.

A noisy disturbance in the ICU, a cacophony that nearly drowned out the steady beeps of the machines. The pain that gripped his head was a vivid memory, a remnant of the accident where he pillioned without a helmet. They were on a bike. The assailants, carrying hockey sticks, emerged from the nearby shops, giving him and his companion no chance to prepare for retaliation. One of them came running, the hockey stick firmly grasped and struck him forcefully in the back. Instinctively, he turned to his side and pushed the attacker with the same hockey stick. Another crazy person tried to pull him off the bike, but he elbowed him before the man could rip his shirt. The most terrifying image, however, was of the person who had aimed to bludgeon him to death. Ajay imagined himself dead. He imagined the impact, feeling the weight of his chest smashing against the pavement as he fell face-first. At that moment, he had been certain that he wouldn't survive. It is strange that he can hear people talking around. He tried to recognize every voice. He began imagining their every action.

A figure approached and placed a tray on the side table. He was aware of the warning bell, a horrible experience that would follow when he heard this sound, which would start after she called a few fellows to help her.

Ajay felt a hand resting on his head, the familiar touch of a closer acquaintance. She caressed his forehead and let out the soothing words, "Again, fever. No worries, boy. I will have you talk to me someday. Now, we are going to give you a sponge bath."

They took out everything. It was too cold. Someone standing far away ordered them bluntly to move to the next patient urgently as he had seizures. Everybody left except the one who was adamant about dressing him up before changing his bed sheet. She threw her arms around him, her head bowed while trying to prop him up. Supporting his back with one arm, she slithered a bed sheet under him with the other. Placing his back gently on the bed, she swiftly went to the other side to pull it before laying it all over the bed. He began to feel the pain when his girdle was turned to one side. He felt his eyes flicker with the pang. Out of the corners of his eyes, he tried to catch a glimpse of the nurse. His face caught the light, and he could see nothing except some blurred features of her face.

All such activities by his side made him draw the assumption that he was fighting his life's inevitable battle. His ability and capability have been vanquished. No longer could he stand by his name, Ajay. He should be thankful for the goodness of the nurse who is still taking interest in his diet and exercises, discussing when to give big meals and calories at the bedside to get a few words out of him.

He wanted to run, but he could not. He felt his legs were no longer under his command, as if they did not exist. The vibrating touch of the physiotherapist's machine made him feel as though they existed in union with his body. His hands moved a little when the stiffness was broken through exercises. The limbs he once felt were nonexistent seemed to exist, and his fingers started moving with his wishes.

The sight of this drew the doctors to the bedside. They saw his eyes open widely before they shut again. They observed his respiration restored spontaneously, and he could protrude his tongue when asked. A wave of happiness spread across the hall, and Aradhana was called in to interact with him first. He was able to write with his hands and express his inner desires through writing on a clip paperboard. The strength in his hands was adequate to grip someone's hand, and on the same day, he was taken off the ventilator.

On the eighth day, he regained the ability to swallow liquids and gradually began being fed through his mouth. He was now able to talk. The physiotherapists provided unwavering support, helping him stand and walk. A week later, he could stand and walk with assistance. The recovery up to this point was remarkably fast, instilling hope in everyone that he would make a complete recovery.

*****

As Ajay was permitted to take an evening stroll on the lawn, he was astounded to spot Ballu sitting on a concrete patio bench, far away from him. Ajay shivered with fury, his face turning crimson until he was assuaged and managed to smother a yell when he saw Pallavi waving at him from a distance. As she walked across the lawn, there was an abrupt discordance in Ajay's emotions. The anguish dissipated like smoke when the coolness of her cheerful, friendly allusion clashed with his intense, red-hot temper, akin to someone pouring water onto a hot pan. He tried to recall a faint memory of her smile from her college days.

Pallavi asked, "How are you doing?" Ajay did a double-take before responding. His sight was unsteady, as she noticed. His eyes glanced towards Ballu, the one responsible for this upheaval in his life. She laid a hand on his shoulder and said, "Yes, he is Ballu. He is also admitted to this hospital."

"Why is he here?" he asked, his voice laced with suspicion.

"He is undergoing treatment for injuries in his cojones. He underwent surgery for that. Doctors drained half a litre of pus from there. The clot there had gotten infected. Now he repents." Ajay retorted, "He should repent from now on for what he did to us."

"I'm sorry! What do you mean by 'from now on'? You sound unforgiving and rude." Her hand slipped from his shoulder, her disappointment evident.

Ajay met her gaze, his voice resolute. "I mean it, Pallavi. I am not rude, but I must tell you he deserved this long ago."

Pallavi's brow furrowed with concern ."After all these lethal assaults, you still have such unsparing and revengeful intentions for him. You both have suffered enough in this life; now you should let it go finally."

Exasperated, Ajay said, "You can't be oblivious to his deeds, Pallavi. Honey and I both love sports. We aspire to become police officers. We never imagined this."

Pallavi sat beside him, turning to face him, saying, "Police officers! That is good news?" Pallavi could sense the unease on his face. "If he apologizes, will you forgive him?"

"Apology! He is the same Ballu who fed us sweets before a final match, and we ended up in the hospital. Mark my words: He will never change." Ajay retorted, his voice laced with distrust.

"Is his guilt unpardonable?" Pallavi asked, her eyes pleading.

"Guilt! You are trying to reconcile between us, but he is not trustworthy. He is like a crocodile who sheds tears but never repents for the hunt he makes." Ajay spat, his words dripping with venom.

Pallavi sighed, "His father rebuked him. He had tears when he learned that his son would have to live with one testicle. He has understood the loss he has caused himself."

"He asked for it, Pallavi." Ajay declared, his jaw set in determination.

Pallavi advised, "On both sides, the injuries are grievous, and a police enquiry has been launched. It would be better if you both patch up this matter and bury your hatchets forever."

*****

Honey chimed triumphantly, recounting how he pummelled Ballu. The excitement in his mind brought vivacity to his actions."Ajay, I gave Ballu a good number of solid punches and kicks to his midsection that day. He will remember that day as his worst forever."

Ajay smirked and said, "Mid-section? You didn't even spare his private section. His father is in a great dilemma if he will ever become a grandfather in his life."

"He deserved that," Honey said.

"That snooty-faced cringed and sought an apology, Honey." Ajay rejoiced.

"I believe he is conscious of his guilt," Honey said.

"Conscious of his guilt! You should have seen his face. You not only changed the course of the ball but also smashed it hard," Ajay smirked.

Ajay was getting better and eager to get discharged any day now after getting a final nod from Dr Gagandeep.

It was fifteen minutes past five on the clock when Pallavi reached the hospital to see Ajay. She saw Honey by his bedside, sitting on a chair and helping him with physiotherapy as instructed.

Pallavi asked Ajay about his health and said, "Natasha didi would meet the patients in the orthopaedic and rehabilitation block tomorrow. She may come here to meet you."

"Who is she?" Ajay asked.

"She is the daughter of our sports minister, Chunnilal."

Honey looked at Ajay excitedly and turned towards Pallavi, asking whether he could accompany her during the visit.

She mocked, "You stone-age man, look into the mirror; you look like a *junglee*."

Pallavi was aware of his grown-up beard and beefy biceps, enough to scare any patient in the hospital. Honey touched his beard, noticing it was well-grown, and looked at his nails, which had also grown.

"Okay, guys, I am going to call Dr Gagandeep for the rounds. He might have come out of the operation theatre by now," she announced as she headed towards the corridor.

Ajay's mind was sceptical, "There is no point in approaching the daughter of the sports minister. I am not going to participate in the selection match in January."

"Don't be stupid. We can ask the minister to postpone it for a month or two," Honey suggested.

"Still, it is not going to change my recovery, buddy. I will not be able to run like before. Now I can hardly lift my legs, and I don't know how long I'll need these crutches," Ajay's voice laced with doubts.

"Don't be a dismissive child, stupid. The doctor hopes you will recover completely if you take regular physiotherapy," Honey reassured him.

"All doctors are like that," Ajay grumbled.

"Can you recall the endurance test where we qualified? Our legs were trembling despite having gastroenteritis, but we still ran five kilometres," Honey reminded him, his eyes gleaming with the recollection.

"Yes, I remember," Ajay's memory resurfaced with a gentle nod.

"Then you must not have forgotten what you said before the race," Honey prompted.

"Yes, I had said, *'Jo hoga, dekha jayega. My goal is basketball.'* We should not have taken those sweets from Ballu," Ajay admitted, his voice tinged with regret.

"That scoundrel didn't even change a fraction of himself after the heavy bashing," Honey exclaimed.

"But this time, Honey, he repented seriously, his face looking at my feet," Ajay said.

"That's his crocodile tear. He must have feared these crutches. You cleverly changed the topic! Why can't you make it by January? Still, five full months remained in between," Honey asked.

"If I can run like before in four months, then a month will remain in hand for practice, which is not enough. I will try next time," Ajay reasoned.

Honey's voice rose with exasperation."Next time... next time. Your cassette player has stuck at next time. Yaar, why can't it be this time? I will ask the minister's daughter if she can aid in postponing the match by one month."

Just then, Dr Gagandeep and his brilliant team entered the ward, and their footsteps drew Ajay's and Honey's attention. The team comprised specialists, residents, specialized nurses, and physiotherapists. He came and stood at the leg end of the bed, slipping both his hands into the apron pockets and his gaze scrutinizing Ajay's face. As his residents examined Ajay's limbs, Dr Gagandeep reviewed the progress notes and diet charts, his brow furrowing with concern. One of his residents gripped

Ajay's limbs one at a time and asked him to apply counterforce to the force he used to stretch and flex all four limbs. The other one noted the findings in the file. The power was normal in the upper limbs and four out of five on the power scale in the lower limbs. He needed some support while walking.

Dr Gagandeep lifted the spectacles from his neck with a band that reached his chest, then placed them over his nose as he glanced through the daily notes. He murmured the critical observations from the record. His eyes settled on the calorie chart. He said that the calories Ajay consumed daily had not been adequate for his weight, and he needed nutritional supplements in addition to his regular diet for a speedy recovery. Ajay revealed his discomfort with a bloated abdomen, justifying his poor intake.

"It happened because you are not going out for a stroll. Your activity record is also not up to the mark," Dr. Gagandeep said with great concern while taking off his spectacles.

Palo said, "Uncle, I insist you give him a big enema now; he will be alright."

Ajay quickly reared up on the bed, his eyes widening in alarm, "Doctor, the former option is better. I do not want any enema. I will increase my walk, but no enema, please."

Saying, "Better you should move your bowels," Dr. Gagandeep left the ward.

*****

Diya felt mushy, killing every romantic thought that arose inside her heart for Honey. She wondered if she could ever express her feelings to him. Will Honey accept her proposal? Can she impress him with her handful of modelling assignments? What will his reaction be? Will he be really impressed by her achievements? Pallavi has nothing to boast about herself, while Diya has her posters shining in every corner of the city. Will he react cheerfully, hug her tightly, and forget about Pallavi? Can she successfully trick him into going crazy about her?

All her hopes of seeing and mingling with him were undoubtedly fading. Her longing for a romantic relationship with him was moving towards a new uncertainty. She was highly disappointed to know that the guy she wanted to make her boyfriend is now dating Pallavi. She presumed the beautiful girl in her wouldn't be able to express her feelings, but she couldn't stop herself from desperately wanting to be close to him. It wouldn't matter to her what Honey would think about her, but for a second, she thought, "With a feeling of love, can she talk to him like before? Can she look into his eyes without shame if he rejects her proposal?" Her confidence was shrinking. She ended up having an endless conversation with herself.

If luck favoured her, she would cross paths with Honey tomorrow. Otherwise, the doldrum would continue to perturb her for another twenty-four hours. These thoughts circled in her mind repeatedly. What would happen if Honey didn't respond to her telephone calls? She had difficulties obtaining his telephone number from the teacher who stayed on her street when the office clerks refused to give her the number. Diya's heart raced with anticipation and uncertainty, her emotions a whirlwind of hope and fear.

*****

Diya's voice rang out behind Honey, "Honey boy, Honey boy." Honey turned around and met with Diya's concerned gaze.

"What happened, Diya?" he asked.

"Honey boy, I called up your home once. Your father picked up the phone and said that you had gone to the hospital. Is everything okay, Honey boy? I miss you," Diya said, her words laced with a subtle plea.

Honey felt a pang of discomfort. He had never wanted Diya as his girlfriend, and her seemingly affectionate tone felt more like an invitation for a close relationship, an intimacy he was not prepared for.

"I had gone to the hospital to see Ajay," Honey replied, his voice guarded.

"Ajay! What happened to him?" Diya asked, her brow furrowing with worry.

"Ajay had a head injury a week ago. Now he is recovering well by God's grace," Honey explained.

Diya's gaze drifted to the stitches on Honey's own head. "Honey boy, you, too, have a few stitches on your head. How did it happen?"

"It happened in a fight," Honey said, his tone evasive.

"I thought it was a sort of sports injury. Honey boy, please take me along when you go next time to meet him," Diya requested, her eyes glimmering with hope.

Honey hesitated, "I don't have a bike to take you along, Diya. My bike is now off-road for another couple of days."

Diya's face lit up, "Don't worry, Honey boy. I can take you in my car."

Honey shook his head, "I am comfortable on my bike. See you tomorrow. I will arrange something."

Diya's emotions were a maelstrom of uncertainty. She watched Honey's retreating figure, wondering how Pallavi might have expressed her feelings to him. A part of her doubted Pallavi's courage, but another part of her insisted that Pallavi could surprise her. That motor mouth can say anything to anyone. It reminded her of the social worker who took a chance with her and what she did with her. The teacher had to intervene finally to stop her.

Diya's gaze swept the crowd, her pulse quickening as she spotted Pallavi exiting the college. Without hesitation, she rushed forward and pushed Pallavi from the side. "Have you gone crazy, Diya? What is this?" Pallavi exclaimed, her eyes wide with confusion.

"Yes, you are right. I am crazy. I am crazy about Honey. Stay away from him," Diya declared, her finger poking into Pallavi's chest.

Pallavi felt uncomfortable with the physical contact, particularly as the gathered onlookers started to surround them. "Honey is my good friend. That will not happen," she responded firmly.

Diya's eyes flashed with possessiveness, "Honey is my boyfriend, so do not eye on him. I won't allow you to eat the cream and leave behind the milk for me to drink. You gold digger."

Diya's words pierced through Pallavi's mind like shards of broken glass. The venom in her voice dripped with malice as she spewed her slanders. Pallavi felt trapped, cornered by Diya's relentless onslaught of accusations in public.

"Stop it, Diya. Are you in your senses?" Pallavi said, her voice laced with concern and disbelief.

Diya's eyes narrowed and fixed on Pallavi, and her gaze was predatory: "You have your eye on Vicky, Your chemistry lab partner. His father is a big fish. You can snare him, and he will give you what you want. You teach Vicky that HCHO means formaldehyde and H_2SO_4 means sulphuric acid. I don't care. Just leave Honey for me."

"What are you talking about, Diya? Are you in your senses?" Pallavi chimed.

"Yes, I am in my senses. The whole college knows how lecherous you are. You speak Vicky, Vicky inside the lab and Honey, Honey once you are outside."

"Stop plucking your theories out of the air, Diya. There is nothing like this between me and Vicky." Pallavi dismissed Diya's words, aiming at her with a twisted sense.

"You plebeians are just bumps in my road. Go out my way. Last time, I spilled formalin on your desk, and you don't know what I will spill this time?" Diya plonked her foot on Pallavi's foot.

Pallavi was astounded, " So it was you who spilled the Formalin on my desk ?"

"Yes, it was me. Complain to the principal. I have many modelling assignments. I am going to say ta-ta, bye-bye to this college." And she left the place.

*****

When a tall poppy emerges in the city, he sheds the inconspicuousness of his familiarity. The watchdogs of another realm set the rules for him. The keepers of this parallel world are a cluster of emotionless dead who dictate the deals, deeds, and directives. The guardians fight there with their best tools and tactics to survive within; the rule is survival of the fittest.

Peter, a tall, slim man dressed in a grey suit and hat with a briefcase in hand, entered the premises of Cheema's palatial house and joined Cheema on his lawn. He was in Mumbai to execute his master's order. He flew from Dubai as a messenger. The message was clear: Cheema can't be left alone to handle a vast business.

"I am so glad to catch you in the morning before I fly back," Peter sat on the chair across from Cheema. The newspaper was folded on the centre table, and Cheema was ready to serve tea to him. Peter seemed in a hurry; he started conversing immediately after a hot sip. "Good news for you, Cheema. Did you hear the morning news?"

"No, what is it?"

"The Narangs were raided last night. Congratulations to you," Peter said.

"That's really good news you brought me, Peter Bhai. We must celebrate." A triumphant gleam flickered in Cheema's eyes as if the downfall of a rival was a personal victory. His face lit up with a satisfactory grin.

"As you sow, so shall you reap. He dealt directly with the Afghans after snipping ties with Dubai for his profit," Peter continued.

"Don't tell me Sultan got him raided? It gives me shivers," Cheema's brow furrowed with concern.

"You need not worry; Sultan will not harm you as he knows I am chummed up with you in your business. I have a plan for your expansion." Peter's words quickly dispelled the unease in Cheema.

"Peter Bhai, I always keep my backyard clean. I can't produce brown sugar like you. Besides, I don't have a huge capital like you to invest in chemical factories." Cheema raised his concern.

"I will arrange it for you. It would be good for our kids. Make your son Vicky a pharma graduate. Jemima will pick up a seat in this course in the UK in the coming year." Peter laid out the vision for the future.

"Peter Bhai, when I see them together, I feel like they are made for each other." Cheema nodded for this alliance, and the air crackled with the weight of their ambitions.

"You come with Vicky once to my place, and I will walk you to Sultan Bhai. He will get investors for your film production," Peter said after the last sip. He looked at his diamond-studded watch and asked, "How is Sameer Malhotra doing?"

Cheema responded, "He is a sinking boat. I am trying to get my money out of his projects. No one likes the films of the '90s.

Poor chap, his wife was his financial advisor, and she passed away long ago. He lost his charm as an actor; even the old, experienced film stars refused to work on his projects. New actors and actresses, much fitter physically, are replacing the old ones every day. After giving three flops in a row, he is now bankrupt."

Peter exclaimed, "Bankrupt! That means you can get his properties in your name at any time, as per the agreement, right?"

Cheema replied, his hopes laced with calculation, "Yes, this is the right time to start getting his properties transferred to my name one by one. These artists always want freedom, so I am not interfering in his work. He has already had a heart attack, and I don't want to give him another one. He has a daughter the same age as my Vicky, whom he is going to launch in the industry."

Peter finished his tea and reached into his briefcase, pulling out a pack of cigarettes. He scattered them across the table, saying, "Here are your samples. Pick anyone and take a whiff."

Cheema leaned in, sniffed hard and replied, "Cigarettes." His nose twitched as he inhaled.

Deftly, Peter snapped one of the cigarettes in half, extracting the tobacco, "Stretch your hand, Cheema. Crush it." He instructed.

Cheema complied, the tobacco leaves crumbling on his palm. When he opened his hands, the earthy scent of brown sugar wafted up to his nostrils, and his eyes widened with understanding. "Brown sugars! Peter Bhai, how much is Sultan asking for this?"

Peter responded, "You pay nothing, but Sultan Bhai wants to make a deal with us."

Peter produced an electronic card and a floppy disk from his briefcase, presenting them to Cheema. "Here are the items for us to explore their utility."

Curious, Cheema asked, "What do we need to do with these?"

Peter's voice lowered to a conspiratorial whisper, "Coming straight to the point, Sultan Bhai wants to see the youth of this country drown in drugs. These cigarettes would attract them. The floppy contains the names of the distributors who agreed to buy this new product. We will get our money paid through a foreign bank. The card is to access our money. The maximum limit is fifty million dollars."

A swift smile appeared across Cheema's face. His greedy eyes gleamed as he stared at the e-card. "A very good offer, Peter Bhai. The deal is done. You are giving me all happy news today."

But then Peter interrupted, saying, "But there is a problem." His voice was laced with a caution.

Cheema's expression evaporated as his eyes fixed on Peter. "What is the problem?"

Peter replied, "The account has been dormant for twenty-five years."

Confusion clouded Cheema's features. His eyes narrowed, he asked, "If the account is dormant, how was the card issued to him? Something is wrong with this deal, Peter Bhai. Sultan is playing a game with us to swindle our money. He wants us to take the risk at free of charge. He won't wire any money into our account; instead, even asking him for a penny will push us into a Narang-like situation. I have a premonition."

Peter's voice held a note of resignation, "Declining Sultan's offer is like declining the breath into our lives."

Curious again, Cheema asked, "What is the problem in activating this account?"

Peter's expression darkened as he said, "Salim Sultan was arrested before he could activate this account. He had written the key number of this foreign bank account in a red diary. After his arrest, the police had sealed all his places, and he couldn't retrieve this diary through his men. He had fifty million dollars twenty years ago in that account."

Cheema said, "How would we search for this diary in all of Mumbai? Any other clue?"

"The red diary bears a picture of Falcon on its spine."

"Falcon !"

"Yes."

"He and Falcon are the same sort of creature. There is no difference between them." Cheema said. "Peter bhai, any other clues or information about his contacts?"

"I have absolutely no idea who all worked with him twenty-five years ago. He was a don and in relationships with many mistresses. I don't know how many have been fed to the crocodiles he kept inside his private pools." Peter said with a ting of desperation in his voice.

"Very dangerous man, rearing crocodiles? Any other way to reject his offer?"Cheema was surprised. There was a tone of uneasiness in his voice.

Peter said, "The deal is for five years. Rejection is like rejecting life."

Cheema contemplated, "Let's see how early we can find a way to use it for our benefit. That scoundrel is sitting in Dubai dictating the terms. We have known each other for so many years. Only you know how much risk I have taken to establish this business. I want to get into politics, and this dog is certainly going to put a dark mark on my spotless image. I don't want any upheavals in any form during my future political journey."

"Think about me, Cheema Bhai. I am in Dubai, and he is just sitting above my head. Like you, I don't even have a plan B to ask him to invest in film production." Peter said.

Cheema nodded, "You hit the nail right on the head, Peter Bhai. This is how we can get our commission paid. This deal suits us, Peter Bhai. If that dog doesn't give us money for five years but arranges financiers for us, then I have no problems. It's enough of a solution to satisfy both of us."

Peter's expression brightened, "That is why I want you and Vicky to meet him to discuss this issue. He wants to discuss this with both of you before me."

Cheema's brow furrowed, "Why is he dragging my son into this?"

"Cheema bhai, think about me. How am I supposed to live with a daughter? I've often considered shifting back to Mumbai, but he is asking for a power of attorney for my estate. That's why I've decided to send my daughter, Jemima, to the UK to complete her higher studies. After her marriage to Vicky, she will settle here in Mumbai peacefully." Peter's face dropped as if haunted by some unpleasant experience from the past.

Cheema said, "Okay, Peter bhai. Tell that dog we are coming there in May once Vicky's first-year exams are over."

Peter shook hands with Cheema and left for the airport to catch his flight to Dubai.

*****

Peter's House, Dubai, 2003

It was late at midnight when the quietness of the night was broken by a slump. Jemima opened her eyes and cringed in fear as she saw a figure looming at the window approaching her. Startled, she realized it was a real person calling her by name and not a part of any bad dream. Jemima pinched herself before she pulled the tassels of her bedside lamp.

Her friend Arshad, a five-foot-ten, wispy-bearded guy, appeared before her. He had climbed through one of the trees fringing her room window to reach Peter's house.

From his action, it seemed he had braced himself for all the harsh consequences of trespassing. When faced with a matter of life and death, individuals may often resort to such risky actions when they see no other viable solution. This was the case for Arshad. His life had recently taken a dramatic turn, leading him to make this perilous choice.

This had never happened to him before. In the past, Arshad would have walked through the main door. However, Peter's men had become very watchful these days. The friends were not allowed to meet Jemima like before. Peter knew Arshad was poor, but he had sensed a threat to his daughter ever since he knew Arshad as the Sultan's man and a so-called nephew. Peter seemed happy that Jemima had understood his warnings about forging any romantic relationship with Arshad.

For Arshad, it was not an easy affair. He had cried dry when Peter warned him and closed the iron gates after encountering special security guards. He couldn't handle it anymore when he intuited something wrong with Jemima. He was asked to make a lot of money, which seemed impossible to earn in a year. He was at a loss for words. He was not resilient enough to handle this burden. A feeling of despair closed in, and he took the chance of risking his life like this.

He and Jemima had become mature enough to understand what was good and bad for them. They had completed their junior college, and in a few years, they would be graduates and stand on their own feet. His father had no right to decide whom Jemima would meet and who she would not.

Jemima sat on the bed with her eyes wide open. Arshad was standing at the foot of her bed, and before she could shout a single word, he swiftly came to her side and put his palm on her mouth to hush her.

In a low voice, he asked, "How could you do this to me?" He removed his hand from her mouth and sat at the foot of the bed, looking into her eyes. When Jemima didn't reply, he asked, "So, should I consider your father's words as your own?"

Jemima responded, "It's all over now, Arshad. Forget about me. You will find many girls better than me. Your uncle will decide whom you are going to marry. Certainly, it won't be me. Don't take this relationship too seriously. It's better for me and my family."

"No, you can't separate yourself from me. I don't care about what Uncle Sultan decides for me. He is stepping down. Javed, my cousin in Pakistan, has completed his training, and he is going to take over his company any day now. I don't see any threat to your family after that."

"You, too, must go for your training, as your uncle says?"

"Yes, I will return soon and ask for your hand in marriage."

"I hope you make a comeback like your so-called brother Javed. That would take a long time. Until then, I must go to the UK for my higher studies as I have promised my father that I would fulfil his dreams. You will always remain a great friend to me. I cannot live without my father. I cannot hurt my father's feelings anymore."

Arshad frowned, and his eyes turned red. "What do you mean by just great friends, nothing more than that? Was our relationship not serious so far? Was it a one-sided affair? No, it's a big no. How can you suddenly declare that it is finished? Are you the same Jemima who promised a lifelong companionship?"

Jemima said, "I don't know what will happen tomorrow, but I am leaving for graduation. I will be in touch with you. If I don't reply to your letters, promise me you won't question why."

Arshad pulled her closer and asked, "Do those words have the approval of your heart? Can you repeat it while looking into my eyes? What about my life?" He had a piercing look in his eyes, and his brows wriggled. "Before you leave, promise to marry me once you finish your studies. I will wait for you."

"Now you go, Arshad. If my father's men see you here with me, they will kill you."

Arshad said, "I would prefer to embrace death by your men over suicide. Your separation will kill me every moment and every now and then as long as I live. I can't tolerate the pain."

Jemima said, "Your Chacha will never approve of our relationship. He has higher plans for you."

"Higher plans! I am a techie; I understand electronic gadgets. I am too much of a bubblehead to understand his business. Not as sharp as Javed, I am a techie. What plans could he have for me? If I must pick up a battle for you, I will. I will not allow anyone to come between you and me."

Jemima said, "Don't be a fool, Arshad. You must stand on your feet first to pick up a battle to claim me. You need to complete your engineering, and then we can talk about us. You may leave now."

Arshad put forth the last stance of a patient lover, "I will wait for you until you come back into my life." The atmosphere was quiet after that. His nerves wept. It made him feel so lonely. He didn't hear her say, "Yes, I will return." At least a few last words she could have spoken to assuage her guilt of dumping him this way; not even a word of assurance came out of her until he turned around and headed towards the window.

*****

Mumbai, 2004

The attachment they felt for each other strengthened, creating a sense of security and belonging. As their love deepened, the attachment they shared grew stronger, cementing their commitment to one another.

They were not seen together in college until their final exams except for linking fingers on a few occasions. The ache was present in both, and the passion was evident in their silence.

The abbreviated exchange of passionate glances between them was visible whenever they encountered each other on the college campus. An enchanting spell descended upon them, captivating their hearts and minds. Pallavi had driven him crazy, and although Honey was unable to express his love verbally, her intelligent mind had almost deciphered his feelings. The adoration for him flourished, blossoming into a profound and unwavering love.

A tidal wave of exhilarating emotion swept across the country's aspiring youth and their parents ever since the much-awaited announcement of All India Medical Entrance Test dates was published in the newspaper.

Pallavi picked up a pen and circled the date on her calendar. Then, she set a desk planner where she crafted a study schedule and carefully allocated time slots for all nonessential tasks. She was grateful for the guidance of senior students who advised her to immerse herself deeply in her studies from the beginning of the academic term. Based on their recommendations, she had bought three weighty, fat volumes in Physics, Chemistry, and Biology. She found them fruitful, albeit time-consuming, in the beginning.

Nevertheless, it ignited her curiosity and sharpened her focus with each challenging question she faced. It fostered a problem-solving mindset, prompting her not to proceed to the next question until the current one was satisfactorily resolved. Pallavi avoided wasting time on trivial activities. She tried not to step outside her house, and inside the house, she declined to visit the drawing room to greet any visitors.

Adhering to daily study objectives, she found her desk planner to be a valuable instrument and catalyst for bolstering her motivation. It facilitated effective time tracking, allowing for productive evaluations of her study sessions. The mental challenges of conquering those three thick, voluminous guides, alongside her regular course materials, simmered with time.

She prepared for the exam with unwavering dedication, adopting the mindset as if it were the eve of the actual test, and she was able to tick off her to-do list daily while setting bigger targets for the days to come. She transformed herself into a more disciplined and accomplished version of herself day by day.

Shivdasnis' House, Mumbai, 31 Dec 2004.

The sorrow in the family had withered away over the years. The Shivdasni family had opened their doors to innumerable guests to celebrate the new year, promising them happiness. Coincidentally, it was Honey's eighteenth birthday.

Pallavi knew why she was invited to the Shivdasni's house for the New Year's party. The gatekeepers warmly nodded as Pallavi entered through the main gate. Diya's devious mind figured out how Pallavi had arrived when she saw an autorickshaw leave the entrance and park beside her car.

"Just arrived, the throwback. Bloody intruder," Diya muttered, one hand on her hip, the other clutching a small bag. She cocked her head and blew at her wispy fringes. She had never imagined Pallavi would be at the Shivdasni's house, and seeing her at the gate ruffled her feathers.

Pallavi was dressed elegantly in a traditional crimson salwar, while Diya wore a resplendent plunging neckline that showcased a diamond piece in the middle of her chest, sparkling brilliantly under the bright luminescence emanating from a chandelier on the porch.

Diya walked up to Pallavi before she stepped onto the porch and said, "Go back." She pointed her finger at the gate and continued, "Look at those Rolls-Royces, Mercedes, and then look at your rickshaw. It's standing weakly beside my car. Go back if you have some respect for the Shivdasnis. "

" What's wrong with you, Diya?"

"Are you sure Honey's father knows about your social status?"

Pallavi replied calmly. "I have no idea. I am here to celebrate Honey's birthday."

"He is classy, wealthy. You are far from his world," Diya sneered.

"I can smell your heart burning, Diya."

"Look at your dress. Too much daydreaming," Diya retorted.

A smile appeared on Pallavi's face, her lips curling at the angle." Do you think this exquisite piece on your chest, which you consider an exciting treasure for your wealthy life, makes you someone extra special at this party? No, that's your bad luck. The Shivdasnis consider me special, and I am here at their invitation."

A shiver ran through Diya's spine. "Special? Stay within your limits, you street girl. Forget about Honey; even your types don't consider you armful."

"Yes, special. Honey is my special friend, and you are an interloper. Cutie, don't dream of being a part of something you're not," Pallavi declared. She presumed this would be a fitting response to keep Diya away.

Tapasee and her twin sister Shreyashi were also present at the party. There was not even a mite of difference in their physical appearances or their hairstyles. Their bob-shaped bouffant had curled similarly, making them look like photocopies of each other. The brigadier's daughters looked vivacious and well-mannered, having arrived in Mumbai specifically for the occasion.

Pallavi was pleased to receive a warm welcome at the doorstep. Shreyashi greeted and ushered her into another large hall next to the living room.

In the eyes of the people at the party, Pallavi was a head-turner, while Diya looked engagingly beautiful, with her face exuding a glow from perfectly layered cosmetics.

Romy's intelligent eyes searched the crowd for Pallavi ever since he discovered the handkerchief and a newspaper cut out of Pallavi as the topper of the All India Medical Entrance exam from Honey's room. The sweetness of her manner had impressed the twin sisters so much that they didn't want to leave her side for a second.

Romy approached Pallavi and asked, "You are Pallavi, right?" He was happy as he had finally found the "handkerchief girl" in Honey's life. He had hoped to meet her once, and by God's grace, it had been fulfilled.

"Yes, uncle," Pallavi confirmed, smiling genuinely. Romy studied her eyes. They didn't lie. She would make a great match, the perfect bride, but it would only be a matter of a few years after Honey completed his graduation.

"Congratulations, Beti, on cracking the entrance test. Meet Shreyashi, Honey's cousin; she also cracked it. When is the counselling process going to start?" Romy asked.

"Uncle, it is going to start in three months. Classes will start by the first of April," Pallavi said.

Pallavi's eyes were fixed on something strange she noticed in the hall. "Wow, uncle, this fountain for the hall looks amazing. Everything is in order."

"These two sisters from Delhi have tidied up the party arrangements." It was ten o'clock when the chocolate gateau arrived from the bakery.

"Chocolate flavour?" Pallavi asked.

"That's my son's favourite. He still loves chocolates."

Sipping a glass of lemonade, she listened attentively to every word her father told her about Honey.

"Shreyashi, show her the house. Honey is getting ready upstairs. He will be here in a few minutes," Romy said and left to invite other guests.

Shreyashi said, "You look very warm in that going away outfit. Where did you get it from in Mumbai?" Pallavi replied, "My mother stitched it for me."

Tapasee interrupted from some distance, saying, "You look very hot in that traditional outfit, sweetie. Hi, I'm Tapasee, Honey's cousin." She tapped Pallavi on the shoulder and left, saying, "You carry on."

The main hall was big and well-organized, neatly decorated with well-polished brass wares, lamps, copper chimes, and more. Pallavi adored the beautiful wall hangings, tapestries, Sekhawati furniture, and rich vases placed carefully on them. The sports medals, trophies, and Honey's childhood photos in the corners also caught her attention. After wandering around the main hall, Pallavi's eyes settled on a sepia portrait. She stopped when she reached the portrait and asked Shreyashi, "Who is she?"

A voice came from behind Honey's father, telling a guest, "I warned him once that you will never leave the house without my permission. And he agreed. You know, how submissive is my son?" "No, Romy, He is not submissive. His bad luck is that you have been a very protective father." A burst of laughter followed.

"Honey's mother, Briksha Roy," Shreyashi said. Pallavi walked closer to the portrait to read the inscription written below.

"How did she die?" Pallavi asked.

"It was a road accident. I was just a baby when it happened," Shreyashi replied. Pallavi's eyes lingered on the portrait. "She looks absolutely stunning in the photo," Pallavi said.

Romy came towards them to ask for drinks. "She is my wife, Briksha. She left us when Honey was three. A brilliant lady, unfortunately, she is no longer with us," Romy said. Pallavi expressed her sadness, "So sad. It seems you still miss her."

Shreyashi walked up to Diya and said, "Hello. "Are you Diya? Honey's friend,"

Diya tossed her head up, puffed some air at the spiky fringes on her forehead, and tried to walk away with a lopsided grin.

"Yes, I am Honey's best friend, Diya. I didn't like you not paying attention to me ever since that ordinary Pallavi arrived at your house," Diya replied.

"It's not true, Diya. Like Pallavi, you are also an important guest to us," Shreyashi assured her.

"Uncle, the portrait is so real. It is speaking to the beholder."

"Yes, Pallavi, you are right. I feel her presence always beside me. Fifteen years have passed, be it morning, noon, or night; she has not left my mind for a second. She is my everything, she is my energy, and she is my success. She was like an angel to me." Pallavi noticed tears welling up in Romy's eyes when he sniffed. He said so in his emotion-filled, wet voice.

In a few seconds, she heard the sound was real. A sudden gush of anger in blood drummed his arteries when he said, "I cannot forget the day when she left me. It was an accident that happened on the highway. A drunk driver from Malad, Sagar Rajhans, was his name. How can I forget his name who killed my wife." Her common sense warned her. It was about her father. The words pricked her ears. She never imagined a sensible man could say, "Like I suffered, Sagar's whole family should rot in hell." She felt awkward. The moment was very unpredictable. She needed some distance to protect herself from the sounds reverberating in her mind. 'Like I suffered, Sagar's whole family should rot in hell.' 'Like I suffered, Sagar's whole family should rot in hell.'

She strained to forget, but it reverberated uninterruptedly. Pallavi froze, her palms sweating. The glassful of drink dropped onto the floor, shattered. There was a moment of silence when the words intensely penetrated Pallavi's mind, and her head was fit to burst. She clutched her head in both hands. She shivered. The eyes in the room that settled on her at that moment could notice that she had a nervous breakdown. She felt like not staying there for a moment.

The parting would be so abrupt. Honey had never expected this. Her manner was not prim and proper and was not acceptable to the Shivdasnis and their guests. Pallavi had left the place before Shreyashi asked her uncle what he had said.

CHAPTER 7

A Dream comes true

Mumbai, 31 March 2005.

She fidgeted restlessly, finding it difficult to sit in one place. She would attend the Dean's address at eight in the morning. It influenced her. Her breaths had become longer out of some excitement. There was a bubbling sense of anticipation in her what the dean would say in the welcome address. He might unleash wisdom from his mind in his speech for everyone's benefit. She was not exactly sure if her feelings were nervousness or pure exhilaration. She knew she had to go. She was certain she would meet Shreyashi, the only girl she knew, but there would also be many other friends from different parts of the country.

She didn't know how often she had flipped through the college's annual report book in the last few days. What struck her the most was that it was one of the most prestigious medical colleges, and in the last fifty years, it had produced many top surgeons in the country and abroad. She had been inside the hospital campus several times, but never as a student. She had never crossed the gate leading to the academic block. The building was an isolated eight-storied structure standing tall next to the main road, covering over a hundred acres of land.

"Will the seniors dragoon her into acting silly, or will they be kind to her, fearing the newly imposed anti-ragging law? Should she complain or not about them for this?" Unlike others, such thoughts never wandered into her mind. On one side, she was delighted to begin a new college career, and on the other side, her mind was recounting the difficult days she and her mother had lived through after her father left. Without Dr. Pradeep's influence, she could hardly have reached this momentous juncture. God is great; somehow or other, the Almighty refills life with new opportunities if he takes away one by himself. She had the highest admiration for Dr. Pradeep since he treated her mother. She desired to start a new career with a blessing from her uncle, Dr. Pradeep.

The worry gets diluted as she stands by the side of the window, staring at the road. She recounts the difficult days she and her mother lived through. Nothing in these years could dull her memories. Standing by the window, she stares at the empty street, hoping that someday her father will come back to her house through the same street. He had left her with a promise of coming soon on that rainy day when she waved goodbye.

She lay on her bed with her eyes wide open. She reminisced about her father, knowing he would never come back to her in life. He would have been happy and blessed her with prosperity if he had been there. She stared at the ceiling, which once evoked a vision of a starry night at the planetarium – a sight she had conjured up countless times before. As her eyes were closing, she found herself sneaking into a dreamland.

She felt as though she was meandering solo among the galaxy of stars, and one of them grew bigger and bigger. Suddenly, a thunderous crash reverberated around her like something had just collided with the big star. Her gaze shifted in that direction, and she saw her father blessing her through the rays for a bright future. The harsh reality was that he would never come back. A sane mind would laugh at her and incredulously question her if she were to narrate what she saw on her bedroom ceiling. However, she never intended to reject these misbeliefs that cropped up in her mind. She had survived all these years with hardships, hoping that her father would come back alive someday. She would wait for him, no matter how long it took. Her eyes were fluttering shut, and her mind was awake.

Therefore, there was no reason to avoid such beliefs that crossed her mind in an awakened state. She knew she missed her father terribly, so his soul always ruled her heart, staying deep within.

The college had summoned them to the auditorium by 8 AM sharp. The new morning would bring her new friends, teachers, and a fresh atmosphere. Her thoughts switched, and she opened her eyes. "What a peculiar experience dissecting human cadavers will be!" She had heard tales about cadavers before. Lifeless and devoid of emotions and pain, still human bodies. How would the seniors behave with her when she would start her first day in medical college? Would she face the dreaded rituals of ragging? These musings were soon interrupted by the pull of slumber.

She woke up at her usual time when the alarm rang. After completing her quick morning ritual, she enthusiastically picked up her new white apron. "What are you doing there, Beta?" Laxmi asked. "Your breakfast is ready. You will miss the town bus."

"Coming, mama. Just getting my bag ready. Mama, should I wear the pink dress?"

"Yes, but don't forget to take the apron." Laxmi had sewn it herself. Pallavi folded it neatly and placed it in her backpack. She quickly ate breakfast and touched Laxmi's feet to seek blessings for her new beginning.

Students assembled at the academic block. A group of senior boys stood at a distance, their casual conversation and body language suggesting a light-hearted exchange. It was not difficult for her to interpret. She overheard one of them giving tips to a less abled junior boy about mate stalking for a successful relationship. The body language clearly showed that he was an expert in such matters. A moment later, a girl, presumably his girlfriend, joined the preacher. After the preacher left with his girlfriend, two junior boys stood there, showing off their charming, well-groomed morning faces. They stared as if they had peeled their eyes to catch the attention of junior girls. One boy called her "Pinky" because of her pink dress, while the other boy complimented her fair complexion by calling her "Gori" (meaning fair-skinned). She wore the white apron to avoid their gaze. From a distance, someone shouted and gave a stern look at them as if to convey the impression that he was more senior than them and knew her as if she lived next door. He said, "Sweetie, they call you Gori because you are beautiful and fair." His eyes seemed to twinkle before he left with a smug smile. She glanced back at him, and his batch mates greeted him for his successful attempt to talk to a girl like her. "Boys will be boys," she thought to herself. She was fair, so it was not a serious compliment. She was prepared to accept such words on her first day, so it hardly bothered her. Having someone like her being raved about might help him gain confidence, as he seemed to be a disconsolate soul buried under a pile of books. She pardoned him for choosing to talk to her as he didn't veer off into a romantic territory.

A senior boy hovered over a girl in the corner of the corridor. His body language was possessive and domineering. The girl's eyes were downcast, her posture tense and nervous, betraying her discomfort. It was clear from their accent that she hailed from the same region as the boy.

The boy leaned in close, instructing the girl on how to carry herself. "Don't walk with your chin up in front of the seniors," he commanded in a distinct Tamil accent. "Keep your eyes trained on the third button of your shirt instead."

The girl dutifully followed his directions, her movements stiff and unnatural. Yet a moment later, when she turned around, a mischievous giggle escaped her lips. To one's surprise, this was all an act - the girl was his own classmate, and their interaction had been a prank orchestrated to teach the new students how they were expected to dress and behave.

It means those sparkling like new marbles in the white aprons are not necessarily her classmates, she understood by now. The seniors have infiltrated into the group to impersonate first-year students. She must be more careful with them while choosing her words. The newly introduced anti-ragging law had created an impact on the seniors, she thought.

A burly figure strode in. A hush fell over the crowd. His charm was undeniable. He was a medicine professor's son and had been enrolled in the first year, as she heard them referring to that hefty guy, the one they spoke about. His gesture was pompous. There was an undercurrent of arrogance to his bearing that set the seniors on edge. The instant consternation she noticed in the seniors when he walked past alongside her, she observed. To her, it was not difficult to learn that any attempt to rag him would cost them their career; they were sure about it. She felt relieved from their prying eyes when she reached the big entrance. The gate was opened, and they all entered the air-conditioned auditorium. It was spacious enough to accommodate thousands. The front row was reserved for the faculty, and the freshers occupied the rest. All eyes were focused on the entry door. They waited for the arrival of the Dean. The watch on her wrist was going to strike eight. Palo was sitting in the third row. She received a tap from behind. She turned around. It was Shreyashi, one of the twin sisters. She had met both once at the birthday party at Shivdasni's house.

Pallavi threw a recognizing smile at her. She uttered, "I am Shreyashi. I have joined here. Do you remember me? I met you at Honey's birthday party. I couldn't speak to you much that day."

The Dean entered in the meantime. All stood up to greet him, and then they sat down as he gestured.

The Dean announced, after welcoming them,

"*Dear students, medical science is an evolving field. With the arrival of new technologies, the standard of disease management has improved over the years. Better than the era when I was a medical student.*" After a brief pause, he said, "*When we were the students,* we didn't have the diagnostic facilities. To diagnose a disease, we used our clinical skills. But remember students, whatever knowledge you acquire here, you must apply it in your practice. The habit will make you an able clinician and help you to grasp the subject better. Tomorrow, you will stand tall in this society as a big name and an able clinician. But mind you, An able clinician cannot become an able doctor unless he shows compassion to the patients. Try to understand the mental state of the relatives who are equally suffering during their treatment."

It reminded Palo about the days when her mother was admitted to this hospital.

It is a test of time; it is up to you how you build yourself up for a bright future. The failure rates so far are almost ten per cent in every batch. So don't waste a single day without thinking about your studies.

Academic discussion at the bedside is very important, so never think of bunking the classes. We have highly qualified teachers to teach you the medicines. It is up to you how you extract the knowledge from them.

As per the request of students, the library is functional for twelve hours, but for enthusiastic readers who learn better by sitting in groups, the reading room is open around the clock.

You can refer to any book of your choice pertaining to your subject and any journals if you wish to refer to them for your research works. There are a limited number of rooms in the hostels, so some of you will have to retain your room outside the campus till next year.

You will have three professional exams in this five-year course and a one-year compulsory internship. I wish you good luck and a bright future." That piece of advice from a man of true intellect was enough to understand the gravitas in the profession.

It was a big hall with about a dozen teaching stations in it. All she saw was six human bodies ensconced naked on six big tables. All looked wizened, as natural as with life. The stations were marked up with roll numbers.

The moment was scary enough to give them an adrenaline rush. A few dragged in their breath. When she saw one of them had unblinking eyes, staring wide open and scanning the roof, the blood thundered through her veins; she was soaked with sweat until someone who seemed to be the caretaker politely said, " Don't worry, child, these are all lifeless cadavers and lain still and supine." They were brought to the hall for dissection. Well-embalmed with formalin, they retained their look but withered with a lustreless skinny cover. The stench of formalin was quite unbearable for many. It had pooled tears in many eyes, the noses filled, and few felt icky. It compelled a few to go closer to the windows to breathe fresh air.

The anatomy professor entered inside and asked each of them to touch the cadavers with their bare palm. In his introductory statement, he said, "Knowing anatomy is like knowing in detail about the body organs. How they are placed inside the body, and how they relate to each other. "One cannot see the abnormal if he has not seen the normal," he spoke. "As the Dean said in the morning, to become a good clinician, you must know all about your body. You must follow the manual while dissecting these cadavers." He picked up a Cunningham's manual to show to the students. He later asked them to use only four things for dissection: a scalpel, a pair of scissors, a forceps, and the last one, your bare hands.

"The resident doctors will help you when required, and the cadavers are all yours. We have given you six stations and divided you into six groups according to your roll numbers. So, you as a team will decide who will make the first incision in your group," the professor said.

Amitav, handsome but slovenly in appearance, was quite uncared about personal hygiene; he grew long hairs dangling over his shirt collar. He was the only son of a professor of medicine. The latter was enough of an introduction to the senior boys to cringe, which is the trapping of power if someone enjoys an influential position in a college. He was non-responsive to the senior's strict instruction to come clean-shaven and keep short hair. He knew well that he couldn't be scowled by them for his unreasonable actions. His conceited mind had already proclaimed his right to give the incision first.

Interestingly, the part in which the group was assigned to be dissected was the thorax.

The assistant professor, Dr Basu, was assigned the table to demonstrate various organs in the thorax. The incision was supposed to be for the breast, following the incision line, to be peeled off in layers to understand the layers inside. The overconfident Amitav made a very deep oblique incision over the mid bone, which landed up directly onto the breast tissue, cutting through the layers of muscles. Pallavi, who had positioned over a wooden platform, piped up from the back, over his shoulder, that the incision was not in the mid-line. Amitav turned around and tried to be a little bossy with the rest, but his approach was wrong. He had not read the manual, so he didn't know where to give the second incision. He somewhat played around the single incision line. Pallavi, by this time, had understood that Amitav had not understood the basics of what the anatomist was trying to describe in the manual. She came forward to help him, but Amitav had to impress his girlfriend, Arundhati, by saying that he knew everything about the breast and the muscles in the chest wall. Pallavi was sure Amitav hadn't read the origin and insertion of the muscles before making the incision. He would not have committed this blunder if he had a little idea about it.

Pallavi stood across the table close to the opposite breast. It was a strict order from Dr Basu that one side be dissected entirely before going to the other side. To teach about the blood supply of the chest wall, the veins, and arteries, he would come to demonstrate on the other side.

After being ticked off by Pallavi, Amitav was not certain about the second incision. He knew Pallavi had read the surface anatomy and the dissection part thoroughly. But handing her over the dissection is like losing the chance for the rest of the classes. Despite her talking about the approach, Amitav stood still and slowly worked on the subcutaneous plane. Pallavi could not stop herself from going again to the right side. She took out her scalpel and gave the other incision below the collarbone, which made the work much easier for Amitav. Amitav didn't like Pallavi's interference in this affair. He tried not to allow her to stand beside him. There were twenty in the group who were trying to find a place to watch. A few had already comfortably stood on the stools to observe the process. The day ended like this in the hall. One thing is for sure: she learned how important it is to learn in detail before making the incision on the body. She wanted to tell Amitav to come prepared next time, but he had left the hall just after the class and was a little bothered about permission from the professor. Will he ever understand that he has an attitude problem? Which has taken him over to such an extent that he is bothered a little about others.

The announcement from Dr Basu stated that the dissection record should be completed before the part completion assignment. So neat and clean diagrams will attract more marks, and cumulatively, these marks will add up to a good number in the final examination.

"Oh, you're here. By the way, I am Pallavi," she said.

"Amitav," he replied, putting his hands in his pocket and not bothering to shake hands.

She automatically put her hand to her side but said, "It's not necessary for people to shake hands every time, but I'm surprised you don't even know how it's done."

She reminded him, "By the way, I didn't like the way you left the dissection in the middle. You should have considered how others would feel if you slipped out the back door. I was expecting you to apologize to everyone who was at the table. You wasted their precious day."

"I had some other engagement, so I came out."

"They waited for you to show them layer-by-layer dissection. You led the team, and you failed, isn't it? Would you mind coming prepared next time? When you left, did you seek their permission?" Her words plunged him like shrapnel. "Look, I am what I am. I know people around here. The teachers know me very well. They all live where I live. It is now none of your business to teach me what is right or what is wrong, okay?" He spoke with an awful temper.

"No, it's not okay. I am not here to bear your nonsense. Look, Amitav, you have an attitude problem. I was expecting some decency from you, but you are simply hopeless," Pallavi said.

"Look, I am what I am."

She chided, "Heard you well. You are what you are, but you have no right to waste everyone's time like this." Amitav stood there, unmoved, quiet. A sheen of perspiration smeared his forehead. "Tell me tomorrow, are you going to stand on the right side of the table or the left side? If you stand on the right side without any preparation, I will complain to the professor. Each part has a fixed number of classes, so you cannot take the other nineteen students for a ride. I didn't like the way you casually gave the incision. What would have happened if a live patient had been lying on the table? In such a case, would you have given an incision like this? Didn't you hear what Dr. Basu said? Your incision must be perfect," she said concernedly.

"I know what I should do tomorrow. You don't need to lecture me. We all learn by making mistakes, okay?" Amitav said. Seeing the medico's son behaving waywardly, she too lost her even temper. Their glares met.

"No, it is not okay. Mistakes! You are not an engineer repairing any machine. He can keep a machine off at any time, but for us, we always operate on living humans with their engines on. There, you cannot saddle a life with your heavy strokes. You are not a butcher," Pallavi said.

"I know that. I have seen more books than you. I am born with medical books around, okay? Don't teach me as my professor," he said. That's a bit rash on his part. Her eyebrows rose up and wriggled.

"Oh, hello. How many of them have you read so far if you are born to be around the medical books?" She cleared her throat, glared at him with terrible eyes, and then pointed a finger at him, saying, "Mr. Amitav Raj, I am Pallavi Rajhans. Your roll number is not going to change for the coming five years. Willy-nilly, you ought to put up with me for five years. Speaking to you for the last time, I warn you as a good friend."

For Amitav, this girl didn't leave any chance for him to say anything except a big sorry. His reaction to her had been buried down in his heart. His attention was drawn to the catering staff, who were present throughout their conversation. To save face, he had no choice but to offer her his apology. Her tone was calm, and her voice was flat. She considered it enough that she had spoken her resentful mind to him. Now, it is up to him to repent for what he did.

"I told you what I had to tell. Many of us study hard to brush up on our practical knowledge, and your bossy attitude with a vacuous mind is neither good for you nor it is any good for us. Bye. See you tomorrow morning at eight for the physiology practical class."

*****

It was 6 PM on her watch. Pallavi decided to meet Uncle Pradeep before leaving for home. She was keen to share her experience over the last two days. He is the right person who can guide her as a mentor.

Disha arrived at the hospital in a black car at 6 PM. The driver opened the door for her as she stepped out. She was dressed formally in a magnificent black business coat and skirt. Her hair was combed back and tightly wound in a bun. She had come straight from the office after a busy day. Her appointment with Dr. Pradeep was scheduled for 6 PM. She entered the hospital lobby and smiled at the guard, who greeted her with a nod of welcome. The guard seemed to know her well, as she always appeared tidy and elegant. She had a charming and sophisticated demeanour. She had a pair of dark sunglasses perched on the pate of her head, and her cheeks still carried a glint of the rose blush she had applied in the morning. A mysterious flowery perfume lingered in the air as she walked. She pressed the elevator button, and the small cubicle arrived on the eighth floor before dropping and stopping at each floor for a minute. While waiting, she took out a mirror from her vanity bag and adjusted her side locks. The elevator returned to the ground floor, and she stepped inside, pressing the button for the first floor. Just as the door was about to close, Pallavi interrupted by pressing the button from outside. The elevator door reopened, and she facilitated the wheelchair-bound patient to enter. Disha noticed how elegant Pallavi's white coat was, mirroring her graceful manners.

The teenage girl in the wheelchair had a withered frame and sunken eyes. Her hands rested on the arms of the chair, and the man pushing the wheelchair was her father. He thanked Pallavi for her kind help. Breaking the silence inside the elevator, the girl asked, "Are you Dr. Pallavi?" Pallavi had never experienced this level of excitement before. Someone addressed her as "doctor" while seeing her in a white coat. She didn't know how to respond. Turning towards the girl, Pallavi tried to sound modest and suppress her awkwardness as she said, "Yes, I am Pallavi."

The girl held her hand affectionately and said, "I read your interview that you gave after passing high school. I have kept your photo. I cut it from the newspaper when I was in fifth grade. My mother and I always talked about you." The girl's grip was weak. Her hand was cold, with suffering evident in her eyes. Pallavi noticed her frail, skeletal body underneath her loosely hanging tea-length garment, giving a glimpse of her slim legs. Despite her weak grip, Pallavi closed her hand over the girl's. Pallavi crouched down, placing her other hand on the girl's cheek, and said, "Yes, I am the same girl. I remember. That day is still memorable for me."

They all exited the elevator when the doors opened and proceeded towards the waiting lobby outside Dr. Pradeep's chamber.

It was a routine operating Friday. Dr Pradeep had just come out of the operating theatre.

The old patients always took the liberty to call him at any time, and few didn't even hesitate to ask for unusual appointments at odd hours to avoid the lineup for a ticket.

He was considerate of patients who were busy during regular working hours and unable to make it to his afternoon OPDs on Thursday. Disha was one such patient.

Disha was quite loyal to her master. She was happy to keep her mind cluttered with work. She was the only secretary who single-handedly managed Sameer's personal and professional tasks. She was self-contented with this corner of the world and never revisited her ugly past in the last two decades to sob. She understood well that she had no better option. It dropped into her lap as a solution to save her womanhood, dignity, and self-respect. She enjoyed Sameer's proximity, so she was more concerned about Sameer than herself. With perfect time management, she could handle situations both on a personal and professional front. She knew well that Dr. Pradeep understood her better than anyone else in the world, not only as a doctor but as a great human being.

To add to her stress, now she had to think about Sameer, who had already had a heart attack, and his angiography of his heart showed three blockages in all three major coronary arteries. He required bypass surgery. She was also aware that Sameer avoided his routine follow-up with Dr. Pradeep. Every time she tried to convince him, Sameer would give a reason for the delay in the surgery. Considering his heart ailments, Disha was more serious about reducing his stress burden from work. No matter what life would bring to him, he wouldn't die without seeing his daughter established in Bollywood as an actor.

Although it was a routine monthly follow-up, she had come to tell him about the uneasiness and easy fatigability. She felt discomfort inside her chest. Is it normal to have such symptoms after so many years of operation? Is the prosthetic valve functioning normally? Many such questions arose in her mind.

With little time spent with her, Pallavi had extracted and was overjoyed to know about Disha as a pleasant lady with a strong will. Her curiosity to learn more about Disha prevented her from keeping any distance from her. A patient hearing can only know so much about others when someone carries a thousand-ton load of emotions in her heart to unload to somebody. She had analyzed Disha's story, with its string of good and bad moments, in a nutshell. Her eyes studied the woman's core, how deep her life was filled with true emotions for her master's ailments, a sensible reason for her to worry.

What she had presumed from Disha's appearance to be a satisfying life, the woman, too, had many upheavals to reveal. When Pallavi went through her file, it didn't even take a moment to know about the lady's medical history. She saw both sides of life that day. On one side was a lady with a sumptuous dress, and on the other was a girl in worn-out clothes who needed solace in Dr. Pradeep.

Dr. Pradeep's face lit up. He was happy to see Pallavi in a crisp white apron. He congratulated her and welcomed her for joining the fraternity. Unquestionably, she had come from the college classes yet looked sporty and energetic. Her enthusiasm was palpable. Seeing her cheerful face, his spirits were lifted. Her positive energy had a catalytic effect. It energized him after a long day's work.

He gestured for Pallavi to take a seat across from him. The next moment, Disha knocked on the door and joined them, taking the chair beside Pallavi. Dr. Pradeep introduced Disha to Pallavi as his student and the future cardiac surgeon of the country. This was how Pallavi was formally introduced to Disha for the first time.

Dr Pradeep suddenly reached into his drawer and pulled out a stethoscope as he reviewed Disha's and Sameer's files. He gently placed it on Disha's chest, listening intently to the sound of her heart. He then asked Pallavi to do so. It confused Pallavi because it was not what she expected. There was a distinct click, something she hadn't experienced with her own heartbeat. Dr Pradeep explained that in patients who have undergone heart valve replacement surgery, the metallic valve creates a unique clicking sound that can be heard through the stethoscope. Eager to understand this phenomenon, Pallavi took the stethoscope from Disha's chest and listened to her own heart. Comparing the familiar rhythmic beats with the distinct click, she uttered, "Yes, it is different." Dr. Pradeep said, "Unless you hear the normal, you cannot interpret the abnormal." She learned that day the importance and practicality of knowing normal before knowing abnormal. The experience of acquiring the newfound medical knowledge left her puzzled with a craving to know more about medicine.

He prescribed some medicines and firmly advised that Sameer should get himself operated on as early as possible. He warned that Sameer would face a tough battle if the heart's pumping mechanism failed. He would end up in hospitals every now and then. It would be better for him to come and get himself operated as early as possible. "Films may come and go, but life doesn't, "Dr Pradeep said.

Disha said, "He is not willing for any intervention at present. He wants his daughter Diya to settle in Bollywood first."

After Disha departed, Pallavi urgently pressed Dr. Pradeep to see the girl first, as her needs were most immediate.

The young girl who met Pallavi in the lift then entered the room. Pallavi could see the distress etched on the girl's face when Dr Pradeep asked her about her sufferings. She had a hole in her heart. It was a ventricular septal defect, and she needed surgery. Dr Pradeep spoke firmly, urging her to undergo the operation as soon as possible. He painted a bleak picture of the challenges she would face if she delayed- a gruelling battle would further her sufferings.

He then turned to Pallavi, imploring her to convince the girl of the necessity of the surgery. With that, Dr Pradeep swiftly exited the room, needing to attend to the operated patient in the ICU. Left alone with the girl, Pallavi learned of her dire circumstances. Her father worked in a piggery and could not afford the surgery. Now, she would have to make do with just the prescribed medications, her future shrouded in uncertainty.

Pallavi now understood that people who have enough money but no time, like Sameer Malhotra, and people who don't have money but time, like this girl, are equally afflicted, victims of their circumstances beyond their control.

*****

Delhi, 2005

Now, it seemed easier to live in Delhi, far away from Mumbai, after his father decided to put a final full stop to Honey's woeful tale of broken romance. The saga of his unrequited love met its end. He felt lighter in his low-spirited mind. It was his own volition to shift to Delhi and stay in the Boy's hostel to overcome his lovesick feelings.

Ajay asked, "*Devdas, Kyun ho tum itna udaas?* Why are you so sad? How long will you sit like this? It is now 5 PM."

Honey heaved a long, weary sigh and said, "I don't know."

He watched the kids playing in Mukherjee Nagar Park in Delhi. The bustling sounds of the park enveloped them. Honey said, "I wish we all should have the heart of a kid as pure as theirs - always forgiving. No matter how bad her friend was, the girl tried not to snitch on him to his mom. Instead, she herself sorted the matter out." It saddled him to look at his life in a new way that interested him in living a life like the kids, finding happiness in everything, be it good or bad. He muttered, "I made a fool of myself over her. My life is my life. She would have no way made my life different."

Ajay's brow furrowed with concern. He said, "It is good as long as the matter is trivial. The kid knew she could manage it by herself well. But in your matter, neither Pallavi nor you tried to solve it. This kiddish approach doesn't work when the issue is serious, like yours. Not everyone is carefree like you. You didn't even bother talking to her mother; you packed your bags and came here. You didn't even try to know from your father what the matter was?"

"I have moved on from that now. There is no point in discussing past things, Ajay."

"Oh, my Devdas. Nothing seems as if you pretend it's done and dusted. Where are those springy steps on the field? I can see they've gone mild before the nationals," Ajay urged Honey to reconcile with the past and focus on the present.

"Nationals in Pune? I am not going anywhere around Mumbai until I become someone," Honey retorted.

"That's a very rude statement. You patch up this matter and come back. Mark my words; you will top the exam when there is calmness in your mind," Ajay undeterredly insisted.

"I am calm. Now I realize how important the present time is. I have learned to live without her," Honey's words, tinged with bitterness, were evident as he asserted.

"Just fooling yourself. It's a competition. And to stay ahead in the competition, you need to be in touch with your near and dear ones for moral support," Ajay argued.

Pointing towards a couple in the park, Honey reacted, "Can you see them there? They come here in the morning to study, and they come here again in the evening. They are friends. The boy knows that the girl is his competitor, and so does the girl. In the end, they must compete in the exam. Are they lovers? No. They met here in the park a few days ago. I witnessed their first meeting. He didn't understand Hindi, and the girl didn't understand Tamil. Still, they discuss and talk about their careers. In the end, they are there to give each other moral support. If you are here with me, I don't need any girl to teach me what subject I should read."

"You can't be so prejudiced about Pallavi," Ajay countered.

"Prejudiced! I feel it the other way. She is a career woman, so she prioritized, or rather I should say, she prioritized her career over me. Perhaps she didn't want the distraction. That's why she stopped talking to me." Honey's voice tinged with anguish.

Ajay's eyes widened, a flicker of understanding dawning, " No, that's not who she is, " he countered. "No way, she is not the kind of girl who thinks about her career. Do you remember when she took us to the hospital, even with an exam looming the very next week? Not bothering about her preparation, she accompanied us."

"Do you think I didn't try? I sent a letter through Diya to know about the matter, but she didn't show up. I am not coming with you. From Pune, you would drag me to Mumbai for the finals. I know you better," Honey stated.

Ajay acknowledged, "If that is the case, then leave everything up to destiny. Let's go to the hostel. Forget what happened on that day. Prodding over it is a waste of time. This city is new but very lively. Soon, you will learn to forget her."

Honey was very much disturbed by the awful memory of his birthday party. Almost a year and a half had passed, and he had not forgotten that night when she left his house without telling him a single word. Neither did she respond to his letter nor come to meet him after that. He was her closest friend in one moment, and she declared him a stranger in the next moment. No one would know more than him how he spent the days and nights after that. After spending many thoughtful days and sleepless nights in agony, he chose to walk alone on a thorny path forward with great determination. There was no father to wake him up from the bed in the morning with a cup of tea at his bedside. Now, with the exams looming over him, he managed to get a few hours of sleep-in patches. Not only once, but often, he had to wake up from sleep. He was determined not to go to the city that snatched away his loving mother and now the girl whom he loved unconditionally. Was it for a career she could not have pursued while in a relationship? Didn't she read his confession of love in the letter he sent through Diya? "I don't love you" was not a good reply to understand. The reason was not told to him.

He saw that it was 6 AM. He strolled back and forth several times in his fifteen feet by fifteen feet room with a book in hand. He was occasionally staring at the walls full of wall-pasted notes, a wide range of newspaper clippings, and book chapters. Except for a tuner, the study space was devoid of anything causing distractions. As I saw him, his head was mostly buried deep in the wodge of books. He couldn't escape his fitness practice in the morning when Ajay was up and ready to go for practice, who stayed in the next room in the hostel.

*****

Mumbai, 2005

The professor in physiology was well-read, as he explained the intricate details of blood cells and their morphological characteristics under the microscope during the practical class. The chalk drawings on the blackboard differed from what Pallavi had read, but his theoretical explanations were captivating and easily understandable. He was insistent on the microscopic study of one's own blood cells before studying others. He ordered the peon to distribute the needles so the students could prick their own fingers to extract blood. Remarkably, the professor demonstrated this process by pricking his own finger. She had never seen a teacher who would get his finger pricked just to teach his students.

In Pallavi's group, everyone was excited to see their blood cells under the microscope while Amitav cringed. He palpated his pulse from time to time, and she could see drops of sweat on his face. None of the signs in him looked normal. Upon close observation, she found him shaky in the exciting atmosphere of the practical hall.

The large quadrangular hall had the tables stretching across its length in two rows. Amitav's fingers exhibited fine tremors as he nervously picked up a needle to prick his finger. He hesitated before selecting the thinnest bore from the tray. She wondered if something was wrong with his fingers or if they were trembling out of nervousness. His actions, like toying with a pen and flipping it between his fingers, seemed to be an attempt to conceal the tremors in his hand.

While he did all this, she had a flash of his fearful mind, which he had cleverly concealed with a gentle smile and slightly contracted cheek. Pallavi noticed that he was neither intoxicated nor incoherent. But there was something amiss. He then moved to his seat but quickly pulled away to the extreme end of the table. It was a non-interfering corner, guarded on one side by the wall. Pallavi wondered if he feared a prick or something else.

She knew Amitav was not the type of person who would fear a minor prick. If it wasn't that, then was he avoiding her after their argument yesterday? She closely watched him and noticed that Amitav feigned to look through the microscope by frequently adjusting its focus. Upon closer inspection, Pallavi realized that the slide he was studying was not smeared with blood but carried a stain of blue dye. Nearly an hour passed, and he didn't let anyone else see through his microscope.

Pallavi approached Amitav and handed him her own slide, asking, "If I'm not mistaken, are you suffering from ITP?"

Amitav was taken aback and asked, "How did you know?"

Pallavi responded, "I noticed the bluish patches on your arms while you were scrubbing in the Anatomy dissection hall yesterday. I went home and read about it. It's a platelet disorder, and you're worried that your count might be less than ten thousand."

Amitav appreciated her observation and said, "You are a genius who could read my mind."

"No, Amitav, I'm not a genius," Pallavi said. "But I am observant of what's happening around me."

Amitav acknowledged, "That is the mark of a genius who can read others' minds. Yes, Pallavi, you're right. I'm not bothered about the pricks. I've been getting them since I was seven. I was worried about the numbers. What if they are less than ten thousand? I fear hospital admissions. Regular steroids, you know, make me feel my heart beat faster, and my pulse throws bounded impulses on my arteries. I know how it feels from the inside to be on steroids all the time. I feel as if someone is hammering me inside my chest ."

After a pause, Amitav added, "Hmm. Arundhati's father is a paediatrician, and he has been treating me since I was seven. I knew my cell counts, so I faked."

Pallavi said, "You stupid, you could have asked me to make an extra slide for you. You didn't need to shift places. I'm sorry for everything I said in the canteen yesterday."

Amitav admitted, "You were right yesterday. It was silly of me to become loutish. I am ashamed of my thoughtless behaviour. The whole batch suffered because of me. By the way, I read about the dissection part yesterday, skipping the first half of the basketball match between Delhi and Mumbai."

Pallavi asked, "Who won?"

"Delhi won the match. Those guys were excellent," Amitabh said, his eyes gleaming with admiration.

"So you have an interest in sports, right?" Pallavi inquired.

"Right, I cannot play contact sports with my platelet count, but I love watching them. Especially when my favourite players play on the pitch."

"By the way, I want to know who they are," Pallavi asked, her curiosity piqued.

"In cricket, Sachin and Saurav, and in basketball, the Delhi players Ajay and Honey," Amitav said.

"Delhi?" Pallavi asked with a hint of surprise in her voice.

"Yes, earlier they were in the Mumbai team, now representing Delhi University," Amitav explained.

"The final is between Delhi and Punjab University. Would you like to go?" Amitav asked.

"Who do you think will win?" Pallavi asked.

"Both are strong teams, but I pray for Delhi to win," he said, his voice tinged with hope.

"I, too, wish them good luck," Pallavi responded, her own excitement building.

The clock in the practical hall struck 1 PM. The class was over, and many students had gone for lunch. As Pallavi was packing her books, a shrill voice from the other row compelled her to turn her head towards Shreyashi. Shreyashi shouted Pallavi's name and excitedly walked towards her, holding a piece of paper. She had a blush on her face as if she had some good news to share. It was a write-up on the last page of the daily news, a statement from the Mumbai team captain praising the victorious Delhi team captain, Honey. Shreyashi wanted Pallavi to say a few words for her brother.

Pallavi looked at Shreyashi's eager, answer-seeking expressions but showed no interest in the news being shared with her. She swung her bag onto her back and invited Shreyashi for lunch in the college canteen. Shreyashi accompanied her as they walked down the stairs together.

As they descended, Shreyashi's thoughts were consumed by the events of the Honey's birthday. "Heaven only knows what happened to Pallavi that day," she mused. "The timing may not be convenient, but today is the day I will ask her and not go home without knowing the reason why she left the party with tears in her eyes. What happened to her in those five minutes? The thought of its consequences has taken over my mind. Either Pallavi will open up, or I will face a disaster."

Shreyashi's heartbeat quickened as she remembered the way Pallavi had glared at her. She was determined to get to the bottom of the issue, regardless of the potential consequences.

*****

Three years later, Dubai, 2008

It was a month of saline-drenching June. The city flaunted its sky-high hotels along Marina Beach Drive. The path leading to the opulent Park Hilton Hotel was well-protected by massive boulders. Rated at a prestigious seven stars, the hotel boasted ultra-luxury rooms and a helipad atop its imposing structure, which stood taller than its neighbours on a man-made island. The parking lot overflowed with sleek, gleaming forms of luxurious Lamborghinis, Ferraris, Teslas, and Bugattis. The view from the hotel was breathtaking, with the simmering sea stretching out on both sides, blending seamlessly with the azure sky. For many who visited during the summer, it was the most enjoyable place on earth.

For film producers, the scenic beauty of the land at the ocean, a true oasis of couples' romance in the summer heat, was perfect for capturing their romantic adventures on camera. The crowd was young and vibrant. Many visitors seeking refuge from the summer heat wore minimal beach wear and displayed exotic tattoos on their backs, faces, and necks. Some people had pierced ears and eyebrows adorned with glittering studs. The nearby theme parks and film studios were major attractions for celebrities in the city. They didn't hesitate to spend nights after their beach activities in such a place.

Vicky noticed a figure lurking around them, recognizing him from the airport, standing near a car. The individual followed them into the hotel, sitting on a sofa, hiding his face behind a newspaper, only to be identified by his distinctive shoes, trousers, and coat. Vicky's wisdom warned him, " Yes, he is the same person."

As they entered the grand hall, they were greeted by gracious women in elegant sarees. Two of them wore cordial smiles and led them towards another hall. The towering gilded pillars in the hall all appeared golden, and the marble floor shone brightly, creating a palpable atmosphere of grandeur. At the same time, the heavy, palatial doors were guarded by tall, burly sentries in well-tailored Sherwanis and regal turbans, evoking the splendour of a royal court.

Everything was in place for the arrival of Salim Sultan, who took great care of his guests. As they had heard before, for both father and son, it was a real experience. Jemima was specially invited for her birthday celebration. Peter had decided that it was the right time to announce their engagement. Though Peter himself was a guest at the party, they were both excited about this new family relationship. Several glamorous film personalities, prominent lawyers, industrialists, and people in business were in attendance.

It was 4 PM, and the helicopter landed on the helipad atop. Sultan disembarked and walked towards the banquet on the seventh floor, accompanied by four security men with sophisticated guns. The security presence outside the hotel intensified, with hundreds of guards circling the area, forming a protective cordon as soon as the helicopter landed. The fire tender was ready, poised to serve its master if needed. The lift stopped at the seventh floor. When the doors parted, a man in a white coat and pants stepped out. Although his dark sunglasses hid the ageing around his eyes, his half-grey hairs hinted at his middle age.

His arrival in the hall prompted a flurry of activities as people surrounded him, seeking to appease his piercing gaze. His merciless, angry eyes had ruined many lives in the past, and a few were still counting their last days in the ICU before the death of their profession and occupation.

Jemmy wore a long red gown with long, slightly curly, dark hair cascading to her mid-back. She always spoke with a British accent, having been born to an Indian father and a British mother. She looked gorgeous and was the undisputed cynosure in the hall. Sultan had taken a special interest in arranging her birthday celebration and her engagement with Vicky. Whether it was part of a business deal remained shrouded in mystery. Jemima was glad to be with Vicky at that moment. It was her primary compulsion to come to the party after an initial denial. She selfishly thought that Vicky would learn the trade better by being a part of this gathering. She had not seen Vicky since last summer, although they had a few phone conversations afterwards. As Jemima approached Vicky, her head was bowed, and her palms joined in a warm namaskar. It was all for Cheema, who stood next to Vicky. Her smile was genuine, and she looked delighted. Jemima's feelings for him were warm but still carried last summer's freshness. She felt the warmth as his arm brushed against her.

The announcement of their engagement was a big surprise to the crowd. It was a gasp-rippling moment for a few in the crowd as soon as Sultan made the announcement. Their booming interest in commerce just shattered. Peter and Cheema, their features radiating cheerfulness, stood side by side, raised hands with their hand in hand. They looked happy to be bonded in a family relationship. Their bond was palpable before the guests' very eyes.

Sultan's gaze swept the room. His goggles were off. A glint of anticipation was evident in his eyes- the alliance, he clearly believed, would grant him a tighter grip as a primary player in the power dynamics of Mumbai. The parents affirmed by accepting his invitation and joining the August gathering. Vicky's eyes scanned the sea of faces, searching, but the enigmatic figure -that man in the black coat was seen nowhere.

Jemima held Vicky's hand and dragged him to the bar at the end. The bartender removed a bottle of beer and poured it into a glass. She ordered tequila and lemonades. They sat by an infinity poolside on the seventh floor and enjoyed the music and the gyrating bodies dancing to the beat.

Peter said, "Look at that couple. They look happy with each other. Very soon, we will be a bigger family. This is the right time to merge our businesses. Sultan has shown interest in being a partner and has promised you some good deals in Mumbai. Experts will guide you to invest intelligently. This would be a more profitable business than your show business. Now is the time to put all your money into one basket. It will yield you the maximum return."

Like a much-awaited reality, the consent was mutual. Vicky slipped a ring on Jemmy's finger before she cut the cake. Jemima considered it more important in life than anything else. Her eyes were dreamy, and she stared at him while she fed Vicky the first bite of cake. The hall was filled with a lot of energy. After his brief appearance and the announcement, Sultan left the hotel, taking the aerial route.

*****

Mumbai, 2008

Cheema stood in his office., adorned in a sharp business suit- a more dignified version of himself. He was expecting someone in the next few minutes. Staff were informed about someone's arrival.

A moment later, a young businessman and consultant from Sultan's legal firm strode in, dressed impeccably in a tailored dark suit and a printed tie, a shiny briefcase in hand. He glanced at his gleaming golden watch before entering.

It was precisely eleven o'clock, the perfect time. Cheema mused, "It was a suitable time to throw out unhappiness for Sultan. He couldn't argue or negotiate when the business deal fell into his lap. In business, sometimes it is prudent to surrender oneself to the tyranny of Sultan's rule." He then realized that at the gathering in Dubai. He had the vibe that refusing the deal would be dangerous. The trailer he had seen in Dubai was enough for him to worry about the agreement. A denial would tamp down his influence in Mumbai and B-town circles. His political ambitions would suffer. Willy-nilly, he had to accept his offer. Sultan was a cunning fox, and he could no longer beat Sultan in the dark business. It will be wise if he remains grudgingly obsequious.

"Here's my card," he took out his business card from the left coat pocket and placed it on Cheema's table. Cheema offered him a seat across from him as both sat together after joining hands.

An obedient custodial worker in the office read Cheema's signal. He placed a glass of water before a cup of coffee. The young man sipped the coffee twice and then looked at his watch again. It seemed he had kept some other engagements before leaving for Dubai. So, he kept his briefing short and to the point. Without wasting much time, he reached for his briefcase and opened it. He took out a property map and a file of land deals with a prominent real estate agent. The plot was not in a marketplace. It was in the city's northwest corner on the coastal line, lining up in that stretch next to a big casino run by Sultan. "You liked it. That's why I came."

Cheema leaned forward, his gaze fixed on the young man. The steadiness in his posture was like someone trying to navigate the complexity of the deal through eyes by reading them. "Who are the sellers?" he asked.

The young man's posture exuded confidence while meeting the gaze of his prospective buyer. His lips curled into a pleasing smile. With a slight, slanting nod, he spoke in a well-pleased voice, "You need not worry about the sellers, sir. Sultan has done the job. All you need to care about is my commission on this lucrative deal."

" How much are you asking for it?"

"Not much, Just eight per cent of the deal price. Sultan will take care of the rest of the legality of ownership. Your willingness is all that I am concerned about to latch myself further onto this project." The gentleman expertly manoeuvred the situation to his advantage.

Nodding his head, Cheema glanced through the property map where the land was circled in red ink.

"So, Mr. Cheema, should I finalize this deal?" the young man asked. His brow contracted while expecting an answer. Raising his eyes at the gentleman, Cheema gave a puzzled look. He didn't even have a clue how to proceed in the chemical business. Cheema said, "Give me assurance that the locals will have no objection if I release the toxic waste directly into the sea." Cheema had to rely on his gut feelings. For him, the biggest objection would be the release of toxic waste into the sea.

Cheema said, "Dealing with public litigations was all included in the deal when we spoke on the telephone, and the final agreement was six per cent. Why are you asking two per cent extra?"

The young man smiled and said, "It is not only for the legality of services that we provide, but also it will provide you a lifetime of protection." He added, "Sultan's firm would provide you with all-time protection, and we will speed things up; the guarantee is ours, and you will get the regulatory approval in a day. You will be surprised to know how it is obtained in a day while others are made to wait months to get their place inspected and their plan approved. It all costs money. All under-the-table deals cost money. Your money is packed in large sacks and spent on this; only those who deny accepting it are dealt with with an iron fist. Those who deny hard cash are lured and honoured with expensive vacations, the welfare of their kids and their family members, and finally an offer of a free elite club membership, a good school in a foreign land." The man maintained a pretty decent cadence of a business executive.

He picked up an envelope and handed it over to Cheema. "These are the lists of drug peddlers who operate around the office buildings, playgrounds, shopping malls, pedestrian malls, business blocks, coconut vendors along the jogger's path, bike trails, dockyards, and airports. This offer is free. You can float your money in casinos, pubs, and drugs." He placed the documents inside the briefcase and snapped it shut. The young man looked at his watch before he left the place.

Cheema took a deep breath as he knew of Mumbai. It was not far beyond the touch of modernities. There were many business options when he came to Bombay. He knew well that it was then the starting point of any global change. He found his customers to be people who spend their lives earning money in casinos and pubs. He lured those indefatigable commuters in local trains and buses with drugs who always found a reason to smoke, and this project, which he just signed, would not be counterproductive if those slick, indecisive politicians did not bend the state rules for any change.

*****

Disha wouldn't have been disturbed if the man, not breaking the tranquillity, had not knocked at her door. The man in a dark suit had knocked twice at the door before coming to her notice. The man had already slipped into her office.

"Good morning, Madam. I am Robert. I am sent by Mr. Cheema to hand over this envelope." Disha eyed the envelope curiously, gaze fixed on the mysterious package, and asked, "Morning Robert, what is in this envelope?" Disha asked when Robert handed over the envelope.

"I don't know. As you see, the envelope is sealed." What captured her attention was the envelope was tightly packed and glued at its mouth. The address label which it bore was her office address. It urged her to open it instantly.

"Thank you." When Robert turned around and started moving away, she stopped him. "I have never seen you before. When did you join Cheema?" she asked.

"Oh, but I know you. I have heard a lot about you from him. I have joined him recently in his chemical plant as a manager," Robert gave her a smile of recognition.

"What is there in this letter?" Disha asked.

"Madam, I am afraid you must see for yourself. I don't know what it has in the content."

"Okay, Robert, I will see it and inform Sameer." Disha could not tolerate the stench of nicotine obnoxiously emanating from his mouth as if he had smoked before he entered her cabin. "You may leave now," she said while taking out the letter.

She tore open the letter and read. Disha's heart sank. Cheema's message was clear: It was an informal notice from Cheema to incur debts. The loaned amount had several zeros towards the end of the figure, which was written in that letter. She had never thought that Cheema would break the partnership unilaterally. He had given one year's notice to Sameer to pay back fifty per cent of the debt amount and the rest fifty per cent in the second year. Any default would attract legal proceedings, and the letter was annexed with a copy of their agreement paper. Towards the tail end of the paper, the amount he had written as the debt is bigger than the value of his estate and the Malhotra house.

Sameer jolted awake, coughing violently. His eyelids still had the heaviness of his mid-sleep. A few more precious hours passed as he looked at his watch; it was two in the morning. He had dozed off at his desk. The script he had been poring over crinkled beneath his forehead as his brow rested on the table. For the past five hours, he had been trying to refine the plot and cut unnecessary expenses for indoor scenes.

The writer's mind in Sameer had envisioned the plots and scenes in vivid detail, but now it wasn't easy to alter them in his memory. He couldn't afford those outdoor expenses. When he reviewed the expenditures, he saw that he had spent quite a bit on airfares, home parties, and hotel expenses. He had spent hours watching dozens of cassettes on a VCR player, but only to end up with a pounding headache through his strained eyes. He realized that a good writer couldn't be a good producer, and a good producer couldn't be a good writer. As a producer, he had to let go of his writer's imagination about characters, emotions, and backgrounds that he had envisioned in high definition. Still, those dialogues were meaningful for viewers to keep up with the story. He couldn't steal someone's imagination from an ancient or Western movie. His visualization was pure, but he had no choice. This would be his last project, where he could recover financially and pay off the goons hounding him. Half a dozen unknown voices were calling him and demanding money. Getting rid of those voices would be difficult until he recovered his investments. His health had not been the same as before. He felt comfortable shooting in Indian hill station locations for the outdoor scenes in the summer. The decorators were nickel-and-diming him for even minor alterations in the set, adding to his woes.

He leaned back, picked up a pencil, and jotted down a few lines in the space between the lines on the draft. He flipped through the papers again from the beginning to set the flow of dialogues right in one breath. Not feeling much satisfaction from the changes, he stood up from his chair and walked from one corner to another. He then returned to his table, picked up a pad, and outlined a new plot within his budget, bypassing the expensive director.

The clock struck four in the morning, and he was stressed and awake. He went to his office to pick up another file from the cabinet. His eyes fell on the envelope with his name on it. With a sinking feeling, he opened it and read the contents, his chest constricting with sudden discomfort. He reached for his medication, took some pills and the pain mitigated. He flipped through the papers in the file to find the places where he had signed an agreement on the stamp papers. Legally, it gave Cheema all the rights to sell off his property at any time if not paid within a year. Exhausted, Sameer managed to catch a few hours of sleep before waking up at eleven in the morning.

Mumbai, 2011

Three years later, Sameer had surmounted the odds and managed to complete the movie. It was a retake of his final scene, a poignant moment where his character would draw his last breath in his mother's loving embrace. Cheema hung around the honeymoon suite in his hotel as it had become the sombre stage of this pivotal scene, the air thick with a palpable sense of mourning. As Sameer had rewritten the script in the eleventh hour without consulting the script consultant, an eerie silence blanketed the set, as if the very walls were paying their respects to the impending demise of their well-known protagonist.

"The movie will turn out to be a super hit. I am speechless, Sameer. What a brilliant performance. Proud to be a co-producer in this film, for now, we need to celebrate," Cheema said, barely able to contain his excitement, dancing on the set as if Sameer had died in real life. He didn't even realize that Sameer had woken up and was watching him dance with happiness in his eyes.

Cheema shouted at the top of his voice, "I recovered my money with the death of Sameer. It will be a super-duper hit." Such a boisterous declaration sent shock waves through the crew. The crew members on set didn't know how to react to his gleeful outburst. The sudden transformation in Cheema's demeanour shook Sameer to his core. His voice was thick, with a disturbing, senseless remark. What was this man up to? It couldn't be believed to be a natural reaction anymore, but that of a greedy mind. To Sameer, he seemed nothing less than a greedy and selfish person. "What a partner, a strange, unusual, and freakish man. He will take everything if I die. What then? What will happen to Diya then? He should clearly instruct Diya on what she should do. Troubled by this revelation, Sameer immediately rushed to his house.

"Where are you going, Diya?"

However, Diya's aspirations had taken an unexpected turn. She said, "I can't stay with you anymore. I need my freedom. It smothers my hope when you say no to everything. I want to fly high in the sky." Her voice was laced with defiance of a rebel.

"You sound like a rebel. I always cared about you. You are going to spoil your career and life. I have seen the industry more than you, my child. Give me your baggage and come inside."

"No, Papa, I have already made up my mind. Your daughter, Diya Malhotra, is unstoppable, as you know. Once she decides to do something, she doesn't listen to her own inner voice. I hope you understand me better. I have bought a condominium and am going to live there."

"I hope you will stand for your father's dignity and won't do anything wrong in the future, my child. I will wait for you to come back soon."

"Don't wait for me, Papa; Diya needs freedom now."

Mumbai, 2018

He wiped the perspiration from his forehead. The room AC was working. His head was aching to burst. He was unaware of how many tablets he had popped to keep the pain suppressed in his chest. The pain was persistent. His left arm, for no reason, was giving him discomfort. He clenched his fist, then tilted his head upwards, not once, but several times. He had a feeling of choking in his throat. He rushed to the window for some fresh air. His throat dried up. He had a feeling that the blood had been dried up.

Upon hearing a knock and the grating noise of a key in the lock, his eyes tried to glance at the doorway. She was not Diya. He was stirred and roused by a touch on his forehead from Disha. He told her, " Diya didn't come !" A curtain of darkness descended, pulling him deeper into the abyss.

There was constant communication between Disha and Dr Pradeep while she was on the road carrying him in the ambulance. The great advantage was that she knew the place thoroughly and where to take Sameer for treatment. Disha couldn't do anything for her mother, but destiny had brought her to a stage where she should do something for Sameer. She rubbed his feet, heedless of his soiled trousers. Her only focus was on getting him the help he so desperately needed.

The vehicle jolted and swayed and finally came to a halt. When the doors parted, they found themselves in front of the emergency room. It was a chilly and windy night outside. Disha alighted, pausing at the door as Sameer was carefully extracted from the ambulance. She buttoned him up properly. The footsteps of the stretcher-bearers were audible from a distance. She turned her head towards them. She recognized Dr. Pallavi behind the mask, who sprang into action, swiftly directing her team to transfer the man on the stretcher to the ICU.

Disha remained at Sameer's side, supporting him as he was wheeled into the critical care unit. Pale and listless, Sameer was lying on the stretcher as if his life was ready to depart for heaven any moment. He gasped for breath. Pallavi touched his hand. It was cold. The pulse was faint and erratic. Pallavi leaned in, pressing her hands against his chest, willing his heart to resume its steady rhythm. After what seemed an eternity, Sameer heaved a deep sigh. His pulse started coming up, returning to its normal volume. Sameer returned to his senses after a few minutes.

When he saw Pallavi, he was stirred, murmuring words that sought forgiveness, "Forgive me, Beti, I am the culprit. Look after my Diya." He clucked several times. Pallavi couldn't understand what he intended to say except for a few last words. He prayed to God with folded hands to spare him for his sin in a broken voice before he was put on a ventilator. His heart lost beats, and the rhythm lost its patterns. Delivering shock after shock couldn't bring his life back, and he finally succumbed.

Mumbai, 2019

Pallavi stood before the multidisciplinary forum and opened her presentation with a front-page news clipping on the screen. The powerful opening slide commanded everyone's attention. "What do you see on the front-page news today? An impressive-looking gentleman, an industrialist, our future political choice, enjoying good media coverage in the country's prominent political gatherings. All he spoke about was economic developments in the state and industrialization. He is powerful, and no one in the print media can question the editor on why his speech is so important to the public. Now, I am shifting your focus to the third page. But Look closely at this picture, a photo of a mother crouched, crying in distress, being grabbed by her arms by a few neighbours, and the place was inside a hospital. These kinds of scenes are just unacceptable odds in our cities. Her unborn baby was an innocent victim of this rapid industrialization. How lucky were those people born in the city when it was clean? The figures of infant mortality rates in recent years might upset you, but that is the reality. Until recently, many projects have been approved in the name of economic development. The reason I bring this up is to protect our innocent victims. The joy of happy motherhood ends when you have a sick child at home."

"Now, coming to the main discussion today, I have a strong observation."

She walked towards the hand-drawn city map on the whiteboard. "In the past six months, I have seen almost hundreds of congenital heart diseases. I analysed that most children I operated on hailed from the northwestern region of the city." Pallavi pointed her pen towards the bunch of red stars drawn on the map. She then moved her pen towards the south and east and said, "Very few cases are from other places in the city, almost a ratio of 90:10. Then I called up Dr. Arundhati, our obstetrician. She, too, had a similar number of cases in her clinic. Many pregnant mothers had stillbirth babies. I also contacted her father. He is a renowned paediatrician in Mumbai. He, too, was worried about too many infant mortalities in his ICU. The majority died of congenital disorders.

Interestingly, Dr Amitav, our radiologist, also revealed that in the last year, he had picked up sixty to seventy per cent of congenital disorders while doing fetal ultrasound. I checked their addresses. They were all from the northwest corner of the city."

Dr. Pradeep said, "The data Pallavi presented is really alarming. I don't deny it. There has been a reasonable inflation in the number of cases. During the initial phase of my career in the mid-eighties, I used to get only one or two cases in a month. The climate was clean, and the pollution was less."

Pallavi said, "Thanks to Dr. Amitav, who set up the fetal medicine clinic and started picking up these diseases early inside the womb."

Dr Pradeep added, " During those days, the diagnostic equipment was not so advanced to detect such diseases. Nowadays, they are picked up while the babies are still in the womb. The number in my ward has increased tenfold. Fortunately, we have been able to treat them at an early stage to save them from a slow, late death."

Pallavi continued, " As per my data, it has almost increased thirtyfold in the last two years. Look at the figures of the neonatal ward; the mortality rate is alarmingly high. I tried to trace their locations. All of them had come from the same region. I blame the water toxicity more than any sort of air pollution in the last few months."

Dr. Pradeep said, "I had never thought of such a problem in the community. It would be best if you dug deeper into this matter. Take the help of friends from community medicine and involve your students in this study. As the department head, I will assign you five students to dig up this issue of infant mortality." Pallavi's eyes burned with determination, and she said, "We must uncover the truth. We must act swiftly, decisively and save these innocent lives."

She called five of her students and asked them to sit across her table. Before telling them anything, she stated with a voice which carried a sense of profound responsibility, "The reason I called you is for a task. The task is vast, and the responsibility is big. In my eyes, none of you is insignificant to the task. What I am going to say is not part of your thesis topic, but it is a matter of professional responsibility to humanity. The very reason we joined this profession. The little effort we put in will significantly contribute to this study. The study is vast, and the number of houses you visit is in the thousands. The water samples you collect from each door need to be studied for toxic chemicals. Would you mind if I made you stay awake until the middle of the night for a few days? I know you won't when every second of your time will save many innocent lives.

" No, Madam. We are ready to work with you." The students unanimously said.

"Students, the mortality rates of infants and neonates have alarmingly increased in the last few months. The spill of organic chemicals, pesticides, metals, and toxic industrial fumes into the atmosphere is to be blamed for this. The cases have outnumbered the hospital beds in the city. All I want from you five is that you visit the medical establishments, the hospitals, and the nursing homes. Identify the cases and record their addresses. You will visit their doors to collect water samples and share your live locations." She trained her students and taught them how to test water for chemicals.

A week-long exercise was almost coming to an end when she received an SMS on her mobile phone. The message from an international number bothered her as it flashed a warning. She immediately withdrew all her students from the field, dialled a number, and said, "The final report would take at least six months to compile all the data. The figure was so big, in the thousands. Some people have travelled to other cities and are being traced."

Corrupt individuals are not inherently corrupt but are shaped by society. Recently, the high court called out certain business groups for supplying intoxicative substances to the public, and news channels broadcasted distressing scenes of women and children suffering in these factories. As a result, government officials launched a large-scale search operation. They shocked those responsible for polluting the roads, water bodies, and air quality with heavy fines and the permanent closure of their factories. This strong stance by the new government was unexpected. Pallavi's articles on health issues in the city profoundly impacted the business community, whose factories were raided and auctioned due to illegal activities. On one side, these groups trivialized the court's verdict to protect their interests, while on the other side, Pallavi emerged as a bold columnist in local newspapers. A clash between the influential figures of the city was inevitable. On one side, a renowned surgeon relied on her expertise in medical science to challenge prevailing practices, while on the other side, business leaders with underworld affiliations disregarded environmental regulations. Various methods were employed to resolve the dispute, including negotiation, punishment, and manipulation, but none were sufficient to bring about an end. Gradually, Pallavi realized that the corrupt individuals in the city were not inherently corrupt but were made corrupt by those seeking to fulfil their own selfish ambitions. The position of power held by certain individuals can either construct or destroy the city. A simple nod of approval to these individuals would have earned Pallavi expensive luxuries such as sandals, bags, jewellery, trips abroad, a new home, or a fancy car. However, these were not her desires. The tension between the head of the department and the business ecosystem was palpable.

Looking at her table, I can say that all the objects were impeccably arranged and remained there as they were when Dr. Pradeep, her predecessor, occupied the office. There was the same desk, same books, same lamp, except for a few bulletins from past days scattered as she had already gone through them multiple times. She was familiar with every object in that room. With time passing and the occupant of the chair changing, the chair itself remained constant. After Dr. Pradeep's retirement, she was elevated to the Head of Department post. Those who believed in the metaphysical laws of the universe also believed that the universe conspires to get you what you desire to achieve through your hard work. Palo dreamt of becoming a doctor about three decades ago, and it all started from this very place. Her life was about to enter a new phase that she was not aware of.

Nearly an hour had passed since Palo had entered her chamber. She had no leisure to observe the exquisite weather beyond her window, as there were other times when she might have cast her gaze upon the city passersby. She was occupied with a crucial task that required undivided attention. Standing by the file rack, her back facing the door, she held a thick file in the flat of her left palm and diligently flipped through its pages with her other hand. She was searching for significant material to study for an upcoming conference.

The door to her office was open, and as she was seriously engrossed in her paperwork, a sudden knock at the open door startled her. Glancing up, she was met with the most unexpected sight. She had never expected this way to be stunned by an unpredictable visit from a friend. She had said, "Come in," as soon as she heard the knock on the door before turning to face the door. The man who stood at the jamb didn't say anything until their gaze met. "Hello, Pallavi." The visitor, wearing a brown coat and vibrant parrot green shirt underneath, showcased a charismatic Duchenne smile. His hair was long and well-lacquered. His overall appearance exuded the demeanour of a thorough gentleman.

With a darting glance, Pallavi looked at him. Following a brief visual assessment of the visitor, a charming dimple appeared on her face.

"Oh... hi." With a dimpled smile, she said, "What a delightful surprise," she exclaimed while ushering him in. She gestured towards the chair across from her desk after a handshake. " Vicky! I couldn't recognize you at first. You have put on a little weight over the years, but it suits you well. "

"How come you are here? Hope everything is okay," she asked.

"Nothing serious. I slipped in the bathroom while taking a shower this morning and sprained my ankle. I saw your nameplate outside, so I couldn't resist stopping by," Vicky explained.

"Sit down. Coffee for you? You like coffee, right?" Pallavi's smile widened as she offered him a cup of coffee, the aroma wafting through the air.

"You still remembered what I like. Pallavi, I am glad you have reached the heights you always dreamed of." She mused on what he had just said, her eyes sparkling with genuine delight.

"You know, Vicky, the metaphysical rule of the universe is that it conspires to give you what you desire most," she said.

"Then I should be thankful to God, the master of this universe who conspired to make it this way. Probably, that is why I am here; otherwise, I would have had to be in London this afternoon," Vicky's Duchenne smile never wavered as he stated.

Pallavi nodded in agreement, her dimple smile reflecting the sentiment. "See his power. You are right here, sitting before me after so many years."

"If I had not come to this hospital, how would I have met this beautiful friend of mine?" Vicky said with an impressive tone.

"Oh... I feel the same. It's all destiny that decides our meetings and existence in this world. But it's not necessary to fall in the bathroom to meet a friend. You could have come straight away," Pallavi teased, her playful tone belied the passing of time. She asked, "What have you done in these years? What about your plans to set up your own pharmaceutical company and chemical plants?"

"I went to London for my graduation. I completed a bachelor's in pharmacology. Then, I jumped straight into my dad's business. Now, I am looking after the business in London," Vicky explained.

Pallavi was impressed by his sophisticated and charming demeanour. She thought, "His persona is still the same, quite charismatic." Vicky maintained his Duchenne smile throughout the conversation.

After taking a sip, Vicky said, "We have now moved towards pharmaceuticals and chemicals."

"That's great news," Pallavi replied.

Vicky asked, "How is everyone in your family?"

Pallavi didn't know where to put herself in this question. She was unused to this question- " Family! Mom is fine."

"How about you?" Pallavi asked.

"All is well here. I stay alone in London. Life is just going as a happy bachelor," Vicky replied.

" Not married yet ?"

" You know, business ventures. I never thought about marriage."Vicky replied.

" Don't you feel lonely?"

Vicky finished his coffee and checked his watch. Looking at Pallavi, he said, "Now, I won't , after meeting a friend like you in the city. By the way , if you are not planning any thing in the weekend then keep it free. There is a small get-together of socialites in my hotel. I would be honoured if you come."

She didn't know what to say. She couldn't decide whether to work on the presentation she would make for the upcoming conference in Goa or to attend a friend's party. Caught in this quandary, she simply said, "I will try to make it."

As Vicky left, limping. Pallavi couldn't convince herself that the person she met was the same Vicky who studied with her in college long ago. She noticed his firm, upright posture, brilliant features, and a rare combination of deep sobriety. It intrigued her. If she turned down his invitation, it might make him unhappy. She was curious to know more about Vicky and his great services to the nation. She was convinced that if she were to marry someone, he should have all the qualities of Vicky. "Falling in love with someone like Vicky would be premature unless he were to express interest in me first," her innate humility urged her to think about marriage after several years. She would try to be useful to him with all her experiences in the field of medicine.

During her presentation, Pallavi shed light on the issues of haphazard town planning and pollution caused by improper waste disposal. "Haphazard town planning has contaminated our streets with garbage. Who cares if the drainage on the road is choked? Where will we grow plants when you have taken all those fertile lands and forest lands under your control? The flora and fauna have difficulty in survivability," she explained.

She also questioned why big business players couldn't use natural gases instead of coal when the globe is facing environmental challenges. She further asked why they couldn't fix their pipelines periodically and why they couldn't set up a chemical treatment plant adjacent to their fertilizer factories. "Is it not their legal responsibility? If it is not, what is corporate social responsibility for?" she concluded with questions for the audience to ponder.

Pallavi was a great presenter, and her presentation carried messages to the bureaucracy, big corporate houses, and politicians to act. She had all the solutions to everyone's problems. Her solutions resonated with the audience and left a lasting impact on those responsible for pollution.

"Vicky, I was always aware of the risk of presenting the facts in a public forum like this. I did it not for me but for my state, my people, and my profession. Vicky, I hope you understand that I have done nothing wrong," she said.

The environmentalists kept mum against the rising industrial pollution in Mumbai. They maintained a whispered hush against the influentials due to their power. Their silence was puzzling, especially when Pallavi's articles were shining a daily spotlight on the issue. However, the reason could be their lack of conviction to gather the necessary data. When she conducted a study, They turned into a pack of hounds, hounding her for the data she had collected.

"They will be shocked tonight when they find out how I collected such a huge amount of data under their nose," she said.

Her words unconcealed the government's inability to tackle the situation and exposed the imperiousness of the so-called eco-enthusiasts who considered themselves the green activists of the century, not letting themselves be discredited for anything.

"I have all the data stored in my laptop. I can show you if you want. It would make them red-faced. But it was your event, and I didn't want to spoil it." Pallavi said.

"I do have a chemical factory right there on the northeast side. I have all the legal permissions to run it. My factory workers live in those hutments next to my factory. I didn't find any symptoms of water toxicity in them."

Do you have a certificate of acceptance for the water safety plan before placing them in the hutments?" Pallavi asked.

"A few labs in the city have certified that the water in the hutments is usable for drinking. I will collect the samples and send them to your lab. You check it yourself. " Vicky said as they strolled out of the hotel lobby.

"Well done, Vicky, my dear," Peter patted him on the back as soon as she left the hotel in her car. "Did you see what she is up to? I am never wrong in my assessment. Didn't I warn you that she cannot be lured? She is a real threat to our society. I can't take her anymore. She spoiled the mood of the party."

"I will solve this matter, Papa. Leave that to me." Vicky said with exuded confidence.

"I hope both of you meet again and solve this matter," Peter said.

"I have made all the arrangements in Goa as per your plans. The conference has yet to receive many participants, but don't worry, Papa. Things will be done perfectly by our management team," Vicky said.

Peter dragged him to a corner of the lobby where the crowd was thin, and the guests were about to leave. "Listen, son, no one would pity us if the data she spoke about gets leaked to the public. You contemplate how to sort this matter out. Sooner is better. After all, we must have a good relationship with Sultan to maintain. Your father is going to get elected by these people. The yokels among these elites may not have understood what she said, but I am sure the well-read elites have gotten a hint out of this discussion. Such a matter doesn't take much time to draw public attention. The press, which is silent about us, may blow the matter out of proportion. It would be enough to put us in the docks. I don't want Cheema's image to get tarnished this way."

Vicky said, "Papa, I always admire your premonitions. Trust me, I am confident. I never fail in my mission."

After Peter left that place, Disha joined him with a file in her hand.

She said, "Diya Malhotra signed the legal documents. Now, the Malhotra estate legally belongs to you, Vicky. You can plan your next project. A production house of your own or a sea-facing hotel."

Vicky laughed, "Thanks, Disha, but I changed my mind. It is a sea-facing property. I don't think like my father. I don't want to waste the land for making films. Didn't my father tell you about the cruise that we are buying? Our import and export business will flourish if we use it best as a dockland. The redevelopment plan of the coastal belt is in full swing. If advice is sought for the best utilization of this land, then my father is a wrong choice. I want it to be decided by the Dubai group in our next meeting three weeks from now."

Disha reacted strongly. Her face turned red, and her voice agonized, "Vicky, you are new to this business. Dealing with the Dubai group means inviting Sultan to your doorstep. Why not a hotel here, Vicky? What is not there with you? Your father will never approve of your misadventure."

"My decisions are final, Disha. You have seen me grow. I always make the right decisions. I adore you. You will be a part of our business adventure."

"Count me out if you deal with the Dubai group. I would rather want to resign from my job."

Vicky said, "Didn't you hear what my father said to the workers in the factory? It would be his first venture to associate himself with Peter. The cosmetic industry is at its peak in India and is hopping well. It will be a collaboration. The chemical factory will be solely ours, and the packaging and distribution will be Peter's. Now, please tell me what is wrong with using waterways as the mode of transport over sea. In my opinion, Dockland is the best idea for this land. You have a bigger task at hand to deliver. You can't think of resigning."

Disha's voice exhibited a perceptible annoyance when she said," Vicky, It should be ratified legally before you plan anything here. Don't go by that, Peter. That man is not trustworthy. He has harmful intentions. His eyes always dart me with an unwanted gaze like a predator surveilling its prey."

My father wants you to be there to handle the delegation of state representatives who deal only with environmental issues and have shown their interest in visiting our factories. He wants them to be looked after well. It would be best if you were with him all the time. His friends from the media and business world would like to join him for an event following their visit. Who do you think can handle them better than you? It is for a social cause. I hope you understand how important this moment will be for him, and your proficiency in such matters is unimaginable. It is not so easy to win elections these days. People in power are familiar with my father. The most suitable time is now. We have only six months left to start our project."

"Tell me, Vicky, Is Peter a fine man to deal with? Does he not have any link with Sultan?"

After a moment of silence, he said, "I can't find a better mentor than Peter in this business today. He is my father-in-law. I hope you understand, Disha. My intention is always inclined to do good for society. It should not matter to you who I am associated with," his tone was soothingly suave, not conspiratorial, which was enough to shunt away the fierce scowl on Disha's face.

*****

Pallavi was all set to present a paper at a conference in Goa. Laxmi asked her to plan a vacation, but she refused. "The workload is so much, Mama, I cannot even think of taking a week off from the hospital. I will catch the next flight after my presentation and come back.

Pallavi's mind was in turmoil. The plight of children suffering to die on their mothers' laps weighed heavily on her heart. "God, someone should tell Mama how important it is for her to be in the hospital when so much work is pending. The string of her heart was pulled taut by the beautiful place. There was no doubt. But vacationing at this moment will be her last priority," Pallavi thought.

As she reached the hotel dining in Goa, Vicky suddenly appeared.

"What a pleasant surprise, Pallavi, to see you here," Vicky said, reaching in no time near her. He was well-suited and booted. The gesture was too friendly. His voice had the softness that soothed her nerves when he asked her to join a group of ladies huddled around a table, engaged in lively discussion as they awaited their lunch.

"Will you go for sightseeing, Pallavi? These girls are from my company and assembled here for a sightseeing trip. The bus is about to arrive. Finish your lunch and come along."

"No, I have to put the final touches on my presentation," she hesitated.

"Then promise me that you will have dinner with me," Vicky said, his eyes gleaming with hopeful anticipation. Vicky's persistence was like a gentle breeze coaxing her. The weight on the heart was momentarily lifted by Vicky's warmth and charm.

"Okay, I promise," Pallavi relented.

In the evening, they met in the dining at his insistence. There was a visible warmth in Pallavi's eyes as he read them. Millions of thoughts crossed her mind, making her speechless when Vicky placed his hand on hers as they sat together. Her heart quickened. She lost track of their conversation topic, as this was not just a casual chat over coffee. They were in a beautiful dining hall in a hotel, with an ambience that could make anyone fall in love. The crowd was young, and instrumental music played softly in the background as their eyes met. They stared at each other silently, their minds filled with countless thoughts that prevented them from having any meaningful conversation. The drink she had consumed had a magical influence on her, and the food had yet to be served. She was impressed by his charm and found him to be nice. However, confusion clouded her expression when he proposed to her, and she willingly offered her finger for him to slip a diamond ring onto. After dinner, they talked, and he walked her to his room. They watched television together, and as the night passed, she fell asleep on the couch beside him.

The sound of the shower woke her up in the morning, and she realized Vicky was in the shower. She felt her deep desire to marry someone like Vicky had been fulfilled. The unexpected waves of emotion had entangled her thoughts. She wondered if it was really her who had said yes to Vicky's proposal. She played with the diamond ring on her left hand as she felt a slight quiver of indigestion. The drink she had consumed the night before still lingered in her stomach, causing her to burp. She quickly stood up and rushed to her room next door to get ready for her presentation.

As she sat on the aeroplane, a thought crossed her mind repeatedly. Was accepting Vicky's proposal a wise decision, or was it the result of impaired thinking? This thought created conflict in her heart. His feelings for her were evident on his face when she said yes. He stared at her, went down on one knee, and proposed to her. Of course, she would have said yes without hesitation. The feeling of being proposed to by him was incredibly tantalizing and couldn't simply be forgotten overnight. The next day, their conversation was pleasant. He was polite and gentle, a true gentleman. "Yes, I made the right choice, Mama," she thought. The engagement was wholeheartedly approved by her, and there were no more conflicts or clashes of incompatible thoughts in her mind. In the next moment, she happily revealed to Laxmi that she was engaged to Vicky and had no difficulty finding the words to tell her.

*****

Six months later-

"I worry about you these days. How are you living? Where do you spend your time? I haven't heard from you in a long time," Disha asked with concern.

Diya's cheeks turned crimson as she frowned and stared intensely at Disha. Those words from Disha shattered her inner silence, and she retorted, "Get straight to the point. I have no pleasant moments to cherish anymore. It all happened because of you. I hate you for going to work with the man who left me on the street. I have nothing left on this earth except this small house. The door is open behind you if you want to leave. I signed all those papers you wanted me to sign; don't ask me for any more documents. After my father's death, our relationship is over. I see you now as a stranger. You can stoop down to such a low level, Disha. I saw you joining hands with the man who threw me out of the Malhotra house. I know your intentions and why you've come."

Disha tried to convince her, "No, dear, I have never been a stranger to you. I still think about you. You've misunderstood me before, and now you continue to think of me differently. I joined him long before your father became a part of my life. He was the one who sheltered me when I was struggling to make a living on my own. My situation was not much different from yours. I had no one in my family, and due to my ill health, I couldn't sustain a career in Bollywood. I went bankrupt and started running a parlour. Your father was introduced to me by Cheema as his business partner. Sameer had high hopes for you and believed that one day, you would become a great star and manage his production house. Unfortunately, he died with unfulfilled dreams. How can his soul rest in peace when you live a life like this?" After a pause, Disha said, "Everyone here calls you Ghost Aunty. The newspapers speak ill of you. You broke your neighbour's windows when he refused to open the door, just for a drink. You've picked fights with security guards. How could you do this, Diya? Look at what is written about you in this newspaper, and look at what is written about your friend, Dr. Pallavi, on the reverse side. She performed a difficult surgery. I have been following the news about you. You look like a withered and less energetic star these days. And your wardrobe choices, revealing slivers of your shrunken flesh, are bizarre. You're at the tail end of your career. What has happened to you?"

Diya's voice softened as she replied, "Don't hold high hopes for me like my father did. I don't want to live much longer. I am suffering from a bad disease called chronic alcoholic pancreatitis. I need alcohol to keep my pain levels low. I cried in pain when there was no whiskey in my bottle, so I barged into my neighbour's door in the middle of the night. The security guards blocked my way, and I hit one of them on the head. I couldn't tolerate the pain. It felt like being stabbed in my abdomen when the pain worsened. The doctors say I have only a few days left to live like this if I don't undergo surgery. After that…"

"After that, what?"

"After that, I will join my father and mother in heaven," Diya burst into laughter to hide the tears streaming down her cheeks.

"Stop it, Diya. You're not going to die. You're saying this because you're depressed. Don't think about ending your life. Let me speak with Pallavi. She can help you with your problem," Disha urged.

"Only Dr. Pallavi Rajhans can operate on me, the surgeons told me. My case is quite complicated. I don't want to undergo any surgery. I don't want to die with a scar on my body. Diya sobbed, "Whenever I wanted something, she took it away from me. In school, the best student award. In college, my boyfriend. And now, the few days I have left, she'll take those too. She'll kill me. She is cruel to me and has a sharp tongue. She didn't even spare her boyfriend, Honey. I hate her. I would rather die on my own than go to her for surgery. I will not surrender my life into her hands. I want freedom."

Disha said, "Stop it, Diya. What freedom are you talking about? Now, you need freedom from your pain. She is the best surgeon in the city, and she is not cruel. The cruelty lies in what you're doing to your own body. Look at me. My story is not much different from yours. I wanted to live a life to fulfil my mother's dreams. I also had to undergo heart surgery and survive a difficult relationship. People spoke ill of me, and the newspapers wrote terrible things about me. They claimed I was a drug addict, the mistress of a gangster, but I was never depressed. I faced all of that at a young age. I understood that it was a state of mind. Don't let bad thoughts creep into your mind. I may drink, but I have control over my mind. I don't create chaos around me or break glasses. I will talk to Pallavi if you can't. She knows me well. The girl you consider your number one enemy has also suffered a lot because of your father."

"My father? How? Tell me, Disha. How has Pallavi suffered because of my father?"

"Mrs Briksha Roy was killed by Sameer in that highway accident. Sagar took the blame upon himself because your mother was battling lung cancer, and you were just two years old. For your information, she is the daughter of Sagar Rajhans, who used to work as a chauffeur in the Malhotra house. I know her as a very kind-hearted doctor. After learning about her, I hope you won't turn her away when she comes to meet you." Disha left her house.

*****

The smell of cigarette smoke filled the air as she took a deep breath and closed her eyes. The wonderful memories of the past danced in her mind. The life she had once labelled as distasteful was slowly shedding its bitterness. Those days were the good old days. The people who encouraged her to smoke and drink in the pub and cheered when she shouted "freedom" were nowhere to be found. They were fair-weathered friends. The most beautiful moments were the ones she had once cursed for their regularity and boredom. She was now ready to let go of her resentment toward love and affection, which she had seen as patriarchal terms and conditions. Now, she realized the true joy of the days she spent with her father. They were filled with laughter and happiness. Her father had passed away three years ago, but she still remembered him calling to ask, "How are things going, Diya?" It felt like just yesterday.

She realized that what she had considered imprisonment was the best phase of her life. She could laugh, chat with friends, and have a set routine for sleeping, waking up, leaving the house, and eating. It was a stress-free life. She even liked her house. Deep down in her past, she was happy and cheerful. The only distressing part was seeing her mother in pain.

"Freedom, freedom, and freedom. What did they all mean after all? She cannot forget the day when she was on a cruise, and her friends laughed at her for not puffing out the "Maal". She later understood that it was not the Marlboro she was told about;

it was pure hashish rolled in papers. The loud laughter of that day on the cruise reverberated inside the four walls of her house, filled with smoky air. "That one mistake in my heyday, spending a whale of time with friends while cruising from Mumbai to Goa, took my life away and snatched me away from my near and dear ones. The 'Hash' they gave me paralyzed my life's most productive years," she thought distressfully.

Diya heard a recognizable warm voice of a lady calling her name on the other side of the door. She knocked and asked her to open the door when she believed that the ring of the bell was not enough to wake someone up from the slumber inside.

Diya ignored the ring of the bell, which buzzed inside like a lazy bee, thinking about the reporters who lately ran smack into her flat without her prior permission in the want of a piece of news for their fashion magazine.

The voice turned louder until she opened the door. She stood stunned to see Pallavi at her doorstep. Pallavi squeezed past her inside before she said anything. Diya turned around and stared at her. She had no interest in starting a conversation with Pallavi. After a moment of silence, Pallavi said adoringly while sitting down on a sofa in her living room, "Dear, if I am desired at your place, let me tell you that an invitation is not required. I am sure I have done nothing wrong by coming to your place uninvited. I know you never expected me here like this. Today, any kind of your behaviour is fine by me. I will not leave this place until you let the turmoils inside your heart out."

Nothing came to Diya's mind on how to react. She walked closer and sank down on the sofa across from her. She lifted both her bare legs to rest on the centre table. She pulled out a cigar from a packet lying on the table next to the sofa, then lit it to take a full puff and blow the smoke into the air. With no obvious sign of a frown on her face, she did it knowingly to show her displeasure. Such a gratifying moment for her to show the enemy number one, the place she had longed for in her life. "I know you are very clever; more than that, you are a devious lady. You will try to outsmart me. I know your habit of tweaking words to monopolize any conversation. I am now fully aware of your intent. You cannot monopolize my time to prove your superiority at the end, but don't think I am in any way less cerebral than you," she pretends to glow with confidence and again blows out a streak of smoke into the air.

" By the way, who told you I am in distress? Who said any turmoil going on inside my heart? " There was a touch of arrogance in her voice. "I am happy and independent. I don't like intruders in my life."

Pallavi's sharp mind began to react responsibly. She looked at her legs, shrunken and devoid of flesh from the thigh downwards. Her eyes shifted to settle on her face. The cheekbones stood prominent; eyeballs retracted into cavities. "You will feel better if you set them free. I am sure today is the day you need my help most," Pallavi voiced tenderly.

Diya grunts, "Unsolicited help! My slippers won't even take that; forget about my foot." Diya showed her scraggy bare feet which she rested on the centre table to Pallavi. Her toes looked pale to Pallavi as they belonged to a patient with gross anaemia. Grumpily, Diya snorts, "Probably you don't know, I am exclusively a creature of myself. I never considered you as my friend. I am still more talented, more sophisticated, and richer than you." Diya's lips quivered in anger. Pallavi saw her cheeks were flushed.

Pallavi said abruptly, "I thought you would sparkle with happiness by seeing an old friend. I don't have the slightest doubt in your sophistication. Your achievements are the result of your prodigious hard work. I have nothing to say about it. You said it right -you are a creature exclusively made for yourself. I know you from school days. You never listened to the teachers, nor even to your father. The whole college heard you disdaining your father with your so-called sophisticated invectives; just because he told you not to sign the 'Pan masala Ad', you signed it against his will despite knowing well that it causes cancer. He had given you all the freedom to choose the right from the wrongs, but you chose wrongs."

"I had no desire to follow his stupid advice. I needed money. I did whatever I liked to get out of his shoes. I wanted to live with an identity of my own. I wanted to be known as Diya Malhotra, not as the daughter of Sameer Malhotra. There is nothing wrong if a butterfly breaks the cocoon; if I did it for my freedom, then it becomes a headline. Highly disgusting," she sounded like a megalomaniac.

"Bravo, your achievements are undeniable. I will not ask you how Diya Malhotra turned into a flop star overnight from a superstar, then to an alcoholic, and then to a ghost aunty. I am not here to disturb your peace at this moment. When I read about you in the newspaper, I thought I must pay you a visit. After all, I am your enemy number one. I have the right to know about you, dear, how you are doing," Pallavi spoke with a pitiful calmness on her face.

"Your words don't attract me. I know who has sent you to me. You are still my enemy number one, and you will remain so forever." Diya puffed out a smoke circle into the air.

Pallavi cleared her throat and said, "Look at this picture in the newspaper. The windows are closed, the room is smoky and must be suffocating! There are a few bottles of whiskey at the bar in the background and a fake diamond necklace around your neck, revealing only your skeleton through these white clothes in this photo. Is that what you meant by sophistication?"

"Oh, I see. The daughter of my chauffeur has a great knack for knowing diamonds. I didn't know when you turned into an aficionado of diamonds. My necklace is fake, be it. I keep them close to my heart. But Honey was a real diamond; why did you then disown him? To you, all diamonds look fake. Disgusting lady, do you think that stupidity is written on my brow, and I don't know what you are up to these days? I know why you chose Vicky for marriage. You snared him for his property. That son of a beast snatched away all my properties and brought me to the roads. Here you again cut across my path but cannot stop me from reaching my destination. I am tired. I want to go for a long sleep. I have lived my life enough, now I want to die." The anger within Diya dissipated to a point of conclusion with these words, Pallavi felt. After a moment of silence, Pallavi stood up and moved towards a portrait hanging on the wall.

Pallavi absorbed the snobbish remarks silently, ignoring the sarcasm. She said, "You have no idea what you are talking about, Diya. You are overreacting. When people called you a flop star, you never reacted. They called you a Ghost Aunty, but you never reacted. When I came here to meet you, you reacted strongly. Am I that bad as a person to you?" Staring at her father's portrait, she asked, "Do you know what your father's last words were? His last words were 'Take care of my Diya'."

Diya's anger flickered away, and her ruddy face faded. She stood up and glided towards Pallavi, then asked morosely, "What do you want to say? Will you take care of me? Don't listen to him, what he said. I am OK. Thank you for your concern. I need no care. Do you understand that?" Her voice had a mixed feeling of gloominess and pride.

"No. You are not okay, Diya. You need to see a doctor. What have you made of yourself? You don't know."

"I know, I am stoved up by pancreatitis. I will not live longer. The little life I have, I want to die peacefully without any pain. These bottles are now my pacifiers. I am sick of this world. When I see the Plough through my telescope - do you know what I think?" Her eyes slinked away towards the telescope she had placed close to an open balcony door. "I want to spend my days with my parents there in the sky. I contemplate staying with them like another star. I am a loner. I now bewail the separation when they left me. I will be better if I am with them.

I have decided to leave this world. I won't allow anyone to put a knife on my body."

Pallavi looked into her eyes and said, "You are contemplating about an imaginary world, Diya. Those are the stars shining since aeons, unlike any film star of today who shines only for a short time. They were in the sky much before your parents came to this world. Pointing to a picture on the wall, Pallavi said, 'Look at the reality in the picture of the sky. Orion, Pleiades, Ursa Major, and Corona Borealis are their names. Look at these stars. Millions of planets. I don't find anything beyond this. They are celestial bodies. You feel differently about them because of your illness. Look at your attire and look at your hair. What have you done with yourself? Never tell me that your life is now meaningless. I am sure my friend Diya will once again glow to dispel the darkness around her."

Diya laughed regretfully, turned away, and didn't look at her. Turning her gaze towards the sky as she heard Pallavi, she was plagued by the insecurity in her life. She couldn't sustain the laughter for long. She swallowed the bitterness. The silence followed for a minute. Pallavi watched the tear spill down her cheek.

Pallavi said, "I am sure you will not yield to your failures like this once you undergo surgery to get rid of your pain. You will think differently. Say only once, yes, I will operate on you."

Diya said with a heavy heart, and the glumness made her voice wet, "I know you don't want to lose me. You care for me. I am telling you the truth: as a loser, I always tried to hurt you. But Pallavi, before leaving this world, I want to know from you - where did I go wrong?" With a deep sigh, she asked, "Why couldn't I stop myself from worrying about failures? Why couldn't I be as successful as you?" She paused for a moment and turned her gaze at Pallavi. She began to narrate, "It all began with you. You gave a blow to my high morale in school. I tried to hurt you for this. I studied hard, but why couldn't I beat you in school?" Her gaze was friendly, and she asked in despair, "What was that wrong in me that Honey didn't like about me? Why couldn't I say no to drugs and alcohol? Why couldn't I sustain success when I got it? I hate you because you snatched everything in my life. Be it the best student trophy in school or the beauty queen tag in college; you snatched away both Honey and money from my life. God won't forgive you for becoming so unkind to me. I was rich, talented, and urbane but still unsuccessful in my career. I could not compete with others in this world. You are a doctor. Tell me why?"

Pallavi replied candidly, "It all happened because you lived a life exclusively for yourself. Nothing mattered to you in your life beyond competition. You competed with me for the first position in school while I was competing with myself for a better tomorrow. In this game of chasing success, you forgot that you were advancing towards a point of reference that was never static. When you couldn't surpass that point, you slipped into a feeling of unfulfillment and vexation. In school, you chased my yesterday while I was advancing for a new tomorrow. You would have been much happier today if you had competed with yourself. In your profession, when you met people more successful than you, you made the best effort to treat them as your enemies. You stockpiled your frustrations when you became tired and listless after competing with your innumerable rivals. You fell into the clutches of bad company. You smoked and drank excessively to calm your nerves, but alas, in the end, you had a nervous breakdown and languished. You spoiled your successful career in your own hands. Now you are left with no desire to bounce back and revive your career."

She threw the cigarette butt to a trash can in the corner of her room, then stared at Pallavi for a moment. She stretched her arms and said, "I want to embrace my life with open arms. Will you be able to give me a second life, Pallavi?"

"What do you mean by 'will I be able?' I am no God. I can only try," Pallavi muttered.

"Yes, you heard it right, Pallavi. I have more faith in you than in God today. Give me a second chance to live. I know you are a brilliant doctor and a great friend. Now, I am sure you won't let me die. Can I hug you now, dear?" Diya kept her arms stretched, and looking at Pallavi, she said, "I don't know whether I can ever live like you, but I am sure you will show me the right direction in life. Embrace me, Pallavi. I am not as bad as you think of me. I miss my papa. I cry in front of his portrait every day. I am not a bad soul as you think. It still disturbs me mentally that I couldn't reach him when he was struggling for his last breath. Help me, please." Diya's eyes moistened.

*****

Mumbai, December, 2020

The nullahs on the side of the factory workers' hutment were full of human waste. The chawl was getting its first pipeline, which would traverse across the nullah. The ragpickers were searching for plastics for the factory in the knee-depth of slush along the sides of the nullah, little aware of the toxic fumes. Only a few were lucky enough to negotiate the price with the factory owner. The opportunity to meet the right person on the right chair for a good deal was bleak, as they were stonewalled by the grey-haired, tired-faced manager who had a special skill of distinguishing a good customer from bad ones. The spectacle had slid down a little over his nose, and his roving eyes always focused on the busy workers packing talcum powders. The rack of recycled plastic bags on the factory floor was being moved to another room for filling of the powders.

A woman entered the factory's main gate. The heavy iron gate in the rear was partly open and waiting to free the truck that would carry a consignment outside the factory. The manager's eyes lit up, and his tired face glowed with a smile, an exaggerated simper. He never wished for her to be there at that time when the powder was being packed. What would happen if she went inside and inspected? Peter, his boss, had warned him not to allow anyone inside the factory when the workers were busy. The security guards could not say no to her as she was their manager once upon a time. There were reports of a few deaths among the workers, and she wanted the workers' signatures on the insurance papers. The social workers blamed the municipality for the pipeline traversing across the pile of filth. The plan could have been executed in a much better way if it had been studied on the ground. It had received a nod from some nonsensical highest-ranking officer. The approval was done hastily on the file as the factory was being established in a place where the nullahs were getting a cover-up. The portion of the nullah that passed through the chawl was only covered to give hawkers a place to sell their food; otherwise, it was mostly bare and open throughout its entire course. The report published in the paper had the officers on their toes. The hospital asked Dr. Pallavi to step down from the project. The government asked for a full report from the hospital.

The baby powder, which was sealed and packed in a compartment, was mostly looked after by the pregnant mothers who worked there for extra money to support their husbands. The owners of the factory showed the public various photographs of how the pregnant women were being taken care of in their factory.

The social workers left the place happily with a note of praise and recommendation for health insurance for their workers. Nobody visited the chemical plant in the basement to see what was happening.

Disha, when she walked downstairs, she was stopped by the manager. He looked nervous. His words skipped the pleasant tonality of his voice, and he throated them out rudely. He could not stop her from going downstairs when it thundered in the basement. It followed the fall of a big object onto an emaciated worker. He was lugging a big machine beyond his capacity to drag unsupported. Through the window of a collapsible gate, she could fairly see four men trying to lift the machine to rescue their fellow workers. They all looked emaciated and weak. They were bare-chested with bruise marks on their body. To her, they looked as if they were captivated by someone for slavery. The man who whipped was a humongous giant. It surprised her when she saw a recognizable shrunken face. She clicked the photographs and tried to go back up through the stairs. To her surprise, it was locked outside. The security was on high alert. The cameras she could see were blinking over her head. The only way left for her was to hide inside the dark room on the left before the camera could trace her. The room was full of packets of cocaine. She almost felt nauseated. The torch lights tried to get a glimpse of her. Luckily, there was no electricity in the dark room where the workers were kept. No natural light could reach the windows as they were sealed from the outside. Disha had never thought of a place where she could end up. It reminded her of the days when Karim Chacha helped her out of the clutches of Sultan. She looked for any back door in the room. As soon as she felt the guards had fled to another room, she groped along the walls in the darkness. Her hands touched many objects which she had no clue about. What were they? The barrels of diesel, probably for the generator, were kept inside. As she slowly approached along the wall, she could feel the rats nibbling her shoes. The light from the lower end of the door was faintly visible; it probably had made these rats able to sneak into the room, she thought. She glided in that direction, and her hands could reach the door. Slowly, she opened the door. It was a toilet, stinking obnoxiously. She could find a window for some fresh air. Her heart pounded heavily, and she started to lose breath when she heard a guard trying to open another door of the toilet opening in another direction. Her hand reached for the pepper spray she always carried in her purse. The door was flung open, and the guards entered the room. They wore masks on their faces, only revealing their eyes, and were armed with sophisticated weapons. The leader called them back to check the truck parked outside. The guard moved outside into a narrow lane. She could see the narrow lane opening into the backyard. She managed to keep the guards engaged until one guard shouted that she had left by the truck carrying the consignment of baby powder. She slowly glided towards the dumping ground in the backyard, where a surveillance camera could barely capture her. She hid under a table until the last light. The security guard at the rear gate had left after the last consignment, and the cameras were not very effective in the darkness. She loped towards the iron gate, mustering all her courage to vault over it. She couldn't imagine herself jumping over a seven-foot gate in no time, something she would never have been able to do easily in normal circumstances.

Before the attackers opened the gate, she vanished from the lane. She dodged them by choosing a dimly lit street. Her only aim was to tell Vicky how bad of a man Peter was. He was a termite for his business, disguising his illegal activities behind packaging and shipping. She feared that Peter's men would be following her. She stopped an autorickshaw and bundled herself into it. The signal on her phone was weak. She called Vicky but could only make out from the conversation that he was at the farmhouse. She reached her farmhouse in a couple of minutes. She felt safe being with her own staff. Immediately, she rushed to her office and turned on the lamp. She switched on her computer and opened her mailbox. She thought about how different Peter was from Cheema. Peter was a very dangerous man. She needed to act now to destroy all his plans.

She heard a knock on the door. She opened it and saw Vicky standing there. "Vicky, they tried to kill me," she explained. "Think again before associating with Peter. He is a potential termite." She explained to him about Peter's men and what they had done to her.

"Don't worry. Just relax. I will take care of it. Get ready for the party."

When Disha joined them an hour later, she noticed a few women of Vicky's age present. "Have a gin and enjoy the party," a waiter known to her said from behind. That was her favourite martini, and he was aware of it. There was a blast of music. Disha got lost with the female employees of Vicky's age.

CHAPTER 8

Justice to Disha

December 2020, Mumbai.

On Monday, at Police station

"Dr. Pallavi, I am ACP Hanumat Shivdasani, the officer-in-charge of Disha's death case. The officer sitting to my right is Inspector Mr Baldev Singh, and to my left is Inspector Ms Charmy Paul. The reason we called you is to know the real story behind this mysterious death. The material evidence recovered from her house so far indicates your presence in her house on the morning of the fateful day. They are enough to be used against you. You were the last person she met before her death. Now, we need your version of the story. Feel free to tell us what happened on that day?" Hanumat said soberly, steady and composed.

"Story!" she exclaimed. "What story? How am I supposed to know who killed her?" Her eyes widened.

"Madam, did I ever say she was killed? I said it was a mysterious death. Tell us what makes you feel that she was killed. Possibly, it could be a suicide, isn't it?"

Pallavi's frustration bubbled to the surface with the twist of her words. She replied, "A dozen of your news reporters hounded me outside this police station. They posed questions to me as if I had done some crime. Through them, I learned that I am being called here as a prime suspect in this case. Any person with average intelligence can guess it is a murder.".

Hanumat met her gaze and said, "They are not my reporters. Even they run behind me for a scoop for their channel. That is their profession. I did not call it murder. We expect your full cooperation and truthfulness. We will ask you some hard questions and some personal questions. We will ask questions until we get a satisfactory answer from you. We may question you to any extent to reach the root of the investigation."

"Ok, officer, go ahead."Pallavi squared her shoulder.

"Everything you say will be recorded, and if you wish to amend your statements, you have twenty-four hours after you leave here. "

"Sure." She affirmed.

"So, Dr. Pallavi, wipe out those tiny sweat beads on your forehead. You look nervous and worried. Make yourself comfortable. Would you like to have a cup of tea or coffee?" Hanumat's tone was soft and friendly.

Pallavi reached for a tissue in the purse, dabbing her brow, "Officer, I am not nervous. I have done nothing wrong." She crumpled the tissue and tossed it into the trash within arm's reach. "The moment I came out of the operating theatre, I was asked to report here immediately. Look at me. I am right here in this police station at the very next moment." She shrugged. "Your man said it was urgent. Hence, I rushed in. I will have just a glass of water."

Hanumat read the tiredness in her eyes. He leapt from the chair, strode up to the fan hanging from the wall, and switched it on. He saw her locks sway with the cold wind. Then he walked back slowly to the table and sat opposite her. He offered her a glass of water.

"Madam, we appreciate your quick response. I know you are a busy doctor in the city, but don't blame us if we take too much of your time until the end of the inquiry. I am most grateful to you for visiting this police station. If you wish, we can question you at your house." He paused and studied the content of what the neighbours had said on that day.

"No, officer. I am okay with it. You can ask me questions." Her voice was steady as she replied.

"According to someone, she was your problem, and you solved it nicely by killing her. Should I presume that the statement given by a neighbour is correct and take her words at face value ?" He asked as he read from those newspaper clippings in his hands.

Charmy interjected, her eyes scanning a newspaper. " I am reading another interview given by the cook in a newspaper". Charmy read out as it was written, *"The cook said, 'On Saturday morning, it was six when I knocked. Madam opened the door, went to her bedroom, and slept again. She appeared heavy-eyed and unwell, so I decided not to disturb her. I left the door open around seven in the morning when I left her apartment. Today, again at six, I knocked on the door but didn't get a reply. The door was open, so I went inside. I looked at the bedroom door, and it was closed. I shouted 'memsahib' many times, but there was no reply. I pushed open the door, and there was a foul stench in the air. I poked my head inside and stood there stunned. I wanted to scream, but I couldn't. For a few seconds, I felt my heart seize beating inside my chest. I had both my palms on my cheeks, and I felt like losing my nerve every second. My head spun. I took a deep breath, then tried to summon up a little courage and dialled 100 from my cell phone."*

"What did you see there?"

"Diya madam was hanging from the ceiling fan. Her dupatta was a noose."

"Is there anything you want to add to this, Dr. Pallavi?" Charmy pressed.

"No. That is the maid's statement. How can I add to this? She said what she observed," Pallavi said.

Charmy asked her, "Is it a new business you have started?"

"What business?" Pallavi shot back.

"Home treatment service. Especially when the client is rich." There was a serious note in Charmy's voice.

"This is an accusation. I can't bear this," Pallavi said.

"These newspapers are full of these advertisements. There is nothing wrong. You can accept gracefully that you went to see Disha for extra money. After all, she was a rich lady, and you are a very popular doctor."

"I don't charge money for any visit. I am salaried. We doctors, too, have social obligations." Pallavi countered firmly.

"Oh, I am sorry. I didn't know this side of yours. I know quite a few doctors charge money for home visits. After all," she paused, letting the words hang in the air for Pallavi to deduce.

"After all, what?" Pallavi asked, her brows furrowed.

"You people are burning the midnight oil to reach this stage. So, mint money. Am I right?"

"Don't put your words in my mouth, inspector. That's the worst sweeping statement for a noble profession serving mankind," Pallavi retorted.

Locking his steely gaze onto hers, Honey asked, "Now, you may tell us in detail. What was the urgency you could not keep yourself from visiting Disha's place on Saturday?" He leaned forward and kept both hands on the table. He had a clipboard on the table where questionnaires were written on paper. He had scribbled something on the paper. After listening carefully to their conversation, Inspector Baldev promptly jotted down the replies on a piece of paper fixed to another clipboard.

Hanumat solemnly said, "I am repeating my question, 'How did you know Disha, and how close was she to you? Did she call you to her house?"

Pallavi replied, "I met her for the first time when I was a student. It was a chance meeting in Dr. Pradeep's cabin. After Dr. Pradeep's retirement, she was under my follow-up care. She called me on Saturday morning because she had missed my Friday OPD. Initially, I thought so when I saw her missed call, but she texted me later stating that she was sick."

"Wait a minute," he interrupted. "First, she called you, and when you didn't pick up the phone, she texted you. Am I right?"

"Yes, you are right," Pallavi said. She showed him her call records on her phone and said, "You can see her missed call and message on my phone."

His gaze shifted from her face to her phone. Honey took the phone, squinted at the call record on the screen, and read the message in the box. "Come soon. I am not well." He shut off the screen and gave the phone back. He felt the soft touch of her fingers. The sweat beads on her forehead did not reappear, but he could see her diamond earrings sparkle when the curling locks billowed in the breeze. He looked down at his note, picked up his pen, and circled a few questions on the paper.

"You dined at a very expensive restaurant on Friday, right?"

"Right."

"With your boyfriend?"

"We recovered a restaurant bill from Disha's house. It seems your boyfriend had an interrupted dinner and left you in the middle. Where did he go?"

"How did you know he left the hotel? He was there with me till nine."

"We are Police. None of the places are out of bounds for us. So, you paid the bill in cash?"

"Yes. He had to entertain a few guests at his farmhouse for his success party in business."

"Very interesting. You were not a part of that celebration. Vicky left you in the restaurant for a celebration without paying the bill."

"I, too, had a call from the hospital, so I decided to leave. But officer, somehow, I didn't like your old-fashioned remark."

"What is old fashioned in my remark?"

"I am an independent woman, I earn. I don't want my expenses burning a hole in his pocket. He hardly waited for the dinner."

"A hefty bill!" A smirk playing at the corners of his lips.

"I chose to dine in that restaurant because it was clean and hygienic. It was surely not a higgledy-piggledy strewn cheapo claustrophobic type of Dhaba with no sense of cleanliness. I don't find any reason for you to ask me if I go clubbing with my friends to such restaurants," Pallavi asserted. Her voice was sharp enough to tear apart Honey's sarcasm.

"What all you discussed?"

"Officer, please, you are getting into my personal space." She protested.

"Sorry, you have no choice," Honey said.

"We talked about our careers, old friends, life in London."

While Honey continued looking down at his list of questions, Charmy said, "We are entering into a more serious zone. Frowning here doesn't work with us, Dr. Pallavi. Every question we ask you is relevant to the case."

Looking at a handwritten sticky note to the right, Honey asked, "Did Disha ever tell you that she had been on any drugs and her real name was Madhubala?"

"No, she never revealed that side to me, but I discovered that in her file. One month ago, she had come to my OPD for swelling in her left arm. I noticed multiple healed scars on her forearms. She had covered them under long sleeves. On her left forearm, she had inscribed 'Madhubala.' When I went through her medical record in detail, I was certain that she was a drug addict."

"Was it written that she was a drug addict?" Hanumat inquired.

Pallavi said, "No, but she had undergone surgery decades ago for an infection in her heart valve linked to her intravenous drug use."

"If I am not wrong, drug addicts inject themselves. How did you conclude that she had injected the drugs herself? Did you examine her right forearm?" Hanumat probed.

She said, "Yes, officer, I did see track marks on both forearms. I discovered those marks when she was moved to the operation theatre for drainage of the swelling. In fact, we struggled to find a healthy vein on the other arm to inject the necessary medicines."

Honey's forehead wrinkled when he stared at the paper on the clipboard. He circled a few keywords and asked expeditiously, "So you knew well that she could only be injected through her leg veins?"

"Yes, officer, on that day, we injected the antibiotics through her leg veins."

"Dr. Pallavi, can you tell us in detail about the swelling in her left forearm?"

Pallavi replied, "She had sustained some injury when hit by a cricket ball during an IPL match, and she developed a large hematoma after that as she was on blood thinners. The hematoma got infected to become a large abscess, which I drained by giving a small nick."

Turning to Charmy, Honey said, "I was right. That was not a suicidal cut on her left forearm."

"Yes, Dr. Pallavi, you continue. We are listening, don't stop." Charmy said.

"After draining the pus, I saw a gush of blood extravasated from the main blood vessel. The wall of the blood vessel had given away. The whole vessel was looking unhealthy," Pallavi said.

Honey showed her the operation note, which had been recovered from Disha's house. "Is this the surgical note? Is this how you always sign on the prescriptions?"

Pallavi nodded, "Yes, officer, this is the operation note, and this is my signature. Her blood vessels looked all diseased. We sent a part of the blood vessel for a histopathological study. The report showed the artery wall was diseased. There were multiple scar marks concealed under a tattoo, which she had made by her maiden name."

He asked, "Any other significant observation? Did she have any other injury marks elsewhere in her body at that time?" Hanumat asked.

She replied, "No, sir."

Hanumat tapped the end of the pen on the table, then scribbled something on the paper and asked, "If she was in such a bad state on that day, then how did she come to you?"

"Vicky, my friend brought her to me," Pallavi replied.

"Who?" he asked with a surprising note in his voice.

"Vicky, my fiancé. He was her employer."

Charmy said, "Sir, it seems this Vicky had fallen completely under Disha's spell while he dated this girl," Charmy tried to ask her something, but before that, Hanumat showed his hand to stop her.

Hanumat asked, "Were they romantically involved? Was there any romantic relationship between them?"

"Between whom?" asked Pallavi.

"Between Vicky and Disha. After all, she was such a beautiful lady; he is a young man," unstoppable Charmy replied avidly.

Hanumat twisted his question and asked, "Had he ever shared his heartbreaking tales with you?"

"Officer, Disha loves Vicky very much."

"Exactly what Inspector Charmy wanted to know from you."

"Sorry, officer, it is not the kind of love that you people think about."

Honey placed a file in front of her. "Look at those photos. She is there with Vicky in almost every photograph. Look at those beautiful pouts. Isn't it looking so intimate?"

She flipped a few photographs. Honey studied her face for a moment to see if there was any reaction. "That's nice of her, enamouring her boss like this while dancing. It is a party photograph with employees."

"Isn't it sort of quite touching type for you?"

"What do you mean? You are as crazy as hell. How can you say this? People pout because they want to look attractive. There is nothing sensual about it."

Charmy put her phone camera on selfie mode and pouted to see whether she looked attractive. Then she closed it and asked, "You don't know what you are talking about. To me, the photographs are sensual. Can someone deny it by seeing this photograph on social media?" She showed her a circulated photograph on social media.

"These days, pictures can be morphed. How did you come to such a conclusion with no evidence in your hand? I have full trust in Vicky," Pallavi frowned.

Charmy said, "Evidence! You want evidence, madam. Vicky had been frequenting her house, are you aware?"

Turning to Honey, Charmy mocked, "Sir, here the scene is like our Hindi picture where the lover bear hugs a girl and stretches his hand for another girl at her back."

Pallavi said, "I don't know which picture you are talking about, madam, and I don't intend to know. My Vicky is innocent."

"Innocent!" Charmy's lip curled. "If he is innocent, then who is guilty? According to you, it is murder. Isn't it? Neither you nor Vicky killed her, then who did kill her? Either it must be you or him."

"If you don't know who killed her, then try not to protect Vicky," Hanumat said.

"I told you my Vicky is innocent and clean. Vicky cannot do this. I know him very well," she replied.

"Dr. Pallavi, how clean he is, the investigations will tell. We do not need your certificate to prove him innocent," Hanumat said. He looked at her hand and said, "The ring on your finger looks very beautiful and expensive. Is it a pure diamond? A similar diamond was recovered from Disha's house, wasn't it Charmy? That turned out to be a fake diamond, do you know?"

"By saying this to me, do you want to say Vicky is not trustworthy, a fake diamond, and he killed Disha?"

Charmy said mirthfully, "Yes, sir, it happens. Sometimes, we pick a diamond, considering it real, but it is not."

"So, this diamond ring is also given to you by Vicky?" Hanumat asked bluntly.

"Yes. What do you mean by 'also'?"

"Oh, I am sorry. I should not have said so," Hanumat said promptly and asked deplorably, "Can you tell us more about this Lucky in your life?"

"Officer, his name is Vicky, not Lucky. My Vicky is a classy guy. Is that not enough for you to know that I am a lady who got engaged, like everyone, before their marriage?"

"No, Dr. Pallavi, it is not enough. Here, we want to solve a death mystery. The telltale signs are crying of a love triangle. When Disha wrangled in disapproval of his illicit affair with you, he killed her," Hanumat replied.

She frowned, "You are taking the matter in a different direction and getting too much into my personal space, Honey. Vicky is a decent man, and I am engaged to him."

In a throaty voice, Hanumat said, "If I am dragging you towards a different direction, then tell me what the right direction is according to you. Sorry, none of your tantrums will work today with me. My name is Hanumat Shivdasani. You must know that I always reach the root of the case to solve any mystery."

"Forget about Vicky; I am asking you a simple and straight question: Why should we not suspect you as a murderer?" Hanumat asked.

"Reasons and motives?" she asked.

He boorishly said, "Reason number one: You were seen going to her house in the morning, and she died in the same afternoon. Reason number two: Blood tests and viscera reports say she was given sedatives and an intravenous anaesthetic agent. You are a doctor, and you know about these drugs very well. Reason number three: There was no mark of resistance on her body, but the mark around her neck indicated a hanging. Can anyone hang themselves after injecting anaesthetic drugs? She didn't know how to inject the drugs because there were marks found on both of her upper limbs. She was not ambidextrous.

Reason number four: The call records and prescriptions which carried your signature. She was prescribed sedatives, as seen in your prescriptions. Reason number five: what I am telling you now. It is a cold-blooded murder to hush her up." He asked with a raised tone, "Speak up now, Dr. Pallavi. Who injected her with the drug? Did Vicky hold her by arms, and you injected her with the drug?"

She shouted back, "Officer, this is a baseless accusation. You have no hard evidence against me except a few OPD prescriptions."

"Please do not become a judge here, Dr. Pallavi. I reiterate that our evidence is sufficient to prove you guilty in court. You need to answer us because you need to prove that you are not guilty. So, without wasting our time, answer what you are being questioned," Honey snorted.

"I had an emergency case to operate on Friday night. I reached home at quarter to four on Saturday. I woke up around seven with a missed call from Disha. I called her back, but she didn't pick up. Later, after a minute, she texted me that she was not feeling well. Around eight in the morning, I attended to her at her house."

"How did Vicky come into this?"

"By the time I was ready to go to her house, I got a call from Vicky. He had come for his morning sauna bath at one of his centres in Malad. He insisted that he would drop me off as he realized I was tired after my Friday night emergency duty."

"When you reached Disha's house around eight, did you notice she was sick?"

"When I reached there, she opened the door, and I found her in a deep oblivion. She didn't have that bright, radiant glow like before. She had a severe headache following a sleepless night. Her tongue was dried up, and her eyes looked boggy, usually seen when someone is fatigued or lacking sleep."

"Is it possible she was without her make-up?" Charmy asked.

"No, Madam. Her natural beauty required no cosmetics to glow. She always looked charming without them."

"Then, what happened?" Honey asked.

"Then, I sat on a sofa in her drawing room, glanced through the previous prescriptions, and then asked her to take one tablet of the sedative. She took it in front of me. Around 9 AM, I left her house. This is all I want to tell from my side. Why would I inject her with any drug, officer? There is no reason. The restaurant bill might have come out of my purse, which you claim as a sort of hard evidence for my presence," she said.

"you said she was confused. What made you think so? Did she tell you why she was restless?" asked Hanumat.

"No, she didn't. She behaved strangely; she was not only confused but absolutely in a state of oblivion. She had no sense of time. She had forgotten that she had called me. It was probably induced by too much alcohol she had consumed the previous night," Pallavi replied.

"Did she mention the party she attended on Friday night?" asked Hanumat, astounded.

"No."

"Did you go to her house alone?"

"Yes."

"Where was Vicky?"

"Vicky waited for me outside. He didn't go to meet her because he was not properly dressed. Later, he dropped me off outside the college gate and headed to his office."

"She is trying to outsmart the police, sir," Charmy said.

"I am not outsmarting you, madam. I am telling you the truth," Pallavi stood up instantly after listening to Charmy's sharp tongue.

"Please sit down."

"My Vicky is not a killer."

"That doesn't work here in this police station, madam. We have enough evidence against you to put both of you behind bars. We are respecting your position in society, so don't take advantage of that," Charmy said.

"Yes, Charmy is right, Dr. Pallavi. Who else knows about the anaesthetic drugs except for the doctors? We checked, and one vial of anaesthetic drugs is missing from your operating theatre. How would you explain that?" Honey asked.

"I am a doctor. I save lives. Honey, why would I kill her? To kill her, I should have a motive," she said defensively.

"I repeat, my name is Hanumat. You are speaking with a police officer. You asked me about the motive. Let me explain that to you. You wanted to kill her because she had sent your father to jail in a hit-and-run case. Am I wrong, Dr. Pallavi?" Hanumat replied crossly. He could see the snoot. Her cheek had turned crimson.

"What!" she exclaimed.

"You mean to say I sought revenge for framing my father in an old hit-and-run case? Bravo, officer. You deserve a police medal. What a brilliant mind you have. I must appreciate that you took no time to reach a conclusion," Pallavi vocalized, making a few short claps.

Honey paused, thinking, "I risked my life to earn those medals, Pallavi. If you are innocent, you will get justice. You don't know who Briksha Roy was and what happened to her child thereafter?"

Pallavi also thought in her mind for a while that Honey was oblivious to the fact that it was his mother, Briksha Roy, who got killed in that accident. Had he known, he would have surely scorned her and put her behind bars. She asked herself, "How would he react to someone like her, whose father served a jail term for an accident that killed his mother?"

After a moment of silence, Honey said, "You may go now," his voice turned guttural, and he said before clearing his throat, "Do not leave this town until the inquiry is over. You must come here again when called."

*****

Charmy said, "Sir, I am a hundred per cent sure that this lady is the one who killed her. She is hiding the truth. We should now bring her in for custodial interrogation. The diamond in her hand was real, sir. It must be expensive. I wish I had a fiancé like Vicky who could propose to me with a diamond ring like this."

Honey asked, "What will you do if he dates a second woman with another ring like in the picture story you mentioned?"

Charmy said, "I will not hesitate to kill the second woman if he cheats on me."

Honey said affirmatively, "Exactly! You don't think any differently from others. You never see any faults in your man. When you blindly love your man, you would rather prefer to kill the other woman to solve your problem."

After a pause, Honey said, "Sometimes, the truth you want to see is hidden behind falsehood. Certain situations compel you to believe differently despite what you see with your naked eye. They often force you not to believe in what seems apparent, as they do not complement each other. There is a thin curtain between them that often prevents us from acting. The truth becomes visible once the curtain is lifted. Did you notice any change in her reaction when I lied to her that a drug vial was stolen from her hospital store? There was not a hint of nervousness on her face when I said so. The Pallavi I know and have heard from others is very honest and dedicated. Her nature doesn't align with the crime she is associated with. The injection of the anaesthetic drug is a false attempt to frame her. That is what my experience tells me."

"Do you think it is a conspiracy against her, sir?" asked Charmy.

"Yes, I sense some conspiracy. Disha had a landline in her main hall, but she didn't make any calls from it. We recovered a mobile phone with a different number and found no text messages. The plan cannot blind us to the truth. The real culprits cannot escape the police. There is someone else who closely knew Disha and entered her house after she left, then killed her and tampered with her mobile phone."

"So, sir, you mean she never called Pallavi to her house," Charmy clarified.

*****

Pallavi hurried out to the corridor outside her office and called Laxmi. After a few rings, Laxmi picked up the phone and said, "Hello."

"Hello, Mama, I am coming home. Don't go anywhere. I am getting your medicines."

"Beta, I wasn't sure you would be free by now. I thought you were stuck in an emergency case. So, I went to the chemist's shop to get the medicines," Laxmi explained.

"Oh, Mama, I have told you many times, don't go alone to buy medicines from the chemists. Now, you stay there. I will come and check if he gave you the right medicines," Pallavi reassured her.

*****

Vicky looked well-groomed. He had tucked his shirt in tight and looked well-primped before leaving his office. His hair was still damp, in a club-cut style, dark and slicked back. He was wearing a new grey coat and shiny black boots. Hanumat looked him up and down, noting that he appeared to be a thorough gentleman.

"Mr. Vicky, please take your seat. You look different today. You look smart with this new hairstyle. Did you apply moisturizer? Which salon did you visit yesterday in the city? If we are to believe, your hair was much longer in these photographs," Honey said, showing Vicky some surveillance camera photos taken in Disha's apartment. "You have been going to her apartment frequently, right?"

"Yes, officer. What is wrong with that? I have known her since childhood. She was an employee of my father and was very sincere and hardworking. I was shocked when I heard about her death," Vicky replied promptly.

"So, Disha was like an aunt to you, right?" asked Honey.

"No, she never liked to be called Auntie because she looked much younger than her age," Vicky answered.

"Mr. Vicky, where were you on this earth when she was murdered?" Honey questioned.

"I was... umm... in my office when I saw the TV news on Sunday. You can check with my staff," Vicky replied.

"I am asking about Saturday morning. Where were you on Saturday?" Honey inquired.

"On Saturday? Umm... I was in my office in the farmhouse," Vicky replied.

"What were you doing in the office on a Sunday?" Honey asked.

"Officer, I had a lot of work. I was at my hotel. I have a room in the hotel that I sometimes use as my office. I had some important business papers to sign," Vicky explained.

"How do you know Pallavi?" asked Honey.

"Pallavi is my fiancee. We are engaged to be married," said Vicky.

"Where did you find her for the marriage? If I'm not wrong, you are settled in London, right?" Honey questioned.

"I proposed to her for marriage in Goa," Vicky responded.

"Ohh... but did she say yes?" Honey asked.

"Yes, she said yes. She accepted my proposal without hesitation, unlike others," Vicky said.

"What do you mean by 'unlike others'? Did you have to propose to many other girls before Pallavi?" asked Honey.

"No, officer. I had expected it to take longer for her to say yes to me. Unexpectedly, she agreed right away," Vicky replied.

"Where did you propose in Goa? Inside a hotel, a park, or a metro station... where?" Honey inquired.

"No... we were both out in Goa for a conference, and we happened to run into each other after our arrival. We were staying at the same hotel. I proposed there. Officer, please don't ask me anything more about my personal life," Vicky said, with a hint of bitterness on his face.

"Okay... you may go now. But remember, you cannot leave the country without permission from this office," Charmy said.

As Vicky rose from the chair and turned to leave the police station, Charmy called out, "Wait a minute!" She had received a report from an inspector, who handed her a piece of paper. Vicky had turned his back and was about to leave.

"You dropped Pallavi at Disha's apartment and left with her after some time. It was caught on the surveillance camera, but the camera turned off automatically when you left. Did you do that?" Charmy asked.

"Madam, when I said I was in my office when Disha was killed, what additional information do you expect from me? How would I know if the surveillance camera was recording properly or not? Even I want to know who killed her. You are looking for a drop of water in a cloudless sky, which you will never find interrogating me," Vicky replied defiantly.

"Okay... you may go now," Charmy said.

Outside the police station, news reporters asked Vicky about his role in the murder. One of them thrust his microphone into the rear seat and prevented Vicky from closing the car door. Vicky's driver slowed down, and Vicky muttered, "I know nothing about this murder. I answered everything I was asked, and I am innocent."

After Vicky left, Hanumat said, "It is a defiant challenge for us to break this, Vicky. One of us should follow him and dig into his past."

Fifteen minutes later, the telephone rang. Charmy picked up the phone to receive information from the team deployed at Disha's apartment. She entered the ACP's office and said, "Sir, the team at the site just informed me that the surveillance camera system was hacked. Someone from Pakistan did it."

"Unbelievable! Can someone hack surveillance cameras to stop recording?" Hanumat asked in disbelief.

"Nothing is impossible for these hackers. You cannot dismiss the incident from your mind. Do you remember how terrorists attacked a hotel after hacking the surveillance cameras installed for security? The intruders knew every detail of the layout and security arrangements inside. I learned that any camera that runs on Wi-Fi is vulnerable. A skilled hacker can do anything. The IP address was traced back to Pakistan once again. The person in Pakistan probably observed Disha's activity before her death. He sent someone to kill her after hacking the system. Vicky may be right. He may not know who killed her. Maybe the love triangle theory we were thinking of is incorrect," Charmy explained.

"Sir, another interesting thing we found during our investigation. Disha's phone records show she received a call from Dubai last night. That could be the reason she felt restless. You know the Sultan gang. All those scoundrels have shifted their base to Dubai since you joined the anti-terrorist squad," Charmy added. "According to the guard, he saw someone lurking around early in the morning. The guard provided a description, and our sketch artist drew a portrait. He saw a man in a sky-blue T-shirt and a white cap in the back of the building. The man quickly hid behind a tree when he spotted the guard."

Examining the portrait, Hanumat said, "Charmy, we should focus on this suspicious man. Search for him in our files. Speak with the Traffic Department and get all the camera footage of traffic signals around Disha's house recorded in the past month. It seems that the murder was planned well in advance and executed on Saturday. We need to see the footage from Disha's apartment to see who visited her in the past month."

*****

Laxmi asked Pallavi, "The operation took so long today. How is the patient doing? Surprisingly, Diya called this morning. She was trying to reach you. Call her some time."

Pallavi replied, "I was called to the police station for a case. You know, the Disha murder case."

"The police station? Why?" Laxmi cried.

"Don't worry, Mama. They called Vicky and me to help with their inquiry," Pallavi reassured her.

Laxmi's heart raced in distress. The memories of the courtroom proceedings from the past flooded her mind. She asked, "Vicky? But why were you two called for a murder case?"

"Mama, I attended to her at her apartment on Saturday morning, and Vicky came with me. She died in the afternoon. The media is after us, blaming us for her death," Pallavi explained calmly.

Laxmi pondered, "You may not like what I'm going to say, but seeing Vicky by your side confuses me. You two moved so quickly into this engagement that I didn't even get to ask him what kind of job he does."

"Mama, Vicky is a very kind-hearted man. As a boss, he always helped Disha with her treatment. I am feeling very hungry now. Don't worry, Mama, I know him inside out. You will be proud of your daughter and tell the world that your daughter made the perfect choice in selecting a groom."

*****

It was 8 PM when Honey returned from the police headquarters after a short media briefing about the day's proceedings. He had spoken with the forensic team for any additional information, but they had nothing more to reveal. The batch number on the vial had been traced down to one distributor who had supplied the same stuff to at least fifteen small and large hospitals.

Sitting on a couch, Romy was watching the news channels. The only headline which hit prime time was "Who killed Disha? Breaking news: use of an anaesthetic drug in the murder is being suspected." A few channels showed "A Lacklustre Police Commissioner," where the anchor blamed the police for their inability to reach a conclusion. At the same time, a few citizens on camera demanded the resignation of the home minister for his failure to provide security to a single woman in the city. The minister knew well that ACP Hanumat's posting into the crime branch had ruffled too many feathers in the underworld, and he just couldn't be transferred out.

Three days had passed, but nothing came to their hand. Honey was worn out both physically and mentally. He doubted his ability, whether he could ever solve this mystery.

Romy asked, "Have you had lunch?"

"Yes, papa."

He sat on the couch and asked his father to change to another news channel. After a moment of silence, Hanumat said, "A part of the rumour also has it that she committed suicide as the young man who she had been seeing ditched her for another woman. The locals accused that girl who accompanied the man."

There was silence in the room for a few seconds. Romy had put the TV on mute.

Romy said, "You look tired, Honey. Sometimes it is good to discuss something else, not about crime... crime... crime always. There is much life beyond this to live."

"No one knows here, Papa, what tomorrow's life will bring to us. My life is inseparably associated with my job. To my seniors, it seems like a dead case—a case of suicide. I have started doubting my ability to investigate this case. The whole nation has been boiling over this case since they knew she was their ancient heartthrob, Madhubala. Why do people have such dubious identities? I can't understand. It has sensationalized the entire issue. The criminals have not left any clue which could lead us to any conclusion?"

"Not all seniors think so. Just an hour ago, DIG Saxena asked whether you could arrive safely. His words were highly praising of you. He was boastful of bringing up a few quintessential breeds of young police officers whom the nation can ever boast of. Even the minister is also supporting you in this death case despite much public pressure on him." Romy's words still carried no impact on Honey's face. His face had unusually lethargic movements displaying all the features of dissatisfaction: a silent face with drooping eyebrows staring just at the big centre table, and his words had no liveliness or energy like before.

Romy said, "You look tired. I was told you didn't have a proper lunch; you've just survived on a few pieces of biscuits and a cup of tea since morning. The food is ready; get refreshed; I will tell the maid to serve the food. Let me watch, and I will join you at dinner."

"I don't feel like having anything, Papa. So much noise in my head today." Honey picked up the towel and went to the bathroom. He drowned himself in the tub until becoming breathless. He thought about the day when his father warned him to stay away from Pallavi. "Show this arrogant and ill-mannered girl, Beta, that you can live without her. If you want to become a police officer, then don't waste your time in Mumbai. Go to Delhi and prepare for the civil service examination." It echoed several times.

A part of his mind said umpteen times - Forget her. She doesn't even deserve to be called your friend. She didn't even turn once after the incident to apologize. She showed her ugly side by disappearing from the party for no reason. She can never be your true love, Honey. She is just a selfish career woman. His other part thanked Pallavi for showing him her true colour before entering a relationship. It counselled him that the breakup, what didn't beget her, was her loss for not getting him, and it did not affect him. The goodness in his mind tried to clear off all the bitterness for her. It nurtured self-control in him, warm emotions for the public, and a strong will to serve the nation.

It helped him to judge people. It showed him the right direction in life.

He towelled off and slipped into a kurta and pyjama. A minute later, he was joined by Romy for dinner.

During their dinner, Romy said, "I know you work hard and wish you will be doing so for the nation lifelong. Have you ever thought about yourself and your personal life?

Priyanshi is coming to Mumbai to celebrate your birthday after completing her Law degree from Delhi University. So Saxena was insistent on keeping your engagement party on your birthday. I said..." He remained silent for a few seconds while chewing the food.

"What did you say, Papa?" He asked.

"I said no."

"Why did you say no, Papa?" Honey asked.

Romy said, "My child, today I realized my biggest mistake. I told you to stay away from Pallavi and forget her if you want to become something in life. I said so because I wanted you to stand on your two feet. I was unable to understand her properly. I never wanted to know the reason why she left you like that on that day. After so many years, I got my answer today."

"Make it clear, Papa. My head is pounding. Don't make roundabouts. I can't take it anymore. What answer?"

"Why did she leave the party and stop talking to you after that? Do you want to know? If you believe in destiny, then believe that destiny made it happen for you, my child. Time has come again after a full circle for you. There is no rose without a thorn. I am ready to accept Pallavi as my daughter-in-law."

"What!" A shocking expression on Honey's face. After a few seconds, Honey asked, "Papa, have you checked your sugars today? Have you taken your medicines? I can't understand you. Which destiny and what mistake are you talking about?"

"Beta, what I saw today opened my eyes. Pallavi is the right girl for you to marry. I know, still, you love her," Romy said.

"No, Papa, I have moved much ahead in life since that incident. What you call today is love; for me, it is a house full of conflicts between my emotions and pride. I can never be a teen. In this conflict, I count my pride over my emotions. You should be happy that I am my own lover." Honey's dry emotions commingled with his devotion to remain duty-bound. Probably, all that happened in the past was for his best.

"It's not wrong to be your own lover, but I still feel that Pallavi is not a wrong match for you."

Telling his father that the chapter he wanted to write for him would have had a complex outcome - was not easy for Honey. Adjusting to public sentiments is more complex than anything. Besides these, for him, erasing her feelings was not that easy.

Picking up a candle from the centre of the table, Honey twisted it between his fingers. "Do you remember this candle, Papa? I didn't light it up that day when she left me. Now, I am keen to light this candle with Priyanshi rather than wasting my life cursing Pallavi for the darkness. If this candle is to be lit, then it should be with Priyanshi on my birthday. I have decided to walk down the aisle with her. Pallavi is already engaged. There is nothing wrong with DIG Saxena's daughter, Priyanshi," said Honey.

"I am not only your father but also to you, a mother and a friend as well. I can read your heart and mind. Your heart says you like Pallavi, and your mind says no, she is facing a trial. You want to avoid mixing up your personal life with the professional one, isn't it? If you say yes, I can go to her mother anytime and ask for her hand for you," Romy said.

Honey said, "Neither can I afford to return to my wretched past, nor am I in my teens to jump from walls or dance around trees to proclaim love. I barely have time to get into the nitty-gritty of love. All these years, I have prepared myself not to accept her in any form by my side. Forget about asking for her hand. I can't think of accepting her in life as my bride."

"Beta, there is no doubt that Priyanshi and DIG Saxena are angels for you. They supported you in Delhi and shaped your career. It's also true that Saxena wants a son-in-law as a police officer as he couldn't make Priyanshi one. She was studying with you and helped you throughout your studies. But don't you feel it's like offering yourself as a symbol of reciprocation for what they offered you in your bad times? Everything will return to normal; just say yes to Pallavi once."

"She has stepped out of my life, Papa. The discussion is finished here. One jolt of pain was enough. I can't take another one. The heartache lingers, Papa. I can't handle it anymore. Now I am okay. I have learned to live with it. She was not on my journey while I was preparing for IPS in Delhi, but Priyanshi and her family stood with me. I didn't know how small or big her problem was to accept me as a life partner, but I am sure Pallavi has found a life mate of her choice," said Honey.

"Beta, I would not have forced you if I had not committed a sin. I repent for what I did."

"What makes you feel that way, Papa? She has found a life partner of her choice. You should feel happy for her."

"Beta, I went to a chemist's shop this afternoon. I was stunned when I saw her standing by my side. She might not have recognized me, but I recognized her in a second. Not much has changed on her face since I saw her in the courtroom thirty years ago. Won't you ask me who she was?"

"Who?" asked Honey.

Romy said, "She was Pallavi's mother, Laxmi. I saw them together in the shop. She is the daughter of the same man who killed your mother. Now, the picture in my mind is clearer. That's why she left us that day from the party abruptly."

"Why?"

"When she learned from me that her father was the murderer who killed your mother, she left. My voice was harsh and scornful. I didn't know then that I was speaking to Sagar's daughter. Now I remember exactly what could have happened to her that day when I cursed ill for Sagar's whole family." He added, "Pallavi was standing in front of your mama's portrait when I told her that she was killed by a man from Malad named Sagar. She asked me if it happened on the highway in 1989. I said yes, then I let out my anger and frustrations on Sagar and cursed his family to suffer like me for the rest of his life. In a sweeping remark, I disdained the inhabitants of Malad for one who destroyed my happy family life. She left that place. I know people at the party thought I said something rude to her, but believe me, I was not impolite to her as a person. Now, I feel I should not have told her about Sagar that day."

Honey said, "Forget it, Papa. There is no point clinging to an incident that happened decades ago. We must learn to live in the present."

Romy said, "Beta, a part of me is not ready to agree with you that you don't love her anymore. I am also certain that she loves you a lot. She wants to avoid revealing to you that she is the daughter of the murderer who killed your mother. I am old, but I am experienced enough to know who is good and who is bad. That day, she was very excited to learn about the antique pieces I showed her. I shared my emotional attachment to those pieces as they were chosen by Briksha. She was happy and cheerful to see the changing colours of the fountain in our house. She was keen to hear from me about our love story. She was desirous to know about your mama when she saw her portrait. She wanted to know more about your bond with Briksha. When I told her about the incident, when it happened, you were merely three years old, and Sagar was the killer; everything changed in her. After saying so, Romy filled their glasses with water. They had finished their dinner. The maid had taken their plates. Romy asked, "Who is this boy Vicky in Pallavi's life?"

Honey interrupted Romy and said, "One minute, Papa. I got my solution. Vicky knew her from college, and he was a pharmacy graduate before entering this chemical business. Vicky can do it because he knows about anaesthetic drugs. He is skilled in how to administer them."

"Beta, I am asking about the Vicky in Pallavi's life, and you are thinking something else," Romy said.

"Oh no, Papa. I am doing this to give justice to Disha. My heart says Pallavi is innocent, but I have no proof to prove her innocence. I am trying hard to bring out the truth and prove Pallavi innocent in this death case. So far, the shreds of evidence are all pointing towards Pallavi as the killer. Before these reporters dig out her past and her family's history, I must bring out the face of the real criminal before the public," Honey said.

Honey rushed to the bedroom, unplugged his mobile from the charger, and hurried back to the dining table. He sat down and phoned Baldev, ordering him to inquire at all the medicine shops around Vicky's house to see if Vicky bought any tablets, sedatives, or injectable drugs.

"Who is this, Vicky?"

"Pallavi's love interest. Today, I took out many old papers from his office. Somehow, I felt that he was not a clean businessman. He is working with some guy named Peter, an organized businessman who plays his cards through Vicky. This Peter was his father-in-law a few years ago. Now Vicky is a divorcee."

"Now I understand why the business community has been giving interviews to these news channels since afternoon. They are very angry at you for taking such action. The whole community has come forward to defend this, Vicky. They have taken the media under their control. They say you are just doing this drama to hide your failures."

"Still, they can't make me feel uneasy. Though I haven't raided his house yet, I will do whatever it takes to catch a criminal. I don't belong to the breed of officers who get manipulated by such industrialists. Yielding to their authority goes against my pledge. My obligation is to my duty and my country, that's all."

*****

Vicky was called to the police station again the next day. He was asked to take a seat. There was not even the slightest hint of nervousness on his face. He looked confident as he sat comfortably across the table.

Honey stared into his eyes and asked, "Why should we not ask for your custodial interrogation in Disha's case? To us, everything is clear that you are a partner in crime."

Vicky calmly replied, "So you mean to say Pallavi murdered her and I helped her in this murder? What nonsense are you talking about, officer? What prima facie evidence do you have against me to ask for custodial interrogation?"

"Vicky, you cannot deny that you have no idea about muscle relaxants and how they act in our body. You have a bachelor's degree in pharmacology before pursuing a master's in hotel management. The circumstantial pieces of evidence, the fingerprints in her house, suggest that you were present there," said Honey.

"If you have all the evidence against me, then why don't you arrest me? After a pause, he said, 'Officer, you are mistaken. I don't deny having a pharmacology degree, but to kill her, I would need the drug. Do you have any evidence against me for procuring this drug? I think not. Your team inquired about me from the chemists around my house. Did they find anything? The answer is no," said Vicky.

Honey frowned and said, "You may go now, Vicky." Vicky stood up to leave. Honey observed a twitch on Vicky's face, which faded with a gentle smile.

"Thank you." Vicky left the police station.

"Inspector Baldev, this man has thrown an open challenge that we cannot reach him. Retrieve his call records from the past month, whom he has been speaking with. It will surely lead us to the criminal."

An hour later, Inspector De Souza came up with information. "Sir, Disha was at the farmhouse on the party night. I checked with the waiter who served her alcohol. She may have been drugged through her drinks. I am sure we will find some leads at the farmhouse. There is a call from Dubai to Disha's number in the middle of the night."

Honey said, "Maybe we can assume a Dubai connection to the murder, or it could have been made to divert our attention. Did you seal the farmhouse as I ordered?"

"Yes, sir. We have encircled it with barrier tapes around a hundred meters from the boundary wall. But no one has seen crossing the tapes from any direction in the past four days."

"Good. My observation suggests that it could be the Sultan gang who killed her. She was the one who sent him to jail."

Honey said, "So you mean to say it's an act of vengeance? I doubt it. Did you recover any mobile phones in the farmhouse?"

"But, sir, the last location where it was active was near Disha's apartment."

"Is it possible for someone sitting in Dubai to text you through someone else's mobile?"

"In this digital world, everything is possible, sir. They can copy your SIM card while sitting in Dubai."

"Look for the phone. Send your informers to all the places they know where old mobile phones are traded. Look for it in all the garbage pits around the farmhouse. Look along the roads, inch by inch, until the main road. You might find some evidence related to the case."

Late afternoon, a stack of files was placed on the desk. Honey was seriously going through the unsolved murder case files to find a trail of Disha's murder case. But in all those cases, the surveillance cameras were functional. The Modus Operandi was quite similar. The victims were all rich and staying alone when they were murdered. The criminals had entered the houses mainly in the late-night hours. In all those cases, they had either used a mask or disconnected the electricity supply. None of the crimes had been committed in broad daylight.

Inspector Baldev reached his chamber, saluted him, and said, "Sir, the informer just called me to say Vicky has a British girlfriend. He found her in one of his cars, and Vicky followed her in another car. Vicky reached the airport, and the lady alighted from her car, then hugged him before her departure."

"This is just news, Baldev, not information. In business, people move from one country to another. It carries no meaning to us. Baldev, I was hoping you could bring me the details of the mobile phones that were active around the farmhouse and Disha's house in those two days. It may give us some clues." After a pause, he said, "Now I do not suspect, but I am confident that Vicky has been closely monitoring our every activity. He even tracks every bit of conversation that we make on the phone."

Baldev uttered in surprise," Sir, how is this possible? We are not on a radio set."

"Baldev, everything is possible for these hackers. If they can hack into a CCTV camera sitting in another country, do you think they are not monitoring our conversations? It is not a big deal for them. How did Vicky know we spoke about the chemists around his house? Now, no more surprises."

Two hours passed midnight; Baldev knocked on the door. Honey opened the door. "The special traffic commissioner, Mr Ajay, arrived at the headquarters around nine and brought along the footage. The team from the site has reported back at headquarters, and we studied the footage."

Honey asked, "Good. Did they find anything worth our investigation?"

"Sir, the side picture of that suspicious man and the bike number. The owner of the bike is in Borivali."

Honey said, "Pick him up, but be careful. Keep one team at the outer cordon. Follow the drill. People must be sleeping inside, so put your cordon tight outside and enter the apartment after the first light. Check the bike in the parking lobby and impound it. Have you been able to get his front photograph in any of this footage? Better you all go in civvies."

"Yes, sir, we also got the front photo, but it looks blurred in the magnified image. It was six in the morning, and the road was clear, so he sped very high," said Baldev.

Inspector Baldev made two teams. He headed one, and De Souza headed the other. Two inspectors went to the complex and inquired about the bike and its owner – "Aftab" was his name, as the security guard said, and indicated towards the open window of a room on the first floor. They discovered the bike in the stilt. The complex was cordoned off by a team of eight, and another team of four entered the complex. Two of them hid behind the sidewall of the stair. Baldev knocked at the door, and De Souza had chambered a bullet taken position behind the pillar.

"Tap, tap."

The door opened. Aftab gave a surprising look at Baldev. He was expecting the milkman in the morning. Baldev took out the pistol from his holster and pointed it at Aftab. He raised his hands in surprise. Seeing him unarmed, Baldev placed the pistol inside the holster.

"Mr Aftab, is it you on the bike?" Baldev showed him a photo and asked.

"No, he is Arshad. My roommate," Aftab said.

"Where is he now?"

"Officer, you are late by an hour. He left for the airport early in the morning, around five."

"How is that possible? We have been here since three in the morning." Baldev stood puzzled. The only person they allowed outside was a uniformed security guard. His identity card was also verified. Baldev rushed past Aftab and checked every corner of the house. There was no one inside the house except Aftab.

"What is there inside this box?" Pointing at the box, De Souza asked.

Aftab said, "A few pairs of clothes and uniforms. Arshad wants to become an actor in Mumbai. To participate in plays, he has a collection of uniforms – police, army personnel, and security guards – which he keeps inside."

Things were becoming clearer to Inspector Baldev Singh. He rushed to the airport with his team in the next moment.

"Sir, Arshad has been intercepted at the airport. Over and out."

*****

Diya watched the news late in the afternoon. Her heart turned heavy as she learned about the news buzzing across every screen. Pallavi, now her dear friend, had become the prime suspect in the murder case. She had something to reveal to Pallavi that she never told her. She wanted to tell Pallavi about her father, Sagar, who was innocent. Disha had confided that Sagar had taken the crime on his head out of compulsion and compassion. The thought gnawed at her – That the secret she had possibly could change people's eyes to look at this case. Without a moment to lose, She hurried to the police station to meet Honey and to record her statement.

As she reached the police station, She heard the voice, "Hanumat Saab has gone home," one constable said, staring at the parking lot inside the premises of the police station and not finding his familiar gypsy there.

Diya asked for the address of his house. It was not in the police line. The constable replied that he stayed with his father. Diya knew his place. The last time she had visited that house was Honey's eighteenth birthday. Almost fifteen years have passed in between.

She reached by car and parked in front of his house. Not the slightest change was seen in the facade: the same walls, colour, and lights. A wave of nostalgia washed over her.

A familiar face recognized her; he was the same watchman whose hair had turned Gray at the temples in these years. The watchman beamed at her and nodded respectfully with a wish. He had a sharp memory.

The watchman said, "Madam, I remember your face. Are you Madam Diya?"His tone was brimming with warmth.

"How do you know me? I came to this house after fifteen long years." Diya asked, surprisingly.

"Madam, I was there around you when Pallavi Madam and you were arguing near the gate on that party day."

That party night was amazing, as if time itself had been awaiting her arrival at Shivdasni's place. She had never been so annoyed with Pallavi until that day. She was ready to hurt her with her bag physically. She was consumed by anger. But now she realized she had overreacted in a moment of insecurity. She was even happy to notice Pallavi rushing outside the Shivdasani house with tears streaming down her face. And now there was a feeling of guilt inside her. However, she was not sure how to tell Honey who had killed Briksha Roy. How would he react? Could she even make eye contact with him after this revelation? Her throat felt dry as she struggled to say something in response to the sentry's words. She hoped Honey, fueled by their previous feelings about her and Pallavi, would behave differently.

When the doorbell chimed, Romy was busy in the office on the first floor. He got up from behind the desk and peered out the window. He descended the stairs to the entrance to open the door. He stared for a while and, with a recognizing tone, said, 'Are you Diya? Honey's friend, the girl at my son's birthday party who grabbed the first piece of cake, right?'

'Oh... Uncle, your memory is very sharp."Diya chuckled.

"You look a bit frail, Diya. Is everything alright?' he asked, concern lacing his voice. 'Make yourself comfortable as this home is your own home sweet home.'

A sweet home-like feeling inside for Diya. She had always desired to be a part of this family. The lip-smacking taste of the food prepared by Romy for that party was still unforgettable.

After she sat on a sofa, the maid offered her a glass of water.

"Uncle, where is Honey? And how is he?" She inquired.

"Ah, Beta, it's hard to talk about him. He is not the same as he was fifteen years ago. He has turned into a piece of metal- cold, emotionless. I worry for his health."

"Uncle, now he is a police officer, taking control of the city's crime."Diya reminded him softly.

"That shouldn't mean that he should neglect his health. Every so often, he works late into the night. He gets hungry but doesn't demand food. At his age, he should be looking after his kids and his wife. He is just killing his youthful days by beating up criminals, punching, and smashing their heads. He is always seen every other day chasing them on the roads. No one is there to feed him on time. How long can a father see him like this? After Briksha, I am working from home. I am available to take care of him at home. But who will look after him after me?"

"You are his close friend, and you can only tell him it is the right time for him to get married." He suggested gently. He brightened from his worries and asked, " Just a minute, I have prepared your favourite kheer today. Coincidentally, you are here. You still like Kheer, don't you?"

He disappeared into the kitchen and returned with a bowl of kheer for Diya.

"Yes, uncle. You remember everything," she said. Her eyes started to well up with the niceness in Romy's gesture. That reminded her of how he served her only kheer when others indulged in ice cream on that day. She realized a mother's heart in Romy when he came forward to serve her on her platter on Honey's birthday.

"Honey never complains- not even when I forget to add sugar. You know I am a diabetic, so I avoid it. He will just eat whatever I make. These days, I have been trying to find a suitable bride for him, but he shows no interest."

"Come, let me show you where he lives." He beckoned, leading her to Honey's room. He opened the door and said, "Look at these medals and a few pieces of furniture. No life...silent and empty. No grandchildren I must play with. There is no Hurley burly in the courtyard. At the end of the day, he is just a lonely person. He is nurturing a broken heart since Pallavi left him without speaking a word on his birthday. He hates her too much these days when he learns that Pallavi will marry a rich businessman. All this happened because of me. I should not have spoken to her like that. She was like my daughter. I want her as my daughter-in-law."

"What did you say?"

"I cursed her whole family to rot in hell without knowing that I was speaking with Sagar Rajhans daughter, Pallavi Rajhans," Romy confessed, regret etched into the lines of his face.

His words penetrated her core. As if the lifeless room suddenly spoke out the words she most regretted to hear. She blamed herself for not revealing the secret to anyone. That moment was there. She should now tell the truth. The very reason she was there was to tell Honey. Now, be it his father.

"Uncle, Pallavi's father didn't kill your wife. It was my father behind the wheel that fateful day."

Romy's brows furrowed in confusion. "How can you be so certain?"

Diya's voice trembled with emotion. "Uncle, I know this because Pallavi's father was our chauffeur. My father then never confessed this guilt to the world as he had to look after me and my Mom, but years later, Disha unveiled to me that my father was at the wheel when the accident took place. He was drunk and racing with another car. Pallavi's father was subservient. He was so innocent to be caught in the wreckage of fate.

Romy's eyes moistened. "I laid bare my anger at Pallavi unknowingly due to a twist of fate." Romy repented.

"That you did because you were ignorant; our ignorance often masquerades as malice," Diya said.

"But, I don't know what she must be thinking about me. I insulted her whole family, and it's my sin." Romy felt a lump rise in his throat after knowing the fact.

"Uncle, Now Pallavi is going through a very tough time. Navigating a storm in her life, I know she is brave enough to face every storm in her life. The media is pressurizing Honey to withdraw from the case as Pallavi is currently undergoing a trial."

"I know Beti. The way these reporters are hollowing out her character day by day because of her relationship with my son in the past is simply unbearable."

"I just came here to tell Honey he should not withdraw himself from this case until Pallavi is proven innocent. There is still a guilt blooming in my heart that she gave me a life, but I couldn't do anything for her except scoffing her for all wrong reasons."

"I know my son is bravely taking on the media alone. Waiting for him is a waste of time, Diya. I want him to settle down in life as early as possible for the sake of his good health."

"Will you do something to help him, Diya?"

*****

Charmy said, "A guy from a Piggery wants to reveal something. He wants to meet you, sir. He has some input about Disha, as he said." Honey nodded after looking at the watch. "Call him inside." It had struck nine in the morning.

Sometimes, a little information turns into something paramount to shape the investigation. At least time will not be wasted gathering irrelevant things. It is the ultimate truth; however good your team may be, the commander only understands the pain of an inconclusive investigation. Honey believed his team was the best in the city and could get inputs by slapping and thrashing. He seldom has seen a guy coming himself to give essential input to the investigation. It invoked a sense of hope.

The middle-aged man had come with his daughter. She was weak. The girl looked at him and studied his ranks on the shoulder. Honey looked at her. She was in college. What interested him more was that he could see a scar mark in the middle of her chest above the halter line, the one like many who undergo heart surgery. Disha, too, had a similar scar on her body. The man who accompanied her seemed to be her father, looking like a middle-aged man. Anyone could guess from his clothes that he is a daily worker. His shoes were untidy, and his clothes had patches of dirt.

The father said, "We have come to meet you, sir, to give you some information." His voice was low. His hands folded in the way when someone speaks to repent for his sins."

"Tell us quickly why have you come?"

"I was scared to inform you, sir, because those people are very cruel." With the tears streaming down and sobbing when he started to narrate, he appeared trustworthy. It seemed to Honey that the man had a near mental collapse.

"The Piggery where I work supplies pig blood. I carried a jarful of pig blood to his farmhouse. I saw Disha Madam in that farmhouse in the evening a day before her death. It surprised me when I saw her photo on TV and that she died. I am not convinced that she would ever commit suicide. My daughter compelled me to come here to share this information with you."

The words of the man somehow convinced him that he was telling the truth. One cannot lie in front of his own kid. And he has not come here as an informer who trades information for money. "My daughter and Disha are great friends. This Friday, she didn't turn up for her monthly OPD visit. She said that Disha had been asking her to stand beside her always while they drew blood for her blood sample. She always liked to get counselled by my daughter during any procedure before being counselled by any nurse."

The girl said, "She is even very scared of syringes and needles."

With the words she said, the bell in his mind jingled. What could have been the motive of these people to get pig blood to the farmhouse? After all, they were not shooting any film over there to fake any murder scene. Honey understood criminals use them to fake accidents on highways to loot innocent passengers.

"How do you know these people?"

"I've been in this business for thirty years, saab. These filmy people were looking for a man who could feed their crocodiles. I took up this job when I was young. With time, I started supplying meat to their parties. They sometimes asked for pig blood for accident scenes. Since then, people in the industry call me whenever they require my help."

"This man can tell us more about Sultan and his crocodile farm, sir." Charmy whispered, "The scene from the movie Shaan. Do you remember, sir? Shakaal presses the button; a sliding door opens, which takes the enemy to the pit of a pool where crocodiles devour his body. Ask him if he ever sees such a sliding door in any of these farms. After all, Toofani was last found in one of these farmhouses."

"You mean she has been fed to these crocodiles."

Baldev said, "Sir, The Sultan guy was a dangerous, notorious criminal. I have also heard this news before. Long ago, as an independent detective, I worked on a kidnapping case. Someone had warned me not to go around Sultan's farmhouses."

Honey asked, "Toofani! Is she one of the girls whose name was mentioned in Disha's diary?"

Charmy said, "Yes, sir, there were two girls she had mentioned in the diary. One is Toofani, the other one is Jeba."

"What about your intel on them, Charmy?"

Charmy showed him a photo: If someone describes her in that black and white photo, Toofani was tall, and her look was terrific, like some vintage glamour of Bollywood. Her face looked familiar to Honey. She had posed with her head turned to the side and one hand at the neck, distracting every attention towards her neck to showcase her diamond necklace, which was fastened tightly around her neck. Her hairstyle was bouffant without an oversized hairdo of the late 1970s, a cute classic look of heroines in the early 1980s.

Showing him a photo, Charmy said, "She is the same girl who worked with Sultan as a secretary in his office. Somehow, my source managed to get her photo from the office record. You seem to have forgotten about her role in that movie, sir. I have forgotten the name of the movie, but her name is Toofani. Just a one-role wonder, sir."

"Of course, I remember that scene, Charmy. I was a kid when she was an actress." Hanumat said.

"What amazing acting, sir!" She exclaimed. "She faked a murder by keeping blood in her mouth. How can someone do something like this for a role? These kinds of films only give ideas to criminals."

"That was a unique scene, sir," Baldev added. "I remember the elderly lady catching sight of her husband, who had a knife in hand and his shirt stained with blood."

"That was a brilliantly executed plan," Charmy chimed in. "The wife followed the blood stains on the hotel carpet. The manager even took photos of the husband standing in a pool of blood. Such plans are insane, putting someone under psychological stress. The couple left the hotel in fear of a potential police case. And they kept paying him money throughout their lives to hide a crime that never existed."

"That was a trap. The couple kept paying him because it was executed in such a great way that there was no reason to suspect anything else," Baldev explained.

"But that doesn't happen in real life, Charmy," Honey interjected.

"No sir, such looters lie down faking an accident on highways. They loot him if someone comes for help. After all, these things put psychological pressure, sir. To create fear in the individuals to get what you want to get." Charmy said.

"What about the other girl, Zeba," Honey asked.

"No trace of her at all in this whole city, sir."

*****

Another day was spent without much action since Arshad was nabbed and thrown into the interrogation room. Police had no additional input to add to their investigation. Arshad was shoved into an infinitesimal room, a pile of rubbish: a few broken chairs, iron rods, bamboo sticks, ropes, wires, nail boards, electrical bells, mops, and whatnot. That room was just adjacent to the interrogation room, which was as terrible as the interrogation room. That tiny room was enough to give someone an idea of what could be used to extract information.

One intense blow from a bruiser had marred his jawbones. He felt the click of its disengagement on his right cheek. There was a twinge of pain when he took a sip of water, and when he spat it out, the porcelain wash basin had all the stains of blood.

He saw his face in the mirror; his face had swollen up. The bruisers in khaki had not left any place where he could see his skin to look normal on the face. A noticeable split in the capillaries over the white of his left eye had reddened it as if it would bleed. Repeated spit balls also carried the tinge of blood. With a closed mouth and clenched teeth, he felt the looseness of teeth ready to fall from their sockets at any time. The striped shirt and the trousers he wore had all stains of blood. He turned his face up, looked at the mirror, and smiled from the angle of his mouth at one of the bruisers who stared at his face in the mirror. With the blood running down at the angle of his mouth, he turned his face to them.

Through the camera, Honey could see that there was no trace of fear. His men had spent more than an hour since morning. Except for giving a blood-smeared tongue and a clot on the faint stubble on the cheek, the punches the inspector showered on his face had no impact on his mind. Honey's biggest trouble was that he was neither constructing any story like others to play a diversionary tactic nor was he bothered to tell him the truth.

The pride of endurance was well visible on Arshad's face. What they had not tried on him yesterday, the calling bells and the electric shock from the live wires did not affect him—a strange man.

Arshad gave the ceiling a look. He could see the iron hoops hanging from it. What more could he get than this? Every nerve, every tendon, and even every bone of his body had been crushed. The pride of a lover to bear the pain for his beloved's family was soaring up with every punch he received. He made a high laugh with it, which made the men in khaki lose no attempt to break him down further. This time, Arshad felt his wrist being gripped. One caught him by his neck from behind. The other one cupped his cheek. He experienced a flash of Disha's plea when she was pinned down. The guilt knocked him down. But soon, the thought of breaking down was deterred by his besottedness for Jemima. What didn't he do to get her closeness?

Arshad uttered, "Kill me, officer. Enjoy the supremacy today. If you can't, then be prepared to get killed in the end."

The bruiser could palpate the pulse at his throat with the crook of the elbow. His breath had turned rapid, and his heart galloped high inside the chest. The guy had a nerve of steel. Arshad lifted his head to look into one's eyes. Their eyes met. He said, "You will not get anything from me, officer. I feel bad for you. I can understand your anger and annoyance. Now, what will you tell the press waiting outside? After all, you get a salary for hitting people like me. Isn't it."

Soon after, he felt his legs tied when he saw Honey unlatched the iron door and came inside. Arshad's hands were stuck inside the hoops. He expected the iron rod, which was kept on a table, to be used on him, but what bothered him more was the silence on Honey's face. More pitiful than his painful imagination. Honey said, "If you have any urge to kill us, do it now." He pulled out the buckle of Arshad's belt. Then he nudged him with a hard shove. The buckle was a folded gun, and it had six live rounds.

*****

In the late afternoon, a woman draped in a sleek black burqa glided into the police station. She was treated with respect by a lady constable. For her, it was a different feeling in the police station. The custodian didn't ask her those unpleasant questions like the ones she was used to after getting caught at every rave party. She hesitated to utter her name, but they were not the same people she saw thirty years ago. She introduced herself as Arshad's mother. When she wrote her name and address in the visitors' book - Jeba Akhtar, mistress of Salim Sultan, and relationship with the prisoner as a mother. Charmy sensed her complicated past with each stroke of her pen.

When she showed her face, Charmy raised a brow. A thin layer of confidence was on her face, contrasting with the fragility of someone's mere presence in the police station for the wrong reason when she stated, "My son is in your custody, officer. Give me a chance to meet him. I have come from Pakistan."

"He is not cooperating, madam. You will have to come tomorrow until we finish our job," Charmy said. Her tone was gentle but not too firm.

"I may be able to convince him to tell you the truth. Give me a chance to meet him." Jeba said.

Charmy looked at her hands clasped in earnest supplication. They looked white and soft. The skin of her face was pale. The little hairs on her forehead still carried the darkness, and there was much resemblance to the photograph she handed over to them. What also clicked in her mind was the name, which had a reference in one of Disha's diaries.

"Sultan is his father, of which he is not aware. I believe you will keep this secret and not tell him the truth. He is an engineer but in the company of dreaded criminals. Believe me, I always wanted him to…"

"you wanted him to become a gangster. Wished for him to follow his father's footsteps, isn't that right?"

"No," Jeba responded firmly, a hint of defiance sparkling in her eyes.

Charmy guided her to a modest bench in a dimly lit corner room.

De Souza mentioned, "Sir, you must praise us. In most photographs we collected from this man's house, he is seen playing with a gun in some jungle—a new trend in the city. Our attention was drawn to this captivating beauty in one of these photographs. We contacted the studio guy who had taken the photograph as a studio number was written on the backside."

"It stunned us when he provided us the information. This woman is the wife of a rich businessman in London."

"What is she doing here in the photo album with Arshad? The background looks familiar."

Baldev said, "It could be one of the arbours in Disha's farm, sir. My source saw her on the Mumbai Road. The sweetheart was lighting a cigarette. My men dodged the traffic to acquire her details at any cost, but she left in a car. They followed her to the airport, and to their surprise, another car followed her. It was Vicky who got out of the car that followed this blonde."

After taking off her headphones, Charmy added, "Relate this dialogue that Arshad just uttered. Not every guy is privileged to have everything you usually have: money, a bungalow, food, and a big car."

Baldev said, "Picture Deewar? But this guy has a mother, too."

Charmy said, "Do you remember the scenes in this movie, sir? On a sunny, breezy day, it would have brought much fun to the little boy busy polishing the shoes of a businessman. And the man throws a coin, but the boy doesn't pick it up."

Honey said, "Yes, I have seen this movie many times."

"This guy has a similar story. There is a page in this man's chapter of life. I flipped through almost every page of him yesterday. There is a broken heart. He held a certain position of attraction in his college days."

"What is that position?"

"A first-grade rank from Kindergarten to his engineering degree."

"Really!"

"I believe some tragedy might have happened to him at some point in time, which is why he chose this path," Charmy said.

"Should I try my emotional intelligence on him before you interrogate him further, sir? I will try to extract as much information as possible from him. Probably, he is under the spell of a lover's pride."

"Go ahead, Charmy."

A strange silence fell over his face when Charmy showed him the photograph they had recovered from his hideout. His hands stopped shaking the hoops. His eyes widened in surprise. His voice carried the pain of a jilted lover, different from the criminals' streak.

"How do you know this girl?" Charmy asked.

"What do you want to know about her?"

"Your story, Arshad?"

"My story?"

"Yes, your story. How did a bright student like you end up in this wrong profession? It all started with a broken love story, right?"

"Let that part be personal."

Charmy looked into his eyes, rested her hand on his shoulder, and said, "Let it come out. You will feel better."

Honey had never imagined that Charmy had the magical power to put someone under her spell. She was as sweet as her name, and her words were too. It was probably the influence of all those romantic movies she watched every day. Honey watched every reaction of Arshad from the other room. The cameras were focused on his face, capturing every expression. The microphone attached to Charmy's shirt captured his emotions well.

There was visible wetness in Arshad's eyes when he closed them for a moment. Until he responded, Charmy stared at his face. Arshad had flashes of memories in his mind. It started when they bumped into each other during a college function. The light, gentle touch of her fingers had sent a wave of romantic feelings to his heart. As he relived their first encounter, their subsequent encounters also flashed in his mind. She held a flower in her hand when she proposed to him. A sudden gush of wind of love passed by when she placed a friendship cap on his head. He recalled the deliberate sound she made once to startle him in the library while he was reading, making all eyes stare at them, from pinching his cheek in her soft hands to drawing love signs in his notebooks and many more such moments.

Arshad said, "I completed my schooling in Pakistan. I came to study in Dubai on a scholarship. Jemima was my college mate. While everyone talked about different subjects, we talked about love. People read chemistry and balanced reactions, and she was solving problems in our chemistry where reactions were the most unbalanced ones."

"Why is that?"

"Initially, our fortress of love seemed impregnable. But not all roads lead to Rome. Who then knew the road to my Rome would be full of pebbles?"

"But that doesn't make someone a criminal. Not everyone becomes a pickpocket when they have no money in their pocket."

"So you have already visited my past before coming here."

"Not in that detail."

"I grew up in a house where eating two square meals was a luxury for me. I was not as privileged as you guys to have all sorts of comforts at home. Three small rooms, that's all. A weeping mother who took every care to fulfil her dream of making her child an engineer, bearing all the brunts of society for not revealing who my father was. There was a culture of playing with guns for every trivial matter in my locality. It was a slummy piece of land, a dumping ground for railway garbage. Not every slumdog can become a millionaire overnight. That was my fate. I was poor, and the girl was rich. Our chemistry was like an unbalanced chemical reaction."

"She liked you because you were a bright student. Where did social class come into your relationship?"

"Books do not feed you. It is the right knowledge and right talent that feeds you and gets you what you want. The right place and the right job could not have given me the money that her father wanted me to possess to get married to Jemima. So, I came back to Pakistan to earn money."

"Was it all for her that you became a contract killer? Didn't you ever think about your mother? Have you ever thought it would have embarrassed your mother more than yourself when caught for petty crimes initially?"

"Only she knew that I was on a training followed by a secured job in the Pakistani Army."

"I loved working with electronic gadgets, and I was paid high incentives to lay IEDs in the streets of Kashmir. I had a real grip on explosives while I worked with the Pakistan Army. My name had been changed, and that way, my identity was secured on the radio set. My mother hardly knew about it."

"How many innocent lives have you killed so far?"

"There is a hard world that sees no rules, terms, and conditions before killing any individual. You get a square slip with the name and address of who to kill and where to kill. How to kill is up to you to decide."

"How did you enter Kashmir?"

"I never intended to come to India. It's a very long story."

"I want to know your story."

"Don't think, inspector, I am telling this story because you asked me. No. It's for my mother to believe that I am not wrong. I can feel her on the other side of the wall sobbing for my arrest, now watching me through your cameras."

"How do you know your mother is waiting outside?"

"I recognize her from her voice and her smell."

"Impossible."

"It is possible. My hearing and olfactory skills are far more developed than those of any normal human being."

"Was it a part of your training?"

"No. Developing these habits is a means to our survival in the jungle, especially when you know that behind every tree, there is a soldier from the Indian Army waiting to hunt us. We don't need dogs to tell us which way you want to move."

"I can't say swaying here. I am tired and need some water and a place to sit."

"Jemima was my college friend, and she had a desire to marry me after I completed my degree in engineering. Striving on a scholarship to pursue my studies, it was not possible for me to fulfil all her promises. I didn't want to discontinue my studies to pick up a full-time job. However, I tried hard to keep her happy by buying small gifts. Through a common friend, I met Javed. He was Salim Sultan's son, who had been pursuing training with the Pakistan Army.

Javed had a big plan to attack India. He suggested a way out that might have caused some incoherence in his mind had it not been for a big sum of money. The risk was as big as the wealth. If I did his job, then he would make me rich enough to buy a car and a bungalow in Dubai. Such things were beyond my imagination. He introduced me to Sultan Chacha. I had never seen such an influential man like Sultan. I respected him more than I respected my own chacha. It delighted me that I might be allowed to meet Jemima if I told Sultan about my problem. It opened all the doors for me to enter Jemima's house as a nephew of Sultan.

Destiny took a different course when Jemima's father learned I was poor. I was not allowed to meet her. Her father, Peter, sent her to London for higher studies. With the passing of time, there was a lot of change in her.

I thought I should go with the flow of time. After completing my engineering degree, I was a loner in need of a job that would give me a hefty salary to be able to ask for Jemima's hand. But I had to leave Dubai.

Javed had given me a card during his vacation. It was a card with the address of someone to meet. It was stamped. When I reached the mountain range of Pakistan, the setting sun had obscured the view. Only I knew the seven people who were also with me in that seven-seater autorickshaw. We stopped at the corner of a village street where the track ascended to the mountains. The upper ridges were not visible. I still remember when the driver said that was the endpoint, and he couldn't drive beyond that point. We stared out of the window and wondered if that was the rest of the track we had to climb up.

I alighted to notice that my feet were burning and my toes had swollen up and turned red. It was the first time I was exposed to frostbite. Somehow, we walked up to a base camp where our documents were scanned and stamped. I was offered an appointment letter to work as an engineer attached to the Pakistan Army. There was intense fog, and only a few meters were visible. The cloud had engulfed the mountains. The base camp was on high alert, with guards in combat dress and carrying big rifles. We were greeted as if we were lions and tigers - was it a reality they saw in us? I didn't know. There weren't even any code words for us. There, the rule was whoever had been sent by Sultan to be recruited. I was addressed as Lion. Everyone around me called out, "Sher Aaya, Sher Aaya."

The camp was impregnable from all sides, with the dense fog enveloping it. We had never experienced such a climatic phenomenon. The faces of my fellow mates changed from chattering teeth to being curious about what awaited them in the ridges. Through the mist, they rubbed their hands until they were provided with gloves and snowshoes. The feathery coat brought them some comfort. A man brought them rucksacks. We wondered what could be inside the rucksacks. They were a load of arms and ammunition that we had to carry to the training camp at Balakot the following day.

The next day, early morning, we left the base camp in a tipper. It seemed to have a balance between its wheels, with one side on the ground and the other on the hedge. As we saw shrubs everywhere, there was no definite pavement and too many dangerous turns that could break our spines. After a few years of rigorous training in Balakot, I came to Dubai."

"Did you meet Jemima?"

"No, I was not allowed to go to Peter's house as her engagement ceremony with Vicky had already been fixed. It was Peter's wish and Sultan's order. I wasn't brave enough to revolt against Sultan's order. I learned through my sources that Jemima's father collaborated with my uncle Salim Sultan on all this. He didn't want me to meet her. Jemima was threatened to cut ties with me. Sultan used me. He sent me back to Pakistan with his son Javed for a special mission. I tried to find out a reason from Javed. He told me that in such military missions, one is considered dead until they return alive. Once declared dead, one cannot have a life of their own.

Javed promised that If I ever came back alive from the mission, he would speak with Sultan about the marriage. I operated in Kashmir until Javed called me to Mumbai during mid-summer in 2008. Javed wanted to plot a terror strike in Mumbai."

"That was brutal," Charmy said.

"No, that was a proxy war," Arshad said bluntly. "What about your Balakot strike? It was a harrowing experience. The extent of devastation and desolation caused by your warplanes and artillery was indescribable. Our camps, which were once filled with laughter and merrymaking, now stand as hollow husks. The deafening roars of aircraft engines and thunderous explosions reduced them to dust and rubble."

"That was a retaliatory response. You perpetrated a blast on our men." Charmy said.

"That was an unprecedented catastrophe we were not prepared for. As a survivor, all I could do was hold onto fragments of hope and solidarity with my fellow soldiers. But somehow, my irrepressible spirit refused to succumb to the tempestuous tides of emotions. I joined the intelligence service to work in Mumbai again. I came here to take revenge for the incalculable toll of the Balakot strike."

"What made you kill Disha? What harm had she done to you? Have you ever realized that you turned from a lover to a murderer?" Charmy asked.

"I am a spy. It doesn't matter who I kill to benefit Pakistan. It was Vicky's plan to terrorize Disha and give her a fainting attack before drowning her in a bathtub."

"Why in a bathtub?"

"No one will suspect foul play as she had consumed alcohol."

"Then why didn't you kill her there?"

"Vicky changed his mind. He had a plan B to execute, where he wanted to hit two birds with one stone. He later dropped Disha at her premises in an inebriated state."

Was that second bird Pallavi, then?

"I was not told that Pallavi was the second target. Peter's order was to kill Disha before she reached any police station. He didn't tell me where she was. So, I alerted my men stationed around the police stations not to allow her inside. Later, my source informed me that she had joined the farmhouse party with Vicky."

"So, you work for Peter?"

"No, I am here to protect everyone who works for Pakistan. Peter is Sultan's man, and Sultan works for Pakistan."

"Tell us about the ingenuity you showed in reaching her doorstep despite knowing it was one of the city's most secure locations. The apartment always had a security guard deployed, and the CCTV cameras were always functional. How did you manage to enter without being caught? Did you hack it?"

"Yes, I did it."

"So, you were the one who helped those terrorists enter our hotels?"

"Yes," he nodded.

"How did you know Vicky ?"

"While I was in India, back in Dubai, Jemima got married to Vicky. I was in deep pain—all my hopes of getting her as my bride were shattered. I was restless about meeting her in London, but Uncle Salim forbade me and insisted I help Javed in his successive missions. At first, I decided to kill Vicky, who snatched away all my happiness. I knew Vicky would return to India someday, and it would not be difficult for me to kill him. No one will suspect me of the crime."

"So you waited for him in Mumbai to kill him, but how he became your companion in crime," Charmy asked.

" I had developed a strong network of informers in India. I collected every piece of information about Vicky. I learned that Vicky is the son of a hotelier. It was then easy to trace him down in Mumbai. Like a douchebag, he changed women like clothes. I followed him to all the pubs he visited and all the restaurants where he ate food. I befriended him in a pub to bump him off.

So why didn't you kill him?

"It was not that easy. Sultan had a direct trade interest in him. That trade indirectly benefited my country. Then I thought, Let me be that dead Arshad for my soil and dead forever."

"But how did you overcome your emotional turmoils."

"Forgiving my enemies, forgiving Peter, forgiving Vicky and forgiving Jemima. I decided to move on."

"So, you patched up. What about your emotions? And what about her emotions for you?"

"Let that be my secret. I don't want to reveal."

Charmy said, "I know you met Jemima in Mumbai. You took this photograph. You have written an important date on the last page of your diary. What was that?"

"No, I won't tell you." Tears welled up in Arshad's eyes. "Let that be my secret."

"Was it that day Jemima wanted to commit suicide? Tell me, Arshad, you will feel better. Did she call you to London?"

"You have already read my diary, so what else do you want to know from me? Jemima was in depression for this Vicky."

"Was Dr Pallavi the reason?"

"Yes."

"So, you planned to frame her in this murder case."

"It was Peter's plan. Peter always thinks three steps ahead. He knows what to do, when, and how to do it well in advance and executes his plans. Vicky is that pawn on the chessboard. I blame Peter today for the problems in Jemima."

"Did you ever get an order to kill Dr Pallavi?"

"No."

"She was a popular surgeon, a public figure. Killing her would have caused unrest in Mumbai. Javed can't afford to lose his men to encounters."

"Have you ever met with Dr Pallavi?"

"After that strike, everything was devastated. It took us six months to reorganise. In August 2019, I came to India; first, I went to Goa for a few days. There, I saw Vicky speaking with a doctor, and later, I learned through my source that he was planning to get married to the girl. I knew about his lecherous character and informed Jemima. That is where I went wrong. I should not have informed Jemima about this."

"What happened on that day?"

"When my men informed Peter that Disha had reached the farmhouse, Peter clued in about the party. It was around 8 PM that day when I reached the farmhouse. Vicky called a few female employees to observe the happy day of the company. Disha was also there at the party. Around 10 PM, Vicky entered with a girl inside a room and closed the door from within. Half an hour later, he came outside and asked me to get in. What I found was the girl was dead and lying in a pool of blood. Vicky had killed her. I was shocked by the reality: a dead body and a knife on her side. I looked down, and my shoes were drenched with blood. The knife was blood-stained. My mind was hard to believe Vicky was that bad as a human. He asked my help to fix the dead body.

"Are you out of your mind, Vicky?" I asked. He laughed at me and said, "It's a fake murder to create a panic reaction in Disha."

"So, it was all planned by Vicky?"

"No, I don't think so. Vicky doesn't have that kind of mind. That mind must be Peter's, who is a storehouse of such plans."

"Why do you blame Peter for every crime Vicky does?"

"Peter introduced Javed into my life to keep his daughter away from me. Javed, in turn, showed me how to earn money to meet Peter's demands. Who else on this earth can have a mind like Peter's?"

"So, Disha was called to that room?"

"No, she was bound to come to the washroom where the plan was to drown her in a bathtub."

"Why was she bound to come?"

"Vicky had mixed a diuretic drug into her drink."

"Ms Disha was drunk, and in the middle of the party, she reached the washroom and saw me there with Vicky."

"She panicked and collapsed."

"So Vicky carried out a Plan B from there. The bathtub was already full, but Vicky had a backup plan."

"How did Disha reach her apartment?"

"Vicky took her in his car as soon as she regained her senses after a couple of minutes."

"As per our Plan B, I dressed up as a courier boy and closely surveyed the apartment from all sides around six in the morning. It was a bit foggy that morning."

"Vicky sent Pallavi to her apartment first by texting her from Disha's phone. Pallavi attracted the guards' attention while entering the apartment. If the police were to explore any murder angle, they would first reach Pallavi's door, not ours. As per the plan, I hacked the CCTV system of the building at 8:30 in the morning. We used the fire escape to land on the first floor and avoid the security during their lunch break. Ms Disha opened the door if Vicky had come to meet her. She was very drowsy when we entered, making it easier for us to complete our task."

"Who injected the anaesthetic drug into her?

"Before she could shout for help, I held her hands, and Vicky injected the muscle relaxants in her vein. She went into paralysis and a respiratory arrest in a minute. Then we hanged her in the bedroom."

"So, you came out being unnoticed after that ?"

"Before we leave the house, Vicky's father opens the door with his duplicate key. He came to the bedroom. We rushed to her kitchen to hide. Through the gap of doors, I found that when he saw Disha had been hanging from the fan, he hastily opened her cupboard, took out all her diaries and left the room with a red diary in hand. Soon after he left, we sneaked away from her apartment."

"How did no one notice Cheema visiting that apartment."

"I don't know. Cheema only can say about it. It may be Peter's plan C."

Jeba entered the interrogation room. She sobbed after a scream of revulsion. She cleaned Arshad's face with her hands. It was swollen up. She gave him a little shake, Why Arshad, why? She steps back. You can't be my son Arshad. She cursed herself for her sin. She uttered repeatedly for being punished for all that she did with Madhu.

*****

Cheema's voice turned dry as he ran for water after reading the letter. It was far from his expectations that the police would clutch him one day by his lapel like this. The stamp on the envelope was distinct before he opened it. He was asked to report to the police station. The mobile pinged with a message: "Delay in Departure." The bearer of the letter was not in khaki, but Cheema's mind could register the stranger as a cop from his brogues after a faint glance.

The police in civvies had cordoned off his house from all directions when they learned from the airport official that a ticket to London had been booked by him an hour ago. The niftiness of the police action at the airport was no different from that used to nab hardcore criminals. The perfection in the drill was not so obvious to a common passenger, but they were in place in and around the airport much before the time when the flight schedule adjustments were announced. To their luck, the delay was undoubtedly no less than two hours. UK Airlines had started the check-in services, and all passengers moved towards the outgoing formalities at the Bombay Airport. All eyes were focused on the escalators carrying passengers to the UK.

Cheema chugged a glassful of water. He jabbed a few contacts in his mobile, but his call dropped after a ring. He knew many police officers of a higher rank but didn't dial any of them afterwards. His sharp mind had woken up, and he smelled the coffee that his phone line was under surveillance.

He reported to the police station after two hours. The sight inside reflected upon the persona of the man who came and sat across from him that he would turn unstoppable if he started pounding his punches. Just a while ago, the swollen-faced man sitting in a corner, upon whom his eyes were fixed, seemed to look like Arshad. This realization came when he heard his deep cry of unbearable pain.

The sight of a blanket and truncheons placed on a table under the surveillance camera made him conscious of the fact that the police use them for kambal parades to work on hardcore criminals. "He will be spared if he sits under the surveillance camera and tells the truth," He thought. He could distinctly read "Satyamev Jayate" written on the wall behind Honey. Now, he understood why it was written there.

"Cheema, now you are going to tell the truth. Why…?"

Before he could start the next sentence, a nervous Cheema said, "Sultan was after my blood for a red diary. Having searched all the places, I learned that Disha was the only girl who could survive in the city because of a changed name and a new identity. Sultan probably didn't want to kill her. It was a matter of fifty million dollars, sir, which gave me sleepless nights. I thought Disha could have that red diary, so I entered her flat using a duplicate key. Sultan wanted his son Javed to rule the underworld in India. I decided to steal it from her place before Javed could become a new commander and get to her throat."

Honey got up from his chair and looked out the window. Not many people strolled around, but the reporters had blocked a gypsy, which honked for a while and stopped. A young couple alighted before it made a U-turn to leave. The police at the entrance walked rapidly towards them for a rescue. He returned to his chair. Vicky and Pallavi entered the room and sat on a corner bench.

"Yes, Cheema, continue."

"Jemima and Vicky were never divorced. Peter wanted to get Arshad out of his way. Arshad was a techie with an engineering degree and a threat to his family. According to him, Jemima still nurtured love for him. Peter knew well that Arshad had a sentimental brain stuffed with a load of unyielding stubbornness, and to keep him away, it was necessary to drag him into our maze of conspiracy. He acted according to our plan."

"Why was Dr. Pallavi dragged into this?" Honey asked.

"It was Peter's plan to kill Disha this way, not mine. And it was Peter who asked me to go to Disha's apartment."

"Why did Peter want to kill Disha?" Hanumat asked.

"Because she had a premonition about a disaster for this city after she saw a portrait of Sultan hung in Peter's newly bought office. She suspected him as Sultan's man and warned me to stay away from Peter. She always had a bitter reaction towards Peter." Cheema replied.

Honey glanced at Pallavi. Her eyes had turned red. Pallavi stared back at Honey. The surprise on her face was as intense as her fury. Her eyes discreetly rested upon him for the first time without blaming him for the cause. It seemed from her face that she had taken the blame upon herself for a paramour relationship with Vicky, for not questioning him about his past life and his wife. Moreover, her gaze carried a reflection of her own mistakes and screaming abuses towards Honey. The glance was interrupted by a scream from the other corner of the room when an entrant carried an ice pack to apply to the man's swollen face.

"So where were we?"

"If ever the police find foul play and dig into the case, Dr. Pallavi will be caught. Vicky faked a murder in the farmhouse to evoke panic in Disha. Arshad's sentimental mind was his biggest weakness. The plan was to send him back to Dubai with no chance of return. Peter and Jemima had already made up their minds to settle in Mumbai, but that was only possible if Pallavi went to jail."

Pallavi rose from the bench and walked up to Vicky, sitting a meter away on the other end with a hand on his face. He was left without any words to protect himself from this case. Pallavi gave a tight slap on his uncovered cheek and said, "You used me... Why me, Vicky? I trusted you more than anyone in this world. Don't ever try to show your face to me. I cannot forgive you, Vicky." Pallavi's throat choked with anger, and her cheek turned crimson.

Honey promptly said, "I will tell you why, Dr. Pallavi."

He took out a newspaper cutting and showed her the news. "For this piece of news that you ever had written against the chemical factory near the Chawl area. I have the whole thesis in my hand that you had written and the materials that you had collected through your students."

"Now, you, Vicky, tell us more about this," he pointed his finger at Vicky and screamed scornfully.

Vicky said, "Much of the information about our company was leaked to the public. The environmentalists were after us to close the business we had built with years of hard-earned money. I wanted Pallavi to write a good review about us, but it was next to impossible without gaining her confidence. It was Uncle Peter's idea from the beginning to kill her. It was difficult for me initially to persuade him not to do so as his son-in-law, but he soon understood the reality on the ground. Pallavi had become the biggest critic of the bureaucracy. She had created turmoil in the political and business circles. Public sentiment was also growing in her favour day by day. There was nothing significant coming out of the relationship I had with her. In fact, Jemima attempted suicide, suspecting my relationship with Pallavi. How long could I continue like this? And Pallavi continued to present her paper in almost every scientific meeting."

Honey exclaimed, "So you decided to neutralize her with this murder. One murder and two enemies out. One arrow for two targets."

"So, what was your plan?"

"I went to meet Pallavi to tell her it seriously affected our business, but I couldn't. She was happy to see me after a long time, and I behaved like an old friend. I was unable to tell her about my deeds. Then..."

"Then what?" asked Honey.

"When I was unable to discuss this matter, I plotted all of this. I invited her to a social gathering for a social cause to create a good impression on her. She agreed and came."

"So, Goa's trip was pre-planned?" asked Honey.

"Yes."

Pallavi rose to her feet and slapped him again and again on his face using both hands. "You scoundrel, you used me for your petty, selfish objectives." She broke into tears.

*****

The gruelling hours she spent in the operating theatre distracted her from the happenings at the police station. She had to rush to the hospital for her job. There was no time for any self-discovery or to think about where she went wrong. She hadn't even taken lunch.

How would her logical mind justify her emotional soul, saying it had made no mistake? Whatever the mind said, she followed. It unravelled a profound conflict, which lingered after she came out of the operating theatre. A string of emotions crashed over her. Her mind sank, unable to find any appropriate answer to her problem. Was he still thinking about what she had told him in a fury to defend Vicky? He hadn't asked any irrelevant questions that day. She tried to go to Honey's chamber to apologize, but her legs froze. She waited for him on the porch until sunset to apologise, but Honey turned down every request she made through the constables. He must feel that she likes him. Their attachments were strong when the relationship grew platonic. Media opinions may have influenced him, but she didn't bother with what they wrote about her being linked with Honey. She has an unaccountable store of love for him but can't ruin his happiness. Though giving away such a feeling was difficult, she had to reconcile the conflict between her mind and her soul. All she could feel before leaving for her house was a built impression of him.

His being respectful towards her had changed. She realized there was a rhythm in her life when Honey came into her life. She was more energetic and vibrant. It was her loss. The dream to become someone's perfect bride had shattered. She was dying to fall in love with him again, while a part of her was in profound disagreement about not accepting the thrill without knowing about the girl who helped him resolve the wound in his heart. Is he married? She didn't even know what tomorrow would bring for her. What's still there for the media to write about her?

She reached her house, parked the car, pulled out a small square mirror from her vanity, looked at her swollen eyes, wiped the tears still welling up with a Kleenex, turned off the light, and exited her car.

*****

In the Shivdasani house, Romy was happy after checking the progress of the case on TV. His son's irregular life would end. For him, if Honey's life was an outer rim, then the core axle was his work ethic. Rise and fall always came in his son's life, but he was proud that no road humps could disintegrate the wheel of his life. He was happy that any unchallenged monopoly of a media house couldn't tune up this machine. What not the press wrote about him, from a rising star to a slacky khaki man. At least he would not be sleep-deprived for another few days.

He still had a supplemental task pending. Now was the best time to visit Pallavi's house to discuss his marriage. At least Honey's actions had renovated the cell that Vicky had once occupied. The girl with overwhelming intelligence, who had the calibre of stitching open hearts, who could read someone from their X-ray, how could she not recognize a hard-hearted man who destroyed the temple in her heart? All that his role would be is to set an idol of Honey on that altar. However, his biggest doubt was Honey. Could he be wishful to lead a life with Pallavi? He looked at the clock. It was half an hour past six. Ajay was supposed to join Honey at the Shivdasani house with the papers related to Pallavi's presence in the classroom while the murder was happening.

The hard wind rushed through the slightly ajar door and swirled into the main hall as Honey left it open after stepping in. He hurried to his room without speaking a word, as if a burden still weighed on his mind before he went through a file.

The news on the TV channels offered a satisfactory view of the day's progress. The reporters had captured the happy ending of the unfolding drama through many ups and downs. Romy padded softly into the hall, sinking into the sofa. He had been eager, waiting for the moment to ask Honey about the case. When Honey came out and sat across from him with a bottle of water in hand and a whirlwind of thoughts in his mind, there was a pause on his lips after he chugged down half the bottle. The intermittent hard wind tried to ease the heat brewing in his mind, giving a gentle touch. Honey ran a hand through his hair, kept his eyes shut, and leaned back on the sofa.

Ajay, too, stepped in with a file in his hand and joined them. He had a satisfactory grin on his face. Honey transferred him half a bottle of water. Ajay chugged the rest. That was how they always drank together from the same bottle, in sadness or happiness.

Romy's voice held a mix of concern and credence as he asked, "Now, have all four been exposed, and they have confessed to committing the crime? Why are you worried, Beta?"

Honey sighed, pointing to an uncertainty, "Cheema's man approached Avinash uncle to accept the case. However, Avinash uncle flatly turned him down. He warned me not to stop here until I collect all the proofs against these people. There is a high chance that these people will get away scot-free."

Romy asked, "If you need to file a charge sheet based on their confession, why can't you?"

Honey said, "Avinash uncle is right, Papa. So far, it's only their verbal confession. Now, we have exposed their motives, but the court asks for hard evidence. We have no concrete proof against them."

"Pallavi is the one whom the neighbours saw going in and coming out. Their motive was to get rid of Pallavi by defaming her so that she would withdraw herself from her research activities and lose all public sympathy after going to jail. Arshad will fly back to Dubai, and Peter will manage the business in India from there. Without evidence, Vicky and Cheema will go scot-free."

Ajay asked, "What made them hang her after the injection?"

Honey said, "Because if a prominent or inspiring figure commits suicide, it catches the attention of the public faster than an accident or homicide. That could be one of the reasons."

Ajay said, "Now I understand; they already knew Pallavi would be convicted in this case anyway, whether it be suicide or murder, because of the traces of an anaesthetic drug in her blood."

"Right. The presence of traces of anaesthetic drug in her blood has sensationalized this case." Honey added.

"So, Honey, what are the chances of Pallavi getting acquitted?" Ajay asked.

Honey said, "Many times, a falsehood is implanted to put someone in trouble so that the truth that comes out after the rise of the curtain will be very sensational. Here, Pallavi is being questioned about the anaesthetic drug even though her fingerprints are not available on the vial and the time of her visit does not match the time of death."

"So then, why are you so worried, Honey?"

"If it were not winter and Disha had not been injected with any muscle relaxant, I would not have been worried. Both delay the rigor mortis. In such a case, the timing of death and her presence would be difficult for Pallavi to defend. To understand a criminal mind, you must think like a criminal here. You are better off being in the Traffic Department, Ajay."

Romy said, "But Vicky was also there within the premises when Pallavi entered her flat. She was alone inside."

"That further justifies the use of an anaesthetic drug, papa. With no marks of struggle. In addition to the route and mode of injection, it strongly goes against Pallavi."

Romy said, "I never got a chance to have a sufficient conversation with her, but whatever time I got, I can tell you that she is a very soft-hearted girl. She is innocent, beta. Try to do something."

"That is why I am worried, papa. For the evidence to convict these criminals, Vicky and Arshad, I must rewind the whole case in my mind. I am going to sleep. I am hopeful we will get some leads by tomorrow afternoon."

Ajay said, "Sorry, Honey, before you go to sleep, go through this forensic report again. We are probably missing something."

Honey said, "The forensic report is complete, Ajay. The cause is the injection of an anaesthetic drug, and such cases can't be thrown into a cold box. But, again, the forensic team will revisit the crime scene tomorrow in the daylight. Baldev is leading that team. De Souza is going to the farmhouse with another forensic team. Charmy is going to the spas where Vicky is going every weekend. I must see if he was taking a sauna bath on that day. How far it is true."

"So, you have a strong team. I think I should also come to join you." Ajay said.

"You are most welcome. I picked Charmy, Baldev and De Souza because all of them had been running their independent detective agencies before joining the police service. And they are the best. A point to note here is that neither Pallavi's nor Vicky's fingerprints are on the vial. Pallavi can defend that in court. The one they found also does not match Arshad's. These scoundrels had worn gloves. As it was a planned murder."

Sleeping with a question in mind was difficult, But finally, three hours of sleep refreshed Ajay. There was something more in this story. He had understood by then, being with Honey. Cheema will not do anything without an ulterior motive. But How do we get down to the truth? What was his real purpose for entering the flat? He had reached the police station.

"How will you convict Cheema?" Ajay inquired. Confusion etched on his face. "I could not understand Cheema's entry into the scene?"

"I hope we will get some leads against him as well," Honey replied.

"Cheema is involved in this murder. His lawyer can argue that he could have taken the diary from Disha at any point if he wished. Why would he kill her? He would discard the fact with this argument that Cheema was not there at all." Ajay said.

Honey explained, "He took the lift from the basement to the second floor where there was no CCTV camera, and to reach the basement, he entered through the rear gate as the guard was not there during lunch. You are right, Ajay; if Cheema had to take the particular diary, he could have taken it at any time because he had the key to her flat."

"How has he got the keys to Disha's flat?" Ajay asked, curiosity piqued.

"Cheema harbours squatters in the vacant apartments and then strikes a deal with the owners through the concierge to buy them at a fraction of the price. That is his old business. Disha's flat was one of those properties. So, he has direct access to many of these apartments. But the question here is, what would he gain by taking the correct diary? Nothing, really. The fifty million dollars would go to Sultan, who could decide whether or not to share it with Cheema. He is not naïve enough to just agree to whatever Salim Sultan proposes. But he grabbed the wrong one," Honey elucidated.

Ajay paused for a moment with a question mark inside his head and asked, A puzzled expression forming. "Are you saying he picked up the wrong diary from her cabinet?"

Honey nodded emphatically. "Yes, Cheema has taken the wrong diary. The red one he mentioned is with us. Disha had kept it tucked away in a suitcase inside the drawer of her bed. Now, our focus should be on Vicky and how he could have acquired such an anaesthetic drug. These are controlled substances. You can't find them at any corner store."

Just then, Charmy entered Honey's room. After saluting him, she shared, "Sir, I went to the spa where Vicky had his sauna session. He was there that morning. I met the girl who does his pedicure. She mentioned that Vicky has six toes on one foot and five on the other and also has a plantar arch issue. Probably, that was the reason he avoided dancing at the farmhouse party. He has corns on his right foot and uses special shoes. Your observation is correct, sir. The right foot in that pair of footprints was found to be half an inch larger."

"Do you have any idea who the shoemaker is?" Honey asked with a genuine curiosity.

"No, sir," Charmy replied.

"Charmy, go to the City hospital and meet the orthopaedician who treated his sprain. He may be able to provide us with more information. Also, you show his footprints to every shoemaker and ask about them. Be careful." Honey instructed.

"As long as Vicky is in custody, I am safe, sir," Charmy reassured him.

"No, it's not just Vicky. The watchdogs of the underworld, patronized by Cheema, may have already received information about your visit to the spa. Don't go alone. Take your team and ensure they are dressed casually. This is a hospital area. Their presence should not disrupt patient care." Honey emphasized.

"Yes, sir." Charmy saluted before departing.

"Ajay, the night's CCTV footage captured the female security guard escorting Disha to her apartment. Vicky didn't enter, but the uneven footprints found at the crime scene will lead us to him. Although the surveillance cameras' recordings from that fateful morning were hacked, we confirmed from the previous night's footage that Disha walked with the guard's help." Honey explained

"How did you suspect this problem with Vicky?" Ajay asked, intrigued.

"Every time Vicky got up from a seat, he had a subtle twitch on his face, which he tried to conceal with a smile. That's why I had him brought to the police station in my gypsy car to observe how he alighted. My forensic experts were prepared to take a footprint in the wet soil. The driver was directed to stop on a damp patch," Honey revealed.

"So, the footprints were unequal?"

"No, they were equal. Vicky recently bought a new pair of shoes and seems uncomfortable in them, likely causing shoe bites or bothering his corns on the right foot. We have his transaction receipt, but the footprints at the crime scene show inequality in size. That's why my forensic experts are revisiting the site to check the soil grass samples. Similar footprints were also found around the basement lift areas, which Cheema used to reach Disha's apartment."

"There are so many shoemakers. How will you reach the real one ?"Ajay wondered.

"Usually, these shoes are customized based on a doctor's prescription, especially for those with polydactyly or any arch problem. And Vicky has both. We may get some information from the orthopaedician who treated him for the sprain." Honey explained.

At that moment, De Souza entered and saluted. "Sir, as you said, we retrieved a partially burnt pair of shoes and a broken mobile phone wrapped in aluminium foil. However, we could not find the surgical gloves and syringe."

" Great job, De Souza," Honey acknowledged.

"The logo is partially charred but still legible, and the sole remains intact." De Souza reported.

"How did you know it was at the farmhouse?" Ajay asked, intrigued.

"It's just a thought, or you could call it sixth sense. If someone aims to evade detection by tracking dogs, they would either burn the evidence or toss it far into the water. That's why I asked for the CCTV footage around the farmhouse. Vicky was in the office after the crime, and he didn't lie because he knew he could be caught if he did. Interestingly, the sole was fireproof. Maybe he worked in a chemical factory, so his soles were customized for fire and chemical resistance, much like others in the field, " Honey explained.

Charmy arrived at one in the afternoon, bubbling with the energy. " Just like they staged a murder at the farmhouse, I staged a sprain, sir."

"So you also went undercover?" Honey asked, impressed.

"Yes, sir." She confirmed.

"The doctor's fingerprints on the X-ray didn't match, but the technician who assists him in arranging operating theatres and manages the stock of his drug store left his fingerprints on my water bottle. I also managed to get the painkiller vial from him that was injected into me."

"So you took the jab unnecessarily?" Honey inquired, surprised.

"My job is more important than a jab, sir," Charmy replied confidently.

"While he was injecting me, I gave him a particularly intense gaze, one of love at first sight. After that, he picked up my bottle and escorted me to the exit to see me off, sir." She concluded with a triumphant smile.

"Excellent work, Charmy. I am proud of your emotional prowess. I trust that injection won't have any harmful effects on you." Honey said.

"Don't worry, sir. Now you will see Charmy's charm and how it works." She declared with a cheeky grin.

"Yes, I am well aware of that. May God bless that poor guy." Ajay chuckled.

"So Charmy, pick him up," Honey instructed.

"I am just waiting for your command, sir. When should I make my move?" She asked, her excitement palpable.

"Soon, If not now, there is a high chance he will either flee or get kidnapped," Honey warned.

"My team is still there, keeping an eye on him. His shift ends at four, and he said he would wait for me for an evening out." Charmy reported.

"A date?" Ajay asked, raising an eyebrow.

"Why not, Ajay sir? That man still has the pride of healing my sprain with his one jab. After all, my appreciation for him to his boss also carries some weightage to bring such a romantic expression out of him." Charmy boasted of her skill.

"Was that merely an appreciation, or was it also Charmy's charm?" Ajay probed.

"Of course, sir, my newly made boyfriend is going to be bankrupt today as Honey sir is going to seize his bank account. His inventory, his briefcase, his bank lockers, and the bungalow where he lives." She teased. A smirk tugged at her lips.

"What do you mean?" Ajay inquired, his intrigue growing.

"Charmy's charm, sir. That man has given me the details of his wealth while walking down the stairs." After a pause, she added, "My sources are all reliable, sir. He is one hundred per cent Vicky's man in the hospital, sir. Mark my words. He is the one who decides when the operation theatres are prepped for emergencies."

"Is that so, Charmy?" Honey asked, intrigued.

"He boasted about it during an argument to prove his supremacy over the surgeons. A charmingly feminine interest in this numb little bug in her man to know what her man does for his living could only evoke a reaction like this, which otherwise would have been hidden and difficult to unearth. Now, he would explain to us, sir, Why Dr Pallavi was being allotted OTs at odd hours. Vicky seems to have her OT schedules monopolized through him."

Ajay chimed in, "Quite possible. And it could be him who leaked it to Vicky that Disha can only be injected through her leg veins. Now your case is solved?"

"Not yet, Ajay, "Honey replied.

"Still, you are anxious. What is the reason?" Ajay pressed.

"No one knows where Disha was before reaching the farmhouse. What her whereabouts were before reaching there remains a mystery. Disha was not murdered for raising her voice against Sultan or for that red diary. We need to see why Disha was murdered. The court will ask for evidence in this matter. Until we have the proof in our hands, the media will continue to vilify Pallavi."

Ajay said, "I have been following the news. They simply echo what you tell them. They don't investigate. If I am to express my point of view, then I can say Disha knew something more about their business. If you combine that with Pallavi's interview, there was something wrong cooking up on that factory side. The chemicals released from the factory were causing health hazards and deformities in babies. You should go and raid the factory now to find out the reason before it gets any later."

Honey smiled and was impressed. "Now you think like a crime investigator. Come to the crime branch. We will work together."

De Souza interjected, "Sir, this tramp was caught with an expensive camera. He is unable to tell where he got it from. This junkie hung about the factory road leading towards the farmhouse. One who saw him said he picked up this camera lying on the road close to a chemical factory. I checked, and the memory card is missing."

Honey urged, "De Souza, let's not divert ourselves from Disha's case to this mind-numbing story. You can go and see that place; I am sure you will discover something else. These days, your ingenuity is expected more in Disha's case; don't forget that."

"Sir, I have taken a few photographs of the place. You can see them," De Souza said.

Honey's disappointment was evident after looking at the photographs. He rudely replied, "Don't be stupid. The factory was empty, with no workers. So, what do you want to say?"

An unpleasant thought crossed his mind for a minute. Honey looked weary. "De Souza is not a new rookie. He speaks his mind from his experience, but this is not the right time to discuss these junkies. They lay like corpses on pavements, and it is difficult to find out who they are and where they came from," Honey pondered.

"I meant, sir, we should not leave any loose ends. We should investigate the possibility of its connection with Disha's case," De Souza clarified.

"Okay, detain him. We will ask this man when we need him. First, you give him a bath. He is stinking. Then, show him to our doctor and bring him to his senses. Who is he, and how much does he know about the camera? De Souza, he is too frail, so don't do anything to extract your tidbits," Honey commanded.

Inspector Charmy responded, "Don't worry, sir. I understood what to do with him. You can carry on."

"A few days ago, a delegation of state officials had visited the factory workers. Now the factory is empty. I checked. The factory belongs to none other than our playboy, Vicky," De Souza disclosed.

"You still believe your camera theory will crack this case open? De Souza, we only have forty-eight hours left to complete our interrogation. Without any evidence, we are vulnerable targets of the media. No one will believe in your camera theory," Hanumat criticized.

"It's a camera, sir. Before this job, when I was a small-time detective, I used to carry a camera like this. I worked solo. You know, without a partner," De Souza explained.

"So what are you trying to tell us, De Souza?"

"The camera was my only companion. It was my defence. It served as my shield."

Ajay's sharp mind grasped the hint De Souza wanted to convey to Honey, but Honey interrupted.

"What dastardly crime stories were you following then, De Souza?"

"Nothing much, sir, just a kidnapping, a few extramarital affairs, or a string of robberies."

"Here, you have one murder case, De Souza. A sensational murder case. Follow it seriously. Ajay is here with us, helping us. Please let us know what is going on in your mind. Now you are in the police. Don't narrate like a detective."

"What I am trying to tell you, sir, is about the missing link. Disha threw the camera because she was being followed. Once, I had to run for my safety. The first thing I did was toss my camera into a pit after taking out the roll. Disha went to the factories in her official car to receive the delegation. The driver couldn't trace her after the delegation left the factory site. He came after waiting for an hour. Her phone was not reachable. He thought she must have gone with the delegation team or was in a meeting. The driver recognized the camera; it was what Disha carried that day. The photographs published in the evening edition of Saturday speak a lot about the camera." De Souza took out the photograph that was published in the newspaper. The driver was standing next to Disha, and she had a camera hanging around her neck.

"What! Why didn't you tell us this before? Stupid! Can't you say everything in just two lines?" Honey screamed.

"One important observation here, sir. One insider said Disha had gone to her farmhouse office around 8 PM. She looked nervous when she reached her office. Around 9 PM, she joined the party that Vicky had hosted. They were all Vicky's friends, except for Cheema and Peter, who were not present."

"What does that imply?" Honey asked.

"I have no answer," De Souza admitted, looking puzzled for a moment. Then he continued,

"That actor girl is missing from her place, sir."

"Did you find out who the girl is?"

"She is a paid artist. Not a single chat was extracted from Vicky's mobile. We tracked her down to a place where she lives with the name 'Haseena.' She was present in the party photograph. According to my informant, her family is worried. Her mobile phone always remained switched off. We will catch her soon. Her photo has been circulated to all police stations. I checked inside to see if there was any computer in Disha's office but found none."

Ajay asked, " What does the caretaker say about it?"

"The caretaker said he knew nothing about the office room. He probably does not want to be involved in any police matters. There is no memory card inside to see the photographs," De Souza added.

Ajay said, "Look, if she were in her senses, she would never throw the camera like this. It means she was aware that someone closely followed her, and she took out the card and threw the camera before being caught. Then she entered her office and loaded the computer, which these guys had hidden somewhere."

Honey said, "Quite possible."

"It is possible that she kept the camera for photography as a few delegates had visited Cheema's factory workers," Ajay speculated.

"What are you thinking, Honey?" Ajay asked

"The postmortem report didn't mention any memory card or chip inside her stomach," Honey replied.

Ajay scoffed, "Stupid! Who would consume a memory card? What would you do if you got caught with it?"

"I don't know what to do. It doesn't seem relevant to our case. Ajay, we are losing track of the investigation," Honey said in frustration.

"Think for a minute. You are Disha, and you are being chased. You run into your farmhouse for safe hiding," Ajay suggested.

"Hiding? Let's have some coffee and take a break from this conversation. All the nerves in my brain are jangled up," Honey requested.

"It means she knew that the person could not enter the farmhouse without permission from the security guard. She considered the place safe for her. It is the nearest place to reach," Ajay deduced.

"It means neither Cheema nor Vicky followed her," said Honey.

"It could be no one. We might be overthinking. It is possible that this man snatched the camera from her at the factory gate and ran away. I feel the driver knows more than what we have extracted so far. If someone had followed her, she could have called the police for help. But she didn't," Ajay analysed.

Charmy interrupted, "Sir, my mobile phone got switched off. I need a charger. Do you have one?"

"No," De Souza replied.

"Yes, Ajay. Probably her mobile phone was switched off. The factory was just a mile away, so she came and placed it on a charger. Then she saw that the party was being organized, and she joined them," Honey proposed.

"What about the murder drama?" Ajay questioned.

Honey explained, "There are two entrances to the main hall, one from Disha's office and the other from Cheema's office. Vicky entered Cheema's office and called Arshad after half an hour. The girl was already inside Cheema's office. As you can see, none of these party photographs uploaded by Jemima has a photo of that girl."

"Wait a minute," Ajay interrupted.

"Disha is wearing a different dress in these photos, which is different from the photos we saw in the newspaper. It means she came and changed her dress in between. According to you, she threw the camera to escape from the place. She couldn't call the police, assuming her phone was switched off. She might have changed her dress if it was sweat-drenched or torn. But her living room was tidy, and no computer was found in her office," Ajay observed.

"If the caretaker is to be believed, then no one gets inside her office," De Souza concluded.

De Souza added, "I am telling you, sir, the driver and the caretaker are hiding something to keep us away from the evidence against these people. I have instructed my sources to keep an eye on the driver. There are many questions in my mind. How could he leave the car keys at the reception and leave? Did he leave the place after receiving someone's instruction?"

"One minute. They could have found something on the computer, so they destroyed it. There might have been some hard evidence against them. Let's connect the dots this way," Ajay suggested.

"De Souza, are you sure the room was dusted when you went inside?" Ajay asked.

"Hundred per cent sure, sir," De Souza confirmed.

"It means the caretaker is trying to fool us. He must have a second key to her office. He must have disposed of her clothes and the computer. He doesn't know who he's messing with," Honey concluded.

"The key makers can tell us more if we call them here," De Souza suggested.

Hanumat's mobile pinged. It was Abhimanyu Bhaiya's text message. The message stated that Javed was planning something big in Mumbai and Delhi after the Balakot strike. They had caught a lady named Haseena at the border and needed more information on her. The message also included her photos.

The telephone rang, and De Souza answered. He jotted down the information and revealed it to Honey."Sir, there is a message from the CBI headquarters. They have received an email from Disha. They want you to meet them urgently."

Honey and Ajay rushed to the CBI headquarters in ten minutes. They clicked open the file in the download folder, but a window popped up stating it was password protected.

"We can try again. The dot swirled before opening another window that said, 'password protected.'

"We're trying to break the password," the CBI officer said.

Honey said. "Let's try with the word 'Madhubala.'"

"Yes, it worked!" exclaimed Ajay.

Everyone who gathered around was stunned by the photographs they saw: emaciated people with bruises on their backs, bags of brown sugar in the corner of a room, workers on machines looking withered and skinny. In another hall, women with minimal clothing were busy packing materials while their children sat nearby. Dozens of them worked in the hall. Along with it are photographs of a few loaded trucks and a register placed on a table while being filled by a security guard.

"Look, these are photographs from a chemical factory. These people are the workers there.

Disha probably knew about all this. They killed her because of it," Ajay speculated. "Let's go raid it. We'll have enough evidence to put them behind bars."

Honey replied, "No, bro... not behind bars, but a tight noose around their necks."

The team broke open the door. The sound of their footsteps echoed in that dimly lit corridor. The flashlights focused on a few objects and the cold stone walls. The sharp smell of chemicals mixed with the faint smell of stale bidies hung in the air—no trace of life.

A strange chain-rattling noise seemed to come from a small cell. The scene sent a shiver down their spine. Honey's eyes fell on the trapped human beings; it looked like something out of a horror movie. It made the goosebumps rise on their arms. The revolver in their hand was chambered, ready to fire. That cramped little cell had no one except half a dozen emaciated people who barely could rise on their legs. Legs tied, they survived only on liquids within their arm's reach.

Ajay's perceptibility to the situation was clear: " Now, Cheema and Peter's game is over. They can't get away from your clutches. They have had enough of themselves to say. Now I understood Cheema had searched for the camera chip, not the red diary."

" Yes, you are right, Ajay. Now Peter and Jemima have been traced in the streets of Dubai."

*****

Papa, don't worry; I have talked to the gym instructor for the coming week, and they have agreed to accommodate me for the evening session so that I will have more time. Getting up for the gym in the morning is difficult as I feel drained out due to inadequate sleep.

"Why not take a week off?" Romy suggested.

"No, Papa, I won't stop until I get to the root of this case and find out who the tormentors in these photographs were. They all fled away from the spot when we raided the factory. I must make Mumbai free from these gangsters," Honey replied.

"When are you going to get Pallavi into this house?" Romy inquired.

"Stop it, Papa. Fifteen years is not a short time. People change both mentally and socially over a decade. When will you change your perspective?" Honey countered.

Honey could sense the hurt in Romy's eyes. His words had struck a deep chord with his father. He was still dwelling on a past incident. And he still believed that Pallavi was the best girl for Honey, even better than Priyanshi. However, Honey wasn't sure if Pallavi still had any feelings for him. He can't even consider meeting her privately until the case gets erased from public memory. It would be better for him to spend time at the gym to work on his physique. He needed to go to the gym right away.

As Honey walked through the narrow corridor of a pedestrian mall, he noticed it was not well-illuminated. The automatic bulbs had not glowed, and darkness slowly crept in through the glass windows. Just before taking the escalator to the first floor, he suddenly swerved into another lane heading to his right. He stopped and looked back to see someone following him a few meters away.

The person had pulled the hood of his jacket up. He fired a single shot at Honey from his pistol. The bullet pinged off a concrete pillar, but Honey zigged a foot away to his side and managed to dodge the second one, although it grazed his arm. He quickly chased after the shooter, who attempted to fire another shot but failed. The escalator was scaling up. The shooter rose and bolted into the gym. When Honey reached the gym, the assailant locked himself in a washroom. When Honey eventually broke open the door, the shooter had escaped through a window.

Women in the gym screamed in panic when they saw Honey bleeding from his arm. One of them, whose voice and face seemed familiar, shouted, "Honey boy, are you alright?!" It was Diya. She sprinted to a table at the far end of the hall, retrieved a first aid box from a drawer, and riffled through it for a bandage. She took it out and swiftly wrapped it around his arm.

"Who was he, Honey boy?" Diya's voice cut through the growing frantic cries as more crowds pulled in, still inquiring about the details.

After taking a long breath, Honey responded, "I don't know."

"Honey boy, you are badly injured. I will take you to the hospital," Diya insisted.

Checking his fingers working smoothly and he could make a tight grip, Honey replied, "I am Okay Diya."

" No, You are not okay. My God, you are bleeding profusely. You need to see a doctor soon. I know a doctor in the City Hospital, and I will take you there."

" I don't want to go to that place. Diya. I am okay."

"Please, Honey Boy," she pleaded. "Your life is precious to this country."

Diya placed her left hand gently on his right shoulder while driving and said, "I know, Honey boy, in no minutes, your team will reach here and take you to another place. But I insist you should get the treatment from the best doctor I know."

" Who is he ?"

" Not he, She."

" She! You mean Pallavi?" He looked at Diya's eyes with a stare of disappointment.

Diya held his left hand with her right as they arrived at the hospital. She dragged him straight to the dressing room and called Pallavi through the secretary. Pallavi rushed to the dressing room, feeling a sudden jerk in her nerves. She couldn't believe her eyes when she saw Honey in such a terrible state, with A crimson stain on the bandage. She quickly opened the dressing after injecting a painkiller. Relief washed over her when she realized that there was no major blood vessel injury. She just ligated a small branch to control the bleeding.

"You should be thankful to God today, Honey. The bullet didn't pass through any major blood vessels. It could have penetrated your chest," Pallavi said. Her words carried a palpable concern for him, but he interpreted her words differently.

"Don't worry, Dr. Pallavi. Whether I live or die, it's all the same to me. As long as I am alive, I won't die. And if I die, I won't live further," Honey responded, his expression filled with sarcasm and anger.

Pallavi placed her gloved hand on his mouth to silence him and removed it after a second. "You can call me Pallavi. How is the pain now ?" she asked.

Honey burst into a quick laughter. Pallavi sensed that his heart had something more painful to reveal through his expression. In the next instant, she noticed his expression was filled with pain. It was as if his eyes were asking her at that moment, "How will you ease my inner pain, Dr. Pallavi?" "That inner pain has made him a man of steel," she realized.

Honey said, " If death stands in my way, I will welcome it gladly. You are asking about my pain ." Pallavi was stunned to hear the untold words as if he had uttered them to her ears, masking them under his laughter. "Oh, death, you are not taller than me. You can't make me cry. I will leave this world happily." " Look at me, Pallavi. Am I having any pain? Am I not looking happy?" He said as his laughter faded. An uncomfortable silence prevailed in the room for Pallavi.

Pallavi stood silently, trying to process his every word that reached her ears into a deep thought. Eventually, she interrupted her thoughts, saying, "Okay, Honey, you can leave now. I will dress your wound again in two days if you come. Excuse me." And with that, she left the dressing room.

*****

Diya checked her watch. It was six in the evening. Without calling Pallavi, she headed to her house to find her. Laxmi arrived with tea and a plateful of snacks for her. She found Laxmi's gestures were adorable. When Laxmi brought it, Diya said, "That's a lot of food, auntie. I can't take them all."

"This is for a long conversation about you and Palo, Beta," Laxmi said smilingly.

Just after Pallavi got home, Laxmi went to the kitchen to prepare dinner.

Pallavi glanced at Diya, surprised, and took a seat on the sofa precisely across from Diya and forced a smile. "Is everything alright, Diya?"

"I can't say things are going alright, but they are certainly much better than before."

"You surprised me today," Pallavi said.

"You may wonder why I have come to your place, but let me tell you, there is certainly an inseparable connection between you and me. You can unquestionably acknowledge that I owe you everything in life, including a common friend with whom you had a prior acquaintance. I sensed the connection between both of you is still platonic. I am just an outsider."

Pallavi huffed. "That was a long past, Diya—more than a decade. Then we were teens. Now I have no feelings for him."

"Two weeks ago, maybe it was not. But, now ." Diya paused.

"But, now what, Diya?" Pallavi looked at her face pointedly with confusion."

"But now, I feel that Honey is still in love with you."

"You are so lost, Diya. What are you talking about?" Pallavi looked at her surroundings with nothing more to add as if irritated.

"I know it's been a long time. Fifteen years have passed. I was a stubborn teen. I had some intention to get him by my side, or rather, I wished to hurt you to any extent. But that did not survive longer in my heart when I discovered his true love, which was only for you," Diya said.

Pallavi made a face. "Stop it, Diya." Palo's hands went to her temples as if the words instantly clung to her emotional nerves without her permission.

Diya noticed that Pallavi's embarrassment-filled eyes had stopped glancing at her. They looked up and down and sometimes to her sides as if trying to conceal the welled-up moisture in her eyes. Diya continued, "The very thought of happiness between you and him had reasonably consumed the happiness out of me, which drove me crazy. Though I knew I was wrong to interfere, then I was out of my mind. It was an age when I understood little about myself and all that about love. Pallavi, he spurned my love because he loved you."

"Why are you saying this to me now, Diya? I don't think about the dead past. I live in the present. I am very happy with my job and my friends."

"I knew you had given your word to my father that you would take care of me. It never meant that you would sacrifice your love for me. You gave me life to relive happily with a friend like you."

"Sacrifice! What are you talking about, Diya? In my remotest memory, I don't consider Honey to be someone important to me. Just say thanks from my side for all the support he gave me during the interrogation."

"You need Honey in your life. He is your first love. He is not like your Vicky, who will cheat on you."

"Please, Diya, stop it for now and forever. I have moved on. You should get your love. Honey is your first love. You liked him more than anyone, more than me," Pallavi said. There was no other way she could get rid of Diya's repeated phrases of love. Her heart was pounding while she stated this.

Diya said, "Okay, thanks. I just wanted to know from you if you still have any love left for him or not."

Pallavi asked, "Why, thanks, Diya?"

Diya blew out a breath and tried to explain her situation so she wouldn't be accused of stealing her love interest in the future. "If it is your wish, I will go ahead and spend my life with Honey, but promise me you will come for our engagement. Romy uncle is going to announce a party for Honey's thirty-third birthday. It would be auspicious to call it an engagement party."

"Okay... I promise you. I will be the happiest girl to see Honey by your side, Diya." Pallavi looked up at the ceiling briefly, and her eyes welled up with tears of a roller coaster of emotions.

There was a New Year's night gathering in Honey's house. A crowd of doctors, lawyers, and industrialists came to attend the party held in Shivdasni's House for a double celebration. One occasion was to celebrate the arrival of a new year, and the other was to celebrate Honey's birthday. Laxmi agreed to a late-night party for the first time at Romy's request. Both Laxmi and

Pallavi went to the party. Laxmi was dressed in a golden-bordered wheatish Saree and looked seraphic and radiant in the glow of bright light.

Palo had wrathed a red peasant top to the ankle with a curled dark ringlet. She looked stunning in the dress. When they reached Shivdasni's house, The party had already begun.

Romy greeted her with closed palms with a smile on his face. He was happy to see Laxmi in a cheerful mood. When he saw her for the first time thirty years ago, she was whining outside the courtroom for her husband. It was then he felt bitterness for the Rajhans family. No number of tears could melt his heart. Briksha's death had transformed him into an idol of stone. He experienced the pain in these thirty years but could not express it through tears. He was shocked to see his world shattered in a minute before him. All he wanted at that moment was the execution of Sagaar Rajhans in that very moment inside the courtroom. Diya's words about the incident forced him to rethink about the Rajhans family. He knew how Sagar had taken the guilt onto himself to prove his subservience to his master. No man can be so honest to protect his master.

Honey was dressed in his pinkish-red long suit and a creamy white shirt. Diya stood close to him all the time. She wore a designer sleeveless golden peasant top with a hemline reaching above her knees and a halter running circularly around her mid-chest, revealing a slight, gentle bulge of flesh above it. She looked fuller with time. Her body-hugging dress made her comfortable enough to display her slimmest waistline on that eve. The curl of her hair was hanging up to her shoulder, and it looked puffy. Her hair appeared smooth and swung when she shimmied down with Honey on the stairs. Persons looking at them for the first time must have visualized a newly engaged couple as if walking closely together, sometimes seen holding each other in the crowd. They reached the main hall, which had a large central fountain. It was the main attraction inside the hall. The ejecting jets gave varied shades of colour, with the reflection of colourful lights focused on these streams. The crowd had circled, and everybody had held a glass of drink in their hand.

Honey was looking very handsome and charming. A group of people from his police circle were complimenting him for his great work. He had exposed the biggest underworld racket.

There was absolute darkness around the colourful fountain after the hall lights went off for half a minute. Romy instructed the guards of the house to do so. The fountain changed its colour with every passing second. The time was half a minute short of midnight. It was desperately climbing to the mark of twelve to welcome a happy new year. In that moment of darkness, Romy gestured for Laxmi and Pallavi to move close to the fountain.

Romy announced, 'Ladies and gentlemen, we are now ten seconds short of the new year's arrival. Everyone is expected to do a reverse count starting now. They all uttered ten, nine, eight, five, four..two, one... And the lights started glowing as before. The crowd started shouting Happy New Year. The familiar faces embraced each other, while a few overcame their unfamiliarity by shaking hands.

Honey looked to his side and was surprised to see Pallavi instead of Diya. Pallavi looked stunning. His eyes narrowed. As the new year was welcomed in the hall, she joyfully clapped and cheered, singing 'Happy New Year.' Their eyes met, but they ignored each other. A surprised Honey didn't have the heart to ask her why she was there. He couldn't help but stare at her. Their gaze locked in a moment, but they quickly looked away as if they disregarded each other. Given the circumstances, Palo hesitated to extend congratulations to him on the engagement. Her mother had brought her to the party for Diya and Honey's engagement. She, too, was eagerly awaiting the announcement. For obvious reasons, she was not keen to attend, but the emotional debt she owed to a son for supporting her during bad times compelled her to accept the invitation from his father. Romy specially invited the Rajhans family, who came personally to invite them. It made Palo uneasy. Consequently, she stood there somewhat awkwardly, evading the gaze of others, as the agony of hiding true feelings behind a facade of cheerfulness in her solemn eyes was difficult, especially when there was a conversation in their gazes.

However, they couldn't resist looking at each other again. They stood closer amidst the crowd, and it seemed like they both wanted to talk and wish each other a happy new year while people around them mingled with everyone to wish a happy new year. Their eyes remained fixed on each other for a while. Diya stood close to Laxmi, hoping there would be some exchange of words between Pallavi and Honey, and prayed for a peaceful resolution of their differences.

Honey stepped back and angrily said, "It's you!"

"I didn't choose to be in this situation, Diya. Did you call her by my side?" He glared at her angrily.

Pallavi tried to sneak away unnoticed.

"I can't bear to be hurt again, Papa. Why did you do this?"

"I'm your father. I've witnessed in these years what you've become. Stop, Pallavi. You're not going anywhere," Romy said firmly.

"Let her go, Papa. I'm alive and happy. That's all that matters. I don't believe in love or marriage. I'm not like you, Papa. I don't abide by love. The Pallavi you see in my heart is beautiful, but I'm afraid of her other side."

"You see things differently than I do, Honey. It's my fault. I shouldn't have told you to stay away from Pallavi. I always thought she was disrespectful, but I was wrong."

Pallavi reached Romy and said, "Both of us were right in our own ways, Uncle. There's no need to feel sorry about what happened."

Pallavi approached Honey, took his hand, and said, "I can't ask why you still love that, Pallavi. It was not easy for me to withstand the storm in my mind. I felt guilty for leaving you without an explanation. The reason I left would have been more devastating for you, even more than our separation. I remember that day; it was the best of my life with you. But one incident changed everything. It would never have been the same for you if I had revealed that my father killed your mother."

Honey's mind was struck by lightning. He stood paralyzed for a moment before saying, "You didn't even consider how I would live without you."

His eyes flickered with a restless energy, betraying the conflict within. Like a kaleidoscope of emotions, they swirled with a love he could no longer conceal. The guarded shutters that had long obscured his heart's true desires now began to lift, granting her a glimpse into his soul.

She watched, gazes transfixed, as their self-constructed barriers crumbled, revealing a treasure of affection that had been consciously hoarded for over a decade and the moment witnessed a great door of their Love-Hate relationship unlocked, allowing the tightly held feelings to spill forth, yearning for an acceptance.

His eyes, which had once been windows to a world of secrets, now shone with an open adoration, inviting her to step inside and claim what had always been rightfully hers. In their shifting depths, she saw the promise of a profound love that had the power to envelop and transform her very being.

Through this unguarded gaze, he offered her the most precious among the gifts – the unveiling of his heart, laid bare and vulnerable, awaiting her acceptance and embrace.

Tears welled up in her eyes; a collective mist of emotion swept through the room. Pallavi gently took his hand, turning it tenderly, and pressed her trembling lips against his calloused palm. "I'm so sorry, Honey," she uttered, her voice thick with remorse. "You're not a bad guy - not at all. But How can I hide it from you that my father killed your mother."

The air grew heavy with the weight of her words. Her glistening eyes pleaded for understanding and forgiveness.

Dropping his hand, she turned to Romy and said, "Uncle, even I let every negative thought away from my mind today. I can't place myself as a queen in your son's heart. Diya loves him. They would make a perfect pair."

Honey replied, "We were more than just friends; we were soulmates. You promised to be with me, but you left me with nothing. We were not strangers."

Tears choked her voice as she leaned against him. He let her hold onto his shoulder. "I'm sorry, Honey. You're not a bad guy, but how can I live with you knowing that the person who killed your mother was - my father. I'm afraid I may never feel the same way as you expect ." She looked down.

He said, " Your words today cannot capture my feelings and emotions ." He let go of her hands and clasped her arms. "You kept everything to yourself. You stole a part of my soul, Pallavi. What else do I have to give you? Even death would have caused me less pain. You made me lose respect for you. Apologizing won't make everything okay," Honey's voice quivered. There was a palpable hurt in the trembling cadence.

She looked into his eyes and said, "I knew what you went through. It's been fifteen long years. I'm sorry, Honey. But believe me; I couldn't bring myself to respond to you thereafter because I couldn't figure things out in my own life for a convincing reply. My soul was soaked with guilt."

Diya got into their conversation. "What guilt, which guilt Pallavi? Honey's mother was killed by my father, who was at the steering that day. It was not your father. I know how much you love Honey. I was kept away from this truth until Disha revealed it to me a few months ago before she died. If you want to see me happy, then you marry Honey. You have promised my father to keep me happy. Now, it is a wish from my heart that you should accept him as your man."

"Fifteen years!" he murmured. The clasp had gone mild on her arms. An unexpected reaction arose in his mind, suppressing all odd memories he was holding onto his nerves. Honey thought, "Pallavi, a part of me wants to tell you how beautiful you are! Today feels like a beautiful dream. How do I express that I waited a lifetime for you to be by my side? How do I tell you I longed to see you all these years? Will your magical eyes feel the same for me? The page where I wrote your name was torn. Can I fill my entire life with your name?"

Honey slowly took her hands in his. A strange feeling surged through her body, leaving her paralyzed. As the thoughts Honey had in his mind battled with her own, her heart started beating for him, keeping aside the conflicts that arose in her mind. It gave her no time to ponder. She began reconsidering his proposal. Honey had already knelt on one knee, holding her hand, and said, "Today, you can't say no. We're more than friends, and we're soulmates. We're not strangers. My heart tells me we've been together in every lifetime. Now, just smile and say yes. Say yes... Say yes, you're mine."

She said, "Yes. Yes, Honey, yes. I love you." Tears filled her eyes as she leaned in and hugged him tightly.

The crowd applauded, and Diya, Laxmi, and Romy approached to congratulate the couple. In their next meeting, they made plans for their wedding and honeymoon in Kashmir, the land of romance.

"Sir, the headquarters has sent the report. One of them has been identified. It matched our missing persons record."

"Who is he, Charmy?"

"He is Sagar Rajhans."

For Special Thanks

I would like to express my heartfelt gratitude to Blue Rose Publisher and their dedicated team, especially Mr. Samar, Ms. Ankita, Ms. Sejal, and Ms. Namrata, for their unwavering support and guidance throughout the publishing process.

I would also like to extend a special thanks to my sister, Ms. Anita Padhy, who resides in the USA, for generously taking the time from her busy schedule to proofread my entire manuscript.

www.ingramcontent.com/pod-product-compliance
Lightning Source LLC
LaVergne TN
LVHW091616070526
838199LV00044B/816